THE RETURN
of
KING LILLIAN

THE RETURN
of
KING LILLIAN

SUZIE PLAKSON

Pilmsthistle & Co.
PUBLISHERS

Publisher's Cataloging-in-Publication Data

Names: Plakson, Suzie, author.
Title: The Return of King Lillian / Suzie Plakson.
Description: Los Angeles, CA: Pilmsthistle & Co., 2019.
Identifiers: LCCN 2019939480 | ISBN 978-0-9884993-1-7 (pbk.) |
978-0-9884993-3-1 (ebook) | 978-0-9884993-8-6 (audiobook)
Subjects: LCSH Kings, queens, rulers, etc.--Fiction. | Amnesia--Fiction. |
Identity--Fiction. | Coming of age--Fiction. | Fairies--Fiction. |
Family--Fiction. | Fairy tales. | Fantasy fiction. | Adventure fiction. |
BISAC FICTION / Fairy Tales, Folk Tales, Legends & Mythology |
FICTION / Fantasy / General
Classification: LCC PS3616.L36 R48 2019 | DDC 813.6--dc23

Cover design by Deranged Doctor Design
derangeddoctordesign.com

First Trade Edition

Printed in the United States of America

Pilmsthistle & Co.
7162 Beverly Blvd. #106, Los Angeles, CA 90036
kinglillian.com

For my Golden Friends,
my lighthouses, my dearly beloveds,
who have shown me countless times, in endless ways,
that Friendship is the sturdiest ship of all.

It is to you, with an infinitude of gratitude, that I dedicate:

The Return of King Lillian

CONTENTS

Prologue:
The End of the Beginning

At long, long last, she was free, free, *free!*
With the wind in her hair,
with the sun on her back,
with the Whole Wyde Whirld at her feet!
How she rejoiced in the majesty all around her:
the hills, the fields, the mountains, the clouds, the trees, the sky . . .

Yes, out there in the middle of Everywhere,
strode and skipped and danced
Lillian, the little vagabond Girl-King.

A spritely, brightly colored figure she was:
purple hat, red hair, white shirt, green leggings, brown boots.
Out there all alone on her very, very own,
cut loose on the whirl of the Whirld,
she was heading off boldly to points unknown.
Why, she'd find out where those mountains got grown.
She was a free bird now and a rolling stone!

Oh, yes, for a while the child was positively thrilling
to the promise of all the possible possibilities all around her.
Until all that striding and skipping and dancing
became just walking.
And walking and walking.
And walking and walking and walking.
And the food was very nearly gone.
And the daylight was very nearly going.

Yes, Lillian had figured she'd feel fine, finally free,
but a dream seems awfully different up close she'd come to see,
especially when a person got to feeling tired and hungry.

At last, she came upon a great, wide stone,
and she stopped to take stock.

She climbed up on top of the stone to see how things stood.
To see where she was and, alas, where she wasn't.
To face, in fact, her Future.

And as she regarded the vastness
that stretched so endlessly before her,
she felt herself to be much, much too small for all of this,
as if she were nothing more than a pebble
that had been thrown away
without a thought as to where it landed.
Then, said she, matter-of-factly, as was her way:

"Well, I best have me one last look then."

And for the first time that day, the Girl-King turned to face her Past.
And she planted her hands on her hips and took one long, last look.
And there it was:

Far, far off in the distance
sat that lovely little ivory-walled Kingdom,
looking so small now, it seemed she could hold it in her hand.
She squinted – was that a swirl of smoke she saw?
Something still smoldering from the fire?
But, no, the Kingdom looked to be the perfect picture of serenity.
As a matter of fact, it looked every bit as if it didn't care one whit
if it ever saw or heard of her again.

And as Lillian watched the sun sinking down behind the castle,
a dark revelation began to dawn . . .
She had long ago spied, from that very castle,
this great, wide stone upon which she now stood,
and, oh, how she had so longed to be standing on it someday, free.
And here she was. Free, indeed.

The girl crumpled into a heap upon that great stone,
and she sobbed until she fell shivering into slumber.
And sunset gave way to dusk, and then to darkness.

After a long sleep, Lillian awoke,
and she rolled over on her back to behold:

The most extravagantly jeweled, black velvet, night sky . . .
fields upon fields upon fields of blinking, winking stars.
Shooting, falling, twinkling, breathing beauty!
And at the center of all that infinite majesty reigned
a big, bright, fat, white Moon, benevolently beaming.

And Lillian was so taken with the firmament above
that she entirely forgot about her predicament below.
And as she lay there, gazing up in such inspired awe,
she felt it all to be so alive, she whispered:

"Hello . . . "

And just as she reached up to touch the stars,
she heard a *rustling*.
She sat up. She looked around. She heard it again.
It seemed to be coming from – the Forest?

"What?" the girl cried. "Why, there sure was no Forest standing
there before!"

But, no doubt about it,
there *most certainly* was a Forest standing there now.
And a tall, dark, and looming Forest it was, indeed,
stretching infinitely to the right
and infinitely to the left.

And as the girl sat pondering the sudden Forest,
still trying to comprehend,
she heard that *rustling* again.

She leapt to her feet and looked all around,
and when she found the source of the sound,
her eyes went round with wonder . . .

The most perfect little creature stood looking at her,
having just appeared from the black of the woods:

A pure white Fawn.

The Fawn took a single step toward her,
then ever so lightly touched the air with its nose.
And the girl said, ever so gently:

"Why, hello . . . I'm Lillian."

The pretty creature stared at her with black, liquid eyes,
and blinked – and then bolted back into the Forest.

"Oh, no! Please don't go!"

And Lillian jumped down off the great stone and gave chase,
running up to the border of the Forest and then alongside it,
trying to follow the Fawn as it went leaping through the trees.
But she soon lost sight of the flashing white
and saw only Forest blackness.
The Fawn was gone.

The girl sighed, then sadly turned her back to the Forest.
And who should now be facing her from just a short ways off?

The Fawn.

And it looked at Lillian and blinked.
And then it ran this way and stopped.
And then it ran that way and stopped.
And the girl laughed with pure delight.
And the girl and the Fawn began to play.
And they ran and chased and chased and ran,
and then the Fawn ran back into the Forest again.
And running so fast and so close on its heels,
the girl had to pull herself up sharply short!

The tips of her boots were now just tickling the Forest edge,
and her toes tingled with whether she would or should or could
ever go into that all-too-sudden dark and daunting wood.

So, there she stood, looking into the dark, liquid eyes of the Fawn,
sparkling at her from the ominous blackness.
The Fawn was inviting her in, and she knew it.

The girl peered into the shadowy night world of the Forest,
listening to the cricklings and the cracklings and the creakings,
as the wind whined and whistled
and wound around and through the trees.

She started to put the tip of one toe just the tiniest bit over the edge,
but a dreadful panic seized her!
And, in a flash, her foot was back on safe ground.
And she declared, most definitively:

"Nossir, going in there would not be good. That is much too big
and far too dark a wood."

And, oh, though she surely felt that sharp bite
of the bone-deep chill of the long, cold night
slipping inside her thin, white shirt,
nip-nip-nipping at her shivering skin,
still she knew she shouldn't, couldn't, wouldn't *ever* go in.
And though she knew she shouldn't go forward,
and she certainly wouldn't go back,
she could find no reason at all to go left or to go right,
since the end of the Forest, in either direction,
was absolutely nowhere in sight.

Why, that poor child was so overwhelmed and so petrified,
she might still be standing on that very spot to this very day
if Fate hadn't made up her mind for her.
(Which it has a way of doing now and then.)

What happened was, it began, all at once, to pour.
Yes, torrents and sheets and buckets and rivers and riots of rain!
Oh, and thunder and lightning too, of course.
Oh, yes, a fierce and terrible Whirld Storm began to express itself.
Like opera, only weather!

And so, of course, Lillian went charging for cover into the Forest,
running right past a carved, weather-beaten sign that read:

You Are Now Entering
The Forest of Forgetfullness
(Might Want to Jot Down Your Name)

And as soon as Lillian crossed over the edge
and into the blackness of the trees,
a terrifying confusion set in,
and everything she remembered of herself disappeared . . .

Oh, the Girl-King suddenly didn't know
who she was or
where she was or
what she was or
why she was wherever it was she was, at all.

And the rain pelted and pounded.
And the wind whipped her and moaned and howled.
And the branches slapped and scratched her and tore at her clothes.
And the little girl wept with terror.

But Lillian, still being Lillian somewhere deep within,
trudged on and on and on . . .
until, finally, she tripped and fell over a tree root
and fainted straight away.

And there she lay,
like a broken doll
in the gathering mud
on the floor of the Forest of Forgetfullness.

Then, all of a sudden, out of the blue,
the temperamental Storm seemed to take pity on the child,
changed its malevolent mood,
went from flashing and crashing
to whooshing and rumbling and grumbling off to somewhere else.

And when the Storm clouds rolled back and away,
they unveiled the once again big, bright, fat, beaming Moon,
sitting ever so placidly in its own little meadow of stars,
as if nothing bad had ever happened to anyone anywhere ever,
as if no night had ever been quite so peaceful.

Truth is, the Moon felt just awful.
There the Rain and Thunder and Lightning were showing off again,
and this time somebody got hurt.

So the Moon sent down a silvery beam of light to search for the girl.
Even for the Moon, it was hard to find her at first,
for there she lay, so covered in mud and leaves
that she looked to be part of the Forest floor.
But, at last, the Moon discovered her
and cast a circle of light around the muddy heap of girl.

And soon, from the blackest blackness outside the light-circle,
there appeared a pair of glowing golden eyes.
Then another pair. Then two, then three, then more . . .

Wolves. Watching. Waiting.

One by one, they stepped soundlessly out of the darkness,
fur gleaming silver in the Moonlight.

And they sniffed at the girl's hair.
And they sniffed at the girl's clothes.
And they sniffed at the girl's feet.
And then each one took hold of boot or belt or bag
and carried her off deep, deep, deep into the Forest.

By the light of the Moon, in the shadow of the trees,
through light and shadow, shadow and light,
the Wolves carried the girl until, at last,
they emerged into a perfectly round clearing,
in the center of which sat a cottage
with a thick, uneven thatch,
with a glow from the fireplace within,
with a crooked candelabra made of tree branches,
all lit up and flickering on the windowsill.

The Wolves deposited their muddy package on the doorstep.
One pawed the old cowbell that hung on a nail,
then disappeared with the rest of his pack
back into the blackness.

And there lay Lillian,
out cold, out in the cold,
on the doorstep of a stranger,
in the belly of the Forest of Forgetfullness.

Then there came the sound of curmudgeonly muttering from within.
Then the sound of something crashing into something else.
Then the sound of the door being fumbled with.
Then the sound of the door creaking open, and then:

Out stepped the fluttery old woman who lived there,
long white hair wisping, beaded shawl over faded nightdress,
looking all around and about.

"Who goes there? *Oh!*"

She frowned at the unconscious creature on her doorstep.
She narrowed her eyes.
She leaned down and looked it over a bit.
She ruminated for a moment.
Then she turned around, stormed back inside, and shut the door.

A few moments later she opened the door again, just a smidge.
Despite herself, she stepped out to investigate further.
She bent over the muddy creature again, sniffing the air around it.
Then she became terribly disturbed.

"Why, you're a human child! Oh, *absolutely not!*"

And she stomped back inside, slammed the door, and locked it.

"I only tend to Forest creatures, which *you* are *not!* Now, goodbye!"

But soon she appeared at the window to scowl at the human child.
Well, that old woman appeared and disappeared
in and out of that window
and went in and out of that door,
until, at long last, she was pulling the girl inside.

"I do not like this at all . . . I am altogether too busy for this sort
of thing!"

And the door slammed with such a slam
and locked with such a lock!
And the wind swept up with such a sweep,
why, it rattled and blew the window open,
whipping out all the flames of the crooked candelabra!

Which, in a moment, leapt up again, once the wind went away . . .

And inside, by the light of that crooked candelabra,
Lillian now lay sleeping, clean and dry and freshly tended to,
tucked into a little bed, just like a little princess.

Alongside the sleeping girl was a gathering
of likewise-seen-to Forest creatures in various states of recovery,
a bandage here, a compress there.
All patients were dozily watching the fire or sleeping peacefully.
All except the human one, that is.
Sleeping she was, yes, but tossing and turning and, oh, so troubled.
(Ah, you see? Where there's a princess, there's always a pea.)

And what a warm, inviting cottage it was,
crowded with the most curious collection
of odds and ends and curiosities,
compasses and keys and jars and sculptures and paintings
and a birdbath and, oh, the most curious curiosity of all, of course:

The old woman.
The lady of the house.
The spinster in question.
Rocking and rocking before the fire,
she was knitting and knitting
the longest, most incomprehensible scarf
that wound round and round and round her chair.
The old woman was muttering intently as she knitted:

"A lost girl, I ask you ... Why, that's the most *bothersome* thing I've
ever heard! How in the Whirld will I be able to concentrate? She'll
always be wanting things. No, she'll simply have to go! I've far too
much to do. There won't be any staying here with *me*, Little Girl!"

The girl moaned and whimpered in her sleep.

"What's that? Oh, heavens *no*, Little Girl, you may stay here for
tonight, don't be so dramatic! Hm? What's that? Well, of course
you can't remember who you are. This is the Forest of Forgetfullness.
Hm? Oh, no, dear, you'll never remember your own name – you'll
have to make one up. And if it likes you, it will stick to you, like
mine has. My name is Mad Aunt Harriet – isn't it wonderful!"

The girl rolled over and sniffled a bit.

"Very nice to meet you too. *Hmmm*, are you a Clarabelle? Are you an . . . Edith? I've got it – Theodora! No. Well, no matter. If you don't really want to stay, any name you pick will slide right off you anyway. Oh, how I do adore my name! How my name adores me!"

And the old woman burst into a loud, tuneless song about her name.
And the girl groaned painfully.
And the animals covered their ears.

"Oh, it's true, Little Girl, I'm not much of a singer, but you'll feel very fortunate, I'm sure, should you hear me play the cello! I am a wildly passionate musician – my gifts develop daily. Hm? Oh, you like to sing, do you? How marvelous! I wonder, does it run in your family?"

At this, Lillian began to cry in her sleep.

The old woman was by her bedside in an instant.
She stood over the girl, contemplating her.
Then she laid one graceful old hand on the girl's head
and the other on her heart.
And she listened.

"*Ahhh*, poor dear . . . Though your past is wiped clear, your little body is remembering – oh, too much pain, *tsk-tsk-tsk!* And only the pain remains. Oh, I don't like that, I do not like that at all for one so young, no . . . Yes, Charlotte? You had an idea?"

A pretty skunk shared her thought.

"*No*, Charlotte! It would not be any *kind* of a good idea to get her drunk! Oh, Charlotte, I'm *ashamed* for you! What's that you say, Little Girl? Ah, '*Take away the pain*,' she says, '*take away the pain . . .* ' My, such a clever Little Girl it is."

And then the old woman brought her palms together.
And, with reverence, she closed her eyes.
And a deep calm came across her face.
And the fire in the fireplace flared up, then flickered low,
and her lovely old fingers and palms began to very softly glow.

Then she whispered:

"Come here to me, Sorrow, come away, come along... She'll take
you back someday, when she's big and she's strong."

And her hands did a little waltzing dance above the girl,
who all of a sudden stretched and yawned,
and let out the deepest, saddest sigh.
And, why, that sigh breathed a *shimmering* into the air,
just above her sleeping form.

And then, rising from the Girl-King's body,
came the most deeply Sorrowful hues,
the onyx blacks and the blackest blues,
gathering just above her in a glimmering pool.
And her Sorrow hovered there, floating serenely in the air,
above the now most profoundly peaceful, sleeping girl.

And the old woman's fingers further coaxed the pool of Sorrow.

"Come along now, don't you dawdle."

And the Sorrow swirled round and round its center,
pouring itself into a single, glistening, teardrop Jewel.

And as it hung there, glittering in the air, she exclaimed:

"My, what a beauty you are . . . "

But, suddenly, the old woman panicked.

"Oh! I must do that *this very instant* so I shan't forget!"

And she plucked the Sorrow out of the air.
Then she hurried over to an old glass cabinet,
lined with miniatures and jewelry and figurines,
and she reached up onto the top shelf and instantly produced
a simple silver setting into which that Sorrow fit
just so perfectly, as if it had been made precisely just for it.

Then, from a carved wooden box overflowing
with snippets and bits and lengths of this and that,
the old woman reached in and drew out
a simple silver chain that suited the setting
in the same perfect way that the setting suited the Sorrow.

She gently fastened the Sorrow around the sleeping girl's neck.
And for a moment, she watched it glittering there
against that pale child, with her mass of long red hair.

"Yes, it's a special Little Girl, isn't it? Well, perhaps we won't toss
you out *right away* . . . "

Then she stood up and addressed her animal patients with vigor:

"Now, I must immediately make a detailed memorandum of these
events, and I must keep it in a very *obvious* place. Yes, I'd say it's
been an altogether remarkable evening, has it not, my dears?
Why, that's exactly how I shall begin my memorandum! *'This
has been an altogether remarkable evening!'"*

And the old woman went off, humming and muttering
as she disappeared into the depths of the cottage.

And then the night sky rolled off.
And the early morning sky rolled in.
And there began a most peaceful, chirping Forest day.
Oh, but on this Forest day, little Lillian was *little* no more!
Why, in the place of the child there slept a tall young woman,
who far exceeded the little bed . . .

One long, green-legginged leg slung over the footboard,
one foot flat on the floor, the other resting on the windowsill,
one big toe poking clean through a hole in the sock.
Sleeping in perfect peace, she was, one arm slung over her eyes.

Then, like a gigantic kitten in the sun,
she started mewing and stretching herself awake,
and knocking things over in this now far more crowded cottage,
packed with so many more curiosities!

Yes, shocking how Whirld Time has a mind of its own, is it not?

Now then, let's talk about *you*.
That's right, *you* who are reading these very words
at this very moment . . .

So, knowing what you now know,
you know that the story that lies ahead
is the story of a person on a journey.
And now, lo and behold, *you* appear.
And you also happen to be on a journey in your *own* story.
Coincidence? Perhaps . . .

Or perhaps there might be Something Marvelous and Mysterious
that weaves all things together.
And perhaps this Marvelous Mysterious has led you here
and is now inviting you to do something rather unconventional,
something altogether out of the ordinary in your world:

To have a rest. Yes . . .
To take respite from all that
hair-tearing, soul-wearing, world-wearying
wondering and wandering and worrying you tend to do.
Perhaps it even asks you to be so bold as to put your feet up,
to let all your troubles drop off you like an old coat,
to let your fancy take flight, in a light, easy way,
like a small bird – say, a skylark – might.

So, O Wondering Wanderer,
whatever clever cosmic happenstance has brought you here,
know this:

You are most welcome,
and have been quite eagerly expected.

Ah, look, see that? Just up ahead?
Yes, that ribbon of Road meandering off
into the unforeseeable distance?
Well, along that Road (why, of course, you guessed it)
lies the tale of the adventures and eventual return of King Lillian.

Most of this history has been recorded in a diary
by the Girl-King herself.
Now, you'll notice that her story begins in the middle.
This might upset you.
Don't fret. You haven't missed anything.
It's just a word, just a name, just a retrospective relativity.

After all, what is Time, anyway?
Just a silly old rumor, so they say.
Besides, aren't there countless "Once Upon A Times" in a lifetime?
Multitudinous middles?
Unending endings?

Well, whatever your feelings on the subject may be,
the fact is, the journey herein is about to begin.

Fare you well, then, dear Reader.
Until we meet again.

1: The Middle

Wherein I Say Farewell and Seek the Edge

Why, Book, that's a mighty exciting beginning, don't you think? Yessir, I do believe I am off to a fine start already!

So, I should tell you that I sit here writing as I pause on my journey out of this most cherished Forest forevermore. I shall herein begin this chronicle by recounting the astonishing events that began yesterday morning.

Now, there are two reasons why I must so very accurately record said events. For one thing, they are the premiere moments of the next chapter of my whole entire life, and, as such, they will never come again. For another thing, since I have no idea whether or not I will recall anything at all of my life here after I leave the Forest of Forgetfullness, a memorandum is most distinctly in order. Though I will not take the time to record anything that transpired before yesterday morning, as in truth, my life in the Forest has been perfectly blissful and almost entirely without incident.

Alright, so here it is, Book . . .

Yesterday morning, I woke up from a dream so glorious, a dream nigh on *effervescing* with lilacs – yes, an endless sea of lilacs. And the smell of 'em wafted right across the border of the dream, and I woke up still smelling them lilacs! Though I didn't remember any more of the dream until I cracked my head on the beam getting out of bed.

So, wait now, let me close my eyes and recall . . .

Yes, there was a very miraculous sort of a person who seemed to be made entirely of light, and she were shining through this sea of lilacs. She handed me something very colorful – though I don't remember what. And she said something to me, something very meaningful that rhymed – though I don't remember that either. Oh, but when she said it, she were so very certain of it and so delighted to tell me about it that I felt mightily inspired – though I can't quite say why.

So o' course I race out of the cottage to tell Mad Aunt Harriet all about this most inspiring dream, and don't you know – even though she's right in the middle of painting a fine miniature of a squirrel – she drops her paintbrush, pulls my head close, and sniffs the air all around me. Then she makes a most extraordinary declaration:

"Oh, yes, Little Girl, you most distinctly smell of Destiny!"

Well, upon hearing such a thing, I am about to bust clean out of my skin.

"I do?" says I. "Well, what do I do about it? Mad Aunt Harriet . . . ?"

But she had already gone back to her painting. Yes, when Mad Aunt Harriet is in the middle of a miniature, well, best leave her be has been my experience. So, off I go, feeling all make and manner of marvelous, quite taken with the idea that maybe Destiny, at long last, has taken an interest in me.

And as I am having a nice, rock-balancing walk through the brook, I am also having me quite a thrilling think, and I find myself recalling all that I have ever read about Destiny. Amongst the ever-burgeoning miscellany that falls through the Skyhole out back come a few books now and again. And in some of them books, folks get to talking about all sorts of various and interesting feelings they have about Destiny. Which makes me wonder what likewise variational feelings Destiny has about the folks that wrote those books and, more precisely to the point, about me.

Anyhow, after having a nice slosh around in the brook in my bare feet, I am all stretched out, a-laying there along the bank, leaning up against a nice round boulder that's all warm and toasty in the sun, just listening to the melody of the water as it flows on along beside me. And I am getting all dozy and heading towards a nice nap, whilst still cogitating upon the natural question of whether lilacs smell like Destiny or Destiny smells like lilacs.

And just as I am about to slide on into sleep, why, I hear the warm, round boulder I am leaning on speak to me in a most polite manner:

"Follow me, if you please."

And then, why, if that boulder don't get up and slowly walk right out from under me! At which time I notice that it ain't a boulder at all, but none other than a massive ol' Tortoise! Well, I were so completely taken aback by his sudden appearance and so entirely smitten by the vastness of his size, the patterns on his shell, the economy of his wrinkly neck and arms and legs, why, how could I *not* stare after him in mute wonder, I ask you? I'd only seen little green turtles before, never someone even nearly the likes of him!

So I jumps to my feet, pulling on my socks and boots as fast as I can. And just as that ol' Tortoise is about to put his wide, stubby foot into the grass alongside the banks, he stretches out his wrinkly ol' neck, looks back around at me, blinks his wise, black eyes, and I hear his voice say:

"No need to rush. Too nice a day."

And then he just keeps a-goin' on along, expecting (rightly, it turns out) that I would continue to follow him. 'Twere odd, Book, but I went right along after him without question. For one thing, because he were so purely fascinating, but also because he were on such a definite course, and his very momentum was undeniable.

Finally, though, my curiosity gets the better of me.

"Excuse me," says I, "but where are we going?"

He stops, and he turns his head all the way back to look a-way up at me. And again I hear his kind voice:

"The Well has something to tell you."

"The Well? What Well?"

"Why, the Well in the Belly of the Forest."

"Aha!" says I. I suppose because I'd never heard of such a thing and "Aha!" is the only thing I can think of to say.

And before I can ask another question, the Tortoise is on his way again. Again, I follow along behind him. Then he takes a sharp turn into dense, dark green grasses, and as I take the same sharp turn, I look down and notice that he is leading us along a skinny little trail – a trail I'd never noticed before, though I'd gone by that very spot a trillion and two times. And as this skinny trail begins to curve, these dark green grasses get denser and higher and the trees grow closer, and I can feel us going around and around, spiraling in smaller and smaller circles until, at last, we come into a small, shaded clearing, which has a very strange, hushed feeling about it.

In the center of this clearing stands a most odd structure, with kind of a cone-shaped wooden roof. The base of it is perfectly round and made of rocks piled and balanced on top of one another – all different shapes and sizes and kinds of rocks, and yet somehow they all fit so snugly and solidly together – why, it feels as if they have been there forever and will stay there just as long.

And, Book, I suddenly feel a little frightened by the silence and the mystery of the place, as it is the very *quietest* place I've ever been to in the whole of the Forest. I hear no birds, no insects, no rustling of any kind, only the slightest breath of a breeze through the trees.

I whisper to the Tortoise:

"What do you think the Well wants with the likes of me?"

"The Well will tell."

And he just keeps on a-looking at me, and so I know there is nothing for it but for me to approach the Well, and so I do. Slowly, I steps up to it – whereupon I note the bucket and the crank and the rope to one side. Then, putting my hands upon the rocks, I look over and down into the circle of cool blackness, and I say:

"Well, hello there, Well!"

I figured I oughta be friendly, at least. But, in response, I hear only silence. So I bend further over into the darkness and call down:

"Hello, Well, it's *me!*"

And it echoes back, *"It's me! It's me! It's me!"*

And after that, why, I don't know how to proceed. So I look to the Tortoise, who proceeds to instruct me:

"Let the bucket down. Get the bucket up. Set the bucket down. Watch the water."

So I do like he says. But as I let that bucket down into the Well, why, it slips right out of my grasp, and it goes falling and falling – far, *so far* – as if it is dropping down into the very middle of the Whirld! Then, finally, in the deep, deep distance I hear a *kerslosh!*

And then, when I see the rope go taut, I begin to pull and pull and pull that heavy bucketful of water up and up, pulling until my arms are trembling and my hands are raw. Finally, I haul that bucket up and out, and I set it on the ground, trying not to spill any of it.

And then I watch the water.
And I wait . . .

Well, all of sudden that bucket of Well water flattens out like a pane of glass. And then, *bubbles* begin to come – very small at first, then bigger and bigger and more and more plentiful. *Ohhh,* there come so many bubbles bubbling up from the bottom of this bucket. Then I gasp, as I start to see flashes of *gold* in the water, and these golden flashings come faster and faster, and then – *oh, my!* – they reveal themselves to be gleaming *golden letters!*

And as these letters pop up out of the water and bob and float around on the surface, all of a sudden a shaft of sunlight shines through the dense leaves above and sets these golden letters to *sparkling*. And then, why, the letters do a sort of dance around each other until, at last, they arrange themselves into these words:

LEAVE
THE FOREST
GO HOME
NOW

Well. You can imagine my agitation, Book.

"What do you mean *Leave the Forest*?" I demand of the bucket. "What do you mean *Go Home?* Why, the Forest *is* my Home!"

But in answer, them golden letters only part and dissolve back into the water. I guess they didn't much like being reprimanded. So I rushes over to that Well and I shouts down into it:

"What do you mean *Leave the Forest?*"

But it only echoes back, *"Leave the Forest! Leave the Forest!"*

"What do you mean *Go Home?*"

But it only echoes back, *"Go Home! Go Home!"*

So I turn to the Tortoise to ask his opinion.

"Well, how do ya like that?" I say.

But he is gone.

So, sure, I go a-tearing out of that clearing and back through the Forest, and I come charging into the cottage to find Mad Aunt Harriet knitting her eternal scarf and muttering to herself. I breathlessly report to her that this big ol' Tortoise took me to see a most exasperating Well. To which she replies, as if I have just remarked that the sky was blue:

"*Ahhh* . . . And what did the Well have to tell, dear?"

Yes, Book, I were amazed, though not in the least surprised, that clearly Mad Aunt Harriet had herself some acquaintance with this here Well, yet she had never said so much as a single word about it. (Likely, she forgot. She's always got so much on her mind.)

Well, when I tell her what this Well told me, she just goes right on a-knitting. But, oh, I *will* have a discussion with her, what with the lilac dream and the whole day unfolding so extraordinarily! So I hammer on at her as she clicks and clacks them knitting needles.

"Now, Mad Aunt Harriet, I put to you what I suspect is a mighty important question: Why in the Whirld would the Well tell me to '*Go Home*' when I already *am* Home?"

"*Hmmm*, now let me think, dear . . . Of course, the Well talks in the most confounding riddles and I – *oh!*"

And she stops. Still as a statue. Knitting needles poised mid-air. And her eyes stare straight ahead, growing rounder and rounder and more and more alarmed. Then she slowly turns to look at me.

"Oh, my, Little Girl. Oh, my, my, *my* . . ."

And she throws her knitting to the floor and right then and there insists that we must put our hands on every last memorandum of hers this very instant. Now, as Mad Aunt Harriet's memorandums have all been written on pieces of cloth and canvas, in the margins of books, and on the backs and sides and corners of endless miscellany – well, fear not, Book, I shall not take either of us through that exhaustive search, but only directly to the result of it, which was this:

At long last, she found and read aloud the following memorandum, whereby a most foundational truth dropped upon us like an anvil.

This has been an altogether remarkable evening! A Human Girlchild was delivered here. At first, I thought she was much too muddy to bring in, besides being dead. But she has turned out to be not in the least bit dead, and is possibly quite marvelous in some way. I have found on her person as follows:

Item 1. A large wet lump of purple felt, which looks to be a hat.

Item 2. A silvery contraption, with tiny jewels and delicate filigree. Palm size.

Item 3. The remaining quarter of an egg salad sandwich, which was delicious.

I have almost decided to keep her, as I believe that if I concentrate, I might manage to make room for her in my schedule.

And with those few sentences, it were made plain to us both that the Forest of Forgetfullness, my most cherished Home, was never my true Home at all.

Somehow, Book, I *knew* that I had always known it. In that moment of truth, I felt as if my restlessness, which had always been there, beneath, like an underground stream, had just broken through into the wide open air and was rushing out to seek some great river. Yes, as profoundly happy as I have been here, in truth, my spirit has always silently yearned to travel and to seek out new horizons. Though I must say, when I first heard tell of it, my heart was anything but fond of the idea.

"You see, that's why a name never stuck to you, Little Girl! You don't belong here! And did I not say that you simply *reeked* of Destiny this morning? Oh, there's so much to be done . . . "

And Mad Aunt Harriet suddenly leaps up and starts searching for things, while I chase after her, trying to continue the conversation.

"Hang on now, o' course I belong here! I love it here, and I feel at Home here and – *awww*, what does an ol' Well know, anyway…"

"Well, the Well knows *everything* – everything there is to know, that's all!" And she whirls around and looks up at me and declares, "And *you*, Little Girl, will be leaving here first thing in the morning!"

All the animals and I most vociferously protest this proclamation. But Mad Aunt Harriet was having none of it, no way, no how.

"She will be leaving *first thing in the morning*, and I shall brook no disagreement whatsoever!"

"But, Mad Aunt Harriet, I – "

And she turns on me with such a fierceness, Book, and I can see in her eyes, it is born of no small amount of heartache.

"Don't be a fool, child! Destiny is calling, and *by gum* you shall answer with head high, shoes shined, and bells on, if I have anything to say about it!"

"But can't it wait a little? Until I'm used to the idea, and – "

"Why, I've never heard of anything so reckless! Trifle with Destiny, Little Girl, and you'll have no end of trouble. Oh, you'll have mountains and avalanches of trouble if you go around being so hubristic! Shame on you, now – *shoo!* I've got to prepare, I've got to – *oh*, where did I put that . . . "

And she was already heading off, searching for this, hunting for that, in the grip of her own voyage and well beyond stopping.

So, alas, there was nothing for it but to go climb a tree. And a-way high up in the branches, I nestle in. And, sure, I takes out my Music Box. I hold it up so the sunlight can flash and play off the little jewels and the pretty, silver filigree.

Then I lift its delicate lid, and I sigh into it . . .

And when it begins to play its lovely, lilting song, I begin to breathe easier. And as I hum along, I am reminded of how something at the soul of this song has so often caused this very ache in me to go and travel the Whirld. And the music begins to soothe me some.

That is, until them birds show up and completely ruin my peace of mind. Oh, first they came to harmonize, o' course, but when I tell them about the Tortoise and the Well and Mad Aunt Harriet and my imminent leave-taking, well, they proceed to alert and inform me, all in a wild, chattering bunch, that I absolutely *cannot* leave the Forest under any circumstances because the Forest of Forgetfullness is a capricious forest – it comes and goes, hither and yon, all over the Whirld and sometimes beyond, and, as such, I will never find it again.

Meaning, Book: I can never, *ever* come back. I can never see Mad Aunt Harriet or the animals or this whole beloved place ever again. Yet another truth landing upon me with a dark and terrible thud.

But, oh, how them birds do go on! And, why, they begin to recount overlapping tales of the many horrible and disastrous fates which will surely befall me once I leave. So, as I make my way back to the cottage, I resolve to make a powerful case to Mad Aunt Harriet for postponing my departure so as to devise an organized plan before I set out. And then I realize that my entire line of reasoning is pointless. Knowing her, she'll forget about the whole thing by morning anyhow.

But it was not to be.
It was to be a morning like no other.

At the very first drop of dawn, Mad Aunt Harriet is poking me to wake up. She thereupon presents me with three gifts that she spent all night creating. They are enthralling, Book, and right then and there these three gifts almost completely and entirely change my inclination about leaving.

Here they are, and here be their particular uses:

First, a Peerless Pocketknife, which not only folds out into a nice sharp knife, but also a fork, a spoon, a toothbrush, a hairbrush, a master key that unlocks all locks, and other such-like handy implements.

Second, a multicolored Pouch of Infinite Coinage that I have only just to reach into and I shall draw forth endless monies where-soever I go in the Whole Wyde Whirld.

Third, an utterly *sumptuous* Scarlet Velvet Traveling Cape that moves and swishes in the most elegant way. Book, this Cape is a transformational *wonder!* It can turn into a hammock, a bedroll, a traveling sack, and it has the most convenient quality of dressing me in the perfect ensemble for any occasion. We tested it, and it put me in the most *beautiful* of ball gowns – a silvery number in which I wanted to stay forever, but Mad Aunt Harriet informed me that I certainly couldn't go traipsing through the forest in a ball gown.

So, you see, on the one hand, these magnificent and astonishing gifts made me feel so all-fired ready to meet Destiny I could fly! But, on the other hand, the moment to depart was all too fast upon me.

And the next thing I know, there I am standing on the doorstep of the cottage, and there is Mad Aunt Harriet handing me my beautiful new Scarlet Velvet Traveling Sack. And she tugs my hair a little. And she smiles at me. Then, all of a sudden, she gets all alarmed and all a-flutter and points to my Sorrow, still and always glittering so prettily around my neck.

"Oh, your Sorrow . . . Oh, for pity's sake, Little Girl, whatever you do, *don't lose your Sorrow!* And you mustn't ever give it away, do you understand? It's yours and *only yours*, like it or not! Promise me, do you hear?"

"I promise," I say. "I hear."

"Oh, my dear, once you've swallowed it, it'll hurt so horribly – why, it'll quite likely kill you stone dead, right there on the spot! So, don't even *think* of taking it until you absolutely have to. But don't ever think of *never* taking it, because of course you absolutely *must!* My . . . it's such an exquisitely *beautiful* Sorrow, isn't it?"

"That it is, Mad Aunt Harriet . . . that it is."

And then we look at each other. And in that look, we see it all – all that we have ever been and all that we will never be again. That, indeed, after this next moment, we will never see each other again in this here life.

Well, it is too much to bear, Book, what with all the animals sniffling all around us too. So, o' course, Mad Aunt Harriet and I thereupon sob ourselves about six buckets of tears. And then we stop, because we both know the time is nigh. And she takes me by the shoulders and looks me deep in the eye.

"Now then, Little Girl . . . Goodbye."

Then she turns on her heel, walks back into the cottage, closes the door, and locks it. And I panic.

"Wait! Mad Aunt Harriet! Which way do I go?"

And she calls out from behind the door:

"Why, any way that suits you, I suppose!"

And so there were nothing for it but for me to go. And as I stood upon that doorstep solo, it came upon me to turn around real slow, so's to *feel* which way would most truly call me. And when I sincerely felt more for one direction than the others, why, I set off taking steps, one in front of the other, until I came upon this here fine, welcoming rock from which I now write.

I cannot yet know if I shall remember anything of Mad Aunt Harriet once I step out of the Forest, but if I do – if I should be so fortune-favored as to remember her – I know that I shall miss her with a great, deep ache as long as I live. Except for her cello playing, Book. That was truly an assault to the senses. And I have the freedom to say that to you now, in confidence.

And, why, it would be out-and-out negligent for me to neglect to record the most auspicious nature of *your* appearance, Book – and at the very moment of my leave-taking too. Think of it . . . How eloquently Life is speaking to me, all at once!

After having just so freshly chosen my direction, I am heading round the back of the cottage, see, and I pass by the Skyhole with its ever-mounting pile of strange and wonderful things. And just as I leave it behind me, I hear the sound of a new arrival dropping onto the pile. I turn around and, oh, what a sight I see! There *you* be, in all your beautifully embossed leatherboundness – so perfectly perched on top!

To be entirely truthful, Book, I picked you up expecting that such an artful creation as you must surely be filled with many magnificent words of inspiration. But to instead find within you the complete surprise of your beckoning blankness, fresh page after page after page... Why, your arrival as an invitation to make memorandums of my own were so fortuitously timed, it were obvious you must come along with me, no questions asked.

And though I most certainly cannot promise you one single inspirational word of wisdom, it appears we are in this together. I should like to hereupon thank you for forbearing to bear the words of one such as I upon yourself. I am most beholden to you.

Now, to make one last note before I depart these most dearly beloved woods altogether . . .

I think it must be, Book, that leaving is something I were always destined to do. Yes . . . Though it is true that I were terribly heavy-hearted at first, I must report that my heart has felt ever and ever lighter inside of me with each step, with each new patch of bright green velvet moss, with the expressive majesty of each new tree, with – oh, listen to that! New birdsong, even!

Indeed, it is already so intoxicating to have gone further and walked differently. Everything feels so fresh – like this breeze just now ruffling through your pages. Why, it smells like lilacs, don't it? Just like that dream . . .

Now then, onward!
To the Edge of the Forest – and beyond!

Wherein the Road Plays a Trick

Book, it has become completely and entirely apparent to me that Life holds extreme unexpectednesses up its sleeve. Just wait'll you hear . . .

So, there am I, on my merry way through the Forest, when, sure enough, I begin to see great big, bright blue gaps of sky between the trees. Well, naturally, I rushes on ahead to at long last make my acquaintance with that fabled Wild Blue Yonder.

But suddenly I pulls myself up short, because – lo and behold – I have arrived at the Edge! That's right, the tips of my boots are tickling the very last blades of grass that grow at the very end of the Forest of Forgetfullness and at the very beginning of the Whole Wyde Whirld! Why, my toes are all a-tingle with the understanding that they now stand face to face with my future.

Well, as I stand there marveling at the monumentalness of this moment, so enraptured and awestruck am I by the wide, wide open magnificence that greets me – the endless high grasses, such a rich, warm gold in the sun, waving and waving with the wind. And, oh, Book, the *sky* . . . Why, I would not venture to even *begin* to try to capture what I feel about seeing so much uninterrupted sky!

Ah, yes, this is why one so longs to be a Poet, so as to put words upon such sights and feelings of such magnitude and import. But I daren't try such a thing, lest I profane such Glory by choosing words that are weak and witless.

Anyhow, I meander from the forward thrust of my tale, which is this: Directly in front of my feet, running along the Edge of the Forest, lies the most beautiful, wide, flat, dirt Road. And it is so beckoning, I takes hold of the branch of an obliging sycamore tree and I leans as far out as I can to have a look-see – and *ohhh*, I can see that this Road ribbons all the way off to one horizon in one direction and all the way off to the other horizon in the other!

But, Book, the strangest thing . . .

Just as I lift a foot to take my first historic and much anticipated step out of the Forest, why, I am suddenly and mysteriously overcome by the pure amplitudinousness of all that suddenly wide open space! Well, I feel so weak and wobbly all over, I find I have to lean up against that ol' sycamore tree for strength. And then, I find myself sliding down it.

And there I sit, in a quivering lump, looking out at all that wide, wide-openness, and then back into the Forest. Looking out and looking back. Looking out and looking back for quite a while.

Oh, yes, *quite* a while, indeed . . .

The thing of it was, Book, I couldn't bring myself to move, pure and simple. Nope, not a single muscle of mine could be coerced into standing up and stepping out onto that Road.

To clarify, sure, my body could move just fine, but my mind seemed to have other ideas. Ideas like: Why should Destiny or some ol' Well I just met care about whether I ever leave this Forest or whether I sit here 'til the end of the Whirld? What business is it of theirs, anyway? And just *why* was I ever fool enough to see myself traveling anywhere, since I don't have the vaguest idea *how* to travel, for one thing, and since I've never even *been* anywhere, for another? And when I *do* step out onto that Road and my memory of who I was before I first came into the Forest comes flying back to meet me, well, what if I remember that I were somebody just awful – and even *hateful* – and then I'll be stuck with her for the rest of my life! *Then* what?

Oh, yes, a torrent of such-like ravenous thoughts feasted upon my fevered brain. You guessed it, Book – I were seized for a prisoner by Fear. Yup, Fear had me in a two-fisted, white-knuckled grip, I tell you! And do you know that Fear would not, for the life and breath of me, let me take one single step out onto that Road? I finally forced myself to stand up, but, nossir, I simply could not take that first step. Why, I might as well have been a *painting* of a person, that's how much I couldn't move. Eventually, I got myself to run, aiming to get me onto that Road by pure velocity – but *dang* if I didn't pull myself up short right at that dadgum Edge every time.

So, there I be, well and truly stuck, and dangerously near to taking root at the foot of that ol' sycamore tree, when, all of a sudden, I hear a *rustling*. And I looks up to seek the source of the sound, and I see, *ohhh* . . . standing directly across the Road from me in the tall golden grass, graceful head held high:

The most enchanting, perfectly pure white Doe!

Well, I am stricken mute by the sudden sight of such a sublimity of an animal. She looks at me with her black, liquid eyes, but I don't hear her voice speak to me at all. So, we both of us just stand there and behold each other from across the Road in a most profoundly companionable silence. And she touches her nose so delicately in the air in my direction. Then, suddenly, she leaps right out into the middle of the Road!

Then she blinks at me, and she runs a few steps one way. Then she runs a few steps the other way. Why, it seems she wants to play! And it is so odd, but I feel as if I *know* her in some way. So, without even thinking, I takes her up on her invitation. And before I know it, there am I, standing smack dab in the middle of that doggone Road – with a big smile on my face, to boot!

"Well, I'll *be* . . . It was just that easy, after all," thinks I.

Yes, there I stand, flat on my fine feet, looking all around me – at the Whirld, at the Forest, at the Road, at the Doe – simply beside myself with delight. And I laugh, and I declare:

"How all-fired ridiculous that I were so afraid! It's not like the Road was gonna open up and *swallow* me or anything . . . "

Well, o' course, Book, that's exactly and precisely what the Road went and did. Yup, you heard me right. This here Road starts grumbling, and then rumbling, and then crumbling completely out from under me! (And this, most particularly, is what I make reference to when I mention *unexpectednesses in the extreme*.)

And through that fast-widening crevice, I am falling and hollering and hollering and falling all the way down to what feels like the middle of the Whirld! And I am just a big bursting ball of pure screaming terror, when whaddaya know but a friendly tree root that happens to be sticking out of the side of this endless cliff suddenly catches me quite neatly by my belt and politely stops me from falling forever and ever, thank you very much.

Well. There I be, trembling, gasping, face all soaked with tears, arms and legs all dangling in the air. And, Book, I am astounded to see – far, far below me, twinkling and sparkling in all its beautiful blue-blackness – none other than the *night sky!* And then I looks a-way, way up above me and, sure, what do I see but the *day sky* shining away, brightly as you please, as if this sort of thing happens all the time. And right then and there, I know that I have, in fact, called it accurately:

I have indeed fallen clear down into the middle of the Whirld!

So, suspended there, halfway between sun and stars – well, what else can I do, I ask you, but laugh my fool head off at the ingenious joke of it all? I mean, there I am plunging headlong towards oblivion in one moment, and in the next moment, why, I feel so infinitely, thrillingly *alive* that there's just not enough of me to hold all of me in one skin! I dunno, Book, it just struck me funny.

Anyhow, after I've had me a good laugh, I reckon it's high time to clamber back up there and head on Home. So, I proceed to climb that cliff, thanks to the hospitality of the many and varying tree roots and rocks along the way. And reaching the top at last, I hoist myself back to the friendly foot of that ol' sycamore tree, whereupon I lean back upon it so's to catch my breath and cogitate awhile.

And as I am a-sitting there, Book – *as I am a-sitting there* – why, do you know that this Road proceeds to close up, right before my eyes? And then it has the gall to lay there acting as if it has been all flat and solid like that the whole time and like nothing in the least bit out of the ordinary has just happened! Now, I do realize that it is entirely unnecessary to point out to you the unexpectedness of *this* development, Book, but I must note that, right then and there, it became patently obvious that I had me an exceptionally *tricky* Road on my hands, and that, frankly, some of my aforementioned Fears of stepping out onto it were not at all ill-placed.

But as I sat on the Edge observing this Road, which had so beckoned me and then made such mischief with me, it comes to me in a flash that it does not matter in the least what this Road has in mind, toying with me like that. The one and only thing that *does* matter is that Destiny is waiting on me, and there is naught to do but go meet up with it – Fear or no Fear, mischievous Road or no. Guess there's nothing like almost dying to clear your head, Book.

So, I figured this Road would surely see that I meant business if I just kept at it. O' course, I had to step out and fall through it another 3,426 times – which might well be an exaggeration, Book, but not by much. In truth, I lost count. Oh, sure, I were plenty terrified the next few times I stepped out on that Road, but after a while, I not only got so's I didn't mind falling, why, I became quite an *expert* faller. As a matter of fact, I got so's I was positively hankering for that big ol' rumbling crevice to open up under my feet! And whenever it did, why, I'd get all wracked with screaming laughter, and sometimes I'd see just how loud I could holler all the way down.

Now, as I am here to tell you the tale, it must be apparent that every single time (sometimes sooner, sometimes later) some friendly tree root would catch me so neatly, just like it did the first time, and then I'd just clamber right on up again. And there were times when I purely delighted in just dangling there, idling peacefully betwixt and between Night and Day.

The salient point here, Book, is that this tricky ol' Road just plumb wore out all my Fear – like water smooths a rock, I guess. So, where I were once petrified, I tell you what . . . I wonder if I won't feel purely *eager* the next time I see an Edge and have to go beyond it.

Oh, and speaking of unexpectednesses, listen to this . . .

So, just a while ago, as the sun is starting to set and the most beauteous rose-gold light is beginning to spread across everything in sight, I steps out onto the Road once more, and whaddaya know – it stays shut! That's right, it just keeps on being smooth, solid ground beneath my feet! Oh, you can bet I watch and wait for it to open up again. But, no, something deep in the core of me knows that something is different. Something is done. And then I look up from the Road to see:

The Forest of Forgetfullness is no more.
It has vanished, silently and entirely.
As if it had never, ever been.

And, sure, I feel suddenly so forlorn, I feel an oncoming river of tears rushing up from inside, threatening to overwhelm me. But then I see before me all the ravishing resplendence that spreads out in place of the Forest. Why, it is so awe-inspiring, it seems to somehow *sing* to my sad spirit, to soothe and uplift me all at once. *Oh, my* . . . all the lush, green hills, all them billowing clouds all a-flame with all the colors of the setting sun! And then I am moved to turn a full, slow circle. And as I behold all the beauty that surrounds me in every direction, I feel myself to be drinking in the welcome of the Whole Wyde Whirld.

And in that moment of communion with all that glory, I hear a sudden rustling in the high grass behind me, and I turn around – and who should be standing there but the Doe. And I laugh and I say:

"Why, hello, you!"

And she looks deep into my soul with those dark, liquid eyes of hers. And I hear her say, in the kindest voice:

"Hello, Lillian . . . "

And then she leaps off and away and out of sight.

"Lillian?" says I. *"Hmph.* What kind of an odd word is that?"

And then I realize:

"Why, that's no word . . . That's my *name!"*

And I don't mind telling you, Book, I became outright giddy with it. Turns out I had so deeply and dearly missed my name without even knowing it. *Lillian!* Yes, of course . . . Lillian. Now, how did that Doe know? Well, I do not know. But what I *do* know is that the name Lillian is my very own, as surely as I know my own feet.

And as I pen these words, with the Forest of Forgetfullness now disappeared and evaporated, having been so anxious and uncertain if I would remember anything at all of my life there, I am so very relieved to report that I am remembering conversations with

Mad Aunt Harriet, and I am recalling all the animals and our cottage and all my favorite spots in the Forest. I declare this vivid memory of my past to be a gift and a solace, a herald of hope for my future, and a vote of confidence in my present. So, I imagine the rest of my memory from before I wandered into the Forest should be along any moment now. Oh, what a revelation it will be when all the rest of who I am comes Home to me!

My, I do feel exceptionally sleepy . . . All that tomfoolery with the Road clean wore me out.

Yes, as I write, I am all camped out and cozy, bathing in the light of the fat white moon, the crowning glory of a starry night sky – *above* me this time, much the way I prefer it, thank you very much.

But I have to laugh, Book, because the Road and I have come to a peace, methinks. Y'see, here I be, lying in my Scarlet Velvet Cape, which I've twirled into a nice, soft bedroll, watching my lovely little campfire crackle and spark, where else but *smack dab in the middle* of this here Road. That's right, I have decided to set up my very first camp right here upon the very spot that feared me, and I just *dare* it to open up while I am asleep. Go ahead and see if I'm not ready for you, Road.

When the sun is up, so am I!

———

Book, I tell you, I am plumb mystified.
I am truly bewildered.
Yessir, I am *thoroughly* perplexed.

I was up with the dawn, see, all set to head Home. And, well, I have stood here and been silent and still for quite a long while now, watching the sun climb higher and higher in the sky, expecting the rest of my memory to come a-knockin' with all sorts of thrilling facts to get excited over.

But, so far, *nothing.* Nary a scrap.
Yet another unexpectedness.
Hmph.

Now, how in the Whirld is a person supposed to go Home if they don't remember a single thing about said Home or where it might possibly be located or who they even *are*, for cryin' out loud? The one and only thing I do know is that my name is Lillian, of that I am certain. Yes, indeed . . . it seems that I have a conundrum on my hands. So, how shall I proceed?

Well, it's as plain as the sun in the sky that it is foolhardy to stand here and fret about when or if or how much or which part of my memory will return *until* it returns, else I will be standing here on this same spot in the middle of this here Road 'til the end of eternity. And I tell you, I have *far* too much of a thirst to see the Whirld, so, by gum, I shall do just that!

Let's see now . . .

This-a-way the Road leads off to Somewhere . . . *My*, will you look at the wonderful way it winds and twirls all the way up into those mighty mountains? And *that*-a-way the Road leads to Everywhere Else. *Oh*, see the way it weaves and wanders so prettily through all them green hills and then goes ribboning right on up to the sky? Yessir, that's the way for me, I'm sure of it!

Wait now, just to be certain . . .

Yup, I just now tested walking a few steps in both directions and the Road to Somewhere didn't seem nearly so nice.

Wouldn't it be fascinating, though, to be two of myself and go in both directions at once? Why, then we could arrange to meet up someplace and have what would likely be quite an amazing discussion! Nonetheless, I am but one Lillian, now heading off, most decidedly, to Everywhere Else.

But I leave you with this last thought, Book, that has just this very moment presented itself:

It comes to me that perhaps all that Fear and all that falling and hollering and such might've just scared off my poor, dear memory. And as it hasn't known me in such an awfully long time, perhaps it feels nervous and shy and is hiding out until it feels sure of me.

Well, I do not blame it in the least.
I expect it will catch up with me when it is good and ready.

Alright, Whole Wyde Whirld, here I come!

Wherein I Meet a Horse

Now, let me just say right off that I pen these words from a stinky old shed where I am all locked up and can barely breathe. That's right, you heard me, Book – *I am held captive!* I write by the light of the moon streaming through the slats, as I wait upon the perfect moment to free myself and free Hank and then hightail it out of here posthaste!

Who is Hank, you ask? Hank is a horse. Oh, he is a most noble animal who has been enslaved and exploited by a pair of idiot villains, and from tonight onward he will be out of their grimy hands forever if I have anything to say about it.

In this moment, Hank is chained up in a corral right next to me, and he and I have been conversating through a loose slat. He has been telling me that these two scoundrels nightly drink and fight and pass out by the fire, so when they are out good and cold, we can make short work of this terrible place.

You know what, Lillian? It's likely to be a good idea to settle down some. Maybe record how it is you've gotten to where you've got – that is to say, all locked up and having to escape with a big tall horse in the middle of the night.

Alright then, here's the how of it . . .

Earlier today I'm a-walking down the Road, see, all hot and dusty, when I pass a little family with two young children walking in the other direction. The man tips his cap, and the woman says to me:

"That poor horse only changes color just a little bit, honey, so don't get your hopes up."

"Why, thank you kindly, I'll keep that in mind," says I, even though I have no idea what she could possibly mean. But I assume I will soon find out, and rightaway I do, indeed.

Just a few more paces down the Road, I behold a huge sign that is so old the paint is faded and peeling. But, written in a pretty script, it says:

- Be Amazed By -

Charlemagne the Wonderhorse

Watch Him Change Into a Thousand Blazing Colors Right Before Your Very Eyes!

Underneath that is a newer sign, painted very sloppily, which says:

HiGGS + BOggs, oWNerS

And in a few paces more, I come upon this ramshackle little shack that looks like somebody slapped the whole thing together with two nails and some spit. That's when I first set eyes upon these two grimy-looking fellas topped by two grimy-looking hats. They are sitting on some boxes and playing cards. And as I get closer, I hear one of 'em yelling:

"Why, I oughta knock your block off, Boggs! You're as big a cheat as your jailbird mother was!"

And he throws his cards at the fella called Boggs, who yells back:

"I'm warning you, Higgs, for the last time – *you keep your big fat mouth offa my mother!*"

Then Higgs grabs Boggs by the shirtfront. And just as Higgs raises his fist to wallop him, Boggs spots me.

"Wait! We got a customer!"

Higgs turns and sees me and calls out:

"Hey, girlie! Howzabout some water? Water's free if you pay to see the Wonderhorse!"

As I am parched, and also quite curious about this Wonderhorse, o' course, I calls out:

"Oh, water'd be wonderful, thank you!"

And this Boggs fella dips a ladle into a dented old bucket of water. And as I walk on over and reach out to take it, he says:

"Hold it right there, girlie . . . Pay up!"

So I give him a coin, and I take the ladle, and I drink the water. Then Boggs brings me around back to see this Wonderhorse.

Well, Book, I am utterly demolished, because what do I see before me but a very tall, drab, grey horse whose ribs are sticking out, who has shackles on his legs and a wide iron collar around his neck, and who is chained to a pole that he is forced to walk around and around.

And this poor horse looks over at me, and, *ohhh,* the endless heartache in his beautiful brown eyes breaks my heart into a thousand jagged pieces. And through my tears, I do note that, yes, he is subtly changing color from drab grey to drab brown. And I head on over to this poor creature with a mind to caress and comfort him, but, right then, Boggs rudely plants himself in front of me and demands that I pay more if I want to pet the Wonderhorse. So I give him another coin, and he leaves me be.

And then comes a quiet wonderfulness, Book . . .

Though I don't think I've made note of it yet, since I left the Forest I have not been able to hear the animals at all like I used to. And I make note of this now because as soon as I draw near to this horse I hear him speak just as clear as clear can be, exactly like I used to back in the Forest!

We introduce ourselves, and he tells me that his real name is Hank and that he loathes and despises the name Charlemagne and that he has been owned by one cruel person after another. This confuses me, as I do not understand how a living being could be *owned* by anybody. But he assures me that he's been bought and sold and bought and sold over and over again, so he is legally owned, and that's just the way of things.

I tell him if that truly *is* the way of things, well, then I will simply buy him and free him, as I have no end of money due to my Pouch of Infinite Coinage. And off I marches to carry out what I think is a mighty fine idea, while Hank calls after me to please be careful, as those two villains are no end of stupid and therefore plenty dangerous. Well, it turns out, Book, that I were the one who were no end of stupid and plenty dangerous to myself. You be the judge.

I go 'round front, see, to where those two nasty pieces of work are *thumb-wrestling*, if you please, and arguing and slapping each other with their hats. And, *oooh*, I am so riled up, I walk straight up to them cruel scoundrels, I plants my hands on my hips, and I says to 'em:

"Mister Higgs! Mister Boggs! You two are the very cruelest of scoundrels, and you have treated that horse worse than despicably, and so I am going to buy him from you and free him. So, *here!*"

And I reaches into my Pouch, and I draw forth a whopping, dripping handful of coins, and I slaps them coins down on one of those old boxes of theirs.

Says Boggs, "Hot diggity, Higgs! That there's a whole *heap* o' – "

"Shut yer fat yap, Boggs!" says Higgs.

Then Higgs turns to me with a sneer.

"Listen here, you! You ain't got near enough money to buy that horse."

"Oh, but you are so very much mistaken, Mister Higgs," says I, "because I got me puh-*lenty* of money!"

And again I reaches into my Pouch, and I draws forth *another* whopping, dripping handful of coins, and I smacks all o' *them* down on that box too.

"There! That oughta do it and then some! Now, I shall take that poor horse outta here this instant, away from your evil, rotten selves."

And as Boggs dumps out the water and starts shoveling that mound of coins into the bucket, Higgs snarls at me.

"You must be looney if you think that's anywhere *near* enough money, sister! We got ourselves a Wonderhorse back there. Say . . . how much money you got in that thing anyhow?"

Oh, yes, Book, I were both furious and witless enough to boast that this were a Pouch of Infinite Coinage, so I had no end of money. And, *oh, yes*, I reach into that Pouch *twice more* to prove my idiotic point. So, sure, those two nefarious crooks overtake me and yank the Pouch away from me and try to get still more money out of it. But o' course the Pouch won't work for them and stays empty. I explain to them that the Pouch's magic were magicked for me alone, but they are in such a wild-eyed frenzy for money, they can't hear anything even remotely sensible. So they thrust the Pouch back into my hands and then start hammering away at me about how I *will* give them as much money as they want and how I *just better* or they will put *me* in chains too!

Well, o' course, I do *try* to give them more money, but the Pouch seems to know that I sincerely do not want to and gets stubborn on my behalf, and then and there it refuses to give out another single coin. So I explain to them two nitwits that the Pouch is exhausted and hates them with all its might. And I very pointedly point out that they already have a whole *bucketful* of my money. But instead of them having a single lick of sense or even *one small dot* of fair play in them, they go on ahead and lock me up in this here disgustingly smelly shed, where I can barely breathe, while they decide what to do with me.

Anyhow, night has now fallen and they've made their campfire and gotten their reprehensible selves all liquored up. I tell you, they sure are making a big fat lot of noise out there.

Oh, no, Book, what I have just witnessed! I am most disheartened to report a deeply dispiriting happenstance . . .

I just now heard them two brutes shouting at each other, so I looks out through a hole in the wood, and there they are, locked in a ferocious tug of war with my poor Pouch of Infinite Coinage! And what with all the punching and kicking and spitting, well . . . there's just no way around it but to come right out and say it: Mad Aunt Harriet's Pouch of Infinite Coinage has fallen victim to the fire, a casualty of their greed and their stupidity. Yes, that exquisite creation is fast becoming mere ashes and memory.

But, wait, what is that fragrance? Such a familiar scent it is . . . Why, it seems to be coming from the burning of the Pouch . . . Oh, I know *exactly* what it is! Yes, it is the aroma of all the herbs and oils and flowers Mad Aunt Harriet invents with as she stands stirring her potions in her big iron pot over the fire. *Ohhh,* I feel so mightily homesick in this moment.

Wait, Book, I have to check and see what all that racket is . . .

Happy news! My captors have taken to bashing each other over the head with bottles! Doubtless they will soon have knocked each other senseless, so I need only bide my time.

Meanwhile, I must make note: I am truly upset that I bungled my fine idea so very badly. I simply did not understand about money and mean people and the disastrous combination of the two. I feel so dadgum *foolish*. How I wish I'd been smart enough to be wise. But I guess you can only know what you know when you know it and not before, eh? Still, it sure is frustrating to have been so dim about something that's now just as plain as paint. I have confided this upset feeling about my foolishness to Hank, and he says to be patient with myself. Book, I already think he's going to be one of the nicest friends I'll ever have, and I simply will not let him spend another night in slavery, that's all there is to it.

Hank just told me them two cruel fools are out stone cold.
Now's our chance – we're off and away!

———

Book, since I wrote those words above, a whole universe of marvelousness has transpired! Oh, where do I even *begin* to begin?

Well, firstly and foremostly, I am most pleased to report that, at present, as the bright blue edges of dawn line the mountains in the far beyond, I myself am languidly lounging 'neath a spreading green apple tree by the sparklingest of streams, breathing in deep gulps of this fresh, delicious night air.

And what of Hank, you may ask? Well, now . . . Hank is munching on green apples. And Hank is drinking long and luxuriantly from said sparkling stream. And Hank is then cantering, just because he feels like it, and then stopping, just because he feels like it, and then, at the drop of a hat, why, he rolls around in the lush, thick grass, just because he feels like it. Oh, Book, what an ecstasy it is to see him! Why, Hank is an utterly and entirely transmogrified horse! You think I exaggerate because you know me. *Ha!* Nope, I merely state a plain truth, and that is this:

Actually and factually, Hank *is* a Wonderhorse!

Now, I shall further extrapolate upon the above declaration momentarily, but first I must not neglect to record yet *another* notable marvelousness, especially in light of the untimely death of my dear Pouch of Infinite Coinage. My Peerless Pocketknife has indeed proven peerless! Though I already mightily admired its toothbrush and backscratcher and other utensils, I must now remark upon the heroism and panache of its master key . . .

Why, Book, I just slips my arm through that loose ol' slat of that stinky ol' shed, and I unlocks that ol' padlock – *clickety-clock!* – and that masterful master key unlocks all them locks on all them chains and shackles. And while I am ever so quietly taking the chains off him, Hank gets terribly fearful for me, and he warns me that I'll get called a Horse Thief, and that could mean a whole heap of trouble. But I tell him that he has every right to be free of their cruelty and that I don't care what anybody calls me, especially not them two wicked chowderheads.

And the split moment he's free of those chains and shackles, Hank tells me to hop on his back so we'll travel faster, and so I do. And as I do, I wonder how *is* it that his coat now feels so satiny sleek, when only just moments ago it had been so marred with sores and scars? But he is urgently telling me to wrap his mane around my wrists and to hold on real tight, and then – with nary a trace of weakness from his long imprisonment – why, Hank simply tears off into the night, as if I am no more than a feather on his back!

Oh, *my*, the ride, Book, the *ride* . . . would that I had the words for it!

Why, sure, I am terrified, and I have to hang on for my dear little life. But, I don't know, some sort of *celebration* from away deep down inside me just leaps right up out of me and starts me whooping and laughing and *yee-haw-ing* and feeling just exactly like I were born to ride, wild and free! Born to it, I tell you! And, naturally, in between trying to not to fall off, I am so exhilarated by the speed, by the sound of his gallop, by the *whooshing* of the wind, and by the sight of the villages and farms and forests rushing by.

And much later, when Hank felt it were at long last safe to slow down, we ambled on into this idyllic valley wherein I now lie, eating these green apples which taste better than I will ever ask any apple to taste ever again as long as I live. Hank says they taste so good because they taste like freedom, and I think he's just exactly right about that.

Anyhow, what was I saying? Oh, *yes!* So, when I slides off Hank, at first I think it's because I am so exceptionally giddy with how much busting out fun I've just had and how free we both are, but, sure enough, I now behold, to my jaw-dropping astonishment, that Hank has somehow become *radiantly* healthy and *immensely* powerful! And as he stands there, so majestic in the moonlight, I see that – indeed, *yes!* – his sores and scars have entirely vanished and his coat is now as sleek as satin!

And, Book, hang onto your hat, because Hank the Wonderhorse has turned out to be, in actual factuality, every bit as amazing as that ol' sign said. That's right, right before my very eyes that big ol' horse is kaleidoscopically blooming into "a thousand blazing colors!" So you see, I do not hyperbolize in the least when I say that this is one *entirely transmogrified horse.*

Oh, dadgum it, one last thing, Book . . .
It's already such a dim memory, I almost forgot to mention it.

As Hank and I were riding off and away, them two vicious varmints did, unfortunately, wake up. I know this for a fact, 'cause a-way off in the distance behind us, we heard them screaming:

"Get back here, you Horse Thief! *Horse Thief!*"

It makes me laugh, Book, truly it does. Why, that's just some dumb, wrong-headed moniker and they are just two ignoble, ignorant scoundrels. I am no more a Horse Thief than I am a butterfly or an elephant. I mean, honestly, can you imagine? They plague this gentle, noble horse with a life of pure exploitationary torture, and then hornswoggle a whole doggone bucketful of coins from me, and then lock me up in a stinky ol' shed, to boot – and they have the gall to call *me* names!

Well, guess what then? They can go right on ahead and call me a Horse Thief, and I will go right on ahead and call them two vile, malodorous, greedy, rotten numbskulls. Furthermore, I resolve not to waste even one more drop of ink or thought upon them two noxious nincompoops as long as I live, thank you very much indeed.

Because I tell you, Book, Hank and I are no end of delighted tonight, here in this perfectly peaceful, pretty place. And I am pure contentment as I watch this stalwart miracle of a creature run and play just exactly as he pleases, all the while expressing himself in an effervescing riot of color. To watch Hank be free and to once again be free myself is a compound bliss that is, alas, far beyond the ken of my pen. Yes, I'm afraid one must be a Great Poet to do justice to such occasions. So, let us suffice it to say, I could lie by this here stream, chomp on this here apple, watch this here Wonderhorse, and think it a mighty satisfying way to spend all my eternity.

Ahhh, Life is happening, Book – can you feel it?
Home must be very close by!

Wherein I Earn a Map

Well, Home, it appears, was not so close by as I expected. Hmph. So, I have decided I must get me a map. All the travelers and explorers I have read about seem to have one, so of course it stands to reason I oughta have one too – even though I don't have a clue as to where I'm going. But with a map, at least I will be well able to determine where I am, and that's something.

Oh, first though, I must record quite a significant decision, which is this: Hank won't be changing color in public any more. It makes us much too conspicuous. Only just yesterday, we were strolling along a riverbank and Hank was having all sorts of fun changing himself into all the colors of the sky and the trees and the river, when a jovial old woman calls out from the porch of her cabin:

"Hello, there, pretty child! *Hoo-eee*, look at all them enchantin' colors he's makin' himself!"

And she gasps and puts her hand to her heart.

"Could it be? Is that the famous Charlemagne the Wonderhorse? My, *my* . . . Why, I been hearin' about this here horse since the Whirld was young."

Well, she is so loving and pure of heart that Hank is more than happy to let her visit with him and pet him. She gets quite teary-eyed and says:

"Oh, the miraculous colors of this creature! Such a balm to my old soul . . . *Ahhh*, the endless glory of Creation!"

And though we were much moved by the old woman's joy, Hank and I had a long talk afterward, wherein we decided to make certain that nobody's anywhere nearby when he's changing colors anymore. We don't want to risk those two good-for-nothings ever tracking him down, nor do we want to risk any other grasping, greedy types taking him into captivity ever again. Nossir. Hank's all through with being famous. All he desires now is a peaceful, everlasting freedom.

Now, before I continue on with my map story, I must record a profoundly flattering thing, which I feel so proud about, and which I know full well to be a vanity, Book, but which I am just busting to tell you: Hank's chosen camouflage color is none other than *the color of my hair!* Can you imagine? Of all the trillions of colors he could've picked! Though I think it looks ever so much more fetching on him than on me and have told him so in no uncertain terms. Someone called him a "chestnut red" horse, which sounds so very nice to both of us. Why, I feel so purely honored about it, I barely know what to do with myself. Alright, so that's that.

Anyhow, Hank and I are passing through a small, scattered sort of a village, see, and I set about inquiring the name and location of this village. And the few folks I ask are vague, as if even *they* are not all that certain where they are located.

Then I spots a little store, and I dip on into it, and I ask the woman who runs it if she has a map, as I need to know where I am so's I can get to where I'm going, wherever that may be.

Turns out she does have a map. So I reach for my Pouch, and then I remember – *oh, my* – well, I'm in a bit of a fix! Hmph. So I says to her:

"Well, I'm in a bit of a fix, y'see, as all my money was just stolen by a pair of nefarious villains. Might I be of some service to you in exchange for the map?"

And she says, "Perhaps . . . I'll consider it, if you, *hmmm . . .* "

The woman, whose name was Delphine, looks around her shop, and she spots some bags of flour that need to be taken upstairs. So I do that.

Then she has me mop all her floors.
Then she has me beat all her rugs.
Then she has me fix the door on her chicken coop.
Then she has me fill in the thatch in a bald area of her roof.
And so forth and so on – that's how badly I wanted that map.

Now, throughout all this strenuous nonsensity, I am noticing that Hank does not approve of this at all, but he just chomps his grass in silence. He later explained to me that, as we had just met and he knew how badly I wanted that map, he didn't want to start off our friendship by giving his opinion without my asking for it.

Well, by day's end, I'd had enough.

"Delphine," says I, "I've had enough. The map, if you please."

I watch her miserably devour the last bites of a chocolate cream pie. Then she crosses her arms and says, all huffy and put upon:

"Well, I don't know where it is. *And I don't care!*"

Can you imagine? For a moment, I don't know what to say to that. And then I *do* know what to say to that.

"Now you listen here, Delphine. It's nobody's fault that your husband left. He just did, that's all. But I must tell you, I think it is downright unkind and dishonorable of you to take it out on a total stranger."

Aw, it were easy, Book . . . I could see by this shirt and that tool that here was a Home a man had left without much care of what he left behind, and none too long ago either. And right I was. Poor Delphine busts out crying a whole bottomless lake of tears and apologizes to me over and over. And she pours out the whole story of how unhappy he made her.

"But do you know why I detest him most of all? Because now I'm in such a *horrible mood* all the time!"

And she sobs and sobs and sobs some more. And I get her a glass of water. (I know where all the glasses are 'cause I washed 'em all earlier.) And I sit with her while she cries it all out.

And then Delphine makes me the most delicious dinner, puts me up in the spare room for the night, and come morning, sends me off with my Scarlet Velvet Traveling Sack bursting with food. And with a sheepish smile, sure, she hands over the map.

People are so interesting, aren't they?

I don't know what to say about the Whirld map, Book. Whenever I look at it, I am overcome by the beauty of it and by all the wonders it represents. It is made of thin, soft leather and rolls up so smoothly. And, oh, the scripted letters of the names of all the places are so intricately rendered. It is truly a masterful work of art! I take it out now and again to befriend it. I run my hands over the names of all the places, and I try to feel if they *feel* like Home. I don't know exactly why, but I reckon this to be the right thing to do with it for now.

Yessir, I am most encouraged to report:
I now know exactly where I am.
Right *here* . . .

That is to say, smack in the middle of Everywhere!

Wherein I Get a Hat

Book, just wait'll I tell you how I came to get this remarkable purple hat, and all on account of Hank's cleverness too! No doubt about it, good ol' Destiny has done me the most generous of turns in meeting me up with Hank. Yessir, I consider myself to be eminently blessed to have found such a wise and noble traveling companion. Sometimes I ride him, sometimes I walk alongside him, and sometimes he vanishes – and I do mean *vanishes*. You heard me right, Book, Hank can absolutely and entirely *evaporate* right into thin air! I know . . . Will the wonders of a Wonderhorse never cease?

The first time he showed me how he could evaporate like that, I asked him why he hadn't plain old evaporated himself out of captivity. Whereupon he told me it were all on account of them chains and shackles. Then he said he's almost glad of them chains and shackles and that whole awful situation, 'cause without it we wouldn't be friends. I about cried.

Oh, you know what? I also learned a little more about Hank's hard history. Somehow, when he were very young, he got separated from his mother and his herd – who are all Wonderhorses, yes – and he were left to wander the Whirld alone and unprotected. Then he got captured by humans, and we all know how *that* turned out. So, now Hank disappears when he wants, reappears when he wants, and is free to run free, hither and yon, all over the Universe. And, so far anyway, when he reappears, he always seems to find me just in time for a ride or for pure good company.

One time, upon reappearing, he told me that he'd been thinking, and he would feel a whole lot happier if I had a saddle and some reins, as I've already slipped off him twice. So, Book, I am ever so tickled to tell you that, with the genius of Mad Aunt Harriet's Cape, I have twirled up the most elegant Scarlet Velvet Saddle and Reins! And, oh *my*, that saddle is ever so plush and so hospitably padded, and my bottom is purely pleasured to get to sit on it for long stretches. So, you see, that's how thoughtful and considerate Hank is. Oh, I couldn't begin to say enough nice things about him, not if I sat here and wrote 'til nightfall.

Anyhow, my long and winding point is: It were Hank who came up with the idea that I should sing for my supper!

Oh, wait, first I have to tell you what happened! See, this is what I get for waiting so long to write, Book. Now there's far too much to fill you in on. Just wait'll you hear . . .

So, there am I, passing through a tumble-down town, see, and hanging above the porch of a pretty wooden dwelling I sees this sign that says:

Savvia the Soothsayer

Beneath this sign sits a small, wild-haired woman in a big rocking chair. And as I am walking by, she calls out:

"You there! Tall Girl! You have money?"

Recalling how I'd helped that four-fingered fiddler pass his hat the other night, and the generous tip he gave me, I reply:

"Why, yes! I do happen to have me a few coins."

"Come here! Give me a coin. Sit, sit, sit . . . "

She motions impatiently to a stool in front of her. And for some strange reason, Book, I go right on along with her, just like that.

I gives her one of my coins, and I sits myself down on that stool straightaway. Then she leans forward and looks me over with a great intensity, taking me in from head to toe. Finally, she leans back in her rocking chair and says:

"*Mm-hmm* ... You are on a very long journey ... *tsk-tsk-tsk-tsk* ... very, *very* long."

"Oh, but I don't have time for a long journey," says I. "I've got to get Home!"

"Well, you won't get there yesterday, I can tell you that!"

"*Awww* ... Wait! Can you tell me where my Home is? Here, maybe you can show me on – "

And I pull out my map for her to have a look, but she pushes it away, "No, no, shush! *Shhhh* ... "

Her eyes are now keenly fixed upon my Sorrow, still and always dangling at my neck. Then she says, of all things to say:

"Your Sorrow, yes ... It could kill you stone dead, you know."

Which, for some reason, she thinks is uproariously funny. And when she finishes laughing, I say:

"Well, I'll tell you what's even funnier, Savvia. My Mad Aunt Harriet said the exact same thi – "

"*Quiet, quiet – be quiet!*"

Why, I nigh on fell off the stool, Book. That woman sure was high strung.

So, Savvia is now tilting her head like she's an animal, as if she's listening to something far away.

"What *is* that? In your bag, your red bag . . . *take it out, take it out!*"

Well, somehow I just know she means my Music Box, so, sure, I fetch it from my Traveling Sack. And the moment she lays eyes upon it, Savvia sighs and clucks at its elegance and beauty, and she claps her hands together in a little ecstasy over it. And as we sit there watching the sunlight flashing off its tiny jewels, it seems to me as if my Music Box is shimmering with being appreciated.

"Make it play!" says Savvia, gleefully. "Make it play!"

So, sure, I open its little lid, I sigh into it, and its lovely, waltzing song begins.

"Well, sing! *Sing!*" she commands me.

And of course I tell her that I don't know the words, but that I love this melody so dearly and so deeply, it sure feels like I oughta. And the instant Savvia hears that, she falls into despair.

"*Ohhh*, how she loved him . . . She loved him *much* too much . . . "

And then she reaches for my Music Box like a mother reaching for an infant. So, sure, I gives it over. And she takes it so lovingly, holds it to her heart, and closes her eyes for a moment.

Then she opens her eyes and glares at me.

"He turned his back on her, and she died of a broken heart. I spit on him! So, where does this thing come from anyway?"

"Well, I don't know where it comes from," says I. "But I've always had it. For as long as I can remember anyhow. Which, well . . . "

And then I look up to see her small, bespectacled husband bringing us tea and pastries. Says he:

"Excuse me, ladies . . . "

"Shhhhhh, Simon, don't move!"

Simon stops stock still, spilling nary a drop of tea, and he winks at me. Then Savvia puts her ear to the Music Box.

"Ahhh, I see, I hear, yes . . . " says Savvia, handing me back the Music Box. "It says it's none of my business where it comes from. It says *you* are its Home now."

And Simon smiles and says, "So, I can move now?"

And Savvia smiles and says, "Of course, my darling."

As Simon sets down the tray and pours us tea, he gives me a kind smile. And then he spots my Music Box, and his face lights up like a child.

"Oh, *my,* can it be?" says he. "Might I please have a look at that?"

So, sure, I hand it over to him, whereupon he takes a magnifying glass from his vest pocket and commences a thorough examination of my Music Box.

"It's not working. Don't worry, he'll fix it for you," says Savvia to me through a mouthful of pastry. "Eat something, you're too skinny!"

"Hush, woman!" says Simon. "And chew before you swallow for once in your life."

After a moment, he puts away his magnifying glass and turns to me with a mysterious smile.

"One bitterly cold night, when I was just a boy, a very tall stranger with a magnificent cloak came through the village . . . "

"Ochhh, your stinking village!" says Savvia, slurping her tea. "It was always so cold in that place. I could never get warm. I *hated* it! Go on."

"We fed him, of course," continues Simon, "and afterwards he sat by the fire with me for a long while. And this man, *he* had one of these. Oh, I never will forget the gleam in his eye as he showed me its wonders."

Then Simon looks at me with a gleam in *his* eye.

"You do not know what you have here, do you, my dear?"

"I suppose I do not, Simon, though I certainly thought I did," says I.

Says he, "You are a lover of music, yes? You like to sing? Maybe dance a bit?"

And my big smile and my wide eyes say it all, I guess.

"Well, my lucky young friend, do you see this – right here?"

And Simon points to a tiny silver switch on the underside of the Music Box that I always thought was part of the filigree.

"This little switch was off, you see. Now . . . it is *on*."

I almost can't keep my hand steady as I write this, Book. I am all a-tremble as I recollect the moment Simon revealed to me the marvel that I have been carrying with me all along, theretofore entirely unbeknownst to me.

"So, *before*, you would lift the lid, you would sigh into it, and it would play just the one song, yes?"

I nod.

"Well, *now*," says he, "when someone sighs into it, the Music Box will play the very song their heart most longs to hear."

And then Simon places the Music Box *just so* in the palm of my hand. And he goes on to explain that because it is *my* Music Box, because – yes, because it feels *me* to be its Home – as I hold it, I will somehow know *all the words of every song it plays!* Well, o' course, we three tried it out straightaway. As I held the Music Box, one by one, we sighed into it, and, *ohhh*, Book, the endless array of glorious accompaniments that poured forth from it – each song sounding as if all make and manner of musicians were *right there in the room with us!* Simon's song was played by a piano and a flute and a cello, Savvia's was played by a lovely, lone guitar, and mine was played by a mighty convergence of many different instruments, all in exuberant harmony!

And I am mute with amazement when I contemplate the marvelous, mystical feeling of songs I've never heard before coursing through me from somewhere deep within, as if I'd always known them and were simply remembering them, each one like a dear old friend come Home.

Well, this astonishing discovery has filled me with a firm conviction that I must make note of here and now. Although it be true that I still do not have the faintest notion where my Home is or how to begin to get there, the facts are as follows:

A) Of all the people in all the Whirld, I have been put in the way of Savvia and Simon, who spotted my Music Box for the wonder that it is and taught me how to use it.

B) The Music Box now feels me to be its Home. And if it considers me to be its Home *now*, it is therefore evident that it must have had a Home *before*.

C) As I have been carrying this treasure with me for as long as I can remember, and even had it with me when Mad Aunt Harriet found me on her doorstep, from whence my Music Box hails may well be from whence I hail. I think this is a mighty powerful clue of some sort, though I have no idea what to do with it.

But my overarching point here is this: Assessing all the evidence at hand, I can only conclude that Destiny has had my back all the while, sees that I am meaning well, and is showing me that I am, in fact, hot on the trail!

So, anyhow, speaking of my Music Box, my Music Box is what got me my gorgeous purple hat! I bet you were wondering when I'd get to that and what in the Whirld one has to do with the other, weren't you, Book? Well, I don't blame you.

Here's what happened . . .

Alright, see, just this evening I were feasting upon a hearty supper in a bustling little pub. Across from me there sits an Old Soldier staring into the fire, hunched over a near-empty bottle of strong spirits. Though he is dressed in resplendent military regalia, he is drenched in a mighty misery. So, there I am eating, and there he is drinking, and I can sense the deepest, darkest, angriest sadness in him. I can also see that his bottle of spirits hasn't nearly done the trick he meant for it to do and hasn't made even a dent in the depths of his anguish.

Now, mind you, Book, had the pub been less packed with people, I would've chosen another place to sit in order to give this fellow a wide berth. Being a Whirld Traveler, I do my best to be respectful of the solitudinous moods of others. So, therefore, I am keeping my head down and eating my stew. And just as I am slathering some more butter onto the last bite of my hot, fresh biscuit, I note the second hot, fresh biscuit just a-sitting there on my plate, eager to be eaten before it gets cold. And though I didn't want to intrude, as I were sitting right across from him like that, I wanted him to know that whatever his trouble was, he weren't all alone in the Whirld, just in case he needed to know.

So I slather up that biscuit real good, 'til it is fairly dripping with butter, and I hold it out to him, there in the periphery of his vision, and wait until he notices. Well, when he finally spots the biscuit, he just waves it away, without even looking to see whose arm it is at the end of, and he pours himself another drink. But then, after a few moments, why, he all of a sudden starts talking to me, as if he were just continuing a conversation. And his story comes pouring out of him . . .

He tells me that he has spent the best part of his life doing terrible violence and killing people at the behest of a rich monarch. And he tells me how fiercely he loathes himself for it, and has done so all along, but had thought all that violence to be his duty. And he tells me how he can't sleep at all anymore, and how all those faces keep coming back to him and all the sounds they made as they were dying. And he tells me how he could not bear a single moment more of that dark and terrible line of work, so he just up and walked out on his king and kingdom, and kept on walking 'til he ended up right here in this pub.

And I don't know why exactly, but it suddenly comes to me to take out my Music Box, and so I do. And I bid him to sigh into it, and so he does.

And, oh, Book, the look on his craggy old face when that violin begins to play . . . the tears that fill his eyes as that melancholy song pours forth through the Music Box and through me! Oh, the power of Music is legion, to be sure, but to watch it work its magic upon such a suffering soul as that tormented Soldier . . . Well, it was something, Book, that's all I'm saying. It sure was something.

When the song finishes, the Soldier does not (I think perhaps cannot) speak for a time. Then he tells me he hasn't heard that song since he were a child, sitting on the porch, where his mother often sang it as she sat sewing after supper, while his father played the violin and his little sister danced. And then, why, that Old Soldier suddenly stands himself up in all his finery and *bows* to me with such a flourish – so graceful and so courtly it makes me gasp!

And then, well, here it is, Book . . .

Because I had so passionately admired it when he bowed to me, why, that Old Soldier humbly presents to me his magnificent purple hat, and he asks if I will please be so kind as to accept it as his gift in return for mine.

Well, I am all teary-eyed, of course. And as I put the hat on my head, all the people in the pub applaud. And I blush to tell you that the Soldier puts his hand to his heart as if it is all a-flutter – and then he full on *smiles.* So, I got two gifts, you see: that smile and this hat!

Oh, Book, the *hat* . . . Why, I outright rejoice in the beauty of it! Not only because I am an absolute *fiend* for the perfect purple, of course, which it ever so perfectly is – tra-*la!* But also because it is velvet and has such a wide, sweeping brim and such an elegance to it. And I do so like that it is a bit frayed around the edges and faded in places. Yes, I love this hat to distraction, and I shall cherish it forevermore. Most especially because of how it came my way.

And so, when I told Hank what happened with that Old Soldier and this new hat, why, that's when he came up with the idea of me singing for my supper – which I think is an exemplary idea, and which I feel suits me right down to my socks!

Hank also came up with another swell idea. He said I oughta make up a sign that will intrigue folks. So I did. It reads:

Songs Sung Here

I think it's a fine sign, indeed, and I shall be proud to display it to signify that I am open for business.

So, Book, here I lie, beneath a fat white moon, hanging in my Scarlet Velvet Hammock in the welcoming branches of this most magnificent tree. It is a Red Rose Oak Tree – a very wondrous kind of a tree that grows on its ownsome, just when and where you'd least expect it. I have fallen deeply in love with Red Rose Oak Trees, I don't mind telling you. I feel we know each other and somehow belong together.

And tonight as I write, my heart ponders the sorrows of that sad Old Soldier, who never did tell me his name. And I send him such love, wherever he may roam. And I pray that he may be surprised by a life full of beauty and long-lasting peace. Yes, that is what I wish for him.

And, let's see, what do I wish for me, as I gaze up at the moon and down there at Hank, already asleep . . .

Ah, yes, I wish me sweet dreams, I do indeed, as I have been having some troubling dreams of late, which I can't seem to recall at all when I wake up – only that they have been troublesome. But I do believe that my sleeping in the mighty branches of this Red Rose Oak Tree may help to sweeten my dreams, as the smell of these roses . . . well, you could never get enough of it if you were me.

But, tonight, mostly I guess I just wish me the cleverness to know how to find my way Home in this vast, lonesome Whirld. I have nary a clue, and I am beginning to feel a mite lost and over-whelmed.

But be not mistaken, Book, what a fortunate wandering one I do know myself to be – me and my new purple hat. And that's a fact.

Wherein I Am a Champion Chatterboxer

What a wildly delightful place the Whirld is, I must say. Yes, on days such as today, I am, without a doubt, the very happiest of Whirld Travelers.

And the cause of said happiness, you ask? Why, I have been declared the reigning Queen of the Chatterboxers! That is, me and my newfound friend Zenzi, who tied with me for first place as the other Champeen Queen. (Y'see, Zenzi is a runaway Princess who purely hates, loathes, and despises being a Princess and rolls her eyes at the very idea.) Oh, how we screamed our heads off and jumped up and down when we won! Anyhow, here's how I happened upon this Chatterboxing Contest . . .

So, Hank is off on his own somewheres, and I am strolling solo down the loveliest curving road lined with orange blossom trees, when I hear something that first sounds like an awful lot of insects buzzing. But then, as I come closer, it sounds like an awful lot of *people* buzzing. And then I round the corner into a big, wide clearing and see a big ol' banner that says:

632<u>nd</u> CHATTERBOXING CHAMPIONSHIP TODAY

And I see that, in fact, it *is* a whole lot of people talking, and they are in pairs and sitting across from each other in chairs, and there are judges walking all around, and the idea is you just talk and talk and talk (and as we well know I can talk a blue streak with my eyes closed), but, y'see, it has to be an *actual conversation*, with no pauses allowed to search around for what you'll talk about, and whichever chatterboxers talk the longest without getting the least bit tired score a whole mess o' points and go on to the next round, see, and then *those* chatterboxers chatterbox against each other (but it's really *with* each other, 'cause like I say, it has to be an actual conversation) to see which one gets tired first, and then, finally, the final two chatterboxers go on to the final round, and me and Zenzi, well, we just talk and talk and talk and talk for *ever* so long without a single sign of wear or tear, if you please, and I think the sun rose and set at least three times while we gabbed and gabbed and barely noticed and, why, they had to rotate the judges at least *twenty-two* times, and everybody else was out cold *days* before, and I guess they finally figured they'd never get us to hush up, so they reckoned they had no choice but to call it a draw!

And here's what is also an amazing thing, Book, that Zenzi pointed out right off when we started chatterboxing each other. She says:

"You know what is so very funny, my friend? I am running *away* from Home, and you are running *towards* it!"

Strangely enough, the only subject that Zenzi did *not* care to talk about was *why* she was running away from Home, so I steered clear of it. But we talked about everything else and then some, and let's face it, Book, there is no shortage of fascinating subjects under the sun – at least, not for me there isn't.

Wait, now . . . I must take a breath and collect myself so that I may accurately report something quite thought-provoking:

I want Zenzi to show me where she comes from, see, so I takes out my map. She looks it over some and frowns, and then she takes out her map. Now, we find that most places have the same name on both maps. For instance, on both maps the town nearby is called "Daffodil Heights," and a faraway expanse of water is called "The Calico Sea" (which I do so dearly long to see someday). But sometimes we see different names for the same place, like say, for example, "Schlufenschlagen" – a sweet little moniker in a very particular spot on her map. Whereas, on my map, in the very same spot it says, "The Biggest and Best City in The History of The Whole Wyde Whirld" – a name which, because it is so long and so very full of itself, rubs me entirely the wrong way.

So, this inconsistency between the maps is . . . well, actually, I don't know what to make of it, Book. I just feel I should record it, along with another salient something, which is this:

I have added a new way of trying to sense where my Home might be. I now like to see how I *feel* about the name of a place, as I feel certain that I will recognize my Home by the peace that I will most certainly feel upon hearing its name. Surely it will bring me the very same feeling that my own name brings me of, "Yes. This is mine. We belong to each other."

Oh, and perhaps you've noticed, Book, that I scribe these here words upon your fine pages with a most extravagant, lush, white plume! It was given to me by Zenzi straight out of her dazzling, jeweled and feathered headpiece. She said it would look just exquisite in the band of my purple hat, and, *boy*, was she on target.

Then I asked her to sigh into my Music Box, and I sang her a song. And afterward she said she felt she would travel faster now, as the song gave her courage and made her feel sturdier somehow. And then we both cried a little and wished each other happy trails.

And so I have now refashioned this plume to act also as my quill pen, and I hereby and therefore rejoice in its usefulness, as well as its wafting white beauty.

Boy, all that yakking . . . I sure am wore out. Guess you already knew I was a champion chatterboxer, eh, Book? No surprise to you!

Oh, *botheration*, I suppose I oughta add a P.S., so here it is:

As I am departing Daffodil Heights, I come upon a most aggravating abomination in the form of a grimy poster nailed to a white picket fence. At the top of this poster, scrawled in a scraggily script, it has the nerve to say:

WANTed:
Evil feMAIL HoRSE Theef

And *this* is what it says at the bottom:

She Stoll OUR WoNDeRHoRSE!!
HiGGS + BOggs, oWNerS

And right there in the middle of this idiotic eyesore is a horrifyingly *hideous* drawing which is supposed to be *me*. Oh, it is jaw-droppingly atrocious! Why, there are about six long, stupid curlicues *sproinging* out of my head and my limbs are all stretched out like *gum* and – well, I cannot stand to look at the thing, it makes me so mad. So I rip down that monstrosity, ball the grimy thing up, and throw it away. The one and only good thing about that pathetic portrait is that no one could ever possibly guess it to be me!

Aw, shucks, Book, the vigorous idiocy of Higgs and Boggs has tromped all over my supremely chirpy mood from just a few paragraphs ago. Well, then, Lillian, shall you allow their nimwitted nastiness to ruin your theretofore exuberant mood? *No, you shall not* – not if I have anything to say about it! I'll tell you what you're gonna do . . . You're gonna straightaway partake of a sure cure, which is to lay back here in this thick, luscious grass and soothe your irritated spirit by staring up at the stars and contemplating their eternal, sparkling mystery to your heart's content.

Ahhh, yes, much better . . .

Ain't it the truth? There's nothing quite so reconstituting on the heels of extreme aggravation as the endless peace of a vast night sky.

Wherein I Dream Dreams

I should like to record the following dreams, as, along with the sound and the feel of the name of a place, perhaps the recording of my dreams might come in handy as a locating tool.

It occurred to me to make official note of my dreams just yesterday, when a nice man named Herbert, whilst repairing the soles of my boots, was complaining about how his wife nags at him and just keeps on saying the same thing over and over and *over* again. So I says to him:

"Well, Herbert, perhaps she repeats herself because she just wishes to be heard and taken note of."

So it strikes me that I oughta take my own advice. Yes, it strikes me that maybe my dreams have been repeating themselves because, just like Herbert's wife, they wish to be heard and taken note of. Mad Aunt Harriet always put great stock in dreams. Anyhow, here they be:

Well, o' course, I have the dream of the Beauteous Lady Made Entirely of Light Streaming Through the Sea of Lilacs pretty regular. But a few nights ago, some things was different. I usually only hear the first few words of something the Lady of the Lilacs says, which are:

"Remember, my dearest darling-dear . . . "

But this time I heard something more. I heard, "Remember, my dearest darling-dear," and then something about a kingdom, I think . . . yes. What a sweet voice she has, Book, sweet like a breeze, and – oh, that's right! This time she handed me a sort of sceptre, like the kind you see in storybooks, you know? Only it was made of all kinds of flowers that sparkled like jewels. But the thing of it was, I couldn't reach it. The sceptre, I mean. It seemed so far away, though she seemed so near. So, that's one dream.

The other dream is of a room – a Heavenly Room, high up. I have been so hankering to write a poem about this Heavenly Room, but my feelings around it grow too powerful and too far beyond my talent to render them with words. I do pray that it is a piece of my memory returning to me, as, alas, no other memories besides my name have yet come home to roost. Truth be told, Book (as we are truth-telling friends, you and I), I honestly do not know if my vision of this room is simply a concoction of sheer lonesomeness.

So, even if it is *not* a bit of memory, but just a wisp of loneliness turned warm and pretty in my imagination, still I shall record it, because it has given me a feeling that feels like Home *ought* to feel. And I believe it is a good course of action to strengthen that feeling as a kind of inner compass, even if it is fancy and not fact. Anyhow, I shall endeavor to try it and see how I fare.

I should say right off, it first came upon me from out of a deep day-time stare. You know the kind I mean. One still afternoon, I am a-leaning up against a tree, staring out at the reflection of the sun on a river, and though my eyes are open, I feel so deliciously heavy in my bones, and just exactly as if I am having a deep and restful sleep. And in my mind's eye, I see this room a-way high up in the air, with tall ivory walls and tall open windows and the bluest blue sky all around, yes, and spectacular views of Everywhere. And out of one of the wide-open windows in this room, I see the topmost branches of a most magnificent Red Rose Oak Tree!

And in this welcoming room, where the dust motes dance through the sunbeams and those sunbeams warm the wooden floor, *ahhh*, there is such a writing desk, such an armchair, such a fireplace, and such a wide, soft bed, with fresh, clean sheets. And there is even a delicate breeze whiffling the curtains.

And, oh, yes, then there's that other dream . . . I downright despise this dream. It's terrible. I don't see anything. It's all black. I hear a lot of men yelling – yelling down at me, like I'm in a hole. They're calling me names, ugly names – I don't know what names exactly though. I can't understand what they're saying, only that they're yelling. It frightens me horribly and has woken me up in a panic twice. That's a new dream. Like I say, I don't like it. Not one bit.

Anyhow, for now, them's all the dreams that's fit to print.

So, here I lie, all tucked into my Scarlet Velvet Bedroll on this fresh-smelling hay in this lovely loft, while Hank sleeps below. Yes, tonight is a night to be grateful for the generosity of strangers and the sweetness of being alive. I fear no trouble from dreams tonight, no.

Let me just make note of one more thing before we part, though, as my eyes want to close and I grow stupider and sleepier with every word . . . Now, Book, I have noticed that when many people speak of Home, it is a thing that brings a smile to their face and a hand to their heart. But here's the rub: I have also noticed that many other people speak of Home with such an emotional and bothered variety of sighs and grumbles and gritted teeth and rolled eyes and tears and more tears – and sometimes even fury! Or, like Zenzi, they just refuse to speak of Home at all. And I must say, I wasn't expecting that, I find it most surprising, and it confuses me immeasurably. Good night already, Lillian – for Pete's sake, stop writing and go to sleep.

Book, my apologies, I must try to remember to write to you more often whilst more alert. I'm sure there is much to be gained by taking stock of one's life while wide awake. But I must now take my leave of you to commence snoring.

Oh, yes, Hank informs me that I have quite a bombastic snore. I just so dearly wish I could be awake so's I could hear it.

Wherein I Have a Perfectly Reasonable Objection Which Is Not Appreciated

First, I put forth in my own defense, Book:

I truly, honestly *do* get on just beautifully with most folks in most places. Really, I do. And I consider myself the luckiest of Whirld Travelers to say so. And as I look at my map and take stock of all the places I have been, I should like to say that some places are so nice I wish they *were* my Home, and some folks so nice I wish they *were* my family.

And then, o' course, there are *other* places, and *other* people . . .

So, there am I, on likely the finest, chirpiest, clearest morning you ever did see in all Creation. And I am riding atop Hank, and I sigh into my Music Box, and I sing just for me and for he and for all the air around us to hear. And some passing birds are sweet enough to stop a while and grace me with their harmonies, and, oh, the sunlight is just so gently caressing every living thing, and Hank and I are smiling with pure contentment as we're moseying on along.

And we keep on a-seeing these signs that say things like:

THE GREAT BIG

SOCK HILL ADVENTURE!

JUST UP AHEAD - BETTER GET READY!

And . . .

COMING RIGHT UP! ARE YOU READY? IT'S:

THE GREAT BIG FAMOUS
SOCK HILL ADVENTURE!

Sign after sign after sign . . .

So I am all excited, o' course! But Hank isn't so interested in socks, so he decides to vanish. Wish I'd've gone with him, that's all I'm saying. I just wish I'd've gone with him.

So, finally, *finally*, I get there, and I am all thrilled to have arrived, and I put in my coins to open the gate. And as I step through, I look up and see the last sign, which is *twice* as big as all the other signs:

CONGRATULATIONS!
YOU HAVE ARRIVED AT:

THE GREAT BIG WHIRLD-FAMOUS
SOCK HILL ADVENTURE!

And, Book, all I see is: a small square store, a flat green meadow, a single cow, staring at me, chewing, and a large, *large* hill of socks – onto which, every once in a while, one or two socks just float down out of the sky. Obviously it's a Skyhole, like the one behind Mad Aunt Harriet's cottage, only this one specializes in socks.

Now, I know you already get my point, Book, but my point is this:

Yes, there is a hill of socks. Yes, it is a monumentally *large* hill of socks, I grant you that. Yes, it's absolutely unique in my experience to encounter a Skyhole devoted exclusively to socks – this too is true. But may I say, there is nothing here that is even close to being any *kind* of an Adventure – *at all!* And you know, Book, if there is one thing that purely steams me, why, it's being tricked and deceived. So I thought I oughta register my objection with someone in charge. I felt it was one mightily worth airing. So I head on over to that small square store, outside of which there is a sign that says:

COME INSIDE!
Learn All About:
The True Origin of The Socks

So I goes in. And, oh, sure, they got all sorts of sock doo-dads and sock this-n-thats hanging everywhere, and sock-shaped sandwiches and such – none of which hold any appeal for me, thank you very much.

And there's this short, squat, red-faced fella behind the counter, see. And I says to the fella, with a light voice and a smile:

"Pardon me, sir, do you by any chance *own* this here Great Sock Hill Adventure?"

"Well, howdy, there! Aren't you tall! What's your name?"

And we shake hands and introduce ourselves, and he says his name's Buster. And Buster says, real loud, like I'm a *crowd*, Book:

"Welcome to the Great Sock Hill Adventure, Lillian! Yes, ma'am, I do own all that you see here outright! And, yes, I'm mighty proud to say that the Great Sock Hill Adventure is my very own idea!"

And I ask, because I just *must*, and I cannot help myself:

"Might I ask you, Buster, just what about your enterprise would you call an *Adventure*, exactly?"

His mouth turns down, and his face turns redder, and he says:

"Why do you ask?"

And I look out the window at the cow, slowly, slowly munching grass next to the Great Sock Hill, just as a little white sock floats gently down from the sky. And I do *try* to choose the right words.

"Buster, I must confess . . . I honestly do not see anything going on out there that looks *anything* like an Adventure."

And then it started, Book. Like an oil fire.

"Oh, I see, Miss *Tall*, you think you're too *fancy* to appreciate my Adventure – and all the hard work that goes into its upkeep, I might add!"

"*What? No*, what I am actually saying here is – "

"Oh, I've got your number, Missy . . . Everywhere you go, you think you know everything!"

"Now hold on there, Buster! I may *not* know everything, but what I *do* know is that what is going on out there is not, by any stretch of the imagination, any *kind* of an Adventure!"

And Buster's face goes about twice as round and twice as red as it was before, and he busts out:

"Well, it's an Adventure for the *SOCKS!* Even *you* can't deny that!"

Book, I draw breath. I *try* to be peaceable.

"No, Buster, I suppose I *can't* deny that. You sure got me there. In truth, I cannot speak for the adventurous spirit of even one sock. Except maybe my own."

Well, when he sees that I am willing to at least entertain his point of view, Buster softens up a little. So I decide to change the subject entirely, as, truly, I do so delight in having an interesting conversation whenever I can. It is one of the fundamental joys of being a Whirld Traveler. So I say:

"My apologies if I sounded overly critical. It's such a lovely place you have here. I was only trying to . . . "

And I clear my throat and swallow my words. And Buster smiles a big, wide smile.

"Oh, that's alright, Lillian, you're entirely forgiven. Y'see, I am an entirely forgiving sort of a person."

"Well, I'm mighty glad to hear it, Buster," says I. "So, tell me, how's business? Do you enjoy your work?"

"I tell you, Lillian," says he, "business is bad. Very, *very* bad. Just so many people seem to want their money back! I don't know what's wrong with folks nowadays – they've just all gone crazy!"

And then Buster proceeds to tell me that folks want their money back because – why? *Because they don't think it's an Adventure!* And he says this, Book, completely and exactly as if I didn't just say what I just said, and as if we didn't just have the most ridiculous argument about it!

Still, I so wanted to turn this headache I was getting into something wonderful so's I could ultimately say, "Look what a nice fella Buster turned out to be! People can be so surprising, can't they?" So I figured the smart thing to do would be to change the subject, dearly hoping to bring us around to *some* variety of pleasant conversation. And then I remember that sign about learning the True Origin of the Socks, so I says:

"Buster, I am so interested in the *origin* of them socks . . . I'm interested in origins, period, as I am on the hunt for my own, dontcha know."

"Is that so? Well, then, I wish you luck, Lillian!"

"Why, thank you, Buster."

Yes, I know, Book. I was hopeful too. So I says:

"Tell me, Buster, what kind of folks d'ya think wear them socks on the other side of the Skyhole? Y'know, from where the socks fall?"

Well, he just stares at me, Book. Then he says, with a smug smile, as if I am to be pitied because I were obviously born just that stupid:

"Were you dropped on your head as a child, girl? Ain't nobody *wearin'* them socks. They just fall through!"

"But, Buster, *from where* do the socks fall? Surely somebody was wearing them socks somewheres else, don't you reckon? I mean, don't you ever wonder about Skyholes? Aren't you ever curious about where everything comes from? Why, what you've got here is a socks Skyhole, for Pete's sake, and, say . . . *Socks Skyhole!* That might be a good name for your – "

"*I AIN'T CHANGING THE NAME!* Now will you clam up about that already? It's *Adventure* and it's gonna *stay* Adventure! Been that way forever. Nobody'd know where to find it if I changed the name after all this time – and, besides, I'd have to change every single one of them signs, and then where would I be, huh? *Missy!*"

I know, Book. Why didn't I just leave, right then and there? I guess because for some dadgum reason I felt like I had to prove at least *one* dadgum point.

"Listen, Buster, I grew up with a Skyhole in my backyard, see, so I've had plenty of time to ponder this question. What's more, my friend Hank goes off traveling to all sorts of places in the Universe, and he told me – "

"Aww, hooey! Ain't nobody goin' anywhere else out there 'cause there ain't nowhere else out there for 'em to go!"

"Oh, for Pete's sake, Buster . . . You mean to tell me you don't think there's *any* possibility that there's *anything* or *anybody else* out there? Not in the whole entire Universe?"

"Not in the whole entire Universe! And don't you even *think* it!"

Well, I quite naturally get thoroughly cantankerous when someone tells me not to even think a thing. So I march myself outside and head directly toward that Sock Hill, with Buster running after me, huffing and puffing and yelling at me not to disturb the socks. And, sure enough, there's another sign that says:

DO <u>NOT</u> DISTURB THE SOCKS

But I am on a mission, and I yanks out a fistful of socks, and as I fully expected, every single one of 'em showed *signs of wear in the heels!* And I go on ahead and point out those worn heels to Buster. And, *oooh,* Book, even though I could plainly see that Doubt had found its way into his entirely numb skull, I could also see that he would rather *die* before he'd admit to even *possibly* being wrong. He would purely rather die and be buried. So I says to him:

"Buster, I see that Doubt in your eye. And what I also see is that you would purely rather die and be buried than admit to even *possibly* being wrong!"

"Just – just *who* do you think you are? I do not have *ONE SINGLE DOUBT!"*

Well, whether he was going to admit it or not, I had made my point, and I saw no further reason to remain where I were so obviously not welcome. So I turned on my heel and walked away, as he continued to shout his fool head off:

"Whaddaya wanna come around here and make trouble for? Business is bad enough. Why, I oughta . . . And another thing – *YOU'RE TOO TALL!*"

And he just kept yelling and screaming until I was entirely out of earshot, all about how everybody was crazy and how I was crazy too.

Well, now, after walking and walking all the rest of the afternoon, I have most fortuitously found this here lovely, calming lake, with weeping willow branches bending over to touch the water all around it, and I have made camp here. The sun is just beginning to set, and here I sit, contemplating whether it is time once again to darn my dear old checkered socks – both of which are, indeed, *nearly worn clean through at the heel.*

I have been cogitating upon my conflagration with Buster, and I am still completely convinced that *he* is the knucklehead, and *I* am not. But you know, I'm beginning to wonder, Book, if me not remembering who I am and not finding my Home is starting to make me ornery. What do you think?

Though I do try to believe it will all surely come out right in the end, Doubt has entered my mind. Hmph. It is sometimes difficult to discern the truth of the tales I tell myself.

Ah, Book, will you just look at that sunset . . .

My, what a masterpiece is that sky . . .

Wherein I Engage in Philosophical Conversation With an Elf

Do you recall, Book, me only just saying that I wondered if I were getting ornery? Well, I have since been steeping in an experience which has made me most *un*-ornery, indeed. I tell you, it has quite cured my heretofore feverish brain, which was still remarkably agitated by my confrontation with that blockheaded Buster. Ah, yes, my mind now feels as if it has been washed clean by a cool, clear river . . .

So, there I be, on foot, on my own, when I come to a fork in the Road. Now, going *that*-a-way, the Road is very wide and flat and well-worn, which naturally commands attention and seems to insist on being followed – surely to lead off to Somewhere Big and Important.

And going *this*-a-way, *ahhh* . . . the Road so delicately curves off and away – like a new leaf – beckoning me to who-knows-where-if-anywhere-at-all.

Well, there I stand at that fork in the Road, still with absolutely no idea how to find my way Home, and mightily frustrated about it, to boot. So, right then and there, I decide to treat myself to some wandering, instead of this ever-and-always seeking, seeking, seeking. So, I sets off a-sauntering down that pretty, delicately curving path . . .

And as I am moseying on along, I note with such admiration that this path is ever so artfully tended to. Why, it is lined with so many varying *lovelinesses*, all in such harmonious flow! I round a bend and come upon an elaborate fountain, then an eye-popping patch of lavender with that heavenly scent, then an exquisite statue of a woman in diaphanous robes looking all serene and wise. And the way this lovely path swirls and sometimes winds back on itself is so delightful – why, it is an uplifting feeling simply to be wending my way along it.

So, there am I, humming a tune that seems to be twirling its way out of me all of its own accord, when I spot a small sign that says:

Welcome to All
Who Follow the Path that Unfurls

Which strikes me as a mighty pretty thing to say.

Then, in this most tranquil of moments, I become suddenly suspicious that this sign might somehow be deceiving me – that's how perturbed I still am by that Great Sock Hill debacle! But, upon contemplating the dainty lettering, so artistically rendered, it strikes me that this sign doesn't seem the type to mislead me. So I continue on with trust in my heart.

Then the trail meets up with a stream that then flows right alongside it, as if they are friends on parallel paths. And then, as I am strolling along, listening to the burbling stream, I come upon a second sign that says:

Once You Get to Where I'm Going
Feel Free to Stay a While

Well, that sounds so warm and friendly, I am now exceedingly curious to see just where this path means to take me, so I picks up my pace. And quite soon, I step out from between two spreading elm trees, and what do I behold, rising so high in the middle of a stately courtyard, but a most majestic building adorned with sculptures and tall arching windows! And I gape a-way, way up at its astonishing architecture, wondering just how unthinkably *high* must the ceilings be!

Well, the entirely unexpected sight of this edifice is so enthralling that I am stunned, and for a moment I stand stock still, just *gawking* at its very existence. But the momentum of my curiosity is far too great, and I am far too captivated by this splendid structure just to stand there with my jaw hanging open like that, so I stride through that courtyard and right on up to the vast, arching entryway of this building.

And there stands a small sign that says, of all things to say:

Big Ideas: Inquire Within

Well, you know how I feel about Big Ideas, Book. Can't get enough of 'em! Why, if you've got yourself a Big Idea, I will slurp it right up and thereupon thirst for more!

So, anyhow, before me looms a pair of massive, ornately carved doors. And just as I reach for one of the huge, iron handles, why, do you know them giant doors sweep open all on their own! And, sure, I steps right on through into – *ohhh*, such cool, airy splendor, such a cavernous expanse – and, why, the entirety of it is lined up and down and every which way with shelves upon shelves upon shelves of *books* and *books* and *books!*

Now, I see no one around, see. No one to inquire to, or to give a coin to, or to ask, "Say, what goes on here?" So I go on ahead and bathe in my sweet solititudinousness, letting the glory and the grandeur of this gargantuan place wash over me. I gape a-way, way up at the arching ceilings, craning as if I am gazing at the highest of treetops.

And I can't tell you why, Book, but somehow I am feeling such a *reverence* come upon me . . . a feeling that, yes, comes very close to how I feel when I am watching rays of sunlight streaming through a glory of clouds. Oh, the *mightiness* of all these books all together like this! Why, I can feel all those Big Ideas reaching out to me, calling me, and I can't wait to get my mind on 'em!

And then my eyes happen to fall upon a polished wooden table and its companion of a chair. Upon the table sits a small sign:

Feel Absolutely Free to Look at Absolutely Any Book

Read as Many as You Desire Stay as Long as You Require

Well, being so very graciously invited, why, sure, right then and there I turn to a shelf, close my eyes and, purely by touch, I pick out one, two, *three* books that feel like they might have something to say to me. And then, well, I walk right on over to this here table at which I now sit, from which I now write, by this here window that looks out onto that stately courtyard. And, sure enough, it has turned out to be my very favorite spot in the whole place.

So, I open the first book, and therein I read the words of a man postulating why folks behave the way they do – some of which I agree with wholeheartedly, and some of which I think is just plain foolishness. But, oh, the *fun* I were having, engaging in the mental conversation of it – as that's what it was, y'see, in its way.

The second book turns out to be a collection of Great Poetry – a distinguished, weighty tome which still sits by my side as I write. I must say, I don't understand a lot of it but, *my*, how them words dance with each other when I read them out aloud! I feel almost as if I am singing – that's how lovely they feel to speak and how musical they sound in the air.

And, oh, Book, the *third* book . . . Well, you just go on ahead and guess what it talks about – I dare you! Alright, I'll tell you. Why, it talks all about *visiting all make and manner of people and places beyond this Whirld, that's all!* So, here it is, in my own two hands: Proof. In print.

"Aha!" says I, good and loud. "Proof! In print! Y'hear that, Buster? I knew it, I knew it, I doggone *knew* it!"

Then, all around me, I hear the sound of tittering. So I calls out:

"Hello? Is anybody there? Is someone here?"

And from somewhere near, I hear a real small voice:

"Oh, we are most definitely here, my dear."

And then I hear the most thrilling, trilling rufflings of laughter, rising and falling from all corners of this cavernous place, and I am put in mind of flocks of tiny, chirping birds.

Then I see a glimmering flash of movement out of the corner of my eye, coming from a shelf right next to this here table. And I turn my head, and what do I behold – leaning up against the spine of a book called "A Treatise on the True Glue of the Universe" – but the most dapper, elegant, pointy little creature!

So, naturally, I thinks to myself, "Why, I'm guessing that there's an Elf!" So I says:

"Pardon me, sir, but if I were to guess that you are an Elf, would I be correct?"

"You would indeed, m'lady!" And he tips his top hat and bows a bit, and he says, "The name's Phineas Phipp. At your service!"

"How do you do, Phineas Phipp," says I, giving him a bit of a bow back. "The name's Lillian. Lovely to meet you!"

"So, m'lady, tell me," says he, "what are your thoughts about the writings you've been reading?"

And right away Phineas and I fall into a deep, delicious discussion in which I tell him what I think about each book. And he tells me why he thinks the author of one book is hilariously funny, and why he thinks the author of the next book is a genuine sage, and why he thinks the book of all the Great Poets is . . . well, suffice it to say, we both rhapsodize about the infinite wonders therein.

Then, after this Elf and I have been conversating for quite a long while, it suddenly occurs to me to ask:

"Say, Phineas, do tell – what's an Elf like yourself doing in such a place?"

And Phineas goes on to explain that he and the other Elves dust and caretake all the books. And *then* he tells me that just above this building there is a very expansive Skyhole leading to all sorts of strange and wonderful locales beyond this Whirld, and that the Elves travel back and forth through it, returning with interesting books and tales and trinkets that they collect on their travels.

And so, o' course, upon hearing *that*, in conjunction with what I'd just read, I find myself telling Phineas about my incendiary encounter with Buster and my consequential exasperation thereof.

Whereupon Phineas tells me that I mustn't mind about Buster. He says that some people are just too deep-down frightened to imagine that there are other Whirlds besides ours, because the very idea of it makes them feel entirely insignificant. I saw the wisdom of his assessment immediately.

So, yes, I've been here for quite a few days now, lapping up all sorts of Big Ideas, and I should like to report that the Elves are the very finest of hosts and companions, and they have seen to it that I am quite well taken care of, indeed.

How many Elves there are here I could not say, any more than I could say how many books there are here. I have had the most marvelous conversations with Phineas, of course, and Chester and Gilda and Sharmila . . . They all bring me books they think I'll be particularly interested in and curiosities they've brought back from other places.

For example, Vincenzo showed me a thing that is called a Clock. 'Twas a strange sort of an object with a round face and with these things Vincenzo called "hands" – though they were made of thin, flat iron and looked nothing at all like hands. Anyhow, every once in a while I'd look up and see that these so-called "hands" had moved and were pointing at different numbers, which were painted around the edge of this here Clock.

Well, Vincenzo then told me that in the place where this Clock comes from, the thing is greatly esteemed and nigh on worshipped, which I found fascinating. And when I asked what this Clock were supposed to signify, he said what it does is – how did he put it? Oh, that's right! It takes the day and the night, see, and chops 'em up into little pieces, so people can meet up for lunch more easily and such. And, oh, it also made a most irritating *tick-tick-tick-tick-ticking* noise which made me very nervous. So Vincenzo somehow stopped the Clock from that relentless ticking, and he laughed and said:

"Ah, yes . . . the people where these things come from, they are also very nervous."

Well, I could sure see why.

Then, why, that clever Elf runs his graceful, expressive hands over the flat, iron hands of that Clock, and he transforms them into hands that look exactly like his own, and every bit as expressive! And then he makes them hands wave and blow kisses and such, and it suddenly becomes so charming a thing, that Clock.

And then one of the hands writes in the air with its finger – in shimmering, silvery-blue letters – the word:

And as I sit here writing, the Now Clock sits on the shelf right next to me where Phineas first appeared. And whenever I look up, them hands wave at me or blow kisses or thumb their nose at me, which always makes me laugh.

How I have adored my time here in this palace of a place, reading anything that suits my fancy and thinking such rich, wide thoughts. My spirit feels replenished and reconstituted, and somehow maybe even a bit bigger or *more* than before – though, alas, not being a Great Poet, I cannot begin to explain how. But I do believe that I have indeed been blessed and *yes*'d by Destiny, who has so congenially led me to this most majestic sanctuary.

Oh, Hank just appeared in the courtyard! I must go invite him to come in and meet the Elves, who will surely admire him mightily and make a big fuss over him. Besides, he might want to read something before we continue onward.

But, Book, before I rush out, I should like to offer you my sincere apologies. I sure do wish I were able to write astute and aston-ishing Big Ideas upon your pages, like those that fill all the endlessly illuminating books in this place. But let us be frank with each other: When it comes right down to it, I really don't know very much. So we must both of us forgive me for being only as smart as I am and no smarter. Though, I must say, all these Big Ideas sure have given me a boost and a half!

Yessir, I tell you, I feel ready for just about anything.

Wherein a Peculiarity Comes in Mighty Handy

Well, Book, it is downright ridiculous that I have not yet recorded a most monumental occurrence that occurred quite a few days ago now. Thankfully, *you* are here, as ever, always waiting, so patiently weathering all my vicissitudes.

Do you know what just occurred to me as I wrote that word? Why, it is that very peculiarity of mine – namely, the savoring of the saying of tongue-and-teeth-tickling words like "vicissitudes" – that were the key to the aforementioned monumental occurrence. *Ha!* Whoever would've thought something so silly would do me such a vast great good? There goes Life winking at me when I least expect it.

But you see, Book, the very reason that I have not yet recorded said event is *precisely* on account of the mind-boggling monumentalness of the thing! Why, every time I even thought of trying to write about it before this, my words just picked up and ran for the hills, feeling intimidated. I can't say as I blame them. Alright, here goes nothin' . . .

I, me, your friend Lillian, Miss Nobody from Nowhere, got herself granted entrance into the Land of the Pink-Purple-Periwinkle Peacocks! (You don't know why that's so wonderful yet, but you will.) See, in my travels hither and yon, every once in a while I'd hear tell of this glorious place called the Land of the Pink-Purple-Periwinkle Peacocks. Oh, sometimes I'd hear the Peacocks was real, sometimes I'd hear they was made up in somebody's fanciful head, and sometimes I'd hear they used to be alive but have been extinct for ages now. But one thing everybody agreed on was that *nobody* knew of *anybody* ever actually laying eyes upon that transcendently resplendent Land firsthand.

So, one night I'm sharing a campfire and a lively meal with a few other assorted Whirld Travelers, when I overhear this dark-haired man with a gold earring mention that the entrance to the Land of the Peacocks is supposed to be somewhere nearby – or so he'd heard. Down this-a-way, or maybe more up that-a-way . . .

Then this piccolo player pipes up and tells us his grandmother always said that in ancient times the Peacocks were happy to welcome human beings into their Land, but then people started taking them for granted and leaving garbage behind and stealing sacred things for souvenirs, even though they were expressly asked not to. So the Peacocks got disgusted with the shameful selfishness of humanity and shut the Door to their Land forevermore.

And when the piccolo player finishes his tale, we all get mighty heavy-hearted about the shameful selfishness of humanity, and we all fall silent and stare into the fire for quite a while . . .

Later that night, though, after everybody else has fallen asleep, I stay up talking to this wonderful old woman with waist-long white hair, whose bracelets tinkle and twinkle in the moonlight, and her name is Genevieve. Well, Genevieve tells me that the dark-haired man with the gold earring was right. Not far from our camp, in the middle of a clearing, stands the very Door that is the entrance to the Land of the Peacocks. And she knows this for a fact because she grew up nearby, and as a child she used to play in the clearing at the foot of this Door.

Genevieve also tells me that she had always heard that humans could still be granted entrance into the Land of the Peacocks, but there was only one way to do it, see, which was to stand before that Door and crack the Uncrackable Challenge, which all through the ages somebody or other was always trying to crack, but nobody ever could, so everybody just gave up.

And whatever might this Uncrackable Challenge *be*, you ask?

Well, Book, here it is: In order to get yourself into the Land of the Pink-Purple-Periwinkle Peacocks, you have to *say* "Pink-Purple-Periwinkle Peacocks" 7,777 times in a row without making *one single mistake!* So, what with my particular peculiarity and all, I figured, sure, whyever not? On my way Home I may as well stop by and see if I can't crack that ol' Challenge: A) for the sake of cracking an Uncrackable Challenge, and B) on behalf of my now voracious desire to lay my very own two eyes upon that pulchri-tudinous place and upon them pretty Peacocks.

So, the next morning, as we are breaking camp and saying our fare-thee-wells, I tell Genevieve of my plan, which prompts her to give me a wide, warm smile, the precise directions to the Door, and a hug for luck. Then she sets off on her way, and I sets off on mine.

Well, I follow the Road until I reach the great, dark forest she told me about. And, sure enough, as I walk alongside it, there I see the last vestiges of an old stone path, so overgrown I nearly walk right past it, just like she said I would. Then I follow this old stone path straight on into the forest until, at last, it leads me into a sudden, round clearing, just like she said it would. And this clearing is encircled by a ring of ancient yew trees, so im-posing, so immense, their gnarled branches all entwined in what seems to me to be a fellowship of mighty guardians.

And just like she said, yes . . .
In the very center of this clearing stands a Door.

That's right, all on its ownsome, without walls or structure of any kind around it, there stands an arching wooden Door in a crum-bling stone doorframe, with three crumbling stone steps leading up to it. Such an artful, venerable Door it is – though its handle and hinges are all mottled and rusted, and its wood is all warped and weather-beaten from ages of nobody caring anymore. Why,

I feel somehow sad for this fine Door, out here all alone in the middle of nowhere, so utterly forsaken.

So I takes me a walk around behind it to see what's what on the other side. But it is just the plain old back of the Door. So I come around front again, and I head on up what's left of the steps, and I have me a look through the keyhole. But all I see is the trees on the other side of the clearing.

Then, 'cause it's the natural thing to do, I try the handle.
Then, 'cause I just can't resist, I put my ear to the Door and listen.
Then, 'cause you just never know, I knock.
Then, 'cause it were worth a try, I try my master key – to no avail.
Then I decide it's time to just get on with it.

So, first I eat an egg salad sandwich to shore up my strength. Then I stands myself at the foot of them steps, I squares myself before that Door, and – whilst keeping track with a stick in the dirt – I starts in saying, over and over again, "Pink-Purple-Periwinkle Peacocks."

On my first try, I get all the way up to 4,268, and then I start thinking about something else and start sputtering P's all over the place, so there's nothing for it but to start over.

On my second try, I get up to 672, and then I *sneeze* right smack dab in the middle of the word "Periwinkle." So, just to be on the safe side, I start all over again.

Then, on my third try – oh, it is so all-fired *nerve-wracking*, Book! I am getting closer and closer and closer . . . And as I get down to the very last seven of them 7,777, I become evermore bound and determined to crack this doggone Challenge, so I make sure to speak each word so slowly, so precisely, with such care.

And, finally, I get down to the very last one. Says I, as if to cast a spell:

"Pink . . . Purple . . . Periwinkle . . . Peacocks!"

Well, sure, the instant I finish, I'm expecting something so wildly beyond compare to happen, I am all a-quiver with anticipation.

Only . . . nothing happens.
Nothing at all.
Oh, a branch of a tree creaks a bit.
A crow crows somewhere far off.
But that's about it.

So, there I am, just standing there, waiting, staring at this pointless, meaningless Door. And as I stand and wait and stare, I wonder if I have done it all wrong somehow. I am even entertaining the notion that Genevieve may have been pulling my leg. And the enormity of my foolishness throws such a bleak, black gloom across my soul.

"Awww . . . it were just the stuff of myth and legend, after all," says I, "that maybe once were true long ago, but is true no more."

Well, I am feeling pretty pointless and meaningless myself, I can tell you. At last, I decide there is nothing for it but to turn my back on that hard-hearted Door. And so I do, feeling such an unutterably deep melancholy.

But wouldn't you know, the instant I lift a foot to take my leave of that clearing, I hear a familiar sound that I cannot quite place – until I do. *Why, that's the sound a lock makes when it unlocks!*

I wheel around in a flash, and, oh, Book, what a sight:

The loveliest, liveliest Light is streaming through the keyhole and out from under the Door, and I am purely *enchanted* by it . . . But then, all of a sudden, this Light starts growing brighter and *brighter* – so bright it lights up the whole clearing, shining deep into the forest beyond! And at the same time – *ohhh*, the Wind is rising and rising and now *racing* all around me with such fierce force, why, it is nigh on whipping the shirt off my back and the hair off my head! And all I can think in my mounting panic is:

"What in the Whirld have I done?"

But then, from some calm space deep within, I realize quite clearly that it is I who have called this Moment forth, and this Moment is now calling *me* forth, and it is testing me to see what I am made of. And I know that I must meet this Moment face to face. Come what may, I must walk up those steps and open that Door.

And so I do. And when I do . . .

All at once, that lovely, lively Light *floods right through me!* I am suffused with strange, lush fragrances, and I hear – nay, I *feel* a Hush so serene that my jangled spirit sinks instantly into a tranquility it has never known before . . .

And then I steps into a lavish, wild garden, teeming with elaborate flowers and all make and manner of plants I've never seen before – all in a profusion of eye-popping color! And everything in sight is softly glowing with that same beatific Light. And as I reach out to pet the nearest petal with the tip of my finger, I see, *ohhh,* my hands, my arms, my feet – why, *all* of me is now aglow with that same Light!

And I look around, and I find myself feeling how it feels to Belong . . . to be just another glowing creature in this brilliantly colorful garden. And as I stand there, drinking deeply of all this gleaming glory, I feel myself to be flowing and overflowing with a sudden, soul-deep knowing: This Loving Luminescence is the Ever-Abiding Truth of All Things Living.

Then I look up and I spot, a-way, way up on a green, green hilltop, a graceful alabaster structure with tall columns and no walls. And just as I am wondering if I ought to head on up there to pay my respects, I am suddenly surrounded by a sound that at first seems to be thousands of . . . tiny *bells?*

Then I realize that this sound is, in fact,
the rustling of all the leaves throughout the garden.
And *then* I ken that this sound is heralding,
from the depths of this lavish lushness,
the spectacular arrival of none other than:

The legendary, the exalted, the sublime Peacocks.
In Pink-Purple-Periwinkle person.

They were ravishing, astonishing, majestic beyond imagining! And, oh, Book, would that you could hear their voice! They spoke clearly into my mind, like Hank does, only the Peacocks spoke as a *flock*, y'see, in a harmonious multiplicity, yet in a single, mellifluous voice.

Why, when they welcomed me in and congratulated me on being the first person ever to crack the Challenge, so smitten was I by the beauty of their voice, I couldn't speak a single word in return. I could only stand there with my mouth hanging open. But they didn't seem to mind my momentary muteness one bit. And they were so warm and gracious, they even apologized for how long it took to unlock the Door and then to come to greet me. Since no human had even *tried* to crack the Challenge for so many ages, they were taken completely by surprise!

So, then they took me on a tour of their Land. And, Book, here is where my words may as well be burps, as they will fall so short they will surely insult the ineffable splendor of the whole shebang. However, I shall endeavor to give you the flavor of it:

Well, first off, wherever they wanted to take me, they caused me to float through the air, which was simply divine – why, I felt like a soap bubble, and – oh, yes, that's right! It is while I am floating through the pink quartz canyon that I first feel the subtle Music within absolutely *everything* in their Land. Yes, there is a lilting melody within the wind, within the rivers, within the rocks. And, *ohhh,* in that luxurious bath I take in a bubbling pool, the caressing effervescence of that water seems to somehow softly *sing* into my body and my being.

And, *oh!* They have this shower of Light there that is sort of a cousin to a shower of rain, see, only . . . Alright, see, there are these trees – a deep, rich *indigo,* they are – and these indigo trees are raining down a soft, steady shower of white-gold droplets of Light.

And when I get floated down to the ground so's I can stand beneath these trees, I feel each drop of Light falling upon me and *into* me. And as each one drops upon the ground and upon me, I hear a tiny, euphonious *chime!* And as I am standing there being showered upon, why, I feel so full of melodious Light, I take to flapping my arms as if they are wings – as if that's all it would take for me to fly off like a bird myself, which makes all the Peacocks laugh.

Anyhow, to top it all off, the Peacocks have a ceremony to celebrate the occasion – that is, this being the very first time anybody ever cracked the Uncrackable Challenge.

And it starts off in such a splendid, stately way! All of us are in a floating procession, see – with me in the middle, which makes me feel so proud, I am near dissolved in happiness.

>   And up, *up* we float . . .
>   . . . spiraling around and around . . .
>   . . . a-way, way up that green, green hillside . . .

. . . right on up to that graceful, alabaster structure with the tall columns that I spotted when I first walked in. And when we reach the top, we float on into that wide open structure whose towering pillars hold up a great domed ceiling of faceted crystal. And all that crystal sends prisms of light glimmering and dancing all around us!

But here is what most wonderstrikes me upon our arrival:

The immensity and the quality of the Silence. Why, it feels to me to be fathomless and benevolent, this Silence. It feels to be the very Silence out of which all the dulcet Music of this Land is born. I'll leave it at that, Book. I don't want measly words to risk offending something so sacrosanct.

Then, ever so regally, the Peacocks encircle me. And what with their warm generosity of spirit, all the glory I've just been witness to, and all that loving Light glowing through everything everywhere, well, sure . . . I can't help but tell them flat out how I so desperately wish this were my true Home, and how I would give or do anything to serve them in some way so's I could live here forever.

And, well, o' course, I bust into a whole waterfall of tears as I blurt all this out, and I am so heartily embarrassed and upset, as I feel I have now ruined their ceremony, and left a bad impression, to boot.

But, oh, those Peacocks . . . they are compassion itself. As I cry, why, they close their circle more closely around me and, in unison, they slowly fan out their tail feathers. And I then feel myself so sympathetically gazed upon by the endless loving kindness pouring forth from *all those eyes* . . . Why, it is a balm to my spirit far, *far* beyond measure.

And then the Peacocks gently tell me that my place is out in the Whirld, and that I must now go back and live out the rest of my life. However, they also say that when I have an inkling of when

I'm a-going to die, I am invited to come on back and visit them again, whereupon they will teach me marvelous and mysterious secrets that they said I am far too young to learn yet.

And get *this*, Book . . . So I won't have to crack the Uncrackable Challenge again while I am in the middle of dying – why, they give me *a key!* That's right, they cause a graceful golden key to appear on a little marble pedestal before me. And as I take their gleaming gift so reverently into my hands, the Peacocks tell me that as soon as I leave their Land, this golden key will change form and disguise itself as a perfectly ordinary iron key. And then they make a very particular point of telling me that this entry key can be used *one time* and *one time only* – so they counsel me to wait until I am exceptionally old and most definitely ready to shed my mortal coil.

Book, as I write, I am now holding this, yes, perfectly ordinary-looking iron key close to my heart. How I do treasure it, both for its golden soul and for its humble appearance. I have made a special little pocket inside my boot to hold it, and you may be sure that before I sleep tonight, I shall sew it right back up into that pocket for safekeeping.

So, anyhow, I vow to them Peacocks that I shall indeed return to their Land when my time comes – to learn their secrets, to be sure, but mostly because I so dearly desire this shining Land of theirs to be the very last sight I see in this funny little life of mine.

And when it comes time for me to go, the Peacocks tell me not to fret, they will never forget me, no matter how long it takes me to return. (They know how humans always worry about how long things take.) And they assure me that when I finally do return to their Land, it will feel like mere moments since I left.

Then we all say goodbye, and I close the Door behind me. And then I sit down on that top step and have me quite a colossal cry.

But just as I am lamenting how sorely I will miss the Peacocks and their hallowed Land for the whole rest of my life, wondering how I will ever be able to live in the plain old ordinary Whirld again – well, I look up, and I behold:

Fields upon fields of twinkling stars in a black velvet sky.
A crisp, white, crescent moon smiling brightly down upon me.
The welcoming canopy of those ancient guardian trees.

And I drink deeply of all that luscious late night air.
And I listen to the soft wind dancing through all the leaves.
And I smile at all the crickets singing up such a symphony.

And, well, I find myself freshly worshipful of the dear, familiar glory that is this Whirld. And I feel ever so glad to be back in it again – a part of it all, after all. And I find myself hopeful that I shall one day cross paths with Genevieve again, so's I can tell her what happened and thank her. And then, why, I decide to make camp for the night at the foot of these crumbling steps, right smack dab on the very spot where I cracked the Challenge.

Now, Book, I'm compelled to report an infinitely less remarkable, yet salient new development prompted by this monumental occurrence:

After all my yearnings to express the glories of Life with my pen, I have at long last decided to engage in the expression of Poetry – though under separate cover. No, I don't ever want to show my poetical efforts to anyone, as I believe they ought to be strictly between me and the Spirit of Art. In fact, I vow to burn my Poetry ceremonially now and again as an offering to the Spirit of Art, which requires sacrifice, I feel, as well as an ongoing ritual of gratitude for its infinite treasures and pleasures.

I should also like to record that on the night I camped out in that clearing, sitting by my happily crackling little fire, I wrote my very first Poem. And even though I know myself to be the most obvious and clumsy of beginners, I shall persevere. Why, I do believe Mad Aunt Harriet would be proud of me. Though if my Poetry is anywhere near as bad as her cello playing, there lies another good reason to keep it entirely to myself.

Ah, but let me return to thoughts of *you*, my silent, generous Friend, from whence I began this entry . . .

Yes, you are here always, patiently weathering my vicissitudes, which means the whole Whirld to me, indeed. So, though I may burn my Poetry, you shall I save, Book, you shall I cherish evermore, so that I will always remember this long and winding journey when I am, at long last, come Home.

Hopefully, these tales of my travels and my ridiculousness will make me laugh when I am old and grey, and preparing to make my pilgrimage back to the Land of the Pink-Purple-Periwinkle Peacocks.

Wherein I Encounter a Troupe of
Theatrical Fellows

Book, today I stumbled upon such a thoroughly enchanting, utterly exhilarating sort of fun that, why, I feel altogether transmogrified from stem to stern! Now I must put my mind and hand to writing smoothly and evenly by this here lovely lantern light, so's I can read what I've written one day when I am wishing to re-live the thrill of it all over again . . .

So, there I sit, outside a small village, under the loveliest trees, beholding something so extravagantly *wonderful* and so achingly *awful* at the same time. And this wonderful, awful something I am beholding is what they call a Theatrical Performance.

Well, this Theatrical Performance is being given by a group of men, some of whom are playing women, which they are down-right astonishing at doing! And they are doing all of this off the side of the charmingest, long, wide wagon that has been flipped open to make a stage. And hanging above the stage there is a beautiful banner with golden curlicues all around it, and the most artful, elegant lettering that reads:

The Troupe of Theatrical Fellows

And to the side of the stage is a smaller sign sitting on an easel, and this sign says the name of the play that they are presently performing. It is called:

"Lamont's Lament"

And, *oooh*, Book, let me tell you, this thing is a *stinker*. Why, I am nigh on dying of agony whilst trying to make sense of the story. Something about somebody being cheated out of their – oh, I don't know, it makes no sense whatsoever, and, on top of that, it is just bad, bad, bad, bad, *bad,* and exceptionally stupid. But, lest I judge the thing too harshly, I give a look around to see how the performance is going over. And, well, there are about eight of us there, and seven us of are asleep.

And yet, Book, *and yet* . . . despite the irritating inanity of the story, I am completely and entirely transfixed! It's true! I am nothing short of spellbound by the captivating, poetical manner in which the Theatrical Fellows are pretending to have such dramatic emotions. And, oh, they have such laudably loud voices and such graceful comportment and such *flamboyant* costumes! So, who's to say what was the precise causation of how I was soon to astonish myself? Perhaps it were the torture of boredom and the thrill of inspiration colliding and exploding inside me (I still can't quite figure it), but suddenly I have this giddy, spine-tingling sort of a feeling come right up over me.

And before I know it, I am sliding off my bench and slipping around to the back of the stage, smiling and laughing to myself and just busting at the seams with excitement! And over by some trees, I see Hank munching away on some tall grass. And when he sees me, he stops munching and just stares at me funny. He told me later he knew something momentous was about to happen.

And, *oooh*, I tell you what I went and did, Book . . .

Why, I takes my Cape and I twirls myself into the most glorious gloriosity of a costume – an ice-blue satin gown with a skirt as wide as a small settee, a monumental hat perched atop a massive white wig, a tall, thin walking stick, and a *monocle,* if you please. Then I run up the little back stairs of their stage, sigh into my Music Box, and out blasts a boisterous brass fanfare. I take a deep breath, and then, well – *I enter!* That's right, I walk my splendiferously costumed self right on into the pretend parlor on that stage, smack into the middle of "Lamont's Lament"! Oh, yes, in a mighty grand manner, I glide on ahead (though my skirt is so wide it nearly brings down an end table), and, why, I positively *float* to the edge of that stage. Then I pound the tip of my walking stick three times, and I declare good 'n' loud to all present, I say:

"It is I, Papa – yes, 'tis I, your beloved Henrietta! I have, at long last, come Home!"

Ha! Well, o' course, my castmates are gaping at me like stunned mullets. So I proclaim again, with still greater vigor:

"I have *arrived,* I tell you! It is I, your prodigal, long-lost Henrietta, come Home at last – and with a whopper of a fortune in tow! Have you nothing to say to that?"

The fella playing the Old Countess finds his tongue first.

"My – dear – *niece!* Oh, ma petite cherie, you are indeed a sight for my poor old watery eyes!"

And from that magical moment on – oh, I don't even know how it happened – but there came the aforementioned exhilarating fun such as I've never, ever had. Delight upon the heels of delight! Oh, one of them accuses me of being a *Courtesan,* see, then another accuses of me being a *Murderess* – and then *another* accuses me of being a *Murderous Courtesan!* Now, as it all turned out, I was indentured to someone, though I can't remember who. Then I was redeemed by my having the secret family birthmark, though I can't remember where. And, oh, we played and invented, and right there on stage we wove the most fascinating story that got so complicated I can barely remember it.

And when we were done, how them seven people in the audience cheered us and threw us coins! And when we took our bows, why, they jumped up onto the benches, clapping and hooting and hollering. And how the Theatrical Fellows and I screamed and laughed and cried when that curtain came down, and how they hugged and applauded me . . .

Awww, I dunno, Book, it sure did feel like a Homecoming, that it did. Even if it were only a pretend Homecoming, and even if it is only a pretend Home, why, it feels so deep and so true. And that is the profound revelation of it.

So here sit I, gazing up at that bright ol' fat white moon, riding along with the Troupe of Theatrical Fellows in this long, wide, wonderful wagon of theirs, as they all snooze and snore away. Hank has been walking along beside us, and we've been discussing this new turn of events, and . . . *Awww,* he just now told me that he enjoyed my performance very much, which o' course makes me mighty proud. Hank just wouldn't say anything at all if he didn't sincerely like it. He's just that way.

And I feel exceedingly honored to record that the Theatrical Fellows have asked me to join their Troupe! Turns out they made more money today than ever before. Consequently, they have been most receptive to my ideas about improving their repertoire, and they asked if I wouldn't mind starting the writing posthaste. How do you like *them* apples, Book?

So, I have already begun to refashion "Lamont's Lament." It shall be our Tragedie. The ending that was invented on stage today was so very touching, it made us all cry when we retold it to each other over a hearty supper. I shall then tackle a Comedie, for I am certain we shall make a fine fortune with a Comedie, and we shall have more fun than we can possibly endure.

Ain't it grand?
Book, I am so enraptured!
I shall never sleep again, nor shall I ever want to.

Wherein I Am Having the Most Wonderful Time

Book, at this writing, the Fellas and I have performed in twenty-seven different locales altogether, and your old pal Lillian is, as aforementioned, having the most wonderful time! I am also plenty pleased to report that we have just premiered our brand new Comedie "The Idiot Harlequin," along with a charming musical interlude courtesy of my Music Box.

And, *ohhh*, how we eat and laugh and tell stories . . . How we *laugh* in the back of the wagon at night after the show! Did I mention that we laugh *all* the time? I think Patrick is the best storyteller – though Leon can downright demolish me, he is so wickedly funny. And Joey and Emile and Marco are so warm and caring and encouraging. And Franklin, our stage manager, is the most kind-hearted, honorable, gentle soul. I can't begin to tell you how it feels to feel such kinship!

Oh, and Hank says he's having a wonderful time too. He watches all the shows, o' course, and o' course we ride out together often, just for the pure invigoration of a great gallop along the horizon.

Now, I must confess something, Book . . . I have been toying with the idea that maybe I oughta give up my search for Home, as it has been so dadgum elusive and unfindable. Y'see, it has come to me of late – quite reasonably, I believe – that this may indeed be where I well and truly belong. Why, it fits all the requirements of *feeling* like a Home, and we sure do feel like a family.

Furthermore, I've always known myself to be a Whirld Traveler, and here I am traveling along with the merriest bunch of Whirld Travelers as ever-oh-ever there was. So, I've recently begun to consider that this may well be a plenty good enough Home for me.

I know, I know … no parents, no relatives, no long lost anybodies, I know … But truth be told, I care not, just now, to ponder too weightily my existence and the whys and the wherefores of it, because I know, just as I know my own name and nothing else:

To enjoy oneself so thoroughly, to feel so useful, and to be so proud of one's work, so uplifted by camaraderie and laughter and Art and by giving folks such happiness – well, surely this is as fine a collection of reasons to be alive as any. And if Destiny doesn't agree with me on that score, well, maybe Destiny and I wouldn't much like each other if we met up anyway.

Yessir, I decree for myself, here and now, that there is only good to be found in traveling along with these most marvelous men, and I see absolutely no harm in giving up my search for Home. Oh, even just writing those words "giving up my search for Home" – what a relief! How deliciously light of heart and fleet of foot I feel to cast off the burden of being Miss Nobody from Nowhere, always seeking, ever wandering . . .

And I've gotta tell you, Book, the most wildly fun part of being a member of the Theatrical Profession is this: I am playing all make and manner of characters, and my Cape is creating the most spectacular costumes. And I simply delight in playing the villain and much relish to make the audience *"Boo"* me – I just *adore* that!

A*www*, dagnabit . . . Speaking of villains, I am most particularly peeved to report that along the Road we have been running into more and more of those hideous Horse Thief posters scrawled by them scurrilous scoundrels Higgs and Boggs. Them stupid posters are everywhere it seems, like a bad rash.

Of course, I told the Fellas the whole disgraceful story, and they were extremely sympathetic and thoroughly outraged on my behalf. Only now they have taken to torturing me about that detestable drawing. Oh, yes, they've started having these "Who

- 111 -

Can Be the Most Hideous Evil Female Horse Thief" contests, where they pass around this preposterous wig Patrick whipped up (that has, yes, long pieces of orange hair *sproinging* straight up out of it), and they black out their teeth and cross their eyes and act all wobbly, as if they are made of gum. I tell you, Book, much as I adore them, they can be downright *merciless.*

Anyhow, back to what I was saying before I was forced to interrupt myself with such annoying stupidness . . .

Oh, yes, I have *so* enjoyed pretending to be vile and bloodthirsty in my new role as the Mean Marauder Pirate Ephraim Crabb in our short dramatic skit "The Blood of the Scorpion," in which Emile gets captured and I make him walk the plank. (Emile is much prettier as a woman than any of us, so he always plays the ingenue.)

Though every time Emile and I do a scene together, it seems that mayhem is not far away. We are a dangerous pair, and we cannot look at each other without getting the giggles if anything at all goes wrong. Well, to be entirely honest, we also start giggling when there's absolutely nothing to laugh at. And, yes, alright, it is usually *my* fault. I can't help it! Something someone will do on stage will strike me funny, and I will start shaking with laughter, and then there's simply no returning for me. I am rendered utterly helpless and theatrically useless.

And, oh, sure, the Fellas always get so hopping *mad* at me! But, as everybody knows, the giggles are notoriously catching. So, despite the Fellas' best efforts to keep a straight face, sooner or later *they* catch 'em too, and then, o' course, the whole audience catches 'em, and at that point, well, you either have to start the whole play all over again or end it entirely.

But, Book, may I say in my own defense, it is also true that, when we are *not* collapsing in fits of helpless laughter, we are knockin' 'em dead. And, by golly, we are even starting to get a bit of a name for ourselves! Bigger crowds come to see us – for the Comedie mostly, but also for the Tragic portion of the evening, because Marco and Joey are so very moving.

I, of course, am not allowed to participate in the Tragedie anymore. For obvious reasons.

Wherein I Have a Headache

Book, I have *got* to get out of here.

Joey and Marco have been sniping at each other nonstop for so long now, they're starting to sound like one person. Yesterday, during the matinee, they actually got into a *wig-tearing* fight on stage – yes, right in front of the audience! They ended up in the lap of an old lady in the front row, and in the scuffle knocked *her* wig off. Oh, it was a disaster.

Emile is *still* sulking because I simply refuse to rewrite his climactic scene so as to extend his monologue. He is stone-cold deaf to the fact that it would make the play drag interminably just exactly when it needs to pick up pace. But he is so impressed with himself that he can cry real tears, he is willing to wreck the entire evening for everyone just so he can chew the scenery.

And then, Book, there is *Franklin* . . . Franklin has become all churlish and resentful because he doesn't want to take the tickets and repair the scenery and do all the things he does anymore. He wants to *act*. He feels he deserves to, as he's put in his time as stage manager, and of course he has a point. He has a point, but he has no talent.

And I don't know if it's his age or what it is, but Leon has become *relentless* in his demands for separate billing. Oh, yes, he counted his lines and figured out that he has more lines than anyone else, and therefore feels he is doing more work than anyone else and insists that this should be acknowledged accordingly. When I calmly suggested that I could easily *cut* some of his lines so that he has *less* work, it sent him into fits of screaming and weeping and great sighs of martyrdom.

And Patrick has begun to drink to excess. I can't *begin* to tell you what a *chore* that has become for us all. The other night he fell off the wagon, and we had to go all the way back to the last town and hunt for him in the bushes.

Oh, it gets worse, Book. Wait for it . . .

Back in Cricket's Bluff, we were supposed to pay some ludicrous fine because we didn't have a License to Act, so they shut us down because we couldn't pay it. So Marco starts right in sobbing and beating his chest because he gambled away all of his and Joey's money – *again*. And Emile *claims* he's flat busted because he just bought himself an entire new wardrobe of wigs and dresses, which he *insists* is only for the good of the show, so we're all supposed to thank and applaud him for being the most philanthropic soul that ever lived. And *Leon* . . . well, Leon has the barefaced gall to stand there and tell us he sent all his money to his sick grandmother – *who we all know is dead and not sick at all* – but he just brings her back to life and kills her off again whenever it suits him. And of course it goes without saying that Patrick is inebriated, incoherent, and utterly insolvent. And, *oooh*, that Franklin . . . He just stands there the whole time with a smug smile on his face and blackmail in his heart, refusing to pony up a single coin unless we let him act.

Like I said, Book, I have a headache.

I would sigh into my Music Box for comfort, only it is sick and tired too, which worries me profoundly. Its accompaniments have sounded strained and off key, so I have chosen to completely withdraw it from the stage and let it rest. And of course the Fellas are all plenty aggravated with me for that, and for other reasons too – though it's all unspoken and sullen and tense.

Ah, yes, listen to that . . . the most immediate reason for my headache:

Marco has taken to doing operatic warmups at the top of his lungs before bed, deliberately to annoy us all. I want to drown him. We all do.

Methinks it's time to jump ship, Book, what say you? I bet it'll bring Hank back. He hightailed it outta here some time ago. He just couldn't bear the noise.

———

Awww, Book . . . The moment I told the Fellas it was time for me to be on my way, why, we all started hugging and crying and apologizing to each other all over the place.

I shall miss them all so very much.
Eventually.

No matter what, though, I will always be profoundly and eternally grateful to them for taking me in, as, during our time together, I have known so much love, such fun, and such sublime artistic adventure.

I would dearly love to meet up with the Fellas again one day. I just hope they don't kill each other in the meantime.

Wherein I Turn Myself In

So, Book, for quite some time now I have had a feeling that some-day I was going to turn myself in to someone of high authority somewhere and clear my name of this horse-thievery business entirely and forevermore. I didn't know exactly when I would do it, but the idea were tucked away in my mind, and I just trusted that the perfect time would present itself. And so it has – by the spontaneous combustion of hot weather and vanity, it turns out.

See, a few days ago, Hank disappears to run wild a while, so I am solo and on foot when I come upon this ramshackle little town, name of Hickory Flat. And *ughhh*, the day is so swelteringly hot, and I am more ornery and boiling and bothered by bugs and dust than I have ever been in all my traveling days put together.

So I am scouring the street in search of some kind of cooling re-freshment, when what do my eyes meet up with, nailed to a wall right in front of me, but that hideous drawing of me on one of those numbskulled "WANTED" posters. Well, sure, I just plain bust a gut inside my brain is what happened, Book. So, naturally, I *rips* that lamebrained lie off of that wall, and I marches myself straight into the town tavern, mad as a whole nest of hornets.

(Now, Book, I must herein make note that I customarily approach strangers in a strange town with a much cooler head. However, for the aforementioned reasons, I didn't happen to have one.)

"Will somebody in here *please* point me to whoever's in charge of this place!"

Now, there are about half a dozen locals scattered about this tavern, all looking so sluggish they seem seconds from sleep.

But the suddenness of my entrance and the bombastic tone of my voice makes 'em sit right up and take notice. In all honesty, Book, I couldn't help but overdo my presentation a little. I was just so wildly overheated, excessively exasperated, and perhaps a bit too freshly out of the Theatrical Profession.

Well, this formerly sleepy little tavern is now all a-flutter, everybody whispering and wondering who I am and what in the Whirld is wrong with me. Then I hear a strong, calm voice say:

"Whatcha all steamed up about, Red?"

The voice originates from a sturdy-looking fella by the bar, who's bending down to give a bowl of water to a big brown hound dog. Well, I know *exactly* what I am all steamed up about, so I tell him without pause:

"Well, sir, I have had just about enough of these pea-brained posters with this horrifyingly *hideous* drawing – which is supposed to be *me*, can you imagine?"

Whereupon I put the stupid thing smack up next to my face to illustrate the obviously vast chasm between the representation and the original. And the locals draw closer to inspect the poster and me.

Says somebody, "Looks just like her."

"I'd say so," says another somebody.

"Mm-hmm," says somebody else.

I cannot grasp it, Book! I am cut to the quick and bleeding! Then somebody looks closer at the poster and says:

"What in tarnation . . . *Horse Thief?*"

And the next instant, they're all hollering up a storm:

"Did somebody say Horse Thief?" "She's a Horse Thief!" "We got ourselves a Horse Thief here!"

And the idea catches fire.

"We *hang* our Horse Thieves around here, lady!" "Hang 'em soon as look at 'em!" "Yes, ma'am, you can bet we do!"

"Now, listen here!" I yell, to no avail. "Doggone it, will you just let me – just – oh, for . . . "

But they are much too lathered up about hanging me to listen. Then, all of a sudden, that sturdy-looking fella walks clean through the kerfuffle like a hot knife through butter and plants himself in front of me, solid as a wall. And they all hush up, just like that. And they all step back a little, even. And then, trying to be helpful, somebody says:

"Horse Thief, Floyd."

Says the sturdy-looking fella, "I got ears, Parnell."

And though he is talking to Parnell, his clear, grey eyes are looking straight into mine. And looking straight back into his eyes, I say:

"The thing of it is, sir, I need to explain this whole mess to somebody in charge and clear my name."

And then this fella says, of all things to say:

"You can explain it to me. I'm the Sheriff."

"Oh, Sheriff . . . " says I, "what a *relief!* Alright, see, these two villains – well, they are just the most despicable human beings I've ever met! Just the – "

"Yup. Let's go," says the Sheriff.

And he takes my arm and steers me out the tavern door, with his big brown hound dog following close behind us.

Now, at first that pack of locals have a mind to accompany us, but the Sheriff turns and just *looks* at 'em, whereupon they obediently stop in their tracks like sheepish children.

Then we step outside, and there stands a real child. She is barefoot, with crookedy pigtails and about ten thousand and twelve freckles, and she stares at me with wide, round eyes.

"Is it true? Are you a real live Horse Thief? Oh, boy, oh, *boy!* I bet you're a terrible *killer* too, ain't ya?"

I laugh, o' course, and the Sheriff quietly says:

"Go on now, Poppy, get on home to your momma."

"Well, alright, Floyd, but I'm gonna bring Doc by to have a look at her! He'll tell you what's what!"

And then she runs off. And as I am wondering why this little girl would want to bring a doctor by to have a look at me, the Sheriff and the hound dog and I walk a short ways on down the street to the jailhouse. The Sheriff beckons me inside, pulls up a chair for me next to his desk, and pours me a glass of cool water. Then we sit down, and in a nice, relaxed way, he listens to the whole story of how I freed Hank, and then he locks me up.

Now, I know what you're thinking, Book. Yes, I most certainly did question whether locking me up like that was the fair thing to do, since I was not *confessing* to horse-thievery at all, but rather *contesting* it with all my heart, and all I had desired to do was to explain to some reasonable person in authority what a terrible mistake it all was, with all the actual facts attached. But the Sheriff said he had to lock me up for my own protection until I have what is known as a trial. And I asked him if by a trial he meant a tribulation, of which I have had some experience. But he said that this sort of a trial is an event they sometimes have to get to the truth of a matter.

He said he shall have to send for a judge, who will be in charge of the whole business. And my two accusers – who he said are called the plaintiffs – will also be there. The Sheriff then informed me that horse-thieving is indeed a hanging offense hereabouts, and that I will need a lawyer, so he will send one by first thing in the morning. And this was the moment it occurred to me, Book, that I've gotten myself into quite a problematic situation here. The Whirld is a constant source of amazement to me.

Now, I am pleased to inform you that this jail cell where I am being housed is clean and cool and has a nice little bed and a window from which I can see a stretch of the main street, as well as an inspiring view of a white-tipped mountain range.

"Why, this is a truly lovely place to be locked up in, Sheriff," says I.

The Sheriff stares at me for a moment. Then he turns to the hound dog, "Otis, you wait here."

And then he departs, leaving Otis and me to get acquainted through the bars. And, Book, I'll be darned if that Sheriff didn't come back a short time later with the most perfect pink lemonade and melted cheese sandwich that I have surely ever tasted. And then he says:

"Gonna leave Otis here to look after you tonight, Red."

Then he leans down and gives Otis a good chin scratch.

"Now, don't you snore too loud, boy. The prisoner's gonna need her rest."

And, Book, here all alone in the jailhouse this evening, I must record that it is the most deeply restorative joy to have the company of this dear dog. Yes, we have become fast, true friends, Otis and I. Especially since I gave him half my melted cheese sandwich. Watching how the Sheriff was with Otis brought to mind Hank and me, and I know that without Otis here tonight, I would've felt no end of lost and lonesome. But with that sweet, soulful face and those long, floppy ears, softer than a petal on a rose, well, I feel peaceful and calm and profoundly companioned.

In fact, may I tell you what just transpired? Well, looking into the pure love that is the soul of Otis, my heart just naturally kept growing and growing 'til it were so overflowing, I had no choice but to get out my Music Box and sigh into it. And, Book, it played such a stirring song . . . 'Twas an ode to the tried and true nature of all the animals in all the Whirld. And as I sang, Otis howled and howled – that's right, he *sang* right along with me, all the way through! I judged him to be particularly fond of the chorus.

And now, as I lie here on this pleasant little bed, with the moonlight shining in, with my arm through the bars resting on Otis's head, well, I have been cogitating upon this predicament I seem to have gotten myself into. Life sure is funny, ain't it, Book? I escaped myself out of one locked-up situation, and here I am in another one!

Naturally, it's crossed my mind that I have only to use the master key on my Peerless Pocketknife and I could likewise escape myself outta *here*. But then I would be an actual, factual outlaw, and that just won't do. Nope, it's time to clear up this mess once and for all, or Hank and I will never have any lasting peace.

Good gracious, Book, the Sheriff did not exaggerate! I must report that Otis does indeed have himself quite a formidable snore. I cannot help but smile, as I wonder how it will sound when I fall asleep and the two of us are snoring contrapuntally. What with all the crickets, I imagine we'll make quite a choir.

———

JAIL, DAY 2: A Visit

This morning, directly after breakfast, I am visited by the person known in legal parlance, Book, as my defense attorney. His given name is Eustace Snodgrass, but locally he is known to one and all as "Skippy." The Sheriff said they call him that because, in his youth, little Eustace never took a single step in any direction without skipping. That's right, he skipped everywhere, anywhere, all the day long.

Now, in the interest of accuracy, Book, I must report that it has almost certainly been a very long time since Skippy Snodgrass skipped a step. Alas, his girth is far too voluminous, and from the rosy bulbosity of his proboscis, I would wager that he has been much too long pickled in alcohol.

As Skippy settles into the poor, creaking chair opposite me, he wipes his big bald head with a big white handkerchief and smiles a big friendly smile.

"So, where you from, darlin'?"

"Well, Skippy, I'm afraid I don't know," says I. "I've been searching for my Home for quite a long while now."

"Ah . . . drifter, eh? Is that so? *Hunh.*"

Skippy seems suddenly nervous that my being the wandering and seeking sort of person that I am might somehow imply something suspicious about my character.

Says I, "It's like this, Skippy . . . I'm a Whirld Traveler, see. I sing for my supper nowadays, though a short time ago I was in the Theatrical Profession."

"But who are your *people*, darlin'? You know who your people are, don't ya?"

And comes the shame I so often feel, Book, when I have to confess to not knowing from whence I come or from whom I hail.

"No, Skippy, I'm very sad to say that I do *not* know who my people are."

Skippy furrows his brow.

"Oh, see, now, this here Judge will not take at all kindly to a drifter – and a *female* drifter, at that. No siree bob, he will *not!*"

And as I am pondering why my being female would cause the Judge to take even less kindly to me, Skippy draws forth a brass flask from his jacket pocket, takes a quick sip, then slips the flask back in his pocket.

"So, now, tell me, little girl," says he, with a sudden gravity, "just where is the horse in question?"

"Well, Skippy, I'm afraid I don't know that either . . . See, Hank disappeared some time ago and is off traveling on his own."

"Hold on now – are you trying to tell me . . . "

And out comes the flask again, from which he takes a sizable swallow before returning it to his jacket pocket once more.

"Alright, darlin', stop dancing with ol' Skippy now. I'm your attorney! You got to be honest with me! *What did you do with that cotton-pickin' horse?*"

Can you imagine, Book?

"I didn't *do* anything with him! Hank comes and goes as he pleases. He appears when he has a mind to, disappears when he has a mind to, and when he disappears he goes off to run free and wild, wherever he wants to. Why, that's just plain fact."

Well, Skippy pulls out that flask and takes quite a big gulp, indeed. He wipes his mouth with that big white handkerchief, then runs it all over his head again. Then he leans forward and speaks sternly:

"Now, you got to listen to me, girl. This here is a *hanging* Judge. Why, he'll hang you soon as look at you!"

"But Skippy," says I, "there's no reason to hang me. I haven't done anything wrong."

Skippy just stares at me for a few moments, in the grips of a mighty consternation. The poor fella seems painfully perplexed by what an incomprehensible sort of a person I am. Then he launches himself to his feet and says, as if we've just shared a nice meal together:

"Well, it sure was nice meeting you, darlin'! I'll be back real soon to see you, so I don't want you to worry yourself about one single solitary thing. We are gonna go in there and we are gonna give 'em what for. Don't you forget now: Skippy's gotcha covered!"

And with a wink and a smile, my defense attorney exited the scene, leaving me more than a bit puzzled. Well, I imagine it will all become clear, eventually.

————

JAIL, DAY 3: Two Visits

Book, today I had two visits which sort of brushed up against each other, but were as different in character as chalk and cheese.

The first was from a convivial group of ladies who tell me that it's been ever such a long while since they've had a hanging here-abouts, so, to celebrate the occasion, they want to plan a big picnic for after I am dead. At their helm is a loquacious woman called Velma Thudder, who eyes me up and down as she talks:

"So, I said to everybody, I said, 'I tell you *what*, we have just got to go straight on over to that jailhouse and find out that Horse Thief's favorite color so we can have a theme for our decorations!' So, here we are! And look at you . . . Aren't you just – so *tall!*"

And as they are all tittering about how tall I am, something about the cheery industriousness of this group – so inspired to throw a party for such a grim happenstance as my hanging, and so audacious as to enlist my help in the proceedings – strikes me as so outrageously ridiculous that, well, Book, I don't know what comes over me, but I start to vision on what I truly *would* like to see at this picnic of theirs if I were a spirit freshly dead and floating by.

So, yes, of course I speak passionately of purple, explaining the qualities that constitute a truly perfect purple – which most definitely does *not* include *fuchsia* – which, though lovely in its place, is never to be considered purple under any circumstances. And, oh, I go on about lavenders and dusty roses and cobalts as accent colors, and sweeping sheaths of fabric, and wreaths of wildflowers. It was all surprisingly fun, really!

Well, Velma and her friends are so inspired by my enthusiastic directives that on their way to the door, they are downright buoyant – burbling and bubbling about whose garden still has those violets, and whose shed has which rose-colored ribbon, and whether so-and-so still has all that purple satin left over from her daughter's wedding.

And, just as I am smiling to myself at how terribly let down they will be if I come out of this trial alive, Poppy, that funny little girl with all the freckles, comes through the jailhouse door holding the hand of a tall, scrawny boy who is likewise covered in a million freckles. And in a blink – so fast it stuns me – Velma Thudder and her friends go from chirping about flowers and ribbons to spitting out venom and spite:

"What do you want to bring that crazy fool around here for, girl?" "Keep him in your yard, for pity's sake, so nobody has to look at him!" "Good thing your daddy's dead, or he'd die of shame!"

And what's almost equally shocking is that these children appear to be completely impervious to it all as they pass through that gauntlet of viciousness. Why, it is as though they have walked through nothing harsher than a light sprinkling of rain.

Well, I am riddled with emotion, Book, and I am so ashamed that I were so stunned and sickened and slow that I said nothing admonishing to those women before they left. And Poppy sees my face, and just as blithely as if she were talking about the weather, she says:

"Aw, don't you pay them no mind at all, ma'am. My momma says they don't know no better, poor things."

And as the little girl goes to close the jailhouse door, I regard her brother, who is standing directly across from me, his sandy-colored hair sticking out at odd angles. And I am about to greet him, but something about his manner hushes me. The whole of him is so very awkward and ill at ease in his form. He is all elbows and knees and feet. But his *hands* . . . oh, his hands are very long and thin and beautiful, and they seem to float in the air by his side. And I find myself to be wonderstruck by a most unique and delicate strangeness about this boy, which I cannot place or put any kind of a name to.

And what is also so curious . . . Even though this boy has been brought especially to meet me, even though he is standing directly in front of me, he never, ever looks *at* me, but rather looks around me and above me and always away from me, as if by some mysterious, internal design. But, oh, how touching it is to see the way Otis simply idolizes him. Why, that big ol' dog presses up against this fragile-looking boy, nearly knocking him over, and licks his hands and whimpers and paws at him gently, all the while gazing up at him in unadulterated adoration.

When Poppy returns to us, she reaches up and lays her hand on her brother's arm. Then she says to me, so quietly and with such pride:

"Ma'am, this here's my brother Doc."

So I say, ever so gently, "Why, hello there, Doc."

And still not looking at me, he only just barely nods.

And Poppy says, "Now, Doc, this here's that lady Horse Thief I been telling you about. Ain't she somethin'?"

Well, at that, Doc turns – not to me, but to look into Otis's eyes – his long, thin hands holding the dog's huge head. Poppy turns back to me and holds up her finger so I'll watch and wait, which I do, though I know not what for.

And after a moment, in the oddest monotone, the boy speaks:

"Otis says Lillian sings with a pretty voice."

Well, my jaw drops wide open, likely never to close again.

Poppy asks me, "That your name? Lillian?"

I nod.

"Didja sing a song that Otis got to hear, Miss Lillian?"

I nod again, because I simply cannot form words, Book. I am much too awed by this boy, this girl, and this dog.

"See that, Ma'am? Doc's the smartest one in all of Hickory Flat!"

Then Poppy proceeds to tell me how all the animals talk to Doc, and how he hears them clear as day. Yes, Book, it does make me wistful for how clearly I used to hear all the animals back in the Forest of Forgetfullness, which feels so long ago now, as if it almost never was . . .

Anyhow, she tells me tales of how all make and manner of animals trust and love her brother. How even the wildest of creatures will come and sit with him and follow him around. How he once mended the foot a mountain lion. How a big black bear once followed him for days, and how he helped her find her lost cub. How he helped a farmer save his last cow who was very sick, and now that same farmer won't let his children throw rocks at Doc anymore.

Book, I end this entry and this day, knowing that when I turn down the lantern and lay back in the dark, I will have me quite a cry. My heart feels so broken open in so many places all at once. To have witnessed such brilliance, such devotion, such innocence, such meanness, such ignorance . . .

Oh, Life is full of so much pain and beauty all at odds with each other all at once, is it not? And perhaps the only thing to be done about it is to have a good cry. That's what Mad Aunt Harriet would recommend, I feel certain of it. Maybe I will write her a poem and speak it aloud into the night in hopes that, wherever she is, she will somehow hear me.

Though it's quite likely she's long forgotten all about me.
Ah, well.

———

JAIL, DAY 13: Three People and a Pie

This morning the Sheriff hung up a sign on the jailhouse door, which reads:

TRIAL TOMORROW

So, there it is then. The trial is tomorrow.

And just in case you were wondering, Book, I have seen neither front, back, nor sideways of my defense attorney since I first met him. Having never been to a trial, I can't think what role he is to play, but I daresay it can't be a very prominent one, as he does not, to say the least, inspire confidence in any direction.

I asked the Sheriff what actually happens at a trial and what will be expected of me. Said he:

"Well . . . *your* lawyer's gonna ask you some questions, then *their* lawyer's gonna ask you some questions, then the Judge is gonna ask you some questions, and you just keep on telling your story, just like you told me."

So, it doesn't sound all that complex, really. But I tell you what, Book, ever since he put that sign up and told me the Judge'll be here by tonight, I keep getting the most unnerving feeling that I am supposed to be preparing for a performance, only I don't know what my lines are, I haven't rehearsed at all, and I don't even know what role I am to play! But then I quiet my mind and remember that I have only to be who I am and to tell my truth, which requires no script and no rehearsal.

Oh, I suppose I must now report – to my supreme annoyance – the arrival of the plaintiffs. It is lunchtime, see, and Otis and I are sharing a sandwich, when I hear these two irksomely familiar voices hollering bloody murder out in the street. So I go to the window, and I look out to see that no-good, grimy twosome, Higgs and Boggs, shouting their fool heads off from the back of a haywagon as it rolls by.

"We have come to get ourselves *justice!*" yells Higgs.

"You heard 'im – *justice!*" yells Boggs.

And they spot me in the window of the jailhouse.

"There she is! The criminal herself!" shouts Higgs.

"Hey! You stole our horse!" shouts Boggs.

Up and down the street, folks are peering out of windows and doors to see what all the fuss is about. And Higgs and Boggs take notice of being taken notice of, so they jump off that haywagon and play it up big.

"Look out, folks, that red-haired dame is pure evil!" cries Higgs.

"You heard 'im – evil!" cries Boggs.

People are now stepping out into the street to watch the show.

And Boggs hollers, "Ya wanna know somethin', Higgs?"

And Higgs hollers, "Yeah, what's that, Boggs?"

"I'm gonna knock her block off, that's what! Lemme at her, *lemme at her!*"

Worry not, Book, the instant the Sheriff and Otis step out into the street, all them cheap theatrics cease straightaway. And Otis growls ferociously because, o' course, that dog knows them two rotten eggs for exactly what they are. The Sheriff tells Higgs and Boggs to quit showing off and informs them that they'll have their say in court tomorrow. Whereupon Higgs sneers and says:

"Ya got that right, pal. We got ourselves a big, fancy lawyer!"

Then he points a grimy finger at the Sheriff.

"Now, get this straight! Before you bump off that broad, remember, she owes us a bundle o' dough!"

"You heard him," says Boggs, "a *big* bundle!"

"We got rights, see!" says Higgs.

And the Sheriff says, "Otis . . . if you please."

Whereupon Otis's growling crescendos into furious barking, and he chases them two good-for-nothings all the way down the road until they are entirely out of earshot. And after the ignominious exit of the odious Higgs and Boggs, why, it feels like the whole Whirld exhales and settles back into a nice, cozy peace.

Then, much later on, as the sun is setting, I hear the steady clip-clop of horses' hooves and wagon wheels rolling by, and I peek out the window just in time to glimpse the thick, white manes of the horses pulling that wagon and the thick, white mane of the person driving the wagon.

And, oh, Book, my eyes then fall upon a most remarkable sight...

Perched atop this long, flatbed wagon is a perfect little house – so charming, so artful in every possible way! It is made of a rich, honey-colored wood with whitewashed shutters, and it has flower boxes in all the windows with bright flowers in each. And in the back there is the prettiest little porch with potted ferns and a white, fan-back wicker chair. Well, I am utterly enchanted! And when the Sheriff hears my gasp of wonder, he tells me that the Judge has arrived, and that he lives in that little house as he travels from trial to trial.

Then the Sheriff and I fall into our now familiar, comfortable quiet, and he pulls up his chair, and the two of us proceed to polish off the most purely perfect strawberry rhubarb crumble pie that ever was. And I cannot help but to declare:

"Sheriff, this has got to be the most purely perfect pie that I have ever had and likely ever *will* have in my whole entire life."

And then, well, we fall into a whole 'nother kind of quiet. See, we both realize I just said "my whole entire life" as if my life were sure to be a lot longer than just one day more, and therefore I'd have no end of time for pie-eating. But when the Sheriff hears me say those words, I sense from his silence that he believes this will quite likely be my very last pie, period.

And when he's ready to go home for the night, the Sheriff gives Otis his goodnight chin scratch and heads for the door. But just as he is about to open the door, he stops, and he digs at the floor with the toe of his boot.

"Chances are, Red, this Judge'll hang you. But, well . . . I sure do hope he don't. You're a right pleasant person."

I feel myself to be most especially complimented, Book – and a good deal anxious too, as I surely hope I don't get hanged either.

Alright now, as for you, Destiny, you and I need to have ourselves a little conversation . . . About this hanging business, I'm gonna be straight-up, flat-out honest with you: If you have decided to end things here, well, I will have no choice but to think you a woefully unimaginative playwright. I mean no disrespect, but that would be my opinion on the matter.

I wonder, is it that you are so very disappointed in me for having failed to find my Home? If so, I should like to point out that you haven't been much help, now, have you? Furthermore, I should also like to point out that I most certainly will *not* find my Home if I am deceased, now, will I?

So, I'm going to choose to believe that you have something in mind for tomorrow that you haven't yet let me in on – something I'm not yet wise enough to see or comprehend.

Fair enough then, I shall simply resolve to:

A) Rise to whatever occasion must be risen to.

B) Set things to rights as best I can.

C) Not let the fear of hanging stand in my way.

I know it sounds like a tall order, but that's what I'm aiming for.

Well, I suppose I best get me some rest.

My, will you look at that sky full of stars . . .
All of 'em ripe for wishing on.

Wherein I Am Trialed and Errored

I bet you're wondering if I went and got myself hanged, aren't you, Book? Well, wonder no more! Here is the whole improbable tale, faithfully told . . .

So, at midday today, with the Sheriff on my one side and Otis on my other, I am escorted from the jailhouse on over to the big ramshackle barn they use as the public meeting place for Hickory Flat. And such a sprawling spectacle greets me! Why, I am nothing short of *staggered* by the *astonishing* size of the crowd!

Evidently, word of my trial has gotten out to all the other towns and hamlets hereabouts, and our path to that big old barn is lined with eager onlookers, all in a happy holiday mood. Oh, they are merrymaking and *music-ing* underneath the trees, everybody bustling with festivity in anticipation of quite a rare and thrilling event hereabouts – namely, the almost certain hanging of an almost certain female Horse Thief – namely me.

And as we walk along, I somehow cannot help but catch the crowd's high spirits. So, sure, I find myself smiling and waving and hello-ing back to those that smile and wave and hello at me, and it all feels perfectly normal to do so.

Though I also overhear choice comments from the crowd, such as, "Oh, see, now she's *entirely* too tall for a woman. I find that unnatural." And, "Doesn't look like she ever combs that hair." And every once in a while, somebody yells, "I hope ya swing, ya horse-thieving hussy!" or some such thing. But it don't much ruffle my feathers. After all, I have proudly played the villain in many of my stage roles, and when the audience heartily dislikes me, why, it just means I'm doing a good job.

Now, I don't want you to think I've gone entirely addlepated, Book. As we three are heading toward that barn, I am acutely aware that this whole trial business is infinitely more fraught with danger than a mere theatrical performance. It's just that, with all these festivities springing up around such a grisly event as a hanging, well, it is all too plain to see that these folks have been much too long deprived of meaningful entertainment. Oh, how *heartily* I do miss the Fellas! How they would be salivating at the size and the crackling energy of this audience! Why, together we would corral the enthusiasm of this crowd in no time flat.

Now, just as I was thinking about the Fellas, something singularly upsetting happens, Book, in the form of a most unsettling encounter. Considering the magnitude of the day, it's mighty odd that such an inconsequential interaction could somehow spook me so thoroughly – but that it did. That it did, indeed . . .

So, there am I, walking through the crowd, flanked by Otis and the Sheriff, when suddenly I am met with *such a stare* – yes, a strange, slight, slick-looking character is *staring* at me! And the instant our eyes meet, he smirks and snickers and starts nimbly weaving his way toward me through the crowd. And soon he is skittering right up alongside the Sheriff.

"Hello-hello-hello, Floyd-Floyd-*Floyd!* Always a pleasure, always *such* a pleasure to see you again. Fine day for a hanging, is it not, Sheriff dear?"

The Sheriff glares straight ahead in response. It's clear he has less than no use for this slick character, who then says, with a sly smirk:

"Now, now, Floyd, I simply must-must-*must* ask our scrumptious prisoner a few questions, now, mustn't I?"

The Sheriff ignores him and says to me, "He's what they call a Hopper. It's his job to let folks know about local events of interest."

Then this Hopper person slips himself in between the Sheriff and me. And walking along beside us, he gawks up at me. And all the while he is writing and writing in a small parchment book, scritch-scratching so fiendishly fast with his quill, yet hardly ever looking down at the page at all.

"Oh, my-my-*my*, yes . . . *you*, my lovey-dove, are the most delicious event what's happened in this dreary patch of the Whirld in an age, in just an *age!*"

I notice a little copper contraption attached to a leather band on his wrist, which turns out to be a little inkwell, into which, every now and again, he dips his quill. And as he is writing and walking and staring and talking and nearly *never* looking down at all, his cuffs and his hands are spattered black with ink.

Then, with a smile as insincere as a smile can be, says he:

"And your name would be Lillian, is that not correct? Oh, I do believe it *is* correct, is it not . . . *Lillian?*"

How I cringe at the sound of my name in his mouth.

"Yes, I thought so. How *coincidental* . . . Y'see, I knew a Lillian once, ever so far back, when I was just a precious slip of a boy. And the very funny thing of it is, this Lillian I knew was a ginger-haired Lillian too, just like you! Oh, nothing good ever came of *her* – or so they say, anyway – *heheheheheh!*"

That laugh, Book. Like a razor blade on bone.

"Now, tell me, sweets, is there any truth to the rumor that you don't know where you're from?"

Suddenly, I have the maddest thought, Book . . . I oughta make up someplace I couldn't possibly be from, someplace I've never been to, a place that doesn't even exist, purely to have the pleasure of lying to him! That's how much I loathe the idea of giving this sly, smirking creature even the slightest true thing about me. But, in spite of my fervent desire to lie, I reply:

"Yes, it's true."

Then, all of a sudden, he ceases that fiendish scritch-scratching, and he lifts his wet little lips much too close to my ear.

"I know you, Lillian..." he whispers. *"Oh, yes, I do believe I do."*

Why, the very idea of it sickens me to my core – that this noxious creature should be the one person who actually *knows* me, after all my searching. I force myself to turn and look into those eyes of his to seek the truth. But, close up, his eyes seem as if they have a kind of film over them – like fish eyes, only a fish has a right to 'em. And search though I might, I see only that film, which is opaque, like slime on a wall.

I stifle a shudder, and stone cold I say:

"You're mistaken. I would definitely have remembered *you.*"

He feigns to fan himself with his little book and says:

"Oh, I am flattered, m'dear, I am so touched! But surely you would have been far too busy to remember the likes of *me* . . . eh, duckie?"

And he chucks my arm, as if he is alluding to some big secret between us. And the Sheriff stops dead in his tracks, whereby we all stop dead in our tracks.

"Alright, Hopper, make yourself scarce."

"Oh, come now, Floyd, don't be so stingy! Our luscious convict here is ever so good for business – look around, look around, look around!"

The Sheriff stares at him, then leans in and says something I can't hear. Instantly, the Hopper backs away.

"Always such a pleasure to see you, Sheriff, *such* a pleasure, as always!"

And that Hopper skitters off without even a backward glance. And when he disappears into the crowd, I find that I can breathe again.

"That's what ya get for being notorious, Red," says the Sheriff. And we have ourselves good laugh and head on into that barn.

How very odd, Book, that such a small encounter should blow such an icy wind through the whole of my being. Even now, as I wonder at the why of it, I hypothesize that there just must be some people in this Whirld to whom our deepest selves are instantly and exceedingly allergic.

Anyhow, as the Sheriff and Otis and I walk through those massive barn doors, I am once again astounded by the fact that the place is just *busting* at the seams! Everywhere I look, folks are piled up – level upon level upon level – on every bale of hay as can possibly be stacked, all the way up to the rafters, which are full to bursting as well. And the whole entire crowd is eating and drinking and having a perfectly marvelous party!

And as the Sheriff leads me down the center aisle, in between these hay bales packed with people, I see that the Judge's little house on the flatbed wagon has been pulled inside and positioned at the front of the barn. And once again, I am smitten by its craftsmanship and beauty. Then, at the end of the aisle, I see two sets of rickety tables with chairs, and at each of these rickety tables sit assorted salient personages.

On the one side of the aisle, holding his big round head in his hands, sits my long lost defense attorney, Skippy Snodgrass.

On the other side sit Higgs and Boggs, along with another man wearing a suit so ludicrous, at first I take him to be a clown. And for a moment I think I recognize him from a circus troupe that me and the Fellas traveled along with for a while on a double bill. But then I realize that this affliction of a suit is such an eyesore, such an unholy concoction of plaids in the most offensive colors, why, no respectable clown I know would be caught dead in it. And *then* it comes to me that this must be the lawyer Higgs and Boggs had boasted about with such a supercilious air.

Well, when those two nimwits spot me, they leap to their feet and start shouting:

"Why, there's the rotten dame that stole our horse!" "She's rotten, alright!" You know, she's this, she's that, the usual malarkey.

Well, then this lawyer of theirs decides to join in. He rises to his feet, and in a big, showy voice, he bellows:

"Mark my words, you harlot, you shall hang today!"

Now, though I know all too well that these three specimens are lower than lowdown and twice as preposterous, *doggone* if that last remark doesn't get my goat! And, *oooh,* I am sorely tempted to haul off and have at 'em, as any respectable Champion Chatterboxer oughta. But the Sheriff puts his hand on my arm, and I immediately see that it is wisest to pay them no mind at all, and to behave as if they are simply a bad smell.

Then the Sheriff walks across the aisle and says something to those three lamebrains that I don't hear, whereupon they all sit down and stare straight ahead without another word.

Then the Sheriff walks over and pulls out the chair next to Skippy for me. I sit down, and Otis sits down on the floor next to me, growling at them knuckleheads across the aisle for good measure.

And then the Sheriff hops up onto the flatbed wagon. He knocks on the front door of the Judge's little house, listens, then opens the door and disappears inside.

So I take this opportunity to conversate with my attorney, who, upon closer examination, I judge to be thoroughly sloshed. Yes, Book, Skippy Snodgrass is nothing short of *spifflicated*. And although I am amazed at the extent of it, in truth, I am not a bit surprised by the fact of it.

"Why, hello there, Skippy, long time no see! Uhh . . . over here, Skippy."

It takes Skippy a moment to determine which direction the voice is coming from, then a moment longer to figure out that the voice belongs to me, and still a moment longer to recall who I am at all. But, at last, he connects the dots.

"Darlin'!" he says, with his big, friendly smile. "Well, it's a mighty fine day for a trial, ain't it, though? And don't you look mighty pretty today! *Mighty* pretty, and that's a fact!"

"Aw, thanks, Skippy, you're sweet. You're also plastered."

And he shakes his finger at me. Well, to the side of me actually, as he is obviously seeing double.

"Now, I do not want you to worry, darlin', I do not want you to worry even one itty bitty *bitty* little bit, y'hear? 'Member now, Skippy's gotcha covered!"

Then, with a wink and a grin, Skippy goes to once again rest his head on his hands. But somehow he misses – whereupon his big ol' bald head bonks down onto the table with a loud *thunk*. And with a smile and a sigh, Skippy sails straightaway into a deep and peaceful sleep. For a moment, I almost envy him.

But I am suddenly distracted, for I now have a clear view of those two boneheads across the aisle who are trying to catch my eye, attempting to silently agitate me by mime-hanging themselves and other such puerile foolishness. Well, there is nought to do but roll my eyes and look away.

And as I do, I see the Sheriff walking out the front door of the Judge's house. He opens a narrow closet next to the front door and pulls out a tall stool, and he sets this stool on the front stoop of the house. Then, from that same narrow closet, he pulls forth a series of wooden planks – flipping this one here, sliding that one there – and by means of hinges and latches and such, he quickly assembles a tall, imposing podium, handsomely crafted of a dark, burnished wood.

Then, opening another closet, the Sheriff slides out a semi-circular handrail, connected by a row of carved spindles to a small, circular floor. Lastly, he touches the side of his boot to the edge of this small, round floor and down come one, two, *three* spiraling steps! The whole of this apparatus – railing, spindles, and floor – is made of the same dark, burnished wood as the podium. Like the house, it is all so artful and elegant, I cannot help but sigh at the beauty of it. And I am rightaway betting that I will get to stand behind that pretty railing and plant my feet on that handsome little floor when I get to tell my truth – and now I just can't hardly wait to do it.

As the Sheriff walks over to us, he sees Skippy sleeping the sleep of the ossified. Shaking his head, says the Sheriff with a sigh:

"Shame on you, Eustace . . . "

And then he turns to me.

"Well, looks like you're on your own, Red. My advice is, when it comes your turn, keep it short. Good luck."

Then he walks up, stands in front of the podium and announces:

"Hear ye, hear ye! The Circuit Court of the Kingdom of Black-wycke, the Province of Tarrymore, the town of Hickory Flat is now in session, Justice Augustus T. Abernathy presiding. All rise!"

And so we all rise. Except for Skippy, o' course.

Then, behind the tall podium, the front door of the little house opens and shuts. And the next thing I see is that mane of white hair that I glimpsed on the wagon the night before, which now reveals itself to be the crowning white glory on the head of a rather feeble old gentleman, who is climbing up onto the tall stool and settling himself in. And I wonder how in the Whirld this rather delicate-looking old man with such a lovely head of hair can have such a fearsome reputation.

Well, Book, my wondering is laid permanently to rest that very next moment. Why, the instant Judge Augustus T. Abernathy lifts his head and looks out from his high perch, oh, *my* . . . What with those fierce eyebrows and that long nose and that high forehead and those black robes – well, it comes to me crystal clear that this Judge is a wrathful, vengeful bird of prey, and all the rest of us, mere mice.

The crowd hushes as Judge Abernathy looks over the lot of us and takes our measurement. And, oh, it is all too plain to see that this here Judge judges me, my accusers, and every last person in the whole entire place to be a bunch of swindlers and ruffians and worse, worthy only of suspicion and contempt. In fact, it seems to me that this Judge is scowling at the whole entire Whirld and finding every last person in it to be the very worst kind of disappointment to him.

And I suddenly feel as if I have an anvil in my chest instead of a heart, and that I don't stand a ghost of a chance of walking out of this mess alive.

The Sheriff says, "Be seated!"

And so we sit. The Judge grumbles to himself. Then, suddenly, in a surprisingly vigorous voice, he roars:

"What in THUNDERATION do you think this is – a CARNIVAL? Get rid of all that food *this instant!* This isn't any *kind* of a carnival, understand? This is a COURT OF LAW!"

Well, everybody drops their sandwiches and cake and chicken legs mid-bite, trying to swallow without choking, rushing to put their picnicking out of sight, so he won't hang anybody else before he gets to me. And the Judge waits crossly as the crowd clears away all evidence of a good time. Then everybody in the place falls stiller than still, too petrified to move even the smallest muscle for fear of rustling the hay.

Naturally, this tense silence prompts a baby to start screaming its head off – which prompts the Judge to hit the roof. He sets about banging his gavel with the force of thunder cracking.

"THAT BABY IS COMPLETELY OUT OF ORDER! Get that thing out of here! And let me tell you something, if I hear one more crying baby or one single solitary fussing toddler, I will *LOCK UP* whoever brought 'em here for Contempt of Court! *IS THAT UNDERSTOOD?"*

And under the Judge's furious glare, a whole river of parents and progeny goes rushing out of that barn, until, at last, the whole place falls into an abject, terrified silence once more.

And someone behind me whispers:

"Hang ya soon as look atcha . . . "

"What's that?" says the Judge. "Who said that?"

Nobody breathes. Nobody moves. Nobody blinks.

Scornfully muttering to himself, the Judge produces a pair of gold spectacles from beneath his robe, blows on the lenses, and polishes them with his sleeve. Then he puts on the spectacles, and he says:

"PROSECUTION! Get a move on – I haven't got all day!"

Thrilled at the chance to stand up and show off that crime of a suit, that preposterous lawyer rises as if he thinks he is the sun.

"Purvis Jenkins, Esquire, on behalf of the prosecution, Your Honor. And may I say – "

"No, you may *not*! DEFENSE, stand and declare yourself!"

And with no reply save, alas, the sound of Skippy's snoring – which has, alas, only just now begun – the Judge raises those fierce brows of his and turns those eagle eyes to glare down at me. And I know not what else to do, do I? So I simply *point* at Skippy.

The Judge stares at him for a few moments, unblinking and inscrutable. Then he looks at me as if it is all my fault.

"Young woman, do you mean to sit there and tell me that swollen carcass is your defense attorney?"

"Uhm . . . I'm afraid so, Your Highness, he – "

"*I AM NOT YOUR HIGHNESS!* Don't you *dare* try to apple-polish me, young woman! I have seen through the very *best* deceivers on my very *worst* day, so don't you delude yourself – you can't get by me with any of that eyelash-batting business. In this courtroom you will address me as 'Your Honor' – nothing more, nothing less, nothing different. *Is that understood?*"

Well, I am entirely and completely flombasticated! How could I possibly not be? I can only just barely nod my head.

Then the Judge turns to the Sheriff and says:

"Please do *not* tell me that is Eustace Snodgrass."

The Sheriff just looks at Judge, and that look sets that Judge to banging that gavel so hard I thought he'd break it.

"EUSTACE SNODGRASS, you imbecilic SOT – WAKE UP! You are in a COURT OF LAW!"

Skippy suddenly snaps awake with such a loud snort, it scares him a little. Of course, he is much too blotto to get his bearings, yet he is bound and determined to heave the tilting globe of his body onto its feet. And wonder of wonders, why, he actually succeeds – landing solidly and most impressively upright! Then, in an admirably strong voice, he declares:

"Eustace Snodgrass for the defense, Your Most Honorable Honor! I am present, I am accounted for, and I am most honored to find myself standing – I say – to find myself standing . . . "

And with that, ol' Skippy just keels clean over onto that rickety ol' table, and that poor table's skinny ol' legs snap like dry kindling and, well, sir, then comes the most perfectly marvelous *crash* you ever heard!

Well, o' course, the whole crowd of us are now just one short exhale away from combusting into a gigantic explosion of laughter, a roar like to bring the barn down, when Judge Augustus T. Abernathy simply *looks up* – and we all instantly forget there was ever anything to laugh at, nor likely would there ever be again.

"Just what in the name of common sense is *WRONG* with you people! Don't you have any sense of *CIVIC PRIDE*? Now, haul that confounded fool out of my sight – *ON THE DOUBLE!*"

About half a dozen able-bodied men leap up, rush over, hoist up that tabletop upon which my defense attorney is passed out cold, and *skedaddle* ol' Skippy outta that barn in a flash! Why, it couldn't have gone any faster if they'd rehearsed it.

And with that, Judge Abernathy bangs his gavel once more, and everybody in the place jumps sky high.

"Prosecution, *state your case!*"

And that posturing peabrain Purvis Jenkins rises to his feet as if he has just been especially appointed to speak on account of his dazzling oratorical skills.

"Your Honor, may I say that I am tickled pink to be standing before your high and mighty self, and I am also pleased as punch to be representing these two fine, upstanding – "

"I said *STATE YOUR CASE,* Counselor. Quit the claptrap and get cracking!"

"Oh! I – *hunh.* Well, Your Honor, I – I – "

The Judge points his gavel at Higgs and Boggs.

"YOU TWO – GET UP HERE ON THIS WITNESS STAND, and *HOP TO IT!"*

They jump to their feet, trip up those little steps, and squash themselves behind that railing.

"TAKE OFF YOUR HATS, both of you – you are in a Court of Law!"

And as Higgs and Boggs whip off their grimy hats, the Judge turns to the Sheriff and says:

"Alright, Sheriff, do the honors, if you please."

"Now, each of you put your hand over your heart," says the Sheriff.

"Ha!" thinks I. "As if they could locate even *half* a heart between 'em."

"Repeat after me," says the Sheriff, "I swear to tell the truth . . . "

"I swear to tell the truth . . . "

"The whole truth and nothing but the truth . . . "

"The whole truth and nothing but the truth . . . "

"By all that I hold sacred."

"By all that I hold sacred."

Which has to be, methinks, a big fat lot of *nothing*.

"Thank you, Sheriff . . . " sighs the Judge, looking suddenly very tired. "Alright, get on with it, Counselor."

With that, Purvis Jenkins puffs himself up, plants himself center stage, sticks his thumbs in that ugly vest of his, and proceeds to showboat.

"Mr. Higgs, Mr. Boggs . . . Please tell the Court in your very own personal words just exactly how you were so viciously assaulted, bamboozled, and horse-thieved by that depraved strumpet!"

"Well, there we were," Higgs begins, "just lying there in our beds, sound asleep, minding our own business, when that no-good dame sneaks up on us with a knife *this long* . . . "

And those scoundrels proceed to tell a surprisingly well-rehearsed and utterly fact-free story about how they were hogtied, roughed up, locked up, and stolen from by my knife-wielding, horse-thieving, evil-doing self.

And as I am sitting there, trying not to gasp aloud at the bare-faced audacity of it all, I cannot help but ponder what could possibly be the point of a Court of Law if you can just go right on ahead and tell lies of any amount or size right smack after you've *taken an oath to tell the truth!*

So, as they come to the end of their long, tall tale, Higgs says:

"And that's the whole story, Your Honor. Jam-packed with facts too."

"He said it," says Boggs. "That's a jam-packed story, alright."

"And a most terrible, tragic story it is too," says Purvis Jenkins, who now begins to *strut*, if you please.

I try not to look at him, for fear I will go blind watching that monstrosity of suit pacing back and forth.

"Now, gentlemen, please tell the Court the most *tragic* part of your tragedy – as to how, as a result of this wanton woman's crimes, you have fallen on such terrible, poverty-stricken financial times, as you were so *EXTREMELY RICH* before she stole your Wonderhorse!"

And Higgs and Boggs then launch into another long and winding whopper of a yarn about how wildly wealthy they were until I purloined their horse and their whole entire livelihood.

"Why, that's quite a dramatic tale you boys tell," says the Judge. "I, for one, was entirely captivated. But, moved as I am, Counselor, I am still waiting for some actual evidence that the plaintiffs legally own that horse. I assume that even *you* have a passing acquaintance with the notion of *proof*?"

Well, that Purvis Jenkins *will* seize a moment by the throat. A wide, smug smile spreads across his mug.

"Why, yes, indeed I do, Your Honor – I do indeed! Allow me to present to the Court cold, hard, paper evidence confirming the up and down legal ownership by my clients of Charlemagne the Wonderhorse . . . "

And he pulls from his jacket a stained old piece of parchment with rumpled ribbons and stamps stuck all over it and waves it high in the air like a flag.

"This here rightful Deed of Ownership is signed by *all* the right people and stamped in *all* the right places, as you will clearly see upon taking a closer examination of it. I hereby submit this Deed of Ownership as *Exhibit A!*"

Book, if he could've, he would've taken a bow.

The Sheriff takes the Deed from him and hands it up to the Judge, who studies it closely, frowning and mumbling to himself. Then the Judge turns to address the crowd.

"Alright now, who here in this courtroom has visited this establishment run by the plaintiffs, and who has seen this so-called Wonderhorse?"

About half the place stands up.

"Now, listen to me *most carefully* . . . I do not mean that your *cousin* saw this horse or that your *friend* saw this horse or that your *sister-in-law* saw this horse and told you all about it. I want to know who here has seen this horse with *their very own two eyes?*"

And with that, almost everybody sits down, leaving four or five poor souls to face their fate. The Judge looks them over and picks somebody.

"You, in the blue dress with the frilly thing . . . "

Well, of all people, it's Velma Thudder, who is, of course, *delighted* to be chosen. Why, she waves at the Judge like she's in a parade.

"Yes, yes, *you*, madam . . . So, you paid to see this horse, that right?"

And Velma says, as if she's got quite a tale to tell:

"*Ohhh,* yes, Your Honor, I most *certainly* did!"

"Well, tell me what happened, what you saw and so forth."

And Velma, in all her glory, sets sail.

"Well, them two fellas have this big sign out front of their place talking about how they have this Wonderhorse out back that's supposed to change into all kinds of colors. So, you pay 'em your money, and they bring you around back and they show you this *awful-looking,* skinny grey horse they got back there chained to a pole, walking around and around in a circle, see . . . "

Oh, how I am remembering the clanking of those chains and all those sores and whip marks and the bottomless anguish in Hank's beautiful brown eyes.

"So, you're telling me the horse is supposed to change color?" says the Judge. "That why they call him a Wonderhorse?"

"*Supposed* to change color, but do you know that horse changed only just the tiniest bit – just from that ugly grey into sort of a *mud* color, which was even uglier! And do you know what else? Well, I paid extra for my little granddaughter Wanda Jean to ride that big ol' bag o' bones, and while he walked around and around that pole she cried *the whole time,* so you can bet your last pair of shoes I tried to get my money back! I said to them two, I said – "

"*ENOUGH, Madam!*" barks the Judge. "*Take your seat!*"

And she shuts her mouth with a snap and sits down. I must say, it sure was gratifying to see Velma Thudder so masterfully silenced.

Then the Judge says:

"So . . . any of you folks care to offer anything different?"

Trembling, the others vigorously shake their heads no.

"Then you may be seated."

And the Judge turns to regard Higgs and Boggs. And he goes on regarding them for a good long while, looking from one to the other and back again, which makes them squirm. Finally, he says, almost friendly-like:

"So, I'm gonna tell you what I think, boys . . . I think the two of you are just a couple of lowlifes, a couple of hooligans, a couple of flim-flammers and double-dealing louts, and if you didn't have this perfectly legal Deed of Ownership, I'd declare a mistrial on account of *stupidity* alone."

Oh, I am so heartened! The Judge sees through to the truth of it all!

"But, alas, I cannot do that. Because, sadly, although there are no end of stupid laws, there is not one single law in this entire Kingdom against stupidity. So, you see, my hands are tied. I am a public servant and I am bound always . . . yes, always bound . . . to uphold the law."

The Judge now seems utterly exhausted again, and the muscles in his face have gone slack. And somehow, why, I find myself feeling sorry for him. Though his exhaustion doesn't prevent him from declaring, in a mighty intimidating manner:

"Now, get off of my witness stand and get back to your seats!"

Whereupon them idiot villains stumble down those three little steps, shoving each other out of the way in a rush to do like he says.

And then Judge Augustus T. Abernathy turns to glower down at *me*. And he thunders:

"YOU! GET UP HERE!"

Well, my moment has arrived.

I feel all eyes upon me as I stand.
I graze my fingertips over the top of Otis's head for luck as I pass.
I walk on up those three spiraling steps.
I step onto that small, circular floor.

And as I rest my hands on that smooth wooden railing and face this crowd, I suddenly and clearly see that everything in my life has led up to this very moment. Yes, after having appeared in front of so many audiences as so many characters, here I now stand, beholding the fullest house I've ever played to – the whole crowd so rapt, so attuned, so attentive! Why, it all feels so deeply familiar and somehow in the perfect order of things. And even though I have no idea if Destiny is for me or against me, I feel strong and calm and strangely ready to perform – only this time as none other than my very own self.

The Sheriff swears me in. And when I get to the "all that I hold sacred" part, as I am looking deep into the Sheriff's clear grey eyes, I am seeing Mad Aunt Harriet and Hank and the Fellas, and all make and manner of marvelous people I have met along the way, and all the trees and mountains and stars and skies and all them sunsets . . .

And even though it were as brief as the few words of that lovely oath, that moment were so over-full of emotion that, in the wake of it, I naturally turn to the Judge a bit teary-eyed – only to find that he is rolling his eyes and already completely disgusted with me.

"Oh, *please* . . . " says he, "I am utterly impervious to the water-works, young woman, so save yourself the trouble. Now – "

And don't you know, that Purvis Jenkins – the plaid-clad *clod* – leaps up to interrupt, convinced that he has spotted his chance to court the Judge's favor.

"Oh, yes, indeedy, Your Honor! We got ourselves one conniving, scarlet female here, do we not? And you can bet I got some questions for *her!"*

And the Judge turns to him and says, with a wry smile:

"As a matter of fact, Jenkins, no, you don't. I am dismissing you here and now from this case. You are as superfluous as you are vexatious. Now get outta my courtroom and don't come back, ya *charlatan!"*

"But – but, Your Honor, I – my – "

"CONFOUND IT, you BLOVIATING BOOB! I told you to CLEAR OUT OF MY COURTROOM! Sheriff, get him out of here."

And as the Sheriff escorts Purvis Jenkins out of the barn, I turn to sneak a gander at the Judge, who is once again polishing his spectacles. Now that I am much closer to him, I can see that, indeed, he is very old, quite frail, and ever so Whirld-weary, clear down to the bones of his soul.

He looks up and sees me seeing him, and promptly resents me for it.

"Oh, you think you can catch me out, do you? 'Aw, he's old, he's foolish, I'm young, I'm charming, I can get around *him.'* Take care not to deceive yourself, young woman! You were fool enough to get yourself into this almighty untenable situation, so you're not near as clever as you may imagine. Now, *WHY DID YOU STEAL THAT HORSE?"*

Well, I am stricken mute! Oh, my mouth *tries* to form words, but nary a one of 'em can find its way out.

"Well?" he says. *"Explain yourself, young woman, and be quick about it!"*

And I hear Higgs and Boggs snickering. I glance over at them, sitting there, shamelessly sneering at me. And do you know what, Book? I find myself oddly grateful for those shameless sneers on their smug mugs, as their mockery instantly snaps me back to my purpose here.

"Your Honor, those men were treating that horse so *despicably*, without a single shred of conscience! Why, they are the greediest, most reprehensible – "

"THAT'S ENOUGH! Now, you listen to me, young woman, and you listen to me good . . . You are gonna give me the facts and only the facts, exactly as they happened, *and you are gonna do it double-quick, DO YOU UNDERSTAND ME?"*

Oh, I understand him alright. Augustus T. Abernathy is a belligerent tyrant, mad at the Whirld and everybody in it, and not what I had hoped a person in high authority would be at all. And you can bet I am plenty furious that he gave that cruel and loathsome pair of numbskulls *no end* of time to lie and invent to their heart's content, but is now in such a rampaging *rush* to do away with me.

But I ain't a Champion Chatterboxer for nothin', now, am I? So, I go on ahead and I give that Judge exactly what he's asking for:

"I understand you perfectly, Your Honor. Alright . . . So, I am walking along and I see this sign, and I am curious about this Wonderhorse, o' course, so I buy me a ticket from them two men, whereupon they bring me around back, whereupon I am sickened and shocked to see this starving animal in chains and shackles, all covered with sores and whip marks, so I give them another coin so I can pet and comfort that poor horse – and then, why, I become determined to buy him and set him free (see, back then

I had no end of money), so I keep giving them more and more and *more* of my coins, but even though them coins filled *a whole big bucket* it were never enough, so they jump me, steal my Pouch of Infinite Coinage, lock me up in a smelly old shed, threaten to do me harm the *whole time* I'm in there, and then they *burn up* my beautiful Pouch, which was a handmade gift from my Mad Aunt Harriet – *but* so is my Peerless Pocketknife, which has a master key on it – so I wait 'til them two villains are passed out dead drunk, and I stick my hand through a loose slat, unlock that shed, set myself free, unlock them chains and shackles, set that dear horse free, and then I hop right on him, and even though I never rode before, well, somehow I held on like I were *born* to it – and, *ohhh,* that Wonderhorse was so ecstatic to be *free at last,* all his sores and whip marks disappeared, and he was *shining,* he was *strong* and, yes, he turned *a thousand blazing colors* right before my very eyes – and I am most profoundly proud to say that we have been the *finest* of friends ever since."

Then I thinks to myself, "So, Augustus T. Abernathy, put *that* in your pipe and smoke it!"

The Judge stares at me for quite some time, as if I am a very odd stick of a girl. Which, come to think of it, I suppose I am.

Says he, "Wait now . . . Are you telling me you *paid* those men for that horse?"

"Oh, yes, Your Honor, I gave them enough coins to fill up a whole big bucket, as was aforementioned."

And here's where Higgs and Boggs decide to make a big fat fuss about what a big fat liar I am, and o' course the Judge gets hopping mad, and the Sheriff sends Otis over to hush 'em up.

And then the Judge turns back to me.

"Where's your receipt?"

"My *what*, Your Honor?"

"Proof, for pity's sake! I need *proof* that you paid them all that money!"

"Well, I'm afraid I don't have any proof, Your Honor."

The Judge frowns and sighs and runs a hand through his hair.

"So, when you couldn't buy him, you stole him."

"Your Honor, *I am no thief*," says I. "I freed him, that's all."

"Oh, so you think it was your right to free him, do you?"

Now, I thought that was a very interesting question, Book.

"Well, I don't know if it were my right, Your Honor. But I do know it were *his* right to be free from such horrible cruelty, so I felt it were the right thing to do."

And the Judge seems suddenly drained and exhausted again, but he narrows his eyes at me, so cynically.

"So . . . now you make your living off this Wonderhorse, eh?"

"Why, I should say not, Your Honor!" says I. "I sing for my supper, and I need make no profit off that noble horse – nor would I."

"*Oh, really* . . . Is that a fact?"

His sarcasm isn't lost on me, Book. I simply refuse to mind it.

"Yes, sir, it most certainly *is* a fact. And here's another fact: It were Hank who suggested – Oh, yes, Your Honor, I should tell you, his real name is Hank. He loathes and despises the name Charlemagne, as it only reminds him of being enslaved by one cruel owner after another."

The Judge just stares at me enigmatically, so I just keep on a-going.

"So, since my Pouch of Infinite Coinage got burned up by them two no-accounts, Hank suggested I oughta make singing my profession, that I oughta put my hat out for coins, and that I oughta make me a sign that says *Songs Sung Here* – all of which has worked out very well indeed."

The mystery is gone from the Judge's expression, and it is obvious that he now judges me to be a liar dipped in lies – just a different variety of Higgs and Boggs.

"Young woman, are you trying to tell me that horse *talks* to you – that you can hear him speak?"

"He does and I can, Your Honor. I hear him just as clearly as I hear you."

And I guess this reminds him to yell at me again, in case I wasn't hearing him clearly enough.

"Oh, for – BALDERDASH! Now stop wasting my time and tell me what in green creation you did with that horse! Where is he?"

"Well, I do not know where he is, Your Honor, but wherever he is, he's running free. I have no hold on Hank whatsoever. Why, he disappears when he wants and reappears when he wants, whenever he has a mind for my company."

"*HOGWASH!* You *sold* him, didn't you?"

"*Sold* him?" says I.

Why, I am purely appalled, Book . . . It seems to me this old man doesn't know anything about anything. So it is apparent that I need to teach him.

"Your Honor, Hank is not mine to sell."

And the Judge points a finger straight at my face.

"Exactly!"

And he picks up that stupid Deed and waves the thing at me.

"That horse legally belongs to those two reprobates, and as you have no proof of purchase, young woman, you have just confessed to stealing him!"

Well, naturally, Higgs and Boggs think this means that they have won the case, and they jump up and down and start hooting and hollering.

And the Judge roars, "If you two don't *SIT DOWN* and *HUSH UP*, I just may see my way clear to hanging *THREE* people today!"

And with that, the whole place gets still quieter and still more terrified. And in that terrified silence, it comes over me quite clearly that this here hanging Judge is going to hang whoever he feels like hanging today. And no matter what I say – right or wrong, truth or lie – he is quite likely to hang me simply because he is bone-deep ornery and in need of a nap. Oh, yes, indeed, this man seems to be of a mind and a mood to be as murderous as he is cantankerous, so I decide I may as well have my say before I depart this beautiful Whirld.

"May I just say, Your Honor . . . I turned myself in, and I took that oath to tell the whole truth and nothing but the truth by all that I hold sacred. Now, you may very well end my life today, and in light of that fact, I am asking only that I be allowed to do what I took that oath to do, which – *dadgummit, sir* – was to tell the whole truth, was it not?"

And of all things to say, Book, do you know what that Judge says?

"Go on."

"Well, the way I see it," says I, "to say that I stole Hank is nowhere *near* the whole truth. Why, it's not even a *quarter* of a *half* of the whole truth. It's just the very smallest *piece* of the truth, which is just that ol' piece of paper you got there."

And I'll be doggoned if he don't hold up that dumb Deed again and proclaim to everybody in the place, as if we must memorize this monumentally important lesson or die trying:

"This is a *LEGAL DOCUMENT* – a *BINDING CONTRACT* – certified by all the proper authorities, and, as such, it is to be honored and upheld!"

To which I reply:

"Well, Hank never signed that contract. He never agreed to be sold or owned or tortured or exploited."

Which stops the Judge cold. He stares at me for a moment. Then he sets the Deed down.

"Young woman . . . has anybody ever told you that you are *impossible?*"

"No, sir. You'd be the first."

The Judge sighs and grumbles and runs his hands through his hair.

"A horse that appears and disappears . . . *Poppycock!* How very convenient! Then tell me, young woman," says he, turning on me, all riled up again, "why didn't he simply *disappear* from the clutches of these two miscreants if they were so all-fired awful to him?"

"Why, Your Honor, I rightaway asked Hank that very question myself, and what he told me was that he *couldn't* disappear on account of them chains and shackles, which he'd had on since he were very young, since he were first captured."

And as the Judge chews on that, well, I cannot help but to turn full out and tell off that Velma Thudder.

"And the *reason* he couldn't change colors, Velma Thudder, was because that poor creature were starved and tormented and entirely *BROKEN-HEARTED!*"

And, oh, how that Judge is banging his gavel!

"Of all the contumacious... *Young woman, you will come to order THIS INSTANT!* How *DARE* you disrespect this Court!"

And I turn to him, my thoughts and feelings all a-tumble.

"I don't mean to disrespect your Court, Your Honor, honestly, I don't. It's just – see, my Mad Aunt Harriet used to say that . . . Well, you know when it truly all came clear to me? It were when I visited the Land of the Pink-Purple-Periwinkle Peacocks, and – "

Oh, *my!* The instant I mention those Peacocks, such a strange, *ferocious* look comes into the Judge's eyes, why, I fully expect him to throw that gavel at me! He looks to be more bitterly angry about this than he's been about anything else all day. And that's saying something.

"Precisely what *is* it that you pretend to know about the Pink-Purple-Pe-Pe-P – The Pink-Purple-Pe-Pe-P – *Ughhh* . . ."

And I mean to be helpful, truly I do.

"You mean the Pink-Purple-Periwinkle Peacocks, sir?"

Ohhh . . . when I speak it so easily after the Judge could not speak it at all, there comes into his eyes a dark flash of such a soul-deep pain and such a withering resentment. He says, so very quietly:

"Please, young woman, *do* go on. I'd like to hear just how *very* well-acquainted you are with those Peacocks."

And though I clearly hear the threatening tempest in his voice, there is nought to do but to tell him what is true.

"Well, Your Honor, I count myself so very fortunate, as I was once granted entrance into their beautiful Land."

And as I speak those words, I can see that I have somehow set a match to dry tinder somewhere deep inside him, and his fury now charges up through him and erupts into a mighty wrath.

"*Shame* on you for such an *ABOMINABLE LIE! NO ONE* has been allowed into the sanctified land of those Peacocks since – since – Why, you are the *WORST* kind of falsifier, the very *WORST* kind of – "

And he goes on to tell me what a liar I am and how ashamed I oughta be. And I am now preparing myself to make a good death, as it is only too evident that this man is mere moments from cracking that gavel and ordering up a rope.

"The sheer *mendacity* ... Why, it sickens me to my very soul. Oh, I am quite ready to deliver my verdict!"

And as he raises his gavel, I bow my head. And he proclaims:

"By the authority vested in me by the Kingdom of Blackwycke, the Province of Tarrymore, the Town of Hickory Flat, in the matter of the theft of Charlemagne the Wonderhorse, I declare – why, *I declare* ... "

And I look up and follow the Judge's eyes, which are now fixed on the far end of the barn. And whaddaya know ...

There stands Hank, having chosen this very moment to appear in that big barn doorway, the afternoon sun just a-glistening off his gleaming coat! Yes, Book, his timing were death-defyingly spectacular, indeed!

Oh, the graceful, powerful size of him as he walks majestically up the aisle toward me. How I exult in the ecstasy of this moment and in the breathtaking magnificence of my noble friend. And as he promenades up that aisle, expressing such a celebration of color, a rush of wonder sweeps through the crowd. Why, they sound like a gathering of angels! Such sweet sounds of surprise and awe and delight as I've never heard the likes of from any audience, anywhere, ever.

And Hank comes up to greet me on the witness stand and gives me a good nuzzle over the railing, and I hug him and kiss him and scratch his neck. Oh, I were so *glad* to see him, I cannot even begin to record how much!

And, naturally, Higgs and Boggs leap right up. "Say, that's *him!*" "Hey, that's our horse!"

And they charge at Hank, who has the good sense to evaporate. And, oh, how the crowd gasps and murmurs . . . And I turn to see that the *Judge* is now the one who is entirely and completely flombasticated!

And you can bet I take full advantage of that moment, Book.

"See that, Your Honor? Hank will have nothing whatsoever to do with those two idiot villains ever again!"

Then Hank appears again right next to me, and again the crowd gasps and murmurs. Floyd and Otis move in to restrain Higgs and Boggs, and I turn to the Judge and forge right on ahead.

"Your Honor, even if you *do* decide to end my life, one thing is certain, and that is this: Hank will never live in chains, ever again. And wherever I go when I die, I go knowing that I freed him, and I'm proud and glad I did. I've been honored to know him and learn from him, and to have his good opinion of me, as well as his kind companionship. Why, he has been the – oh, alright, Hank . . .

Hank just said to please quit chatterboxing about him, so I guess I best hush up and let you get on with things . . . Your Honor?"

Well, Book, during the course of his flombastication, it seems that Judge Augustus T. Abernathy has undergone quite an extraordinary transformation. No longer is he that fractious, furious bird of prey, nor is he that much depleted, disappointed old man. Why, he seems so much *younger* now, and so much more vibrant! And his face has softened in such a way that he looks like – well, like an elegant old gentleman who travels in an artful little house with whitewashed shutters and a pretty little porch with a fan-back wicker chair.

The Judge looks at Hank, and then at me. Then he takes off his spectacles and runs his hands through his hair, and he says:

"Get me some water, will you, Floyd?"

And as the Sheriff does so, the Judge turns back to me.

"You see, young woman . . . What was your name again?"

"Lillian, sir."

"Lillian, yes . . . Y'see, what I need here is what is known as *corroborating testimony*. This horse, will he – will he speak to me?"

Whereupon Hank says he'd be happy to tell the Judge anything he needs to know.

"Hank says he'd be happy to tell you anything you need to know, Your Honor. Did you hear him?"

"No . . . I'm afraid I did not," says the Judge, with a touch of sadness, I think.

"LET DOC TALK TO HIM! DOC'LL TELL YA WHAT'S WHAT!"

Sure enough, it's Poppy, yelling down at us from way up in the rafters. And the Judge turns his gaze skyward and locates the little girl waving both hands in the air. And, do you know, I think I see a smile twitching at the corners of his mouth, though he remains altogether stern and imperious. Then he swiftly goes about the business of finding out from the townsfolk who Doc is and what, if anything, he might contribute to the proceedings. In order to vouch for Doc's amazing gift, people tell such touching tales, testifying how Doc saved their animals and them in the bargain.

Then people help Doc and Poppy down from the rafters, and the children step up in front of the Judge. And I note with such admiration that this Judge, though he is such a naturally loud sort of a person, instantly senses that Doc needs to be addressed with a very soft voice and even, yes, with tenderness. And as I stand there on that witness stand, listening to Hank and Doc and the Judge talking quietly amongst themselves, as Poppy gazes worshipfully up at Hank, I am so deeply moved, Book. At one point, Hank tells Doc and Doc tells the Judge that he wanted only to die before I happened upon him, and that I saved his life, and how eternally grateful he is. And, sure, it's all I can do not to stand there and blubber.

So, after they are all through discussing things, the Judge sends me back to my chair, and Poppy and Doc and Hank gather round me. And I notice that Higgs and Boggs now sit hunched and scowling and refuse to look anywhere in my direction.

Meanwhile, all alone up there on his high perch, the Judge commences to ruminate, as if he is the only person in the whole place.

He picks up the Deed of Ownership and studies it.
He studies the ceiling for a while.
He studies Higgs and Boggs, then Hank, then me.
He drinks some water.

Then, at last, he says, "Will the defendant please rise?"

And that's me, and so I do.

The Judge looks down upon me, and then out at all the people waiting breathlessly for the verdict. And then he proclaims:

"By the authority vested in me by the Kingdom of Blackwyke, the Province of Tarrymore, the Town of Hickory Flat, in the matter of the theft of Charlemagne the Wonderhorse, I declare the defendant . . . "

And, oh, I can see it in his eyes, Book . . .

"GUILTY AS CHARGED."

Everybody in the place gasps in shock. Higgs and Boggs start hooting and hollering, and the Judge starts banging his gavel.

"I WILL HAVE ORDER IN THIS COURTROOM!"

Well, he's got everybody so well trained, the whole place hushes in an instant.

And me, well . . . the only truth I now know is that I don't understand anything at all about anything at all. And as I am blinking back tears, the Judge is glowering out at the crowd. And then he sets down his gavel and begins to speak:

"Ladies and gentlemen . . . I am entrusted and commissioned by this Kingdom to uphold the law. That is my sworn duty, and in this case I have fulfilled that duty. *However,* I am answerable also to a different kind of law, a deeper law – some might call it a moral law. And this most hallowed of laws mandates the honorable, decent stewardship of our fellow creatures in this Whirld. Now, I must tell you, there are two beautiful, powerful mares who pull my little home all over this Kingdom so that I can be a circuit judge, so that I can try to dispense justice whenever it may be possible to do so. The three of us have been together – well, a very long time now – over the hardest of roads, through the harshest of weather. They are steadfast, they are stalwart, and I like 'em a whole lot better than most of my relatives. And though they are not, strictly speaking, Wonderhorses like Charlema – like Hank here – they certainly are a wonder to me. And I consider it to be my sacred responsibility to return the honor of their devotion with my own. So . . ."

Well, I don't know where he's heading, Book, but it sure sounds promising!

"I thank you for your whole truth, Lillian. I thank you for teaching a tired old man that he has *not*, in point of fact, seen everything, and that he does not, in point of fact, *know* everything. Now, I can give no verdict other than the one I have given, but with regards to the sentencing, I do have some – free rein, shall we say. Therefore, I am hereby commuting your sentence. *You shall not hang!*"

A deafening cheer erupts from the crowd. And the overwhelming relief that floods through me so nearly undoes me that I have to lean on Hank just so's I will stay upright.

And the Judge bangs his gavel.

"SILENCE, Y'HEAR ME? THIS COURT IS STILL IN SESSION!"

The crowd hushes. The Judge turns back to me.

"It is this Court's decision to instead impose a fine. Therefore, young woman, since you have heretofore testified that you, in fact, sing for your supper, this Court has determined that your fine shall be: one song! Payable by sundown."

And he bangs that gavel, and the crowd cheers once more. And then . . . Judge Augustus T. Abernathy smiles down at me, and, why, it is like the sun shining directly into my soul. Yes, I do believe it is one of the warmest, most kind-hearted smiles I shall ever see in all my life – which looks to be a whole lot longer than it did mere moments ago.

And, wouldn't you know, Higgs and Boggs hop to their feet, mad as hornets! Why, they kick their chairs and holler at the Judge all the half-witted things you'd guess they would:

"Whadda *you* know anyway, y'old geezer!" "I'm gonna knock your block off!" "We'll *sue*, that's what!" "*Yeah*, you heard him!"

Instantly, the Judge transforms back into that vengeful bird of prey. He glares down at them two cruel fools, and then and there decrees that they are to be locked up for Contempt of Court, starting right this very moment! Then says the Judge, *with a chuckle*, as if he's having such fun:

"Let's see now…how long can I lock you two disgraceful dunces away? What's a nice round number? Hmm… *One thousand days!* Yes, I like the ring of that. Sheriff, would you be so kind as to get these vile scoundrels out of my sight?"

And do you know, the Sheriff outright *laughs*. Then he shoots me a wink and a smile and hauls Higgs and Boggs right on outta there, with Otis nipping at their heels.

Then the Judge bangs his gavel one last time and proclaims:

"This Court is officially *ADJOURNED!* Now, y'all go on, get outta here! Go home!"

Why, the crowd fairly floats outta that barn, like a thoroughly satisfied audience. When it comes right down to it, Book, I guess all they really came for was a good show. And, no small thanks to Hank, why, I do believe they got one.

But in this moment, somehow these folks seem to me to be much more than just a happy audience. There is now such a lightness of heart, such an uplifted spirit in the air! And as I look around at all their faces, it truly feels that kinder people are coming out of this barn than them that came in.

Outside, Poppy and Doc are standing with their quiet, pretty mother, who I am so happy to meet. And how lovely it is to watch folks stop to say nice things to her about her children and to gently pat Doc on the back and Poppy on the head. And as Hank and me are strolling side by side down the path, free as birds once again, quite a few people pat me on the back too. And of course everybody wants to pet Hank and talk to him.

Though I must make a pointed note that *some* people get entirely too grabby, and Hank doesn't like that one bit, and neither do I. And when Hank turns himself his chestnut color once again, do you know that some of those people get all snippy about how Hank oughta change into the colors *they* say, and at *their* say-so? And Hank asks me if I see why he has no use at all for being famous. Of course I see. How could I not?

Well, sure, he and I agree that we are both in need of a great whomping gallop. So, with my Cape, I twirls up my Scarlet Velvet Saddle and Reins, which always look so handsome on him. And as I hop on Hank's back, all is right with the Whirld once more, and my spirit feels as if it's nigh on billowing! But, just as we are about to ride off and away, who should appear, pressed right up against Hank's flank, but that *horrible* Hopper fella. He is smirking up at me ever so slyly, that quill of his scritch-scratching away.

"Why, you tricky wench, you went and cheated death, didn't you? Cheated death yet *again*, I should say, eh? Care to comment, lovey-dove? What may I tell your public?"

And as I look down at that Hopper, I notice the frayed edges of his hat and the holes in his coat and the dull greyness of his person, inside and out. And, well, I feel a touch of sadness for him.

So I smile, and I look him right in the eye, and I say:

"You can tell them I am glad to be alive."

And with that, Hank decides it's high time we leave this crowd behind. And with a few quick, powerful steps, we are off on our ownsome once again. And he lopes, and he canters, and then we break out into a full-on gallop down that wide open Road, lined with endless fields of wildflowers on either side. And every particle of my being is bristling with Life, as I am remembering our first wild ride on that first glorious night, and, oh, I am *howling* with the rip-roaring rush of pure, sweet freedom!

And, far behind me, I hear that Hopper's voice fading in the wind:

"Death don't like to be cheated, duckie! Mark my words, Death will catch up with you one day!"

What a ridiculous thing to say.
As if I didn't know.
Death catches up with us all, does it not?

But not today, Book!
Not today!

Wherein I Attend My Own Funeral Picnic

So, Hank and I gallop our hearts out on this most marvelous afternoon, and then we take ourselves a nice, leisurely stroll back to Hickory Flat. After having been cooped up for so long, how *delicious* it is to drink my fill of all that freedom and fresh air once more!

And you'll laugh, Book, because what we then come upon is none other than my Funeral Picnic. Yep, the very shindig that Velma Thudder and her pals cooked up to celebrate my hanging. I'm surprised to see they're still having it, as the evidence would suggest I'm still very much alive. Guess they just didn't want all their food and decorations and scavenger hunts to go to waste.

Anyhow, as Hank and I walk out into this wide meadow dotted with trees, the whole place so vibrant with folks laughing and dancing and merrymaking, well, who should I straightaway see but Velma and her gang making a busy beeline straight for me. And the moment he spots that bevy of biddies heading our way, Hank, in his wisdom, trots straight off to where the Judge's horses are standing, well out of earshot.

As she approaches, Velma has at me:

"Well, if it isn't Miss High and Mighty! Now, you listen here, you did *not* have to holler at me like that in front of everybody. I didn't do *jack rabbit* to that horse! Besides, he's fine now, isn't he? So that was just some nasty bad manners on your part! Obviously, nobody raised you right – but I suppose that's not your fault, since they say you're an orphan. *Anyhow*, what do you think of our decorations? Aren't they just the most perfectly *gorgeous* things y'ever saw?"

Now, being that I were in such a cheery frame of mind, I might've overlooked the fact that their decorations were created especially to celebrate my death, simply replied that everything looked very nice, and then gone on about the business of celebrating my aliveness. But as I see that woman's face all pinched up with spite, I remember all too well the poison that she and her friends spewed at those children in that jailhouse. And, truth be told, I suppose I had a little stored-up outrage in my craw. So I takes me a good look around, and I decide to unleash my unbridled opinion on the matter.

I begin by pointing out the Purple Problem, in particular, as it is nothing short of a *travesty*, Book, pure and simple. Every which way you look, Velma and her cohorts have mistaken the most sickly shade of *fuchsia* for purple – yes, *exactly* as I'd specifically specified against – smothering everything in sight with it, including themselves! You heard me, these silly creatures have gone and bedecked themselves in *fuchsia* from head to toe!

And I am most heartily dismayed to report that there are poofy, lopsided fuchsia *bows* insulting all the trees. And, of course, they have likewise ignored my recommended use of cobalt and dusty rose and lavender, and their copious use of yellow is nothing short of a slander to that poor color. That's all I'll say about it.

And, oh, sure, as I hold forth, Velma gets all mortally offended and goes on to lecture me about how nobody has to teach *her* just what a color is or isn't and how *she* has the finest taste in town, I could just ask anybody – whereupon I notice several of the ladies stealing smirks and glances at each other. But, undeterred, ol' Velma rolls right on about how if I can't appreciate beauty when I see it, well, that's just plain too bad for me, as I was supposed to be dead and not get to have an opinion anyway. That woman sure could've held her own in a chatterboxing contest, Book, I'll say that much for her.

But it is such a splendid, dazzling afternoon that I am not inclined to spend a single moment more of my hard-earned happiness trying to straighten out ol' Velma Thudder. So I just do what needs doing in the name of accuracy, expediency, and artistic sanity. Says I:

"Ladies, please observe . . . "

And I twirls my Cape, which dresses me up in a diaphanous, pointy-sleeved, pointy-hemmed number, in pointedly *perfect* purple. And with a pointedly theatrical flourish, I announce:

"Now, *this* is purple!"

The eyes of all her friends light right up. But Velma purses her lips, looks me up and down, and says:

"Oh, see, now I make dresses like that *all the time*, but the ones I make are so *ladylike*, and *this* – well, this just makes you look like you belong in a brothel."

Why, I can only gape at that shameful, spiteful woman and wonder what in the Whirld could have made her that way.

Well, just then, Poppy comes skipping up, picks up one of the embroidered points of the hem of my dress, and dances with the diaphanous material, chanting:

"Miss Lillian, Miss Lillian, why, you look just like the Queen of the Faeries!"

Which causes Velma to huff and puff and stalk off in disgust. Poppy looks up at me and beckons me to lean down, and so I do. Then she whispers:

"Don't you worry, Miss Lillian. Every once in a while, I go pee in her well."

Well, I bust a gut laughing, and I pick Poppy up and swing her around, feeling entirely reconstituted. What a fine cure-all is a great big belly laugh, eh, Book?

And you know, despite Velma Thudder and that unholy proliferation of fuchsia, why, it turns out to be just as fine a Funeral Picnic as ever there was, I bet. There is such a lot of laughter and rejoicing, the food is mouth-watering and generous, and the company couldn't be better if it tried.

And I tell you, nothing tasted sweeter than the Sheriff's strawberry rhubarb crumble pie, which he'd made special to celebrate my living. Handing me a whopping big slice, he says:

"Proud of you, Red. And, uh . . . well, I'm mighty glad you didn't get yourself hanged."

And he lightly tweaks the tip of my nose, and we smile at each other, and Otis paws at my hand so I'll pet him. And I feel so moved and honored that we happy three have come through such a very big event together, and have formed ourselves such a fine fellowship along the way.

Then the Sheriff walks over and sits down beside Poppy and Doc's mother, and they take to quietly talking, as if they are simply picking up a conversation that they are always in the middle of. And out in the meadow, Poppy runs and plays with the neighboring children, while Doc sits in quiet communion with a gathering of all the animals in the near vicinity.

And as for me, why, I get to sit and sip lemonade with Judge Augustus T. Abernathy on the porch of his little home – which Maude and Maybelle, his two marvelous mares, have pulled into this meadow. The Judge sits on that wonderful fan-back wicker chair of his, and I get to sit on the identical fan-back chair that he keeps especially for company.

My, oh, my, how we *talk*, Book! We talk about Life and Justice and Destiny and all the things he's seen and all the things I've seen. And, of course, I talk about Home and how it is the aim of my life to find my Home, having lost it somehow.

And when he hears that, the Judge smiles a small, strange smile. And after a moment, he tells me that his Home is far, far away, and that he barely ever sees it anymore. Then he says:

"Lemme tell ya, Lillian . . . Home isn't always everything it's cracked up to be. But you listen here: It does not matter if this long lost Home of yours is good, bad, or indifferent. You must seek and you must find."

Then he goes on to tell me that the reason I must find my Home is because, at our roots, at our very beginnings, there lies buried treasure, waiting to be discovered. And also because maybe, just maybe, somebody is missing me terribly and dearly hoping I'll find my way back again, even after all this time.

And, oh, how we *laugh* about how furious we were with each other during the trial! And, of course, I apologize to him for mis-guidedly judging him for all make and manner of offenses, such as not really caring about or even knowing right from wrong. Then the Judge gets very quiet. And then, why, he comes right out and apologizes for having been so horribly harsh with me when I mentioned the Peacocks.

Well. When the Judge tells me what he next tells me, I under-stand everything . . .

You see, ever since he could recall, ever since he were a very small boy, Augustus T. Abernathy's ruling passion in life was to learn anything he could possibly learn about the Pink-Purple-Periwinkle Peacocks. He wanted to live in their Land. He wanted to study at their feet. When he grew to be a young man, against the adamant wishes of his family, he moved to live near the entrance to their Land, and he devoted himself to being granted admission. And he practiced and tried and tried and practiced, but he could never say *Pink-Purple-Periwinkle Peacocks* more than 2,627 times. So, one day, he decided it would be best to give up on his dream, go earn a respectable living, and make something meaningful of his life.

Says he, after a moment, "Hmph. Still quite a sore spot, I guess. Having such a grand passion come to, well, nothing at all . . . "

And though he is looking at the horizon, I can see that he is watching memories. Then, all of a sudden, a whole other sort of a look comes over his face. And he turns to me with a sly smile, as if we are playing a game.

"Do you know what, Miss Horse Thief?" says he. "It is nearly sundown . . . and unless I am very much mistaken, I do believe somebody around here owes this Court a fine."

And then the Judge calls what remains of the crowd together. And standing there on the porch of his little home, as the sun is taking its long, sweet time to set, I open my Music Box and beckon the Judge to sigh into it.

First come the dulcet sounds of a harp, then joined by a flute, then by a lute, and then . . . why, I find myself singing about the Land of the Peacocks. And as that song sings through me, I close my eyes. And the moment I do, all the sublime, shining visions of that Land come rushing back to me: the glowing garden, the pink quartz canyon, the Light-shower, everything everywhere breathing its own Music . . . all that luminous, numinous glory! And all the while, inside of me, it feels as if I am floating again, surrounded by those Peacocks and their endless loving-kindness.

As the song ends, I look up to see the Judge wiping his eyes with his handkerchief. Then he folds his handkerchief, puts it back in his pocket, and looks at me for long moment. The corners of his eyes crinkle up, and he gives me a small smile. Then he clears his throat, rises to his feet, and he proclaims:

"In the name of the Kingdom of Blackwycke, the Province of Tarrymore, and the town of Hickory Flat, I hereby declare the defendant to be all paid up and free to go!"

And everybody laughs and applauds, and then they all break off into their little groups once more. Likewise, the Judge and I return to sipping our lemonade and taking in the sumptuous sunset and the play of shifting colors all across the sky.

After we sit silent for a stretch, I say:

"I could watch a million and one sunsets and never get tired of 'em, *ever.*"

And gazing off at the horizon, the Judge murmurs so low, I wonder if he even knows he's speaking aloud:

"Gotta soak up every last one of 'em now . . . "

And something in his voice makes me suddenly understand why, during the trial, he went from being so fiercely energetic to so thoroughly exhausted. And as I turn to look at him, tears jump into my eyes. And when the Judge sees my distress, he smiles softly and pats my hand.

"No, no, now . . . I have lived a long life, and that's just the way of things. Though I must confess, I had hoped to go on a good deal longer. But my body seems to have other ideas on the subject."

After a bit of a silence, I quietly ventured to ask if he'll be heading Home now. And so many emotions crossed his face as he watched the last of that sun slip away, he never did get around to answering me. But, by that time, I was thinking of something else entirely. Yes, just as that day was giving way to dusk, a remarkably fine idea was dawning on me, clear as a morning sky:

Why, sure, I'll give him my key!

So I come right out and tell the Judge my fine idea, and I retrieve the key from the compartment inside my boot, and I happily offer it to him. Oh, o' course, he protests and refuses and argues with me for a good long while. And let me tell you, don't *ever* try arguing with a Judge – it nearly killed me.

I finally won the battle, though, by means of the only lie I told him all day. A lie by omission, in fact. See, I selected to neglect to inform the Judge that this here key is a one-and-only-one-use-allowed kind of a key. And to give my lie some legs, I asked him if he would please make sure, after he has opened the Door, to hide the key between the stones on the top step so's I can find it upon my return.

It was a worthy fib, Book. I'm glad to have thought of it.

And when the Judge asked me what the Peacocks will think of him having the key when they so clearly intended it for me, I says to him:

"You just tell 'em Lillian sent you. They'll understand."

And they will, Book. No question about it. Aw, I can always go crack that ol' challenge again! I'll just likely have to sit down while I'm doing it, as I will be so very old and not feeling up to snuff. In the meantime, I'll just have to keep in practice.

So, tonight, here am I, a-way up high in this welcoming treetop, lying in my Scarlet Velvet Hammock as in days of yore, looking down upon Hank and Maude and Maybelle, who stand sleeping under this here tree. The meadow is silent now, the moon is high, the Judge is fast asleep inside his house, and everyone else is long gone Home.

Long gone Home . . . That has a nice, warm ring to it, eh?

Alright now, Book, I have something to say, strictly between you and me: Though I am elated to have seen justice done, and though I know how wildly fortunate I am to be free as the wind once more, I must confess, I am feeling pretty exhausted underneath it all and would very much welcome a rest.

There, I've said it.

I know, you must be thinking, "Well, if you are in such a great, deep need of a rest, Lillian, then for goodness sake, close your eyes and go to sleep."

Right you are, Book.
Sweet dreams to us all.

Wherein I Am a Glutton and a Dreamer

Oh, Book, you should see me! I am *lying abed.* You heard me, I am a-lying in a wide, soft, delicious bed, with white sheets so fresh, I feel like I'm floating – 'cept that I'm all cozied up and warm.

Oops . . . Those splotches on the page are drops of peppermint tea, which I have been sipping and which has been most medicinal. Thusly fortified, I shall now commence to explain to you just how I came to be laid up in such a lovely place, and in such a sorry state as to necessitate the sipping of peppermint tea.

Well, there am I, coddiwompling on along, on a day as blue and as fine as a fine, blue day can be – notably without Hank around to talk some sense into me. So, when I come strolling up over a bright green hilltop, I am amazed to see, spreading out before me, an endless expanse of cherry trees . . . rows upon rows upon *rows* of 'em, carpeting the valley and the hillsides all around. And as I descend the hill and begin to walk amongst these trees, I notice that all the cherries are so perfectly ripe – why, they are such a deep rich maroon, they are just about *purple* – and each one is nigh on as big as a plum!

Well. I came to consciousness, Book, flat on my back on the ground, groaning, next to a veritable mountain of cherry pits. My stomach was so big and round and stretched it were fit to pop, and the shooting pains in my belly – sheer agony. Yes. I had done myself in entirely.

Then I hear a few footsteps on the grass behind me, and I look up to find myself in the shade of a very tall, big-shouldered man, with unruly thick hair sticking out every which way. Right off, he puts me in mind of a sheepdog. He looks me over. Then, dry as crackling leaves, he says:

"Did yourself in, eh?"

Well, Book, I have eaten so much I cannot sit up, so I am forced to introduce myself from this prone position.

"Hello, how do you do? I'm – *oof* – Lillian. *Ow* . . . "

Whereupon he tells me his name is Jonas, and he offers me both his hands, which look and feel to be made of oak, they are so thick and strong. And, why, this oak tree of a man pulls me up onto my feet as gently and easily as if I were just a sack of feathers. Then he tells me that his wife Clara will fix me right up, and he leads me on over to his horse cart – towards which I am *waddling*, mind you.

Says I, "I only meant to eat a few – *oof!* I guess I'm just a glutton, pure and simple."

"Looks like. G'on, lie down now."

And he gives me a boost so's I can lie down on some blankets in the back of the cart. Then he climbs up onto the seat, picks up the reins, and proceeds to say nary a word the whole way back home.

And, Book, in spite of a corresponding stab of pain in my belly for every bump in the road, I lie there so contentedly, listening to the cart wheels turning and watching the clouds glide by, until, at last, Jonas pulls up to a big, welcoming house. Oh, such a *beautiful* house it is, with tall windows and a wide, wraparound porch and a garden on all sides!

So, Jonas brings me shuffling into the kitchen. And there stands Clara, round and red-headed and smiling, with her hands on her hips.

Says Jonas, "Present for ya."

And she shakes her head as she takes me in, and she says:

"*Awww*, you've gone and done yourself in entirely! Poor lamb…"

"Pig, more like," says Jonas.

And I laugh, and then I groan because it hurts so much to laugh. And Clara swats Jonas lightly with a dishtowel.

"Husband, look at her! Isn't she just the spittin' image of your sister?" says Clara. "His sister could never be moderate with the cherries neither. Come with me, love. You'll have yourself a nice lie-down in the back room."

And before I knew it, Clara had bundled me off to this, oh, most perfectly peaceful picture of a room, with its dark wood floors and its fireplace and its armchair and that beautiful roll-top desk. And the lush scent, Book! Why, there are lilac bushes outside my window, *mmmm* . . . It is *so* restful here.

So, Clara pulled off my boots and put me to bed and puffed up the pillows and pulled the covers up over me. And then she brought me a pot of her peppermint tea – an old family recipe specially formulated for cherry gluttons.

And ever since Clara left the room and closed the door, I've been sipping this tea and gazing out the window, watching the gentle breeze playing with the curtains. Why, I can only just barely keep my eyes open. I don't think I've ever felt so weary, so way down deep in my bones. I feel so

———

I didn't finish that sentence, Book, because I fell asleep. I must have slept for . . . well, the sky outside my window has gone crimson with sunset.

I have just had a dream so potent, I must write it out immediately: I dreamed that I was lying in this very bed in this very same position in this very room. Yes, in the dream I am lying here watching the breeze gently playing with the curtains, yes, just as it were doing before I fell asleep . . .

But then, what starts to happen is this breeze becomes a wild wind, which blows the curtains away completely! And then, why, *it blows the window and the walls right along with them* – yes, just as if curtains and window and walls are all made of the same light, fluttery fabric – *whoosh!*

And then, as I am a-lying there, it seems that there is suddenly much more sunlight in the room, and I see that the bed has grown bigger and wider and there is a canopy above it. And I see many tall, arching windows all around the room, and through one of the windows – why, I see the topmost branches of a Red Rose Oak Tree.

Yes, Book, I am *in* the Heavenly Tower Room! Yes . . .

And the next thing I know, I am standing in the middle of the room. And, *ohhh*, how comforting is the warm, wood floor that greets my bare feet, how familiar it feels to be standing here, watching the dust motes dancing through a shaft of sunlight.

Then I turn to look around me, and, yes, of course . . . there be the armchair, there the fireplace, there the writing desk, all of it so big and beautiful and ornate. And then I turn to behold the wide, soft bed . . . and the *moment* I lay eyes upon that bed, I am once again *in* it, under the covers, back where I started.

And then I wake up in *this* bed, in the very same position. And that's it. The dream is over.

Well, I don't know what to make of it . . . My mind feels like pudding. All I know is, I've never felt a dream feel so real, *ever.* Yes, I've dreamt of the Tower Room, but it always felt so far off, 'til now. Surely it must be of some great portent. I was *in* that room, Book – *in it*, I tell you! – just as sure as I am writing these words upon this page at this very moment.

I must sip some tea and have a think on it.

———

I am back. More awake now. Thoughts are rushing into my mind, one upon the heels of the other.

Now, I've come to use that dream of the Tower Room as a measuring stick for what Home oughta feel like. And now, as I look around me, I am realizing something:

Everything in that Tower Room is in *this* room in this good farmer's home. Why, except for the size and the ornateness of everything in the dream, sure, there's the fireplace, there's the armchair, there's the writing desk, and here's the wide, soft bed. And just outside my window, there is a lilac bush . . . *lilacs*, yes! And Jonas is so very tall, and Clara has red hair. And she even said I look just like his sister!

I am afraid to write what I am thinking, Book. No, I cannot bring myself to scratch with my quill what I hope against hope to be true. I heard once that hope can break the heart, hope can be too strong . . .

Clara just popped her head in and asked me if I feel well enough to have dinner with them, as she's made me a nice, big bowl of her special vegetable broth. And she told me that I will stay the night here, and that she won't take no for an answer.

Fear not, Book, at dinner tonight I will be entirely circumspect.
I will hear what I need to hear.
I will see what I need to see.
And I will know.

I will just allow myself to say this: I would give my very Music Box for this to be my true Home, so's I could finally rest. Hank would be so happy here too, I know it. And I do believe I could learn to be moderate with the cherries.

However, my mind will not jump to conclusions.
Though my heart has already leapt the fence.

———————

Well . . . I am a fool, Book.
I am not come Home. I am not come Home, no.
I were just dreaming, pure and simple.

Oh, we had dinner, and when the moment presented itself, I told Jonas and Clara my story. But I knew immediately. There was no rightaway talk of a lost little redheaded girl. There is a prodigal child though, it turns out. Their son, whose room I am sleeping in, has been gone for a long time and is expected back any day now with his wife and their brand new baby.

No, I am not come Home. It was just my mind playing tricks on me – I suppose because I were so tired and such.

Fear not, Book, they never guessed what I was feeling. In all these years on the outside of things, I've gotten myself a darn good poker face, that's for sure. And I haven't been in the Theatrical Profession for nothing, now, have I? So, to feign that I were thoroughly cheerful, I told them all the funniest stories of how Emile and I were forever wreaking havoc on the stage, and I expertly pretended that all was well with me.

But tonight, back in this wide, soft bed, gazing into this fireplace and at the desk and at the armchair, I must record that hope can . . . well, hope can most certainly be too strong. Nope, they're not mine, and I'm not theirs. I'm just a glutton and a dreamer, and that's all there is to it.

Oh, they are so generous, they've even asked me to stay on for a while, and they told me how their son would be so glad to know me, as it's always the more the merrier with their family.

Finally, I relented, and I lied, and I said I would stay. But I will be gone when they awaken. Truth is, Book, I cannot bear any kind of a goodbye or to be hugged by them. Of course, I shall leave them a note of thanks.

But I should like to record our last moments together, because I'm certain I shall want to remember Jonas and Clara and their kindness and hospitality when I am old and I read this again. Perhaps I shall even smile when I remember who I thought they might have been to me.

So, we are sitting in front of their big stone fireplace and we are talking about our favorite flowers, and I tell them how delightful it is to have those lilac bushes right outside the window. Which prompts me to talk about my Lady of the Lilacs dream. Which perks Clara right up. Which provokes Jonas to say:

"Here we go . . . Her grandmother was a gypsy, so every darn dream is a revelation."

And Clara says, "Oh, *hush*, ya big buffoon. What else goes on in your dream, love? Does this Lady say anythin' to you?"

And then I tell her how the Lady always says, "Remember, my dearest darling dear . . . " and then something about a kingdom. And then I tell Clara how I always smell lilacs in the dream, and how the smell stays in my nose even after I've woken up. And her eyes go wide, and she rubs her hand over her heart.

"Oh, now, Lillian, a dream that follows you around like that is surely tryin' to tell you somethin'!"

I didn't have the heart to tell her that I wasn't going to be putting any more stock in dreams from here on in.

"What does the Lady want you to *remember*, I wonder?"

"That it's late, and it's time to turn in. Come on, ya Gypsy Queen," says Jonas. "Sleep tight, little piggy."

By that he meant me, Book.

And Clara kissed me on the cheek, and Jonas threw the blanket up over my head, and we three had our last laugh together. And then they went on upstairs to bed, and I came back here, to this perfectly peaceful room that belongs to somebody else's life entirely.

Ah, well . . .

Book, I tell you, if I did not just look up and see Hank outside, waiting for me down near them cherry trees . . . Well, I just don't know what.

I ride at dawn.

11: The End

Wherein I Am Aimless

Well, Book, I have returned!
More awake and ringing with life than ever before!

"But, Lillian," you may say, "when last we left each other you were in such a terribly *sorrowful* sort of a state."

Ah, 'tis true – true, indeed. But that was then, and this is now. Yes, I have altogether refashioned my point of view . . .

Y'see, after I left that farmer's house, I cried and cried for days and days, about not having a Home, about not having parents, about this, about that, until at last I got all them tears out – a whole ocean of 'em, likely. "Cry until it's all cried out," was what Mad Aunt Harriet used to say. And, Book, I have come to believe that all them tears cleaned up some windows inside of me, and I can now see things a little more clearly somehow.

So, first things first . . .
I hereby officially declare and record:
I have entirely and eternally given up my search for Home.

That's right, you heard me – I am well and truly *free*, see. No more always trying to figure out how I got to where I've gotten, and how I haven't got to where I haven't gotten. No more forever feeling let down and led on and left out. I declare the Whole Wyde Whirld to be my Home now. Yessir, I am like the birds! Why, I'm "Lillian of Everywhere," which suits me infinitely better than being "Miss Nobody from Nowhere." The plain fact of it is, Book, I'd begun, without ever really knowing it, to feel so very failed and foolish, what with all my everlasting seeking and not finding.

Remember that time I gave up my search for Home for a while, when I were traveling with the Theatrical Fellows? How I felt so light of heart, so fleet of foot, so full of feeling useful? Well, I am now filled to the brim with that very same feeling, only much more – well, much more *in tune* with everything. 'Tis a feeling far too deep and wide for words, that's for sure.

Ah, yes, which reminds me … I am likewise compelled to report that the one thing which has *not* improved is my Poetry. It is still largely drivel. Though I continue to burn my poems as an offering to the Spirit of Art, which does seem to lend them a certain loftiness that is otherwise so sorely lacking.

Oh, but speaking of being in tune with everything, Book, how my Music Box and I do thrive! I am mighty gratified to tell you that I do believe we uplift and comfort folks quite a bit wherever we go. And we make quite copious coinage, might I add!

And now, I must record yet another declaration of momentous import: *I have forgiven Destiny entirely and completely.*

"Forgiven?" you ask. "Was there a need to forgive?"

Oh, yes, indeed! I had grown such a mighty big chip on my shoulder, Book, because I felt Destiny to be so hard-hearted and unfeeling – calling me to leave the only Home I'd ever known to go out and find my real Home, then never giving me my memory back so's I *could* find it, then continuing to withhold any and all clues as to its whereabouts, and then callously breaking my heart when I thought I finally *had* found it.

Oh, I were cultivating quite a sizable grudge, no doubt about it.

But slowly, as my heart mended, I began to take into account the vast variety of people I've met, all the bona fide wonders I've seen, and the showers of sheer *interestingness* that I have encountered all along my wandering way.

So, nowadays, I surmise that perhaps Destiny and I somehow got off on the wrong foot and then got tangled up somewheres with our expectations of each other. Maybe ol' Destiny just got frustrated with me for some reason I'm not wise enough to see, and jumped to conclusions, and judged me unfairly. And in return, well, maybe I secretly judged ol' Destiny right back, supposing it to be unsympathetic and uncooperative to a wondering wanderer such as myself.

Whatever the truth of it is, Book, I'm all through with hard hearts and shoulder chips and grudges. I open the doors of my spirit wide-wide-wide, and I say:

"Alright then, Destiny, let's start fresh. You go ahead and do what you will – whenever, wherever, however it suits you. I am but a humble leaf, and you, the Sovereign Wind!"

That's right, Book, I am entirely without destination.
I am only a wondrous *journey* of a person,
let loose on the whirl of the Whirld.

Why, I gaze at my map and I marvel at all the places I've been, and at all the places I have yet to be.

I purely marvel.

Wherein I Am Plagued
by a Vicious Pernicious Narcissus

Mmmm . . . Here I lie, ever so grateful to be, once again, safe and sound of mind and spirit . . . reclining and snoozing and otherwise reposing upon these mossy, velvety banks of this here slow-flowing river.

And, *ahhh*, there stands Hank, 'neath that most majestic Red Rose Oak Tree. The two of them make quite a picture. Times like this, I'm awful glad I can't paint, 'cause I'd want to paint 'em both together just like that, and I'd never even come close to doing 'em justice. And I tell you, Book, what a rare and auspicious gift to have happened upon a Red Rose Oak Tree on the heels of such an unsettling experience as I've just had. Oh, I can't tell you what a cure-all it is just to smell those big, fat, red roses.

Anyhow, yes . . . I do believe my senses are soothed and settled enough at last that I am now able to recount this tale without agitation, which lingered on for far too long after leaving the strange place about which I am fixing to tell you.

So, there am I, emerging from a lush, dense forest, when I am staggered to behold on the hilltop beyond – sparkling wildly in the sunlight – such a spectacular sight! As I stand there a-gazing and a-gazing, my spirit swelling more and more at the splendor of it, I then recall that I have, in fact, heard tell of the much-vaunted beauty of this place, which is called The City of Mirrors.

And as I walk through the valley that lies before it, I am so captivated by the brilliance of this splendid city on the hill, I can barely tear my eyes away to look at anything else – not even to look where I am going! Oh, yes, I stumble quite a few times (which

I nearly never do), that's how enraptured I am by the endless glittering, which grows ever more entrancing the closer I get. So, yes, Book, I suppose I was, in a manner of speaking, enchanted. But it truly felt to me to be the Spirit of Art beckoning, so I ran into its arms as I always do – though usually not to such hazardous effect.

Anyhow, as I pass through the towering gates and step inside the city and begin to make my way through the streets, why, I nearly put my jaw out of whack, I am gawking so much at the masterful means by which everything, but *everything*, is so artfully covered in mirrors! The buildings and the streets and the people, oh, the *people* . . . My word, every one of them is so ravishing, so magnificently coiffed and polished and haberdashed – and they are adorned head to toe, yes, in *mirrors!*

But, oh, I am beginning to feel *so very hot,* what with all that sunlight flashing and flaring off all them mirrors. So, sure, I am overjoyed to spot a sign that says, of all things to say:

The POOL →

Well, without hesitation, I follow the arrow. And as I am making my way along, up ahead of me I spot a beautiful little boy who's got a bucket and a rag and who is washing and polishing the mirrors on the sidewalk. For some reason, he completely stops what he is doing when he sees me walking toward him. And, oh, how he stares at me, with a pair of deep brown eyes near as big as his head! He is the most angelic, curly-haired little boy you ever did see, and I cannot help but smile at him, o' course.

But he looks up at me quite solemnly and says:

"Careful of the Pool, Miss."

"Why, thank you, good sir," says I. "I promise to be *very* careful."

And do you know what, Book? I were so taken with how ador-able it was that this little boy were so concerned for my safety (when o' course we know I swim like an eel) that I paid not a *single* moment's attention to what he said.

Anyhow, I then come upon another sign that says:

THIS WAY TO

The POOL
→

And I round the corner, and I there behold such an extravagantly long, turquoise blue Pool, surrounded by intricate mosaics made of mirrored tiles.

Well, I go on over and flop myself down by side of this Pool, and I yank off my boots and peel off my socks and roll up my leggings. Then, just as I am about to stick my big ol' feet in the water, I become *transfixed* by the sparkling tiles at the very bottom of this Pool, so I am compelled to lean out to get a better view.

And as I do, the water suddenly becomes so *uncannily* still . . . and there be my own red-headed mug reflecting back at me. Well, I am so alarmed, so dumbfounded, I am utterly *combastulated* by how *horrible* I look! Why, the me that I see in this Pool is simply the unholiest mess that ever was!

And as I begin to examine all of the many things that appear to be so suddenly and appallingly wrong with my physical form, which I'd always been so mighty friendly with before, I notice a *whirlpool* start swirling in the water. And from this swirling whirlpool – *ohhh, my!* – there comes a-rising and a-rising this . . . why, this . . .

Creature!
Who looks exactly like me!

Only her hair's shinier and much more flowing, and in every way she's so much more beautiful than I am, though I cannot quite put my finger on *how* . . .

And as she is rising up out of the Pool, this Creature is berating me – that's right, she is spewing a relentless stream of insults, all about the felonious failings of my physical personage. She is haranguing me about my looks, calling me the ugliest, fattest, *ugliest* thing ever in the history of the Whole Wyde Whirld – and all of this, mind you, in the most piercing, *awful* voice!

Well, sure, I am so startled, I can only stare at her as she grows ever more menacing, looming larger and higher above me, all the while castigating me in that *agony* of a voice. Soon she has backed me into a corner, see, where it comes to me that I oughta make my way over to my Cape. Sure, if I can think straight enough with all her nonstop jabbering, maybe I can twirl myself into some sensational creation – maybe somehow out-dazzle her or out-frighten her and shrink the hateful thing back into that Pool.

But, doggone it, what with the pernicious potency of her meanness and that vexatious *voice* of hers, why, the Creature has me so rattled I cannot get my Cape to work! And in that moment, I feel myself to be purely trapped in this corner, so I have no choice but to curl up into a ball and wait here until a better idea comes along.

Well, all curled up like that, in the dark of myself it dawns on me: What in tarnation am I doing all curled up in a ball like this? Am I or am I not Grand Champion of the 632nd Chatterboxing Championship? Well, o' *course* I am! So, sure, I jumps to my feet, I stands my ground, and I have at her:

"HOW DARE YOU! How *dare* you terrify and torment a completely unsuspecting person like that? Have you no shame? Why, that's just plain mean-spirited, that's what that is! And let me tell you something else . . . "

Well, Book, this is why I won the trophy, ain't it?

And in a matter of mere moments, why, the silly Creature bursts into a shower of tears and wailing lamentations:

"*Ohhhhh*, why are you being so mean to me? Why are you being so *cruel*? You don't appreciate me – you don't *love* me!"

Can you imagine? And I thought *I* had a flair for the dramatic.

"Alright, now," says I, "you can just stop all that boo-hooing you're doing and tell me what you want of me and why it is you are compelled to be such a spiteful, wicked Creature."

Well, this sets off another storm of histrionic whining and weeping.

"*Ohhhhh*, you're attacking me – you're *attacking* me! And all I'm trying to do is *help* you!"

This stuns me for a moment. Why, I've never heard anything so preposterous in all my life.

"Wait now," says I, "you're trying to *help* me?"

"Of course! You're so *ugly* – I have to help you be beautiful! It simply won't *do* for you to be walking around as ugly as you are!"

Well, this just plain irritates me, Book.

"Now, you look here," says I, "I'm *just fine* the way I am. I thank you for trying to be helpful in the way you seem to think best, but it simply does not suit me. So let us just bid each other farewell and – "

She panics at this, and her eyes get all round and frightened.

"Oh, I can never *leave* you – you *need* me! You need to know how *ugly* and *fat* you really are!"

And what with the petty idiocy of her words and this sudden greedy neediness of hers, why, my patience evaporates entirely.

"Why, if that isn't the most outrageous, addlebrained load o' bunk!" says I. "I am *not* ugly and fat! And if I am, that's *my* business. Now, you just go on back to your watery home over there and leave me be!"

"You don't understand – I am your Narcissus! I belong to you, and you belong to me, and I will be with you always, always, *always!*"

"Why, you wretched, pointless Creature . . . *I CAST YOU OFF, do you hear? BEGONE, I SAY! And that's FINAL!*"

(I must say, Book, it felt quite rejuvenating to give vent to my big fat Stage Voice again. I hadn't used it since my last performance, when I played the Arch-Villain Hester Nambrin in "While Away the Willows.")

Anyhow, much to my surprise, the Narcissus vanishes, just like that! And, oh, you can bet I am not waiting around for any more possible perniciousness to plague and torment me, thank you very much. So I yanks on my socks and boots, and I thereupon aim to hightail it out of this city this instant, if not sooner. But all that glaring, flaring light off all them mirrors somehow muddles my inner compass . . . because when I leave the Pool, I take a wrong turn, and I find myself plunged into a far more densely populated street, packed with far more dazzling people. Why, it is all so blinding and stifling, I tell you, I am feeling nigh on *frantic!*

Well, I then come upon a group of gentlemen gathered in front of a tailor's shop, and I ask the nearest one for the quickest route out of town.

And, *ohhh*, Book, here is the chillingest thing to tell . . .

The street noise is so loud, I must lean in close to hear the gentleman's response over the din. And then I notice – *ohhh*, his eyes! Where eyes are blue, they are not blue, where eyes are brown, they are not brown, but *mirrors* – yes, *he has mirror eyes!* And I see myself in his eyes, which is *so* disturbing. And as I glance around at all his friends, I see that they *all* have mirrored eyes, and that, as they speak to each other, they are all posing and admiring themselves in each other's eyes.

Well, this gentleman I asked for directions has just caught sight of himself in some mirror behind me. And he has become so engrossed in adjusting his collar and his cravat, he is now so very *irritated* as he grumbles at me to go this way, then that way, then this way, then that.

And so I turn away from him and continue pressing on, trying to make some sense of his directions. But in the glaring confusion of it all, I get hopelessly lost. So I ask somebody else which way to go, but I get lost again. And then I ask somebody *else* which way to go, and I get lost *again*. And then I stop asking anybody anything, and I race through the streets on my own steam, dead set on finding my way out of this place, one way or another, now and forever.

Well, I then take a turn and find myself in the midst of a loud, crowded party in a banquet room. And because everything is mirrored, mirrored everywhere, and all is gleam and glare and flash and flare, well, each person is multiplied over and over and over again. Oh, it is *such* pandemonium! People are bumping into each other and banging into the mirrored walls – and yet they are blithely unconcerned, as if all this chaos is the perfectly natural order of things! And in this profusion of confusion, I can no longer discern what is real or just a reflection, or *who* is real or just a reflection, and I become so dizzied, so discombobulated, I am suddenly feverishly fretting:

"Which reflection am I?"

And in that horrible, harrowing moment, for the life of me, I cannot make out which is the *real* me . . . *Ohhh*, such an ice cold panic is coursing through my whole being!

Then, at that very moment, who should appear before me, hovering there in the air, but that nasty, nattering Narcissus! Only she is much more *menacing* now – her beauty much more sinister, her malice much more savage. She is competitively scrutinizing everyone around us. And as she snarls at me, her teeth look shockingly sharper!

"You are so *embarrassing*. You're the ugliest person here! Look around, every single person is absolutely beautiful. But you wouldn't listen to me, no! *You* have to be *ugly* – *you* have to be *fat!*"

And what with her hateful voice and all the chaos and the noise and the still fresh terror of me not recognizing myself, well, her fiendish attack cuts through me, piercing some soft part of me deep inside. And I feel myself weakening . . . Yes, I can feel myself teetering on the verge of a tormented madness from which I fear I may never return . . .

But then I decide *I will not court it.* I simply *refuse* to lose myself to it!

> "Why, you whining, wicked lackwit . . .
> Whatever you may think of me,
> I simply *DO NOT CARE.*
> You are nothing more than *AIR!*
> *NOW BE OFF WITH YOU! BEGONE!*"

And then, why, I *roar* at her – like a fearsome warrior, like a wrathful beast of a Creature myself! And, oh, of course, such a woeful, wounded expression comes over her pretty face, as if I have stabbed her in the heart, yes, as if she has been brutally betrayed by her dearest friend. And she quickly fades to nothing – the nothing she were made of.

And I turn to behold that all the glamorous, glittering people at this party are staring at me – all of them now silent and still, so stupefied are they by my extraordinary outburst. And in that moment, I too am somewhat stupefied, as I find myself being gazed upon by all these mirrored eyes. Oh, it is most disconcerting to see so many tiny reflections of myself staring back at me.

Then I hear someone say to someone else, "Who *is* that?"

And someone else says, "Nobody."

And they all go back to their party.

Just then I feel a tug at my sleeve, and I look downward. And who should be looking back up at me but my curly-haired, angel-faced little boy. He crooks his finger, beckoning me to follow him, and he leads me out of the banquet room. Then he takes a right into a parlor, then a left into a kitchen, then a right down a long, dark hallway – at the end of which is a door, which he opens.

On the outside of the door, in faded letters, are the words:

Service Entrance

And as he holds the door open, I look out and see – *ohhh!* – a *salvation* of a view . . . rolling green hills, billowing white clouds, and the spectacular Wild Blue Yonder! Well, I could just about bury my head in my hands and cry, I am so overcome with relief.

And I look down at this angelic little boy, and I kiss him on the brow, and I thank him. Whereupon he looks me in the eye, shakes his head and says, quite sternly:

"You should've listened, Miss."

Right he was, eh, Book? Right he was! And off *I* was . . . Yes, I got me to running – that's right, *running* – as I couldn't put that mad, mad place behind me far enough or fast enough.

And, *ohhh*, what more welcome sight could possibly appear just as I round the bend but good ol' Hank. In a blink I am upon him, and we gallop and gallop, and with the sound of his hooves pounding the ground and the wind *whooshing* by me, I can feel myself coming Home to myself again.

So, yes . . . my senses and my spirit are now quite thoroughly soothed, and I feel deliciously in tune once more.

    Ahhh, will you listen to that river flow . . .

         . . . and the breeze dancing through the leaves . . .

             . . . and the birds . . .

                 . . . *mmmm* . . .

Wherein I Run Out of Ink and Into Faeries

So, Hank and I are sauntering along down the Road, see. And me, well, I am seeking a shady spot at the friendly foot of a spreading tree under which to arrange myself and formally invite the Muse. Yes, I have plume and inkpot and parchment at the ready, and my eyes are combing the sides of the Road for the perfect place to settle in, when suddenly, in my mind's eye, I see the first few thrilling lines of what I instantly recognize to be my first respectable Poem!

That's right, there be those first few lines and the very *shape* of the whole Poem in my mind, ready and waiting to be born! And the thing of it is, Book, it is not my usual limpid, pedestrian fare, no . . . Oh, these pearls of profundity are obviously being gifted to me directly from the Muse! So, o' course, I whisper:

"Thank you!"

And straightaway I stop seeking any spot other than the one I am standing on – that is, right here, smack in the middle of the Road. So, sure, I sits down without a moment's hesitation, trembling with anticipation.

But, *doggone* it, just as I uncork my inkpot, the dadgum thing goes flying clean out of my grasp, and then proceeds to go bouncing and rolling off down the Road! Well, I leap up and chase after it until it flips and lands upside-down in a ditch. And all I can do is stand there and watch helplessly as the last of my precious ink sinks into the dry dirt. Why, it were nigh on tragic, Book.

And I simply cannot help but to stomp my foot and vociferate:

"Awww, doggone it . . . *doggone it, doggone it, DOGGONE IT!"*

So Hank ambles on over to find out what all the fuss is about. And when I explain the perfectly valid reason for my tantrum, he reminds me that I can buy ink in the next town, which we can get to fairly soon if we feel like picking up the pace and having ourselves a gallop.

But, in reply, I can only *harumph* and kick the dirt. I know perfectly well that Inspiration does not like to be jostled, so galloping is out of the question. And, for Pete's sake, the Muse *certainly* cannot be prevailed upon to wait for me to get to the next town! But I know it will sound petulant if I speak these things out loud, even to Hank, so I just kick the dirt again, utterly disheartened that my first respectable Poem is going to die of thirst.

And then it comes to me that the only possible remedy may be to return to that very spot in the Road where I first received them first few lines in my mind and pray they'll be gracious enough to present themselves again – and if they do, I'll *memorize* them, sure! So, I rush on over, and I plant myself to receive them perfect pearls of profundity once again.

I get real still. I close my eyes. I open my mind and . . . *there they are!* Well, I am so excited and relieved and nervous all at once that I decide I better speak these words out loud to Hank so he can help me remember them. And when I open my eyes to let him in on my plan, what do you think I behold, Book? Well, you'll never guess, so I'll tell you.

Tucked cozily into a gathering of trees, there sits the most *charming* little Store! Which surely wasn't (or *was* it?) there before . . .

The sign above it reads:

GENERAL STORE

And another sign hanging in the window below says, of all things to say:

INK SALE: TODAY ONLY
Exquisite Ink, Fresh From the Glen

Well, I am absolutely amazed at what a *coincidence* this is! Here I am out of ink and here this Store is – and they are even having an Ink Sale, of all things to be having! Then Hank points out that there is likely no coincidence involved at all. And we look at each other. And we both of us know the same thing at the same time:

Faeries.

So, Hank being Hank, well, he goes right on back to sauntering along down the Road. He knows enough about Faeries to let them be. And, me being me, well, I saunter along down the Road for a while too, *pretending* I have as much common sense as Hank. But, Book, the raw truth is: The one and only thing I can think about is *getting my mitts on that ink.*

And though I can still remember bits of those first shining lines of my first respectable Poem, I am now fretting up a storm, as I can feel it slipping back into the ethers, unembraced. So I stop dead in my tracks, and I announce to Hank that I simply *must* have that ink, that my whole will and desire is bent upon it, and that I cannot be reasoned with or redirected, no way, no how.

Well, Hank is mighty unhappy to hear that, to say the least. He's known far too many instances of folks disappearing forever once they cross over into the Land of Faerie. Or if they *do* come out, they have the head of a goat or they dance until they die or other such-like life-disturbing afflictions. Then Hank initiates what turns out to be a very short conversation about patience, with which I am thoroughly *im*patient, as I am mad for ink the way some folks are mad for gold.

So I present my perfectly reasonable reasoning to Hank:

"Hank, truly, I'll be just fine. It's very simple. All I have to do is remember the rules: be courteous, be kind, be calm, be complimentary, eat nothing and drink nothing, no matter how delicious it looks or smells. Fear not, I shall get me that ink and be right back here on this very spot in a blink. You just watch."

Well, Hank looks at me for a while. Then he says he'll wait for me right here, but not forever. And these are Faeries we're talking about, Book, so when he says "forever," he is not hyperbolizing. And with that, I turns on my heel and I most decisively stride through the high grass toward that Store, leaving Hank in the Road watching after me. Oh, sure, for a moment I feel a bit trepidatious, so I turn and wave at Hank to give us both more confidence.

And then, when I turn back around and head toward the Store again – wait now, can it be . . . ? *How* can it be? It seems that as I am walking *toward* the Store, why, the doggone thing is moving farther away! So I stop. And, sure enough, the Store stops too. Then I walk toward it once more. And once more that tricky Store moves still farther off! And I can't tell you how but, *oooh*, I can just *feel* them Faeries watching me.

So, I stands my ground, and the Store stands to face me. And I remind myself to be calm and courteous as I address it:

"Greetings, pretty Store! Now, I see that sign in your window, quite plainly advertising that you have ink to sell. And, *ohhh*, I am so deeply desiring to buy said ink, because, y'see, I am a fledgling Poet in the midst of what is nothing short of an artistic emergency! Alas, I have only one coin left, but it is gold, and I will most gladly pay it. So, Store, if you are sincere about selling your Exquisite Ink Fresh From the Glen, please be so kind as to allow me to enter and make that purchase. And if you do not wish for the sale, well, then I will wish you good day and be on my merry way. So . . . whaddaya say?"

(Everybody knows that Faeries love threes and rhymes, so I thought it couldn't hurt.)

Well, when next I walk toward it, that Store stays stock still! Why, it even settles in some, letting many curling vines grow up to prettify itself, and letting even more flowers bloom in its front garden.

And then the most delicate dirt path rolls out from the Store door, right up to the tips of my boots! And as I step upon this path, it lines itself with tiny, purple flowers . . . *soooo* pretty, *soooo purple* . . . But, no, I stay strong. I simply *refuse* to be taken in by their color or by the sweet charm of their sudden appearance. I am complimentary. I am courteous. I am the essence of dispassionate detachment.

"How very lovely," says I, ever so coolly, as I walk up the path.

And when I open the Store door, I hear such a fanciful, musical flutter of tinkling bells! Now, Book, this General Store has been concocted by Faeries, so of course there is an *unimaginably* enchanting assortment of ribbons and fabrics and wondrously shiny this's and thats, and such smells and, *oooh,* such eye-popping, mouth-watering pies and cakes – but I refuse to succumb! I will *not* be sidetracked, nossir. I stick to my mission and keep my mind on ink – which I don't see *anywhere.*

So I head straight on up to the counter, I ring the dainty silver bell, and, wouldn't you know, the tone is so inspiring that I have to forcefully wrestle down the urge to sing.

"Think *ink,*" says I to myself, quite sternly. "Ink and *only* ink."

And I ring the bell twice more. Still, the Store does not respond in any way. I say, "Hello" three times. Then I ring the bell three times more. Still, nary a clerk appears.

So, calmly, courteously, I announce:

"Alright then . . . Sadly, I shall take my leave of you, O Most Charming General Store. I did so long to buy your fresh ink in the service of Art, but, alas, I see that there is no ink here after all. I surmise that you are all sold out and have simply forgotten to remove the sign in the window. Ah, well, so be it . . . I'll be on my way now."

And as I turn to go, well, what should be standing right there in front of me but a towering display of delicately stacked, gorgeously gilded inkpots! And on each exquisite little pot of ink there is a vivid stripe of the most vibrant color. The colors – oh, the *colors!* – such a feast of luscious colors as I have never seen. It feels as if I must have them all . . .

Then, suddenly, I am *transfixed.* I have spotted *my* pot of ink, sitting at the very tip-top of this towering display!

Why, I nearly swoon when I read the label:

The Most Perfect Purple Ink
Anywhere Ever
~ with a tidge of ~
Opalescent Iridescence

Well, it is patently obvious that there is nought to be done but to speak openly to the Faeries.

"O most marvelous, gracious Faeries, I greet you! With the greatest of admiration for your exquisite merchandise, I am going to leave the aforementioned gold coin on this here counter in exchange for that there pot of Perfect Purple Ink. Oh, I do realize that I do this at great risk to life and limb, but I am a servant of Art and can do no less. However, I do most humbly ask that you do not disappear me forever, as my dear friend Hank waits nearby, and he will be so terribly worried about me. And it's not his fault, as he were never foolish enough to want to write Poetry."

With that said, I kiss my gold coin and, with a flourish, I place it on the counter. I then turn back to that tower of inkpots, I take me a good, deep breath, and I set my sights upon that little gilded pot of Perfect Purple Ink.

Did I know better as I got on tiptoe, Book?
I did.
Could I stop myself?
I could not.
Did I even *try* to stop myself?
I did not.
Not for so much as a breath.

And even on the very tips of my toes, reaching up with even my long arms and fingers, I can only *just about* grasp my pot of ink. And, o' course, I *do* grasp it for a moment. And, o' course, it slips right out of my fingers. And, o' course, I teeter, and I totter, and then I *crash* full on into that towering display!

And, sure, all them delicately stacked inkpots make such a fantastic *fuss* as they come clattering down on top of me, and all them gorgeous colors of Faerie Ink Fresh From the Glen pour and pour and pour all over me – and the more the ink pours over me, the more I *laugh*, as it is all so audaciously funny and such a first-rate joke on me! Yep, them pots keep pouring and pouring, and there I sit, drenched in Faerie ink, in an ever-deepening puddle that spreads and spreads and rises and deepens and then begins to lift me up . . .

And the next thing I know, I am *swimming* around the General Store, laughing and sputtering! And then, why, this pool of swirling color suddenly *surges,* and I am *whooshed* out of the Store door, carried along on a rushing river of riotously colorful Faerie ink that goes ribboning out into the forest – *swishing* around this tree, *swooshing* around that one!

And *then,* somehow, suddenly . . .

There am I, sitting by a stream, trying to catch my breath, and I am watching the last of the Faerie ink drip off my hands and clothes and disappear entirely. And I can do nothing but shake my head and chuckle with admiration.

After a moment, I look up into the air – oh, yes, I can *feel* them out there! – and I calmly, courteously declare:

"O Ingeniously Humorous Faeries . . . Alright, ya got me! I am but a foolish mortal, who too ardently desires to be a Great Poet, with too little knack for the art of it. Have your fun with me then, as I surely do deserve to be made sport of."

And with that, Book, they turned me into a rock. Oh, how *nice* that was . . . to feel the cool water streaming by, to feel myself nestled so deep and cozy into the dark of the ground, to feel the sunlight sparkling through the trees, so warm and friendly on my face. I simply *adored* being a rock, and while I was being one, couldn't imagine why I'd ever want to be anything else.

That is, until they turned me into a rabbit. Whereupon it became perfectly clear that there is no more fun to be had in the whole of the Whole Wyde Whirld than running as fast as *that*. Why, I ran and ran and ran and ran and ran and ran and ran and ran and ran and ran and ran and ran without a mite o' weariness or heaviness of limb. "Nothing more marvelous to be than a rabbit," thought I, when I was one.

Oh, but *then* the Faeries had the most generous genius to turn me into a tree. I tell you, Book, being a tree in that Faerie forest, well, that were a moment of the most profound peace, and such a harmony of spirit and form, which I would have most contentedly enjoyed forever and ever and then some, had it not been for the distant thought of Hank waiting out there on the Road for me.

And it were whilst I was being a tree that the Faeries first appeared to me. Yes, that's right, they were discussing me and laughing.

But, being a tree, I could not talk. And, being a tree, I did not mind in the least that I could not talk or that I were being discussed or laughed at.

And the Faeries began to gather all around me, dancing over my roots and flitting through my branches. I remember that beauteous blur of flowing hair and glowing skin and wings, and deep, liquid, twinkling eyes that caressed when they gazed ... And were they dressed in beautiful clothes that looked like the forest? Or was the forest dressed to look like their beautiful clothes? I couldn't say.

Then, the next thing I know ...

One of the Faeries has turned me from being a tree into being just me, and I find myself plopped there on the ground like a rag doll, trying to get used to being in my own form again. Well, this starts them laughing themselves silly. The gist of it, see, is that I am their funny new toy. Then, in a flicker of a moment, they look altogether bored with me. And they pout, and they don't seem to know what to do with themselves.

Then one of them perks up and says, "Let's dance!"

Then another one says, "Fiddlers! Play!"

Then another looks down at me and says, "You stay there."

And as I am watching their revelry, I am thinking, "Oh, that's right, I know all about Faerie Circles. *Do not join the Circle, Lillian, do not – oooh,* but look at the candle flames all dancing in the air like that, in time to the music. How beautiful they look, with all the stars sparkling behind them ... *Wait!* It must be *night!*"

And then I remember that Hank is waiting out there on the Road for me, and that I only came to get ink, and I am wondering just how long I've been here.

Just then, a Faerie with long blue-black hair goes waltzing by in the air, and when she sees me sitting there, she stops and says:

"Oh, that's right, I forgot about her."

Then another Faerie flits in and says, "I know what let's do! Let's bring her to the Empress! Since she turned Ziegfried into a hamster, she's been *so* upset, as she loves him so, and so hated to do it."

"He needed to be taught a lesson," says one.

"He refused to apologize," says another.

"He tore her heart apart," says a third.

"Which is why she requires cheering up," says the first. "Yes, this one will make her laugh. She's sparky."

And *the very next thing I know* . . .

There am I, sitting in a high-back chair in the center of an opulent room, all ivory and golden. And I know, without anybody having to tell me, that I am seated across from none other than:

The Empress of Faerieland.
Throned and crowned and sublimely sparkling.

Ohhh, such enigmatic elegance. Such endless, luminous, silvery hair. Why, her gown looks to be made of the night sky, shimmering with moonbeams. And could those be *real* stars sparkling in her crown? But as I gaze into her glistening, sapphire eyes, I see that this radiant being is feeling downright woebegone deep inside, and that she is putting on a brave face. And I *think* she sees that I can see . . . but I cannot be sure, I am too gobsmacked.

And as I steal a glance around the room, my eyes are treated to a glorious gathering of Faeries. Oh, the gleaming, the glimmering, the wings, the whisperings! And in this moment, though I know I am just a plaything and they can squash me like a bug if they feel like it – or *make* me a bug and *then* squash me if they feel like it – for some reason, I don't begrudge them, what with their being all mysterious and wondrous and immortal as they are.

But then I remember – with the whole twinkling crowd of 'em staring at me as if they are waiting for something to happen – that I have been brought here especially to cheer up the Empress. Why, it appears that I am expected to entertain! Well, for the first time in Faerieland, I feel like I've got my sea legs!

So I stand, and I bow to the Empress, and I say:

"How do you do, Your Most Majestic Majesty! Allow me to introduce myself: I am Lillian of Everywhere, and I am most humbly at your service."

There is a flutter amongst the Faeries, and I hear one of them say:

"Ah, a professional!"

And with that vote of confidence, I continue on:

"That's right, Lillian of Everywhere am I, and for a single, sweet sigh, I shall sing you the song your heart most needs to hear."

And with my usual flourish, I produce my Music Box.
And there is such a horrified gasp!
And then such a fierce flurry of whispers!

And, suddenly, the Empress is holding my Music Box in her long, elegant hand. She regards it for a moment. Then she regards me for a moment. Then she says:

"Where did you get this, Mortal?"

And I am now wondering if I will *mind* having the head of a goat, and if it hurts very much to dance yourself to death, and I am thinking how awfully sad Hank will be when I do not return, and that I should have listened to him.

"Well, Your Magnificence, I can't say as I know. But I've always had it with me, and always cherished it, for as long as I can remember."

The Empress regards me for a moment, then tilts her head a bit.

"Lillian . . . *hmmm* . . . From whence do you hail?"

"I do not know, Your Grace. All I know is, when I were a child I somehow wandered into the Forest of Forgetfullness, and I was raised there. Then one day I left the Forest, aiming to seek my true Home, but I never found it, so I have been a Whirld Traveler ever since. But the Music Box has been with me all this time. Why, it were found on me the night I was discovered in the Forest – and, well, I've always felt it to be a part of my very soul."

The Faeries are silent. They seem to be breathing and listening as a single, glowing creature. The Empress speaks again:

"'Tis Faerie made. Did you know this, Mortal?"

Well. How could anyone be more wide-eyed with astonishment in this moment than me?

"So *that* is why it is the most marvelous miracle of music in the entirety of the Whole Wyde Whirld! Why, *of course* it is Faerie made!"

I can see that what I've just said makes all the Faeries feel very much appreciated indeed, but the Empress's face does not move a muscle.

"If it has always been yours, Mortal, then you must know the original song of the Music Box. Let us hear it."

And my Music Box is suddenly in *my* hands again. Trembling, I turn it over, and I flip the little filigree switch that was switched so long ago. And I open the lid, and I sigh into it, and *ohhh* . . . that lovely old song of longing begins to play.

And as I sing, and as the waltzing melody floats through the air, I sense that this beloved old song is somehow saving my life.

And when it is finished, I open my eyes to see that all the Faeries are weeping. 'Tis a most heart-rending thing to see one Faerie in tears, Book, but to see a whole audience of Faeries in tears . . . well, that's something.

Then, in a flash, I find myself somehow kneeling, and the Empress is standing above me, with her hand lightly resting upon my head. She tilts my head up, and she says:

"We thought you were dead, my dear. How clever of you not to be."

And *the next thing I know* . . .

I am lounging on a luxurious divan of the softest, plushest cushions, and my feet are being washed and oiled and rubbed, and my toenails have been painted *gold!* And next to me, the Empress is lounging on *her* luxurious divan, while all her attendant Faeries comb and coif her silky, silvery hair.

Oh, yes, that's right . . . I remember asking if someone could please get word to Hank and tell him that Lillian's alright. And the Faerie massaging my head says, so gently:

"Fret not, Lillian . . . "

And then I smell amber. Is it amber? *Mmmm,* yes . . .

And then – here it comes, Book – as I am lying there, the Empress tells me the story of who I am:

"Let's see now, you are the daughter of Lilliana. She was my 6,422nd cousin, yes . . . She was only *half*-Faerie, mind you, on account of her mother – or was it her father? I can't remember, but she *adored* her father. Oh, yes, that's right, *he* was the mortal one, so she always *loved* mortal men, and she ran off and married that fool who was your father, King of . . . something, somewhere. We all warned her, but she was in love, and you know how that is . . . "

"Oh, no, Your Wondrousness," says I, "I am entirely relieved to say that I do *not* know how that is. You see, in my profession I am all too often witness to the disastrous aftermath of love, and I tell you, it sure looks to be for stouter hearts than mine. Why, I fear it would rend me into pieces."

The corners of the Empress's mouth curl up ever so slightly.

"For a three-quarter mortal, you are very wise. Love can be the most profound pain, even for us . . . "

Whaddaya know, Book, even Faeries get lovesick.
Now, that is a revelation.

Though, as she speaks, I feel so sad for the Empress, as I can sense how sorely brokenhearted she is 'neath all that eternal elegance. And I *think* she sees that I can see. And she looks away from me as she continues telling me of my origins:

"Well, your father was insistent upon a *boy* to inherit the throne, but your mother gave birth to you. So the fool refused to speak to her, or even to look at either one of you ever again. And soon after you were born, Lilliana died of a broken heart. That was *her* Music Box, my dear, and that was her favorite song."

Of course, when she tells me all of this I am nearly moved to tears, but I am absolutely determined to keep my wits about me so's I can later recall it all, as the telling of her tale feels so like a dream . . . yes, just like a story in a book about somebody else.

"Ah, how we loved our Lilliana. She was quite the pet of the court. Oh, and she *loved* lilacs, yes, it was always lilacs with Lilliana . . . everything had to be lilacs . . . "

And suddenly, that Beauteous Lady from my Lilacs Dream flashes into my mind, and I finally understand that she is *my Mother!* And in that flash of recognition, I see those fields of waving red hair, that light streaming all around her, and I inhale that heavenly scent. So present is she in this moment that I actually feel her *kiss my head.* But then the vision vanishes, as I hear the Empress saying:

" . . . but she was never happy, no. She never felt beautiful enough or perfect enough, being half-mortal around full Faeries. Of course, being half-Faerie, she was much too fragile to live so much of her life out in the Whirld. She was so lovely, so delicate, skin like gossamer . . . Ah, well, she died. And though of course we'd heard about you, and we wondered . . . Wait, I could have sworn that someone was supposed to – "

And the Empress sits up, and she calls, "Albertina! Come here!"

Albertina appears out of nowhere, shimmering in a thousand shades of pink and looking mighty worried. Says the Empress:

"Was it you or was it your sister who was assigned to look in on Lilliana's baby? She *is* your 448th cousin, you know."

Well, Albertina is just plain put out. She rolls her eyes and says:

"I have *so* many cousins, Your Majesty. Oh, wait, that's right! I asked Irmalinda to look in on her. Remember, Irmalinda?"

There appears Irmalinda, iridescent lavender and hopping mad.

"You did *not* ask me! She did *not* ask me! I *knew* you would say that you had asked me when you never *once* – "

Then a third Faerie, glimmering green, appears and interjects:

"If I may? May I just say that I personally reminded both of them *three times*, Your Majesty!"

And then they all chime in:

"You *lie*, Catrinetta!" "Oh, be *quiet*, Catrinetta!" *"Three times!"*

The Empress vanishes all three of them, and, with a sigh, she turns to me.

"You were forgotten. No matter. You managed quite well. We are impressed by you, Lillian of Everywhere."

Then, ever so languorously, she reclines back onto her divan again, and I recline back onto mine. Says the Empress:

"Now, where was I . . . Oh, what was the name of that ridiculous kingdom? It was ever so long and ludicrous. Did it begin with an 'S' or . . . Oh, no, that's right, it's called 'The Biggest and Best City in the History of the Whole Wyde Whirld.' Such a filthy, *grey* place. So provincial."

So *this* was why, the few times I'd heard it in my travels, I'd always had such a peculiarly strong aversion to that name, which went beyond and beneath the puffed-up pomposity of the name itself.

And the Empress turns and smiles at me. And as she gently scans my face, I can see that she is remembering my Mother in it.

"Ah, yes, how we adored your sweet sprite of a Mother . . . But then, we are Faeries, we love everything beautiful. That is, until we don't. Yes, until we don't . . . "

And the Empress stares off into nothing, looking so very forlorn. Whereupon I am seized by such a strong desire to help this sublime immortal – as silly as it may be to think that one such as me could be of service to one such as she. Says I, softly:

"O Most Marvelous Majesty, I humbly ask that you allow me to try to repay your benevolence in the only way I know how."

And I see that she sees exactly what I mean.

And *the next thing I know* . . .

She and I are all alone in a small, round clearing in the forest, seated opposite each other upon the most graceful, swooping chairs that look to have grown straight up out of the forest floor. And as I behold her sitting there, the Empress of Faerieland, for all her gleaming glory, puts me in mind of a purely brokenhearted mortal woman.

Lovesickness. It levels 'em all.

Yes, I have noted in my travels that lovesickness is what so many folks need soothing songs for, and it appears that the Empress of Faerieland is no different. And so I open my Music Box, and the Empress sighs into it, and, *ohhh* . . . I have never heard *nearly* the likes of such a melancholy melody before, and the words I sing are in a lovely language I do not understand.

And when I finish the song and open my eyes, I see that the Empress is weeping. And I go to her and take her hand and hold it 'til she is through. And afterward, though we neither of us say a word about it, I can see she feels ever so much better for it. I ask you, what greater privilege could an ink-mad three-quarter mortal ask for?

Then the Empress stands, and I feel her cool hand upon my cheek. And she gazes deeply into my eyes. And we both of us know that it's come time for me to go. But then she takes a few steps back, gives me the once over with a critical eye, and frowns a bit.

"Oh, no, no, *no* . . . We simply cannot have you walking around like *that*. You'll give us a bad name."

And then, with the arch of an eyebrow and a sweep of her elegant hand, the Empress entirely *transmogrifies* my traveling costume! Then she pops a long oval mirror in the air so's I can appreciate her artistry, and, oh, what I behold in this mirror:

Well. My leggings are now the most *luscious* shade of forest green. And you should see the sleeves of my shirt, the way they *flow*, and the elegance of the cuffs . . . And I now have a *scarlet velvet vest* to match my Cape! It is tunic length, with capped sleeves, and it so flatters my form. And Cape and vest are now both delicately edged in gold! And my boots – oh, my *boots!* – the leather is richer, the soles are stronger, the insides softer. And I am ever so happy to add that the whole ensemble is weatherproof and will never, ever wear out.

And, Book, these last two things'll knock your socks off: First, my plume pen has been filled with eternal ink, so it will always be at the ready whenever Inspiration has a mind to strike! And, oh, Book, *my hat* has been ever so sumptuously *re-purpled!* And truly, once a purple has been re-purpled by the Empress of Faerieland – well, I think we can safely say that I now own *the* most perfectly purple hat anywhere ever, period, end of discussion.

Why, the only thing of mine the Empress did *not* spruce up was my Sorrow. She pointed to it dangling at my neck, tickled it with the tip of her finger, and said:

"Yes, your Sorrow . . . One day you must swallow it, you know."

Then she gestures for me to twirl around, and the very last thing I remember of the Empress of Faerieland is her smiling and saying, "*Ahhh, much* better," whilst I am twirling and twirling . . .

And *the next thing I know* . . .

I am walking out the door of the General Store and down that dirt path lined with all those pretty purple flowers. And then I am striding through the long grass, smiling at dear, patient Hank, who is standing in the *exact same spot* I left him, with the sun in the *exact same place* in the sky. Why, it turns out that I *have* come back in a blink, just like I said I would!

Well, Hank just stares at me with a mixture of astonishment and relief. Then he asks me if I got my ink, and he compliments me on my spiffy new getup. Boy, did I give him an earful!

And, Book, I should like to make a special self-congratulatory note: I somehow managed to steer entirely clear of food in Faerieland – which, considering my aptitude for gluttony, I'd call nothing short of a miracle! And though I am therefore absolutely famished, I am nevertheless compelled in this moment to posit a mighty big question for cogitation:

Now, ordinarily, I would have been in complete accord with Hank about the foolhardiness of risking life and limb adventuring with Faeries, and we'd've gone right on sauntering along down that Road. But the thing of it is, Book, from the very first moment them lines of that Poem emblazoned themselves in my mind, why, it felt like I were *harpooned* – first by Inspiration, then by ink, and then, perhaps most pointedly, by Destiny.

So, I wonder, were Destiny and the Muse somehow in cahoots to help me? And if they *were*, well, what if I'd *resisted* my mad, unquenchable desire for ink and just continued obliviously on down the Road? I mean, would I have remained forever ignorant of who I am and from whence I hail? Or would they have collaborated on some other clever means to –

You know what, Book? There's plenty of time to ponder this, and I'm so hungry I could eat my hat. And what with the pure *perfection* of purple it is now, that sure would be a crime.

Wherein I Take Stock

Well, in striking contrast to the glories of Faerieland, here I sit, on this ordinary mortal bench, enjoying my fourth fresh, hot, mortal, blueberry scone, feeling deliciously, mortally content. And as the butter and the blueberries melt in my mouth, I find myself contemplating this series of recent revelations:

> To know that my Mother has been following me all along.
>
> To know that she has always seen me and sees me still.
>
> To have felt her tender kiss upon my brow.
> (Yes . . . when I close my eyes, I can still feel it!)

Knowing all this has brought me the very deepest sort of peace, a peace that reaches all the way down through me and on into the belly of the Whirld, it feels like. And, oh, how elated and proud I feel! From now on, every time I sing I shall know: This is my Mother's Music Box, made in Faerieland, from whence she hailed.

Remember the cherry farmer's wife, whose grandmother was a gypsy? Turns out she was right, wasn't she? That Lilac Dream *was* the key to my lost life! And I now know what my Mother was prompting me to remember all along:

> That I have Faerie blood.
>
> That my Father was a foolish king who'd have only a boy for an heir.
>
> That since my Mother gave birth to *me* instead, he despised and condemned us both for my offending girlhood.
>
> That she died of heartbreak.
>
> That I am a cast-off princess.

Well, there it is, Book.
The mystery of my history has been solved.

Ahhh, yes . . . I now completely comprehend why the subject of Home can bring such dark emotions to so many that speak of it.

Yes, I suppose I must have run away because I were so unwanted and despised. And maybe somewhere in my soul, even then, I sensed myself to be a Whirld Traveler, and in my childish mind thought it best to get started without delay. And, oh, how fortune-favored was I to have happened upon the Forest of Forget-fullness and upon my dear, long-lost Mad Aunt Harriet. How achingly I miss her in this moment. My, what *would* she say to learn that I am related to Faeries – and royal, to boot!

Royalty, Book . . . Dear me, it's a bit worrisome.

Well, no matter. Royalty cast me off, and I certainly don't want anything to do with them either. Good riddance to them, say I, as they surely said to me all that long while ago. That's alright, I shall remain myself unto myself, always and forevermore. That feels exactly right to me and in the perfect order of things.

Anyhow, I do not remember or miss that ugly city with the pompous name, and I know that it certainly does not miss me. And I assume the King remarried long ago and has all the sons he wants by now, which suits me just fine. I have no use for a Father who has no use for me, nor do I need to beg for entry into some unappealing place just to say, "This is where I was born." What of it? I am only just barely curious, anyhow.

Nope, it is as plain as the nose on my face that my place of Origin and my Home are not the same thing! *Not nearly.* And where I'm from is *not* where I am going. My true Home will always be the Whole Wyde Whirld, where I am most happy and where I always feel most welcome.

Case in point: As we speak, I am a-gazing at a most magnificent mountain range in the near distance, jutting so high up into the wild blue, so thickly carpeted with trees of green and of gold and of a deep, rich burgundy I've never seen before.

Now, I've never been to those mountains, and yet I tell you, I can *feel* them calling me! Yes, I can feel them inviting me to come and meet them, to meander amongst what grows there, to encounter whoever goes there. Yup, that settles it . . . Tomorrow morning I head upwards, into the mountains, in the direction of the sky.

Now, though it is not so significant a subject as my past, I must make mention of a subject that is most certainly significant to my present:

How I ever more adore my recently Faerie-ized traveling costume! For one thing, I feel light as a feather and infinitely more fleet-of-foot in my much more marvelous boots. And the rest of my clothing feels so deliciously soft against my skin that, well . . . somehow, all of me feels fresh and shiny and new. I tell you, Book, for a three-quarter mortal, I feel downright *divine*.

Oh, yes, Life is very good indeed.
Everything has worked out just perfectly, has it not?

Wherein I Encounter Someone From Long Ago

I must say, Book, I'm feeling more than a bit at odds and ends . . .
I was feeling just fine, thank you very much, and now I am all a-
tangle inside. Sure makes me wish Hank were here. He is always
so clear about things. But, alas, he is off on his own for now, and
I am left to untangle these feelings about this very (shall we say)
remarkable encounter entirely on my own.

So, here's what happened . . .

Now, you know how whenever I see a glorious view, I feel called
to sit upon the furthest edge of an inviting cliff, with my legs
dangling over the side, to all the better gaze at some beauteous
vista of sky or land or river or such? And if I have never before
made note of it (and as I write this, I am quite sure that I have not
and would like to), often the edges upon which I sit are rather
perilous indeed. Whenever I mention this predilection of mine,
the thought of it tends to make folks squeamish and anxious. I
had always supposed that my delight and comfort with such
edges were due to my long-ago experience with that tricky Road
at the Edge of the Forest of Forgetfullness. Now, though, I find
myself wondering if it isn't my Faerie blood that makes my body
so fearless, as it so recently remembers the possibility of wings.

Anyhow, yesterday I came upon such a vista and sat upon such
an edge of such a cliff – as a matter of fact, the very one upon
which I now sit as I write – where there grows a wondrous, wide,
strong tree, with lots of lovely, thick vines winding round it
and through its branches. So, as the sun is just starting to set, and
as I am beholding this vast canyon, with all its risings and fallings
and formations and striations, I am much inspired by the beauty
of the colors shifting and deepening with the setting sun . . .

And, sure, a sort of a rapture moves up through me, so I draw forth my Music Box and sigh into it. And right off, it becomes evident that something extraordinary is in the air, because a soft, sentimental tune comes out, instead of the sweeping, symphonic sort of an accompaniment I were surely expecting. 'Tis a slow and simple song of memories sad and memories lovely, of light and of shadow, and of sorrow, even.

So, there am I a-singing, when all of a sudden I am *joined* in my singing by a beautiful *tenor voice* in the most beautiful *harmony!* The voice is coming from – well, I don't know where it's coming from at first. And our duet is so soulful, and I am so carried away by the sweet-sounding music, for the first few moments I do not think to question my good fortune.

But soon my eyes begin to naturally follow my ears, and I look around me, listening. And then I look down. A-way down . . .

And, lo and behold, I find myself looking down into the merriest green eyes, set in a freckled face, with a crookedy, busted-up nose in the middle of it, the whole thing topped by the messiest mop of black hair. You heard me, Book! Smiling back up at me and ever so happily harmonizing, is a perfectly calm-looking young fellow, hanging by his hands from the bottommost root of this aforementioned tree, above a sea of jagged rocks *far* below, as if he doesn't have a care in the Whirld. I gasp when I see him, o' course.

"Why, *hello!*"

And he says, "I'm mad for your singin', lass! C'mon, let's have another!"

"Why, sure, if you like!" says I. "Although . . . maybe you'd rather join me up here?"

"Love to, darlin'! But first, have a bit of a look around for me, would ya?"

"And what might I be looking around *for*, pray tell?"

And he says, "A rich bastard in a gilded coach, who might appear to be . . . upset."

I regard him for a moment. Then I have a look around.

"The coast is clear!" says I. "You wait right there."

"Gladly!" says he.

So I takes out my Peerless Pocketknife, and I cut and unwind and unwind and unwind, and I throw him down the end of a long, strong vine. And on account of his strength and his slightness of stature, why, he pulls himself up and over the top with such superb speed and agility that he were quite quickly safe from the gaping jaws of oblivion.

But as he starts to stand, he falls to the ground in a heap o' pain.

"*Aaugghh* . . . A lifelong weakness," he says, with a wince. "I see a redhead and me legs go right out from under me."

I can see by the way he grimaces that he's truly in pain, and he pulls back his pant leg and reveals the reason for it – a bruised, badly swollen ankle.

"Lucky thing I got me ankle medicine handy," says he.

And he reaches into his jacket, pulls out a flask, and takes a swig.

"Ah, for pity's sake, here I am entirely forgetting me manners . . . Forgive me not givin' you a proper bow and a kiss of your fair rescuing hand, oh, most marvelous lady. I myself am none other than Jimmy the Dodger, Prevaricator and Pilferer Extraordinaire! I am forever in your debt. Yah, y'ever need something stolen or somebody swindled, I'm your man – you've only to ask."

"Why . . . thank you!" says I, astonished at this rather singular introduction. "I myself am Lillian of Everywhere, Singer of Songs and Whirld Traveler at Large. Mighty nice to meet you!"

And as we shake hands, he peers at me and tilts his head.

"I know you from somewheres, surely I do . . . Or perhaps 'twas another lifetime, eh?"

And then he picturesquely tells the tale of how he ended up over the cliff, escaping an angry lord whose coin purse he'd pilfered. And I get a good campfire to crackling just in time for dark, and we make a nice meal of my bread and cheese and apples. And he offers me a swig of his spirits, and I decline, and he says:

"*Ahhh*, shame on ya! Y'give me no choice but to do all the drinkin' for the both of us!"

And he lifts his flask in a toast.

"May trouble neglect ya, Jillian!"

"Uhh . . . that's Lillian," says I.

"*Lillian*, o' course!" says he. "Me mind knew that, but me mouth forgot."

And we have a fine laugh together.

Now, Book, I must make note: Different though we may be, Jimmy the Dodger and Lillian of Everywhere are, in fact, of the same Whirld Traveling tribe. And as the tribe naturally do, we trade our tales at such times, mine for yours, yours for mine. And the longer the night gets, the truer the stories get. So, we trade ourselves quite a few tales of the Road and have ourselves quite a few laughs, while Jimmy has quite a few swigs. And he tells me the story of himself:

"Knuckle Alley . . . that's the name o' me birthplace. I shoulda known, eh? When ya come from a place called Knuckle Alley, the writing's on the wall. I run off as a child for the reasons most children run off. They're never nice reasons, are they? And I got by then how I get by now – only now I'm *enormously* better at it. Oughta be. Been practicin' all me life!"

And he winks, and he drinks, and he goes on:

"Yah, for a long while I lived like a gutter rat. And then I fell in with this con artist. Slick sorta fella – a weaver, y'know – full o' big schemes. He had use for me talents and use for a sweet-lookin' lad he could push around. And I sorta looked up to 'im, y'know, as he were so clever and smooth – and, o' course, he fed me regular. Yah, at first he was *real* good to me, to reel me in, y'know. But he's a stone-hearted fiend and nothin' else, and I wish him an *exceedingly* unappealing death, I tell ya that."

Then Jimmy takes a long pull from his flask. And as he looks into the fire, I look into his eyes, and I can see the pain of unspeakable memories there.

Then I tell him the story of myself. And to end it, I say:

"So that's how I found out about my origins. And let me tell you something, I don't care if that ugly city *is* my birthplace, I will *never* call that place my Home."

"My sentiments *precisely*. You know what I always say? I always say – and I'm tellin' ya I always say this because I truly *always* say it – I always say that the Whirld is my Home!"

"Why, that's exactly what I say!" says I, and I raise my cup. "To the Whirld, our Home!"

And Jimmy raises his flask, "Spit on it, friend!"

And we clink, and we drink. And, no, Book, I have no idea what "spit on it" means either, but Jimmy is more than a little snockered at this point.

"So what's the name of *your* rotten birthplace, then?" he asks.

"Such a ridiculous name . . . It's called *The Biggest and Best City in the History of the Whole Wyde Whirld* – can you imagine? And from what I hear, it's a grimy, *grey* sort of a place, so, frankly, I'm relieved that I don't remember anything about . . . Jimmy? What is it?"

He is suddenly staring at me, Book, with his eyes gone big and round and frightened. Then, sounding like no more than a boy, he whispers:

"*No* . . . In a pub, a while back now, I heard some filthy rat of a Hopper claiming you were still alive, but . . . I can't believe it."

And he stares and stares at me, and soon, why, there are tears brimming and beginning to overflow. Says I:

"Oh, my friend, whatever ails you so?"

"You don't remember any of it, do ya?"

And he buries his head in his hands and gives way to quiet sobs. And as I put my arm around him, the rest of his story comes tumbling out:

"That bastard I worked for? Well, he conned the King and stole the throne and drove the whole place into sheer misery. But it's my fault too, y'see – I was his shill. And I was smart and I was fast and I coulda . . . Oh, Lillian, I couldn't be sorrier. I just couldn't . . . "

And I hug him, good and strong.

"Aw, Jimmy, whatever you did, you were just a boy. Whatever it is, it's alright, I promise!"

And as I hold him, I can't help it, I begin to weep along with him. And I can't tell you why, but somehow when we shed tears together like that . . . well, I feel something deep inside my soul growing stronger. And though I don't know why that should be, I feel I must note it. And soon the worst of it passes through him, and he calms. And I ask, because I can't *not* ask:

"So . . . is my Father still alive then?"

Jimmy looks at me with red-rimmed eyes and drooping lids.

"Still in prison, last I heard."

"*Prison?*"

"Aye. And still barkin' mad, o' course."

"He's *mad?*"

"Oh, cracked in the upper story, love. Without question."

And with that, he finishes off his flask. And, Book, I've just got to know:

"So . . . did he ever remarry? Did he ever have sons?"

Suddenly, Jimmy points angrily into the air.

"And do y'know why that scum bastard changed the name of the bleedin' place? So nobody'd remember he poached it – *that's* why!"

"But, Jimmy, did my Father remarry? Did he have any sons?"

"Hm? *Nahhh* . . . Never had the chance."

And with that, his eyes fall shut. I wrap his jacket around him, and as I do, his eyes flash open once more, and he smiles broadly and he says:

"*Ahhh,* I shoulda *known* it was you! Y'still fancy purple hats! I'm the one that threw it over the wall, y'know ... Did ya ever get it?"

And then he falls to snoring.
And I go lie down and stare up at the blue-black sky.
And I behold the moon, half-hidden behind a veil of clouds.
And I wonder what Destiny could *possibly* be thinking.

Then I fall asleep, and I have an absolutely terrifying dream. It's the one with all those old men yelling down at me – only this time I can feel their hatred burning through my being and their sour breath on my face. I see glimpses of watery, bulging eyes, and spit flying out of mouths that snap and snarl, calling me a traitor and a liar and a witch!

It is only a vivid flash of a dream, but that's all a quaking, horrifying nightmare need be. I wake up scared and shaking and sweating. And Jimmy hears my distress, and he crawls over and puts his arm around me.

"There, there ... You're alright now. There now ..."

And even now I am knowing, so very deep within me, that such a pure, good, wide open heart has Jimmy the Dodger. In that gentle moment I felt it, and I was much healed by his tenderness.

I say "even now" as I woke this morning to find ... no Dodger there, just air. That's right, Jimmy is gone, plain and simple – having stolen my Peerless Pocketknife, to boot! Yes, I am a good bit cut to the core and more than a little perturbed. Aw, Book, I shall miss my Pocketknife most dreadfully, that I will.

But other issues press upon me in this moment, and I have a question to put to myself:

Am I frustrated or am I relieved that I cannot ask Jimmy anything further about what goes on in that Kingdom? Hmph.

Well, the answer's easy: I am *relieved* – entirely and completely! Why, this city of my origin sounds more and more nefarious the more I hear about it. And I am now more certain than ever that it is none of my affair, and that I were infinitely fortunate to have washed my hands of the place long ago.

And, alas, it has become more than apparent that whatever it was that was wrought there was brought there by my fool of a Father. Who is mad. And I suppose that's sad. Though I also suppose that the measure of the sadness depends upon the manner of the madness.

Well, like I say, it's got nothing whatsoever to do with me!

And, for Pete's sake, Jimmy outright *introduced* himself as a liar and a thief. He certainly has proven himself to be a thief, alright, so it stands to reason that he is also a liar.

You know something, Book? Everything he told me?
I bet not one single word of it is true.

Wherein I Meet a Monster

Oooooh, Book, I am so *upset* and so *aggravated* and just so – *ughhh!* Well, I have no choice but to discuss it with you, because every time I've asked Hank what he thinks about all of this, he says he has no opinion either way. Oh, he is being just so *maddeningly* inscrutable!

I really must try to calm myself . . . If I read this later and my handwriting is as raggedy and ratchety as are my nerves in this moment, I will not be able to make out the details, and I will be extremely annoyed – though not *nearly* as annoyed as I am right now!

Alright then, I shall pause for a moment. I shall drink deeply of this rich, delicious night air. I shall gaze at the moon a while, which is so oddly fat and golden, and seems so much closer by somehow. I have never seen it like this before. Whatever the reason for it, I dearly hope these marvels shall soon soothe me, whereupon I shall commence to relay these events to you reliably and evenly.

––––––

Alright then, I have returned, with a rather reasonable thought as an appropriate point of departure . . .

Reputations are a funny thing, eh, Book? As is so often said, where there's smoke there's fire. And then, as is so often discovered, there's usually barely any smoke at all – and sometimes none, save what's in the pipes of those who dreamed up the doggone fire to start with. I suppose that's because a reputation is a flat, thin thing, and the truth of a person's character is round and endlessly variational.

For example, Egbert, who I met a while back, is so kind and *such* a gentleman – yes, he is a fine illustration of the Truth Versus

-235-

Reputation Discrepancy. By all who lived in his vicinity, he was pointed out to be the village idiot, yet I found him to be easily one of the most original thinkers and dreamers I've ever had the good fortune to meet! What a rich afternoon we had philosophizing about the way things play in the Universe. Dear Egbert, how I thank him for making me smile tonight.

Alright, I've steadied myself, Book, and I believe I can now be trusted to give an even-tempered account of events. And here it is:

So, there sits I in a pub, having me a mighty tasty nutbutter and raspberry jam sandwich, when I overhear a conversation amongst a few locals about this Monster who lives a-way up on the mountain. Well, being an experienced Whirld Traveler, I am not foolhardy, and if there's talk of something or someone well and truly dangerous, naturally it behooves me to investigate.

"Please forgive me for my intrusion," says I, "but I am traveling through here, and if there is a Monster about, I'd be most grateful to know more about it."

"Oh, this man is a terrible Monster!" "Aye, he is!" "A terrible Monster!"

"Ah, I see…" says I. "So, he is a *man* then, not an actual Monster."

"*Ohhh, noooo,* he is a terrifying Monster!" "He's a horrible, *deformed* creature!" "Cold-blooded!" "He's gruesome, he is!"

Yes, they all agree he is a terrifying Monster. But I tell you, Book, they didn't feel to me to be truly terrified of this Monster at all. It seemed to me that they were only truly bored and just lathering themselves up over any topic that came into their range. To illustrate: Earlier I'd overheard them savaging a local girl whose hair was too blond and too long for their liking.

Still, I am curious about this supposed Monster of theirs.

"May I ask what manner of Monster might the man – I mean, the *Monster* be?"

"Well, for one thing, he lives in a *cave!*" "Aye, a big, *black* cave!" "A dark and *dreadful* cave!" "Oh, yes – *terrible* dark!"

They all agree he lives in a cave.

"And he hates everyone and everything!" "Aye, everyone and *everything!*" "And *everybody!*" "Terrible monster, terrible cave . . ."

Once again, they are all in agreement.

"I wonder," says I, "just what might happen if I were to go near this terrible Monster's terrible cave?"

Well, this causes a great stir, as you may well imagine.

"She wants to know what'll happen!" "I'll tell ya what'll happen, he'll yell so loud, he'll scare ya into a million pieces!" "A *million* pieces!" "And then he'll take every single one o' them pieces and *eat* 'em!" "And all while you're *still alive* to watch him do it!" "Aye, that's what'll happen, alright . . . "

Now, upon further inquiry, I deduce that no one ever actually goes near that cave, nor does anyone know of anyone who's actually been eaten by this Monster. For that matter, no one has ever even seen him up close – though they are all absolutely sure he is covered with hideous hair from hideous head to hideous heel.

I thank them, and I wish them good day, and I can see from the way the women are eyeing me up and down that when I turn my back and walk away, I will likewise be labeled some variety of monster. I am most relieved to be free of them.

So, directly thereafter, I head off to the baker's, and I buy me two big slabs of fresh, thick, moist, chocolate layer cake, because, Book, it has been my experience that the way to open the heart and mind of many a fearsome beast is through the sweet tooth. And then Hank and I head on up the road that the baker told me leads directly to this Monster's cave – which is, as you may well imagine, none too heavily traveled. The way is rather steep, but both Hank and I are nimble of foot, and as I walk ahead of him I am ashamed to say that my gluttony gets the best of me, and, well, I simply cannot help but devour most of my piece of the chocolate cake.

The higher we get, the more expressive and dense the trees seem to be and the more rich and pungent is the smell of the soil. And when we get to the top, where the cave is situated, oh, such a *revelation* of a view . . . Way off in the distance on the one side, a majestic, white-tipped mountain range climbs high into the sky, and way off in the distance on the other side stretches a long, bright, beautiful, blue sliver of what must surely be, at long last, the Calico Sea!

Ohhh, just to stand there and drink in that view and the miraculous mix of sea and forest air . . . Why, I am so smitten with the sight and the scent of it that, for a moment, I clean forget why I've come here! That is, until the smell of chocolate rises to mix with forest and sea.

So, I turn to regard the cave. And what greets me is a most surprising sight: a massive wooden door that fits the opening of the cave so precisely and so very artfully. What also greets me is a shouting male voice from behind said door:

"IF YOU VALUE YOUR LIFE, YOU WILL CLEAR OUT OF HERE!"

I am ready for this, Book. So, though the furied power of his voice definitely unnerves me some, I stand my ground and I speak up:

"Well, I most certainly *do* value my life, and I heartily apologize for disturbing you! The thing of it is, though – "

"WHATEVER IT IS YOU'RE SELLING, GO SELL IT SOMEWHERE ELSE!"

Well, o' course, I find this funny, so I laugh a little, and I say:

"Why, I'm not selling anything, sir! I am simply a Whirld Traveler passing through, and I heard the most ridiculous things about you from the people in the village, and I thought, 'Now, there's got to be a rather singular fellow at the bottom of all that, and perhaps he'd like a piece of fresh chocolate cake – and, if the spirit moves, perhaps a bit of philosophical conversation to go along with it.'"

I can feel him listening. I wait. I watch the door.

And then a slot within the door slides open, revealing the two most astonishing Eyes I have ever seen in all my life . . . wide open Eyes, shining like blue-grey moonstones, staring and staring at me. And I am helpless but to stare back.

And then the slot slides shut!

Well, first, I have to breathe again, 'cause I'd clean forgot to, so stunned by the beauty of those Eyes was I. Then, though I don't know *what* to say, I feel compelled to say *something*, so I call out:

"I can . . . personally attest to the deliciousness of the cake! I know because, well, I ate quite a bit of my piece on the way up."

Silence.

"But don't worry, your piece is . . . untouched."

And I just stand there, feeling ever so stupid – a feeling of which I am not fond *at all*. Then Hank reminds me that I have a perfectly valid question to ask.

"Oh! Yes, uhhh . . . Say, will this road lead down to the Calico Sea? Of course, I could've asked those people in the village, but

I didn't want to let on that – that – well, that I was on my way up here. I figured they'd make a mighty big meal of it, so . . . well, here I am!"

Silence.
I wait for a bit.

Then, figuring I best be on my way, I turn towards Hank. And just as I do, from behind the door I hear, with a *mite* less bite:

"WHAT WOULD YOU BE WANTING WITH THE CALICO SEA?"

"Why . . . " says I, "to *see* it, of course!"

Then, silly words start tumbling out of my mouth, all of their own accord:

"See, I only just saw it just now from up here for the first time, and it's just so *beautiful*. And I've never swum in the Sea, y'see. Oh, I swim like a fish, but I've only ever swum in – well, y'know, only in rivers and lakes and pools and such. Though I tell ya, *some* pools ya gotta – well, just give 'em a *wide berth* would be my advice . . . yes, it would . . . hmph."

It were most alarming, Book! I have never sounded so dim-witted in all my life!

But the slot slides open again. And again, oh, there they are – those Eyes! Only now they look like *skies*, clear and beautiful and *so blue* . . . as if the weather has somehow changed behind them. And, somehow, I manage to remember my name.

"I'm Lillian . . . How d'you do."

And do you know he shuts that doggone slot *right in my face!* Why, I am stung clean through, and completely embarrassed, to boot. The Monster obviously does not want to know the likes of me. Well, that's alright, I'm not to everybody's taste. Some folks want to be left alone and, indeed, have the right to it. So I says:

"My apologies for having disturbed you, sir. I'll just leave your cake . . . right here. Fare you well, then."

And I place his wrapped piece of cake in front of the cave door. And 'tis odd, Book, but I feel so deep down *sad* as I head on over to Hank.

And then, just as I am lifting my foot to the stirrup, I hear a sort of a *creaking*, and I turn around to see that a small, square, door-within-the-door has opened to reveal:

A most marvelous, most *un*-monstrous masculine face . . . that, yes, appears to have itself a beard, and wild waves of wheat colored, not *remotely* hideous hair. And those Skies of Eyes still stare, but with a sparkle in them now. And his most marvelous mouth moves, oh, most marvelously to say:

"That road does lead down to the sea, yes."

Well, it were all too much at once, Book. I were purely stupefied. And of all the words in the whole of the Whole Wyde Whirld, all that comes to my mouth to say is:

"Oh."

And then, for a Monster, he says a most amazing thing:

"I do . . . like cake."

And he looks at me, and I look at him. And then, sure, I walk over and pick up that slab of cake, and I set it into the palm of his rough-hewn hand, which is now reaching through the small square opening in the cave door. And he draws the cake inside and steps back a bit to eat. And I can glimpse him eating, which, for some mysterious reason, is downright *enchanting* to watch.

So I backs up little by little, see, smooth-like, while he eats, so as not to startle him. And I sit myself upon the wide, warm rock right across from the cave, with the sun on my back, and I eat what's left of my cake along with him. And in between bites, me on that big ol' rock and him behind that massive cave door, we talk in tiny morsels – mostly about cake. And I must make note that it was easily the shallowest conversation I've ever had with anybody. Still, somehow, I couldn't have moved from that spot for all the Whirld.

Finally, I venture, "And so, good sir, might I know *your* name?"

And the Eyes flash at me.

"You can call me Monster."

"Well, that's not your given name, so I won't be calling you that."

"Well, it's my *taken* name, and I'm telling you to call me Monster."

"Oh, *don't* tell me your name then! I just won't call you anything."

"Suit yourself. Just don't be calling me *sir* – and especially not *good sir.*"

"I was only trying to be polite!"

"Well, it's wasted on me, see. I'm no longer fit to live where people are polite."

What a thing to say, eh, Book? I don't know what to make of it.

Then he says, of all things to say, "Good cake. You're a good cook."

I roll my eyes and raise my eyebrow, because we both know I *bought* the stupid cake. He stares at me and says:

"See what I did there? I made a joke."

And, no, it weren't a funny joke but, doggone it, I cannot help but smile some, because I see that *he* is smiling some, and these crinkles are crinkling up around the corners of those Eyes, and, well, it just undoes me, and I nigh on fall off that rock. Which he then tells me is where he likes to sit to carve things. Which gives me the courage to tell him that I think the cave door is very beautiful. Which makes him flush. Which is also very beautiful, and which, for some reason, makes *me* flush.

Then we trade one or two bits of this and that about nothing much at all, and, in between, we fall into a sort of a peace underneath the silences. Then, out of one particularly deep, wide silence, just as the sun is desiring to set, he tells me why he thinks those people from the village are right about him, and why he really *is* a Monster. He tells me he was in the War. He says that he saw monstrous things, and that he did monstrous things.

"And, well . . . " says he, "it made me a Monster."

And our eyes are looking deeply, one into the other's, and I nod a bit, and he nods a bit, and then he gently shuts that small square door. And *then*, oh, the massive wooden door of that cave opens, leaving a space just wide enough for him to step outside. The vision of him were too much then, and even now, as I write.

Yes, there in the dusk, by the faint golden glow of a light shining from deep within the cave, I see those Eyes, yes . . . but I am also now beholding his height, his might, his wild waves of hair! And as he stands there, in boots and belted breeches, he almost seems to me to be a tree. Yes, there be the gleam and the shadow of skin, there be the long, strong form of a most magnificently made man . . . who then most purposefully takes one bold step further out of his cave. And, *ohhh* . . . the savage violence done to his left forearm and hand is laid monstrously bare.

And as I behold the whole entire wonder of him, I am – well, I barely know what I am. I have never before been awash and near drowning with so many bewildering, ungovernable feelings all at once. Now, as I recall it all, I suppose I must've looked purely terrified, as I were trembling, with tears in my eyes, which I felt to be open wider than they've ever, ever been.

Says he, so sourly, "I *told* you I was a Monster."

I am dumbstruck.

"*No* . . . you're so . . . "

"What?" he snaps. "I'm so *what?*"

And, for the life of me, I cannot find a single word. And rage contorts his face.

"Right. So, now you've seen the Monster, you can *clear out!*"

And he's back in the cave in a flash, and he slams that door so hard I swear I feel the whole mountain shake. And, somehow, I find my legs underneath me, and I rush to the door.

"*I'm sorry!* I'm – I'm – "

"*Damn and blast . . . CLEAR OUT OF HERE! GO!*"

Well, Book, I have never been so confused and shaken and panicked in all my life! But I couldn't just stand there and beg, could I? And I couldn't just stand there and yell, could I? And I couldn't just *leave*, could I?

"So, sure," thinks I, "I'll get out my Music Box – that always works! That'll soothe that raging beast in that cave – sure it will – and me in the bargain."

And so I sighs into it (a mighty shaky sigh, might I add) and, why, the most mysterious, haunting, soothing song begins to play, and I start to sing. And do you know what he says to that, Book? Well, he *hollers* at me, and I quote *verbatim*:

"AWWW, WILL YOU QUIT THAT CATERWAULING, WOMAN!"

You heard me, Book. "Caterwauling," if you please! *"Caterwauling!"* Can you imagine? Well, when I hear that, my jaw drops wide open and just about sticks there, I am so *insulted!*

But, owing to my vast experience in the Theatrical Profession, I soldier on most mellifluously, yes, as if he is merely a drunken heckler! And all the while he is shouting at me that I am "tone deaf as a stone," if you please, and that I have a voice "like a chicken being strangled," if you can believe *that!* But, fear not, I am expertly affecting to be entirely unaffected by any of his nonsense, as if he is merely a distant breeze.

So, sure, I finish the song – *marvelously,* I might add – and I climb this here tree, and I hang my hammock and, *ooooh,* I tell you something, I could just spit! I really could. After I brought him *cake* and was so *nice* and everything! Obviously, he has no taste and no manners *whatsoever.*

And, Book, as I lie here and stare down at that stupid door of his stupid cave, I will confide that I am mightily frustrated with Hank too. He is still refusing to offer any opinion about this most aggravating situation, when it is quite plain to see that he has one. *Ughhh . . .* I just don't know what's *wrong* with everybody today!

Well, I tell you what, I am gonna hightail it outta here the moment I get even a *hint* that the sun is even *threatening* to come up. *Oooooh,* that insufferable, *ignorant* man has wore me out entirely!

And what in the *Whirld* is wrong with the moon? It looks much too big, and it's the wrong color, and I just want to *kick* it!

Wherein I Am Attuned to the Music of the Spheres

Donovan . . . His name, Book, is Donovan.

I cannot say it enough, just to feel the word against my teeth and on my lips and around my tongue, as it is one round, oh-most-perfect prayer of thanksgiving for being alive and in a form.

It had been so very long, he said, since anyone had spoken his name to him. Yes, and who better, we agree, than me, who knows so well and so deeply what it means to welcome one's name Home to one's long lost self again. Then, when the heart hears another speak your name, oh, you feel such a "Yes!" so deep within.

And so we each say the other's name over and over, whispering, caressing, blessing, *yessing* . . . And, Book, I could not begin to describe why, but I tell you, though it is but two words we use, it is easily the most profound conversation I've ever had with anyone. Except perhaps the one in which we use no words at all.

He sleeps now, and I gaze upon him as I write. Oh, how I wish that I could write without ever having to tear my eyes away to look down at the page. (No offense, Book.) Ah, yes, awash in bliss as I be, I must make certain that these particular pages will not be completely indecipherable scrawls, and I must pay some extra mind to my script.

Look at him, glistening in the firelight. He is an angel, I know it, fallen from the sky, who badly burnt a wing in falling past the sun.

And, oh, he has let me see the rest of his remarkable, wondrous face. We shaved his beard – what *fun* that was! – and now all I do is marvel at the lovely expressiveness of his face and kiss it.

I did not know, Book.
I understand now.
I understand so much.

I did not realize – how could I, of course – that this manner of Love, this kinship, this melding, were not any kind of a *sickness* at all! And no wonder so many so desperately seek it, as it is such a healing grail. It is a vast, eternal Truth, so sanctifying, so transporting – nay, so *transmogrifying*, that I tell you, Book, I absolutely know and feel every particle of my being to be reverberating with the same resonance as all living things throughout the Universe.

The sound of the Universe is a music, so they say – that is, them that think and say such things. 'Tis a synchronous symphony to which I am now one more creature most perfectly attuned. Ha! Yes, the singer has become the song within a bigger song within a bigger song, and on and on forever.

And perhaps when parts of the symphony are out of tune, all becomes discord and chaos and wounded like his arm. And when *in* tune, all breathes harmony and glory. And what do I behold now before me but glory, glory, and more glory . . .

Well, I just turned back the page to read the end of my last entry, and I busted up laughing so hard, I could only just barely smother myself enough so as not to wake him! I will read it to him the moment he awakens, though. I can hardly wait to hear how hard he'll laugh.

Oh, yes, we have done heaps of laughing, and how we have clung to each other in this cavernous, astonishing cave of his these last few days – is it three, is it four, is it less, or more? *Ohhh,* look how the firelight plays upon his hair and his skin and . . .

I forgot what I was writing, Book. I was drinking him in.

Ah, yes! It turns out that he loves my singing, after all, and now he asks me to sing to him all the time – isn't that funny? He said that at first it drove him mad because it was making him feel things he didn't want to feel and fought ferociously against feeling and swore he'd die rather than feel. And having now felt them fully, he says he feels stronger and better by far than he has felt in all his life.

Oh, yes, I should tell you that I stuck my head out of the cave after my first night here and met Hank's big brown eyes all a-sparkle. Do you know that he knew exactly what sort of sparks were flying between me and Donovan the whole time? Donovan says that he knew too. I daresay *you* probably knew as well, eh, Book? 'Twas only I who did not know. Which, I suppose, further proves how alarmingly obtuse I am when it comes right down to it.

Anyhow, Hank has told me that he has decided to go off and have some adventures of his own for a while, and that we should each of us make sure we have many marvelous tales to tell one another when he returns.

So, Book, do you want to hear what stopped me from galloping off and away forevermore as I had planned? Well, just as the first light of the sun were beginning to dawn, I jumps from my hammock to the ground, and what do I see but a rough piece of parchment hanging in the opposite tree. And what it says is this:

Dear Lillian,

I said brutal things to you last night. I used my wound as my armour, which was cowardly enough. But then to have turned it into a weapon and used it against one so kind as you was a most disgraceful act.

I am very much ashamed. I hope you can forgive me.

Donovan

Well, o' course, upon reading them beautiful words, I burst into tears, and he bursts out of the cave to come to me. Yes, he had been wracked with remorse and worry all night, waiting for me to find his note, watching through a little lookhole in the door.

And, oh, how *nice* it felt to be a damsel and to be rescued by this marvelous male creature – why, I was mute with the joy of it. And then, yes . . . he led me into his lair and closed us in, and here we've been ever since.

He just opened one eye a tiny bit and smiled at me, and I am therefore dissolved into a puddle of happiness. Why, the fact that I can move this plume with any direction or sense at all is a complete marvel, as being a puddle, one does not collect oneself so easily. So you will forgive me, Book, if this entry is as liquid as I am.

Oh, and I must report that there are so many unutterable wonders in this here cave. Donovan took us on a walk along a long and winding path by torchlight, and – you will not believe it, though it be true – there is a *lake* within this very cave, with a vast expanse of space soaring high above it. And we swam in that lake and, oh, it was so *cold* and the water so fresh! And would that you could see his carvings and his woodworkings – they are nothing short of breathtaking! Why, he even carved the bed!

Oh, Book, the bed . . .
Why did no one tell me?

Or perhaps they did, but what they told me weren't what this is. To love this way is to pray, after all, isn't it? To adore in every way is surely the prayerful flesh-expression of the Soul.

Mmmm . . . my, how soothing I find it to gaze upon the hills of his shoulders and the valleys of his back rising and falling with his breath . . .

Now, what should I like to say to myself about this series of revelations? Well, for one thing, I *adore* my body three times more than ever before! Who knew it were such a marvelous animal creature I am? And *his* body . . . Yes, it's like he just now heard me writing this and stretched like a lion just so's I could admire him, limbs and paws and all of him.

He has oils that he rubs into his wounds to help the scars. Last night I got these here hands o' mine on them scars with those oils and, *ohhh,* what a journey we had . . . At first, he were horrified and mortified that I should even want to touch his scars. And, well, I can't exactly say why it is that I feel proud, but I have to say it: I am so *proud* that I found such a holy use for these here hands of mine. I healed my Donovan some. I know I did, and I know I do. Like I say, we did this just last night, so this is why he sleeps and sleeps today, and that, too, makes me proud.

My Donovan is what royalty *should* be, you see.
He is my Prince.
He is my King.

What was I meaning to say, though? Oh, yes, that first night, he told me his tale:

He was born and raised by the shores of the Calico Sea. His mother died giving birth to him, so it was only his father and him, living in their stone cottage by the sea, fishing. Then he and his friends heard of the Great War and determined they should go. His father begged him not to go, and they argued, and Donovan left. And then all that happened to him . . . happened. And while he were gone, he heard that his father had died. So he never went back, and he won't and he can't go back, but can only bear to look at the Sea from afar, from a-way up here.

And I told him what I know of my story, and why I won't go back. And so, of course, now we are *both* going back – to both places, together – and both of us will come to our reckonings. We are sure that this has been Destiny's long and winding plan all along, and, therefore, we are most willingly conscripted.

I am now convinced that I must go back because I've learned that the man who gained control of my Father's Kingdom is the same man who started the War in which Donovan were wounded and his friends were killed. And we discussed it, and it now seems imperative that I take the throne, not for the mere act of throne-taking, but for the sake of justice. And he is to be my champion and my general and my army. And then he kissed me, and that ended *that* discussion for a nice, long time.

And he is now convinced that he must go back and make peace with the soul of his father. And I told him that I would go with him as his Faerie Queen and his darling and his singer of devotional songs. And then I kissed *him*, and that ended *that* discussion too.

I should also report that he is very happy and intrigued that I have Faerie blood, and he wonders if our children will fly out the window, and how will we ever find them, and will they love threes and rhymes and be very temperamental and drive us to distraction.

He's quite funny, my Donovan.

Now, I shall spend no more time recording our discussions regarding these leave-takings and journeyings. We are both profoundly certain that Destiny has the reins. And we have also agreed that, although we must indeed proceed, 'twould be profane to rush to get further and faster down the path we see before us. It is our mission now to relish this great gift of each other, and to weave ourselves together with such a potent power that we can prevail and prevail and prevail . . .

My point is, after this one last bit of reverie, I will end this entry, and I will return to pure, pulsating Life.

Book, you know me, and you know that I have always felt it to be a glory and a gift to be alive, I have indeed . . . But never before have I felt my soul to be *gleaming* so, seeming to grow so far beyond my physical form. Never before have I felt every last particle of myself to be ringing to the furthest reaches of an Everywhere farther than mostly mortal me will ever travel. For we two have now become a third creature, in humming harmony with all the Universe. I am experiencing this absolutely, and I know it to be Truth.

"What have you done to me?" I keep asking him. "What have you done?"

And I never wait to hear the answer.

By the Shores of the Calico Sea

No matter what happens, from now until the day I die, whenever anyone asks me where I was born and raised, I will say:

I was born in a Cave,
and raised in a Cove,
by the shores of the Calico Sea.

I feel thoroughly and completely new, Book. It's true. Why, the mere fact that I am so fortune-favored to be such a proud part of a "We" gives you an idea of how truly newly born is your old pal Lillian. Let's see, I have been: first Lost, then Seeking, then Wandering, then Loved, then Found, and now Reborn as Lillian of Donovan's Cove. And whosoever she may be from here on in all her journeys, this last is who she is firstly and foremostly and finally.

Aye, so very many days and nights have passed since I last put pen to paper, but here in this perfect, private place, by the vast, magnificent, tempestuous creature that is the Sea, I did not want to miss the slightest whiff of a single salty breeze, or a droplet of a wave, or a bubble of foam, or a grain of sand that is everywhere and in everything, or one wisp of a moment in this most miraculous stretch of life with my Donovan by stopping to write about it. Thank you, Book, for being, as always, so eminently understanding.

But, yes, I take this moment to let it all wash over me, as I watch him through this window do whatever he is doing with the nets and the boat, as the sunlight has started to turn rosy-gold on his deeply tanned back and shoulders, as I write this here entry on this carved wooden table, and now and again remember to stir the stew for our dinner.

We leave in the morning at first light, with the aim of setting many things to rights. And now I cannot help but to gaze over at the very bed where his father and his mother dreamed him up, and at the mantelpiece, at the fireplace, at every cup and every chair . . . I am memorizing, memorizing, memorizing . . .

With regard to the journey we are about to undertake, and the now apparent imperative thereof – that of taking back the throne – why, it is downright absurd how my perspective has shifted in a blink! Before Destiny brought me to Donovan's doorstep with chocolate cake, I wouldn't have cared half a quarter of the smallest whit about attaining redress for any kingdom, any way, anyhow – much less for that awful place that cast me off without a thought, as we know. Nope, not if the Whirld broke in two. But what was unthinkable before is now somehow "of course." I know, Book. I am a constant source of mystery to myself.

But, yes, it is so. Since that short stone's throw ago, I am sensing this is likely the very thing I were born and now reborn to do – yes, with the same inevitability in which I were never meant to be a Great Poet, no matter how hard I tried.

And speaking of Poetry . . . I have not felt remotely inclined to write even one small word of Poetry of late, as I am most assuredly *living* a Perfect Paradisiacal Poem with every moment, with all the moments strung together here, with Donovan and me and the Sea. No, it is plenty poetical enough to watch how his Eyes match every single shade and shift of Sky and Sea. And to have the gift of continually looking into those Eyes and the gift of continually feasting on the breathtaking beauty all around us – well, it is an embarrassment of riches, is it not? Yes, it is now apparent that to truly pay tribute to the Spirit of Art is to simply appreciate its gifts, and not irritate it with what would only be, after all, pointless piffle.

I tell you, Book, although I am sometimes profoundly a-feared of this journey for a thousand perfectly reasonable reasons, I now

- 254 -

recognize it to be my duty. All I have to do is look at his wounded arm and all my questionings quiet.

What's more, I have only just been given this even deeper inspiration . . . As we lay on the beach looking at the stars the other night, Donovan told me he feels that helping to restore the Kingdom to rights may be the only way he can redeem and forgive himself for his dark deeds in the War. Well, if anything could make me courageous, it is the chance to win my Beloved redemption and peace.

He had, I now know, a very fine father. Ah, yes, too much to tell, and I must be wise about selection at this most significant threshold between Now and Then, as fleeting as it is eternal. But the reason I mention his fine fathering is because I can tell from the way he teaches me, with so much encouragement. Why, he looks at me with such belief and love that I feel I could lift a mountain, balance it on my pinkie, and *twirl* it. I do not exaggerate, Book, not one bit. It is an accurate rendering of his ability to inspire me.

I have no idea what he is doing with the nets by the boat right now, but I tell you, I would wait in line and pay good money to watch him do it. It is thoroughly astonishing to me to see how *alacritous* he is! Not only is it as if there were no physical impediment at all, it is as if – because he has taught himself how to use his feet so intricately and so powerfully, as well as the elbow of his wounded arm – he is like some many-legged, sun-drenched sea creature. And the uncanny strength of him! And big as he is, when he walks or runs, he is somehow as light and fast as a wildcat. In point of fact, I could watch him do *anything* all day – and I have!

And it's no question he was a leader of men, because he can be so exceptionally *bossy* and, oh, *so stubborn* – with a head like a boulder of granite! We have had two whopping, loud, stormy arguments during this time, both of which I'm proud to say I have utterly *ruined* by getting the giggles in the middle of them. The first time it happened, he nigh on burst into flames with frustration, which, of course, sent me into an even more catastrophic fit of laughter. The second time it happened, although he kept trying to stay mad, in the end he failed miserably and chased me out of the house and into the Sea.

Oh, we have been such jubilant, boisterous children in this perfect place amongst all the perfect places in all of the Whole Wyde Whirld – for we are Home, and that's the perfect truth of it. I know every corner of the Cove so deeply by now . . . when the tide is in and when it's out, the round rocks, the endless seaweed, the ever-present breathing of the waves in and out, in and out, as they rush to us and wash over us and renew us, again and again and again. We shall come back whenever we can, as Donovan says it's not too far from my place of origin. And, of course, when we have passed the Kingdom on to our children, we shall return here and be merry old people, playing in the sand.

How I love and adore this big stone cottage in this here Cove, which has been passed from father to son for so many generations. Yes, with such camaraderie and efficiency did we clean and care for this house, and how warm and welcoming it has become once again, how vibrant with the light of being so lived in and so well loved. We came upon it looking so sad and abandoned, and we will take our leave of it happy and alive and expectant of us evermore.

On our first night here, we made a big fire on the beach. Donovan took his most cherished toy that his father had carved for him – a simple little boat that was sitting on the mantelpiece when we first arrived. 'Twas the first thing he were moved to pick up, and he carried it with him all the while we looked about the place.

So, as we sat by the fire, he held this little carved boat. He said he felt it to be calling forth the spirit of his father. And he spoke of what a generous man his father had been, and what a great teacher and giver of courage and confidence and kindness he was, and he called his father a king amongst fathers.

And then he broke down and said how eternally grateful he was to have had a father that loved him so much, that had argued so hard against him going to war because he felt so sure that his son was being lied to and were going to be used and hurt. And then Donovan spoke out how sorry and torn apart he is that their last words were spoken in such anger when their lives were spent in such friendship, and how heartbroken he is that he didn't get to see his father again. Then he said that he hopes his father can see Lillian from wherever he is and love her too.

And then, when Donovan said all that he had to say, he took some twigs and dry grass, tucked them into the little boat, poured a bit of lamp oil onto the twigs and set them ablaze. And we walked out into the water, and Donovan set the boat upon the waves, and we stood and watched as the tide carried the little funeral pyre out to sea.

So, before we depart, I here and now must record what absolutely must be recorded – that is, what I would most like to remember of this most magnificent stretch of life . . . *Ha!* Well, it cannot be done, can it, Book? How can I possibly select from such a sublime avalanche of images – endless visions of love and silence and silliness and sand and sea. No, I am a fool. There is no point trying to choose one perfect pearl when they are countless and all gleam with such everlasting glory.

Ah, look at that . . . There be my Donovan, covered with a whole beach full of sand, smiling and singing to himself, coming Home now for dinner. Oh, yes, I know that wherever we may go, though I will always cherish the Cave, I will always crave the Cove.

I am newborn.
I am strong as all the Whirld.
I and my Donovan.

Onward, indeed.

Wherein I Die

I do not know or care to understand the force by which the quill moves across the page, or how these words form beneath it, because, you see, I am dead.

My body lives. This I see. This I am told. So these two kind souls who found me tell me. They bring me soup and comfort me when I wake up screaming.

But I am dead, you can be sure of that. I am dead because he is dead, and because he is dead, everything is dead.

So, why do I write? I write because these two kind women, one with gold-brown eyes, one with green, found this book in my things. And the one with the gold-brown eyes tells me that if I write what happened it will get the horrors out of my mind some, and I won't see it so much because it will be further outside of me. And she doesn't even know what happened, because I cannot speak it, I cannot say it, I cannot form my mouth around any words at all. I suppose it must be because the dead cannot speak.

Yes, she tells me that writing it out may help to heal my mind some. But whether it does or doesn't, I do it for her and for them because they are so giving and generous, and when they see that I am trying, it seems to make them feel a bit better for their efforts, as it does when I sip this or that.

So then, let the quill tell the tale . . .

There were three of them. We had only just set out. We were only one or two hundred paces away from the Cove, no more. And then there are three of them, suddenly there – come up from the side of the road like phantoms. They laugh and say how glad they are to have found me and how they can't wait to spend all that money. Then something about some Hopper, something about some weaver, some weaver who wants me dead . . .

Then I hear a blood-curdling *howl* – and my Beloved blasts by me, a ferocious warrior-animal, slashing away at them! In an instant, all is clashing and flashing of metal! And when I step forward to help, he yells at me to *stay back, stay out of it* – so I just stand there, frozen, terrified to distract him.

Then there lay two of them on the ground, dead, and it is just he and the last one, the third one, battling, savagely battling . . . Then, somehow, he is on the ground, still fighting, but I see that he is tiring. And then I hear someone screaming – it is *me* screaming as I grab a dagger from a dead man's hand and grab the greasy hair of the third and slice across his thick throat and – *ohhh*, that *sound* – and *so much blood.*

I drop the dagger, I fall to my knees, I look into my Beloved's eyes, and though they be the darkest blue they've ever been, oh, he is *so alive!*

But he keeps saying that it is his thigh, his thigh, so I rip his shirt, and we wrap it, we tie it so tightly around his leg. And he is fine, he is so *alive*, he is *fine* . . .

He says to get us back to the Cove, and he calls me his fine warrior queen. And as we are making our way along with his arm around my shoulder, I feel the power of his muscles, and his grip is *so strong* – and he even says something funny, and we laugh – we *laugh!* He is alive, and he is *fine* . . .

But then, he isn't. We cannot stop the bleeding. We can't stop it. Then he says not to bring him to the house, but to lie together on the beach, like always. And as I lay him down on the sand, he says to please just lie there with him and to listen very closely . . .

And I beg him not to leave me, and he says it's the last thing in the Whirld he wants to do, but it can't be helped, so listen, *listen* . . .

Then he smiles, and the corners of his eyes crinkle up the way they do, and he whispers that I must always remember that I brought him peace, perfect peace, and so much happiness. That he feels honored to have set me on my path. That he did what he were meant to do.

Then he kisses me . . . and he looks deep into my eyes, and he bids me never to live in anger and bitterness, not for even a moment, because he feels so clean and new again, and because he is so proud to die a fine warrior's death defending his queen. And he makes me promise to keep on, to press on, to never, ever give up. And the last word on his lips was *love*.

And then his soul slipped away . . . and his Eyes, those Eyes closed. And I died.

I don't know how long I lay there holding him. All I know is that the sun has slipped away, and I am shivering, shivering. He is ice cold, and I feel as cold as he. So, yes, of course, I build a fire to warm us, like always. And as the fire grows strong and the flames leap, my eyes fall upon his fishing boat, and I know what must be done.

But he is so *heavy*, I can't lift him. So I run into the house, I tear the bedclothes off the bed, I grab a rope and the lamp oil. Then I go back out to him, and I wrap the sheets around him and tie them with rope, then wrap the rope over my shoulders and around my torso. Then I drag him a few steps, and I fall. Then I get up and drag him, I drag him toward the water, toward the boat.

And when we reach the water, the Sea helps me buoy him up and, finally, I get him into the boat. Then I take the twigs and the dry grass and tuck it all around him and pour the lamp oil over it all. Then I grab a branch and douse it with the oil, and I go back to the fire. And as I plunge the branch into the flames to make a torch, I look up to see – *oh, no!* – the Sea is sweeping him away, sweeping him out too far, too soon . . .

So I grit my teeth, and I run, *I run* – my legs feel like lead in the sand, but I *run*. And bless my aim, *bless my aim*, I throw that torch and it sails over the waves in a long, wide arc and falls into the boat, bursting into a powerful blaze, a fine funeral pyre for my King!

And then I hear somebody screaming – it is *me* screaming. I feel the flames, yes, I *feel* the flames consuming him, consuming me, so I run into the Sea to be with him . . . And the last thing I remember is the sight of the fire and the feeling of my body sinking as I let myself give up swimming . . .

But the Sea spat me out, I suppose, because they found me.

The woman with the green eyes just came in with some soup and fed me a sip and kissed my head. The woman with the gold-brown eyes told me to rest as best I can, and said that they are happy to have me here and that I mustn't worry about anything.

The Whirld has ended. It has broken in half.

And I have fallen into the bottomless blackness in between.

Wherein I Write Because I Said I Would Write

I lie here in this long, wooden chair, with a blanket over my legs, on this expanse of green grass behind the cottage. It is just a stone's throw from the cliff, which falls off steeply to the beach, so, yes, I can see the Sea. I have sat out here and watched the Sea all day, nearly every day, for all these many days. I know not how long I have been here. I have lost track entirely.

And even as I write this, I realize that I may have finally forgiven the Sea for spitting me out. It is so vast and eternal, it must surely know everything, swallow everything, birth everything . . . So, I suppose it must have had its reasons for throwing me back to the shores of Life.

And here's a thought behind that one, which I suppose I ought to note, as well: Though I have no real desire to live, I no longer so very much desire to die.

As I watch the Sea and Sky endlessly shifting and changing, I cannot help but see his Eyes shifting and changing. And there have been moments when it feels to me as if Sea and Sky *are* his Eyes, now grown eternal.

I still have not spoken or attempted to at all. And, in truth, I have not missed speaking. Not even a little. Connie and Bonnie do not behave as though this is anything to be alarmed by, but perfectly understandable, and they say that speech will come of its own accord, when and if it has a mind to.

Connie is the one with the gold-brown eyes and Bonnie is the one with green. My head could not hold even those simple rhyming names when last I wrote. Even in my silence, we three have knit together as such friends, and my little nods and small smiles and such are somehow quite clear to them. They are so good-hearted, they often act as if I am actually adding to the conversations. And the two of them are quite funny together. Which makes me remember that laughter and I used to have an awful lot to do with one another.

I should record these facts, as well: Bonnie and Connie are the nearest neighbors to Donovan's Cove. They spotted us on the beach when we first arrived, and they were so relieved that Donovan was alive and so obviously happy. And they saw that he was in love, and resolved to let us be for a while.

And then, on that night, when they came to stand at the edge of the cliff to watch the moon, they saw the flaming boat on the water and ran down into the Cove, and they found me there in the seaweed . . . yes. And, yes, I showed the two of them those last few pages I wrote so they would know what happened to Donovan. And to those men. And to me, I suppose.

Anyway . . .

Neighbors have come by, one by one mostly, to pay their respects and to sit with me and grieve for Donovan. They all knew him from the time he was born and loved him. They have told me stories of him. They have sat silently with me and held my hand. Most of their sons, who were his friends, were killed in the War, and though they had heard rumors that Donovan still lived, they did not know where he was. They have been so accepting and gentle, and they do not seem to mind one bit that I don't speak or even try to. They have lived in the same valleys of grief, and they understand the language.

One night, an old fisherman stood at the foot of my bed and sang a song in memory of Donovan. I had never before been on the receiving end of a song sung, and I must make note of how moved I was by it. Said the fisherman, when he finished:

"When he was a lad, how our Donovan did love that song . . . 'Tis known hereabouts to be a song of mourning, and we all thought it so curious that a child would have such affection for such a song."

And his wife, a little slip of a woman, added:

"We thought it was that his mother had died giving birth to him, and he missed her."

When I heard that, I thought, "Or his soul were so clever, he sensed all the death that lay ahead of him."

Bonnie told me that she'd known Donovan from when he were newborn, and as he had no living mother, and as she and her parents lived so nearby, she was an ever-present big sister to him. She too has been sorely heartbroken, and though I am by no means glad for her grief, the comfort of the depth of it has somehow helped save me from a completely bottomless despair.

Sometimes, when she is knitting in her chair nearby, she will look up at me and her eyebrows will raise in a certain way, and I will give a little nod, and she will tell a story of Donovan as a boy. And it is always just exactly the right story to soothe our souls a bit more. In my near madness of missing him, I imagine him prompting her from invisible realms.

Yesterday, she laughed as she told me, "Oh, he was forever giving us all such a fright! You'd turn around and there'd be Donovan jumping off something that was altogether too high to be jumping off of. No matter what we said, that boy was convinced he could fly!"

And when I heard that, I thought, "That is because he were an angel, and he were practicing."

And just as I think that thought and get so achingly sad because I cannot kiss him or hold him ever again, why, Cynthia jumps up on my lap, stares straight into my eyes, and yowls at me reproachfully. So I cannot help but smile and scratch her chin.

Yes, Cynthia is a cat. Three things must be known about Cynthia:

1) She is a queen amongst cats, and she knows it.

2) She is, of all things, a Calico cat, living here by the Calico Sea.

3) She is fat. *Very* fat.

Cynthia lies in the sun "like a beached whale," Connie says, as she rubs that wide, white belly. And after Cynthia bakes herself so hot in the sun, she jumps up and lies on me and warms me clean through. She has slept with me and purred on my belly and followed me everywhere since I've been here. Connie and Bonnie tell me that I should be flattered, as Cynthia is so certain she is the very center of the Universe that, usually, she pays nobody much mind, not even them.

Ah, the sudden weariness has just fallen upon me, as it does, like an anvil. When I walk, it sometimes pulls me clean down to the ground, and in an instant I am drained of all life force. It's as if my body and I are only distant acquaintances now, instead of the dear friends we used to be Before.

But now it is After, isn't it?
Now there will always be Before and After.
Yes . . .

So, there. I have been a good girl, dear Connie. I have done as I promised you. I have written something. I'm going to close my eyes now. I am entirely and completely exhausted.

Wherein I Am Saved

I have just this moment awakened, just as the sun is starting to set. Something thoroughly miraculous has just happened.

I must marshal my forces and record the event this instant, lest a single shred of it evaporate out of the reach of remembering. Wait, let me close my eyes and retrieve it all . . . Yes, *yes*, it were just like that dream I had in the bedroom at the cherry farmer's house . . .

I was lying here convalescing in my customary spot behind the cottage, overlooking the cliff, gazing out at the mighty vista of Sky and Sea. Well, I must have slid into a sort of a sleep, see – a sleep in which I am dreaming that I am lying here looking out at this same mighty vista. Then, suddenly, there comes this swirling breeze . . . so gentle at first, caressing even.

But soon this swirling breeze whips up into a wild wind that sweeps away this vista of Sea and Sky – as if it is merely *blowing away curtains* – revealing, once again, my Heavenly Tower Room!

And then I feel myself to be lying once again in the wide, soft bed of that warm, welcoming room, with its arched windows all around, with all that sunlight streaming in. And who should be sitting on the window seat across from me, gazing out at the Red Rose Oak Tree, but *my Mother!* Why, she is as clear and vivid and present and solid as you are beneath my hands, Book. And, oh, she is loveliness itself, so sparkly and pointy and porcelain, with a diaphanous green gown and those fields of red hair and a delicate crown of white lilacs.

And then she turns and sees me, and she claps her hands, so gleeful is she to see that I am awake! And in the next instant, she is sitting beside me on the bed, with her cool hand lightly stroking my forehead. Yes, I can actually feel the weight of her on the bed next to me. And I look up into her sublime lavender eyes, and, *ohhh*, I feel such love pouring out of them, flowing into me . . .

Then, with a soft smile, she says:

> *"I died of a broken heart, my darling.*
> *But that won't do for you."*

And then she points to the Sorrow at my neck, and she tickles it with her fingertip, just like the Empress did. And in the next moment, the dark jewel is dangling from her pale, elegant fingers by its silver chain. Together, we watch it glittering in the sunlight.

Then she turns to me, and she says:

> *"You soon must swallow your Sorrow, my love.*
> *You must learn the Truth, at last.*
> *You see, you cannot claim your Future*
> *until you claim your Past."*

And in the next instant, my Sorrow is back around my neck. And I look down and grasp it, my fingers feeling its familiar facets. And when I look up, there she be, at the window once more, standing sideways to me. But this time my Mother is round with child! And she lays loving hands upon the globe of her belly. And she looks over at me, and she smiles, and she nods, as if to say that everything has gone just right.

And then, why, her belly is flat again, and she is holding a new-born baby, swaddled in white. She kisses the infant's brow so tenderly, and I in my bed across the room feel that tender kiss upon my brow!

And next, *ohhh*, I must steady my hand to write this . . .   As she whispers into the babe's ear, I hear her sweet voice whispering into *my* ear, ever so clear:

"Now, remember, my dearest darling-dear,
you are the rightful Emperor-King.
And a Girl-King for this Kingdom
might be just the thing."

The whole rhyme! After all this time . . .

And then I wake up.

I am overwhelmed and overcome, to say the very least.
I had a visit with my Mother, Book . . .
I had a visit with my Mother.

It is just coming on dawn. Connie and Bonnie have only just gone to bed, and here am I in my room, still wide awake.

So, here's what happened next . . .

There am I, a-lying there in my long chair, basking in the wonder of that dream visit, when Bonnie calls me in for dinner. And, sure, I feel myself fairly *floating* back to the cottage, so transported and uplifted by the dream am I. And so I sort of drift in and stand there in the doorway, smiling to myself. And what do my eyes fall upon but Cynthia, curled up on the sideboard, sleeping, with her chin resting upon none other than: my Music Box.

I expect it's been sitting there all this time, but I never noticed it or missed it or thought of it even once until this very moment. Naturally, I am pulled to it, so I ease it out from underneath the sleeping cat. Oh, the dazzling beauty of it – I'd quite forgotten!

I then turn to Connie and Bonnie, holding the Music Box up to the light for them to see how it glimmers and flashes. Well, they are so accustomed to my melancholy that they're mystified by my sudden good spirits.

And Connie says, "*My* . . . It is so *beautiful!* We've been wondering what it was."

And Bonnie says, "Yes, it's so pretty! Does it do anything?"

Book, she asks me, *does it do anything?* Well . . . the old Lillian of Everywhere, who somewhere deep down I still must be, strikes a showy, theatrical pose, as if to say, "Ladies, hold onto your hats!" And the two of them laugh, as they've never seen me be even remotely theatrical, o' course.

And then, natural as breathing, I turns over the Music Box, I flips the switch, I sighs into it, the old song sings, and the point is, Book – *so do I.* You heard me. Right then and there that song flows through me and from me, smooth as a swirling breeze. And the looks on their marvelous, expressive faces as they listen – oh, their eyes get so big and round and teary and absolutely amazed!

And when the song is over I bow, and they applaud and rush to hug me. And then, why, I sit right down and tell them the extraordinary dream I just had about my Mother and the whole extraordinary history behind it. And then, right in the middle of telling them all of this, I stop and I say:

"You know something . . . *I'm talking!*"

And Connie says, "You are indeed, my dear!"

And Bonnie says, "Yes, and you're very good at it!"

And we laugh and we laugh and we cry, and then we laugh some more. That's right, *we* – meaning *me too.*

She sings, she speaks, she laughs!
She lives, I suppose, eh, Book?

So, o' course, Bonnie and Connie and I have been up all night talking and telling, with the aid of much coffee and many fresh scones and such-like sustenance. And now, writing here in bed, I feel a potent truth a-rising, which I must close my eyes and receive . . .

Yes, it has made itself known to me, and here it is: Deep down inside me, right next to where all this time I have felt only cold and dead, there now, once more, lives Lillian. And I am only just this moment realizing that, well . . . I've missed her.

Oh, there's so much to report! Alright, so first I told Connie and Bonnie the dream, and then I told them what I know of my history. And, yes, it surely did take a while, and, yes, they were astonished by my rather astonishing ability to talk a blue streak. It was as if I myself were only just then remembering that I were once a Champion Chatterboxer. So, I tell them my whole story, including, of course, where Donovan and I were going and why.

Well. What I next hear shocks me to my core . . .

First, Connie and Bonnie tell me that everybody remembers the Emperor-King's firstborn child – a girl called Lillian – but nobody knows where she is or what happened to her, and everyone assumes she's long dead. And then they tell me that, just like Jimmy said, my Father had no other children and that I am the one and only true heir anywhere, and that, indeed, my Father is quite mad and has been long locked up in a jail cell – and not a nice one neither.

And *then* they tell me that, indeed, a fiendish tyrant has seized power and given himself the title of "Emperor-Regent," and that he trots my Father out for special occasions in the shameless pretense that everything's on the up-and-up, and that he hired a bunch of Hoppers to spy for him and to spread lies far and wide about the glory of his reign, and that he married a very young cousin of my Father – a Duchess – in order to annex her family's land and wealth.

Says Connie, "He is plotting to weave his way into the dynasty, and, of course, he is convinced that only sons will do. But the little Duchess keeps giving birth to girls."

Says Bonnie, "Yes, poor thing, they say she's had at least a dozen baby girls, but they've all been . . . "

"The official story is that they all died at birth," says Connie. "But it's common knowledge that *despicable* man had every one of those babies killed."

And they go on to tell me of the despair that now reigns in the Kingdom.

"Oh, the people are so miserable."

"Yes, the place is so depressed, so repressed in every way."

"And, *ohhh*, there is a *Cloud!* Tell her about that dreadful Cloud!"

"Yes, a dreadful grey Cloud hangs over the Kingdom and completely blocks the sky."

And as I listen, I feel such a terrible sadness for all the People there who cannot see the sun or the moon or the stars . . .

And then, suddenly, inside my soul I can hear my Beloved roar like an angry lion! I can see his Eyes flashing with fury! And then, well, I suppose it were seeing his whole being so clear like that but, *ohhh*, such a monstrous wave of missing him comes rushing up from deep inside, sweeping up and over me. And then, rising up too close behind it comes such a *treacherous* wave – a wave of guilt and shame that has a mind to pull me under and drown me. For I am suddenly and entirely overwhelmed by a most horrible certainty that has been lurking underneath, ever since it happened: It was *me* those three men meant to kill, and therefore it was *me* who well and truly killed my Donovan.

Well, all those waves of anguish come sobbing out of me right there at the kitchen table:

"Why did I move so slow? *Why was I so slow? I could have saved him.*"

And bless my friends, how they help me, how they hold me, how they comfort me . . . Oh, they say so many things to soothe me, like how I'd never fought in a battle before, and how brave I was to kill that man, and how I brought my Donovan home to die in such peace, there in my arms, feeling so clean and whole again at the last. Then Bonnie takes me by the shoulders and looks me deep in the eye, and she tells me that I most certainly did *not* kill Donovan, and she knows for certain that Donovan would be heartbroken if he knew I were blaming myself, when, in fact, he felt so proud to have died a fine warrior's death defending the woman he loved. Oh, yes . . . these wonderful, warm, wise women have once again pulled me to shore.

And so, Book, it seems I have finally returned to my old self once again. And I now fully recall my duty to my Kingdom, to my Donovan's great sacrifice, and to my promise to press on and never, ever give up. Much as I could cry a whole ocean of tears for the loss of him and still have oceans left, I know that now is not the time to give in to endless weeping. He would not have that be. And I will not have that be. No, this is a time to get me strong, to get me to my Kingdom, and to see what I can do about setting things to rights.

Oh, my mind is whirling and humming with so many possibilities! Yes, I know it would be sensible to try to get some sleep now, but before I do . . .

Ahhh, look at that! The first flame-gold light of morning just splashed across this here page, and I wonder

---

Book, the reason I did not finish that sentence was because I ran – that's right, I threw my plume pen up in the air and I *ran!*

You know how I was just writing that last bit about the first light of morning splashing across the page? Well, sure, it were so beautiful, I looked out to see the sun, which were just getting ready to rise from behind the Sea. And as I look, what do I behold, so majestic on the cliff, *ohhh*, there he be . . .

My own dear Hank come Home to me.

So, *o' course* I ran! And though my body felt so weak and weary, my spirit sure remembered running, and I was out there with him in a flash. I threw my arms around his warm neck, and I hugged him and kissed him and put my head to his. And, sure, right there in my nightgown, barefoot, I climbed up onto him, and we had ourselves a long, gentle, beautiful ride along the shores of the Calico Sea.

Yes, we even went down to the Cove . . . Not for very long. But I wanted Hank to understand. And I wanted Donovan to see that I now had my big, strong, noble friend with me.

Then, as we come a-strolling back, with Hank turning all manner of marvelous colors in celebration of our reunion, there be Connie and Bonnie waiting in the doorway, arm-in-arm, with beaming smiles and a warm, hearty breakfast ready.

I tell you, Book, I am seeing miracles glistening all through the fabric of my existence – miracles which have, until now, gone unseen on hidden threads. Oh, the body, the spirit, and all the different I's that I am shall surely still take time to recuperate and organize and harmonize, but let there be no doubt:

I may indeed be wounded, sire, but I am not dead, after all. Nossir.

Wherein the Time Has Come

Hank and I rode for three days and nights, and we crested this here hilltop a short while ago, where we came upon this idyllic round clearing surrounded by – of all things to be surrounded by – these spreading green apple trees. Hank noticed right off that these just happen to be the very variety of apple trees we happened upon that first night we got ourselves free together. And after having sampled them, he and I agree that these apples *still* remind us of the taste of freedom. And I have developed such a special partiality for round clearings throughout my travels that, I must say, I feel it to be a most auspicious portent to have come upon such a place at such a time.

Ahhh, look, there's Hank yanking yet another apple off a tree . . . Yes, whatever happens, I shall always remember this lovely, tranquil setting, with its sheltering trees and its green apples and its carpet of thick, soft grass.

Anyhow, allow me to record the most epic fact of the here and now . . . As I sit here, perched in one of these fine trees, I am beholding on the hill opposite me, none other than:

My City of Origin.
My Birthplace.
My Long Lost Past.

That's right, as we speak, I am a-sitting here, chomping on this here apple, gazing upon "The Biggest and Best City in the History of the Whole Wyde Whirld."

Now, I must point out straightaway that the place is small and sad and drab and could not be *less* deserving of its ludicrous hyperbole of a moniker. And I do not say that to be sour or curmudgeonly, but merely to state a plain, grey fact. To be plainer and greyer still, there is a tall, thick wall that encircles the Kingdom, which appears, even from here, to be coated with layers of grime. The only distinguishing feature of this grimy, grey wall is a wooden door in the middle of it. I must say, I feel an intense dislike for this door, which seems odd. It looks to be an ordinary, run-of-the-mill door – nothing more.

But odder still (and far more ominous) is the remarkable phenomenon of which my dear friends spoke. Alas, yes, there is a gigantic grey Cloud hovering over the city that stops right at the edge of the wall! Why, if this Cloud were high up in the sky and behaving like a reasonable cloud, it'd be the source of a sensational storm – that's the color grey it is. But this Cloud just . . . hangs there.

Now, the sky *outside* this immense Cloud is its usual, wide open, wild blue self, which makes it look as if the Cloud – oh, dear! – *crowns* the Kingdom. Good heavens, whatever could be going on beneath such a Cloud? Well, I will know quite soon, won't I?

Having just written that word "soon," well, I now feel stricken through with feelings of complete inferiority to the task – the very task that, at the same time, I know I were born to. And I quite reasonably assess myself to be so terribly untrained and totally untried. Well, what's to be done about it? Nothing I think, but to make note of the feelings, maybe chew 'em over with Hank some, and then enjoy the peaceful, graceful beauty of this hilltop while there is still some afternoon light left.

Because, quite simply, there is no turning back now.

You know, Book, I would customarily ask Destiny to weigh in at a moment like this, but, well . . . suffice it to say, we are no longer on speaking terms. Oh, I know it'll play whatever tricks it has up its sleeve regardless of my wishes. So, Destiny shall do what it has a mind to do, and I shall do what I have a mind to do, and we'll just have to see how it all turns out.

Book, will you look how far we've come?

I mean, here I be in this here tree, recording this wildly historic moment in the funny little life of Lillian of Everywhere, who so very long ago left the Forest of Forgetfullness in search of Home. I do wonder . . . who will she be after this?

Well, she will always be Lillian of the Cave and Lillian of the Cove, that much is certain. So, should this venture of mine prove to be the end of me, I can only hope my spirit will be canny enough to head on Home to the Cove to meet Donovan and spend eternity with him.

But what if I should come out of this enterprise alive? Will I ever again be the same Lillian of Everywhere who goes where she goes when she wants, how she wants, whichever way the wind should blow? Will I ever again be the Lillian who lies lazily under any ol' tree that'll have her, beholding the good ol' sky, sliding into a nice afternoon nap, while Hank munches on some tall grass nearby?

You know something, it almost makes me want to write a Poem. But I would be nothing but irritated with myself if I sullied this most monumental of moments by writing bad Poetry. No, when I light tonight's campfire, my only offering to the divine Spirit of Art will be my thanks for expressing itself with such transplendence all throughout this perfect pearl of a Whirld. I am ever so grateful for the privilege of having walked and breathed and lived in this three-quarter mortal coil o' mine so's I could behold it all.

So, yes, I'm going to relish this sunset. And then, when the last red-gold glimmer slips away, I shall take my Sorrow.

How I tremble as I write that, Book.
It is, after all, quite large.
And it is, after all, a *jewel* . . .

———

Book, the jaw-dropping, mind-boggling *genius* of Mad Aunt Harriet is an infinite source of wonderment to me! You see, I have just this moment freed my Sorrow from its lovely silver setting, and, in doing so, what should fall out of the setting and into my palm but a tiny, pretty piece of paper that unfolds and unfolds and unfolds and unfolds to reveal a note in Mad Aunt Harriet's wonderful handwriting!

Why, sure, I had to blink away no small amount of tears when I saw it. Here is what it says:

Greetings to you, Little Girl!
Well now, ready for our Sorrow, are we?
Read and take heed:

Your Sorrow is the rest of you returning,
so it well knows what to do.
Though in taking it, you may feel as if it's killing you,
in point of fact, the very opposite is true.
If you resist, it will break you.
If you surrender, it will make you.
So, swallow your Sorrow with some sweet, hot tea,
as a Sorrow should be swallowed just as sweetly as can be.
Now then, down the hatch, child!
Fortune favors the bold!

Well, I would wax emotional and philosophical here, Book, but the tea has steeped, the sun has set, the time is nigh ... And I don't mind telling you, I'm a big ol' ball of *scared*.

There, I've said it.
And now, well ... here goes nothin'.
Hopefully, I'll be back.

———

I am back.

It is just before dawn, and I feel as clear as the sky! Why, compared to losing Donovan, my Sorrow-Taking weren't but a sneeze. Fear is such a funny thing, ain't it, Book?

Anyhow, here's how it went . . .

I hold the Sorrow over my heart for a moment.
Then I kiss it, and I put it in my mouth.
Then I drink the whole cup of tea to wash it down.
Then I wait.
I look at Hank, who looks at me.
Then I begin to feel dizzy, so I lie down and close my eyes . . .

And then, out of the blackness, comes the sweet, soft voice of my Mother whispering that old rhyme – only this time she sounds so weak, she barely has the strength to speak. But her words resound through my whole being:

" . . . and a Girl-King for this Kingdom might be just the thing . . . "

As her voice fades away, a heavy tower bell begins to toll, so slow, so low . . . and in between each toll of the bell, *ohhh,* there come such cutting shrieks of mean, mocking laughter . . .

And then I see a boy standing across from me in a spacious hallway. Why, it's Jimmy! Yes, of course it is, with those big green eyes and that mop of wild black hair – only he is so docile and so *frightened.* And then a tall, dark shadow falls across him, and suddenly, he is *slapped hard across the face* with – what *is* that? Why, that's my hat! My hat when I were child – yes, crushed in the fist of a grown man.

And then that tall, dark shadow falls over *me.* The man hovers above me. Then he leans down, and he puts his lips right up against my ear, and I hear him whispering – though I don't recall the words, no . . . All I feel is the ghastly threat in that *nasty, needling voice!*

And then I am running and running . . .
I am somewhere else . . .

Ohhh, there is my Father, so sad and broken, sitting on the cold stone floor, up against a cold stone wall, wrapped in a blanket. But he doesn't seem to see me or care that I am standing there. And then I hear all those angry old men from my nightmares – yes, there they are, all of them glaring down at me with such rage, such loathing, as if I have done something so unspeakably evil – all of them snarling and snapping, calling me *traitor, traitor, traitor.* . .

But then, from out of the blue, comes my Father's voice, roaring through:

"LET HER GO!"

And upon hearing those three words, suddenly everything I'd forgotten about myself comes rushing back to me – rushing through me in a cascade of sights and sounds and names and faces of people I loved and people I loathed and people who were wicked and people who were wonderful. And I saw and heard and felt and knew the light, the shadow, the beauty, the heartbreak – the Everything that was my Childhood.

And then I drifted into the deepest, most restful sleep I ever did have. And I awoke knowing who I am, why I left, and why I have returned.

I am come Home.
Like it or no, welcome or no, I am come Home.

Now, Book, this may very well be my last entry ever, and if so, well, it was sure nice knowin' ya. I am so very much beholden to you for so patiently putting up with all my ponderings and wanderings and wonderings. Oh, I do not say this to be dramatic or poetical, but only purely practical. You see, one of the most essential facts I have remembered is this:

-279-

I were *banished!* And when they were doing their banishing, they told me in no uncertain terms that if I should ever dare to return, they'd kill me – *and the horse I ride in on!*

So, when I told Hank what I saw and heard upon swallowing my Sorrow, I left out that horrifying bit about the horse-killing. I could not bear to go on living if something horrible happened to Hank on account of me. I'd be a tree cut down dead, that's all there is to it. So, sure, I told Hank that my plan is to enter the Kingdom on my own at first, so as to recollect and reconnoit my way around the place as inconspicuously as possible. And even *he* had to agree that, no matter what color he turns, he is anything but inconspicuous.

Well, Book, the time has come.
Onward it is, then.

Oh, wait, one last thing: Remember when I said before that I so disliked that wooden door? Well, no wonder! *That's the very door they threw me out of.*

How do you like that?

Wherein I Claim My Throne

Book, I purely marvel at the way all of Life works out so perfectly. What a wondrous, mysterious Poem . . .

Well, here's what I did, and here's how I did it:

So, Hank and I head on up to that grimy, grey wall (which used to be such an elegant ivory color when I were a child). Then, as we ever so cautiously follow it on around, encountering no one – *ahhh*, yes, there it be, mightier and more magnificent than I could ever have hoped to see: my very first and favorite Red Rose Oak Tree!

Now, Book, I expect that all this time you have likely thought me to be plumb nutty when it comes to Red Rose Oak Trees. But now you see how this variety of tree and me have ourselves quite a substantial history. Why, sure, all throughout my wanderings I must've felt such a kinship with these trees on account of this beloved Tree that still grows, thank goodness, right here by the Kingdom wall. Oh, I'm ever so glad to see this ol' Tree again – and, my word, it has grown *so tall!*

Anyhow, I looks a-way, way up into it, and I think I can see that – *yes*, a few of its branches look to have grown directly into the foggy thickness of that Cloud. And, Book, deep in my directional bones, I get the distinct feeling that one o' them big ol' branches might just get me *exactly* to where I am desiring to go.

So, Hank and I agree that he'll wait right here until I know the coast is clear – or in case I come barreling outta the place in need of a speedy getaway. And with that, he wishes me luck, and I leaps right on up into that ol' Tree, and I climb and I climb with *such* familiarity, just as smoothly and easily as when I were a child.

And, I tell you, despite the danger that lies ahead, what with the sun on my face and the wind in my hair, I am feeling so *alive* and so *light* . . . Oh, to be climbing this mighty Tree again with full memory of who I am and from whence I hail, at last! And how them Roses glow, like rubies in the sunlight, big as wide-open hands they are! And I find I must stop for a moment to inhale deeply and fuel myself with their sweet, delicious scent. And as I continue on upward, it occurs to me that I've always slept most soundly in Red Rose Oak Trees, and that this here Tree were the primordial reason for it.

And so, at last, I've climbed high enough that I find myself face-to-face with this menacing grey Cloud . . . and, *ohhh*, I feel such a fierce *foreboding*, and I am seized by a sudden panic! But I've learned enough about Fear to know that *I must keep on moving*, that I must concentrate solely upon the task at hand, which is to choose the branch I believe is most likely to take me where I aim to go. And so I make my choice. I head on into that Cloud.

And, oh, Book, what happens next is so *insidious!*

Well, there I am – slowly, carefully feeling my way, pulling myself along the branch like a caterpillar – and this Cloud is so *dense*, why, I am unable to see anything at all in front of me. And suddenly, out of nowhere, I am overpowered by the most oppressive *exhaustion* . . . In an instant, I feel as if each and every one of my bones is made of solid lead. So heavy, *so heavy* is my head, I can barely hold it up, barely keep my eyes open . . . Why, I feel so profoundly weak and weary, I can't even remember what it is I'm supposed to be doing up here, out on a limb in mid-air, and, what's worse, I can't bring myself to care . . .

I only know that I just *must* rest my head.
I just *must* close my eyes.
And I cannot help it, I do . . .

And the moment I do, I think I hear – is it coming from way off or is it quite near? I cannot tell, but just like a bell, I hear a young girl's voice ring out, pure and clear:

"I'll be back some day, you wait and see!
I'll remember you, if you'll remember me!"

She sounds so familiar . . . Why, that's *me!*

That's right, I remember . . . When I were leaving this place so long ago, the last thing I did was to call out to this here Tree. Could it be that this Tree is now calling out to *me?* Urging me to *wake up,* to *press on!*

Well, Book, I can't say if it were the Tree or if it were just me, but right then and there, I recall my sense of mission. And I *force* my eyes open, and I raise my head, and with all my might, I *pull* and I *push* and I *push* and I *pull* myself onward, *onward* through that sinister Cloud!

And soon, I feel cold stone against my arm. And as I continue forward along the branch, I venture to reach out my hand to determine where I am. And as I move ever so slowly forward, feeling my way along the wall, I feel – *aha!* – the top of an arched window, edges of broken glass, and I know *exactly* where I am. And so, hanging onto that branch for dear life, I let my legs slip off, and I swing and I swing and I *swing* – and I land like a cat, clean onto the window seat of none other than, you guessed it:

My Heavenly Tower Room!

And I jump down into this room that has been calling and calling to me, all throughout my journeying, to come back to it some day. And *yes*, it's all here, just as I've always seen it: the fireplace, the writing desk, the armchair, the wide, soft bed. But, *ohhh*, how saddened am I to see this dear room cloaked in cobwebs, covered in dust, and so heavy with grey gloom. To say the very least, I am overcome in so many ways.

You see, Book, this Tower Room were my most cherished place in all the Kingdom, as it used to be my Mother's private room and *her* most cherished place, a-way up here in the highest tower of the Empress-Queen's Wing. After she died, the whole wing were locked and boarded up. But once I were old enough to learn that this wing of the Palace had been hers – well, you know me, Book – I just squoze my way in through a side window, explored and wandered through all the halls, and then I came upon that steep, spiraling staircase that led me right up into this warm, welcoming room.

And I tell you, from the moment I walked through that big oak door, I felt this here room to be my very own sanctuary. Why, this is where I first found my Mother's Music Box, under the armchair, right over there.

Ahhh, how nice it is to sit in this old window seat again . . . Yes, this is where I used to sit and watch every sunset I could watch, and gaze out at my favorite view of anything anywhere:

That Great Big Beautiful Whole Wyde Whirld out there.
Oh, how I dreamed of traveling through it, everywhere.

And now I can glimpse through the battlements, now that I am beneath that dreadful Cloud, the glorious green and the wild blue off in the distance. I lean out and look a-way down to the ground, where my dear friend the Gardener secretly taught me to read and to reason and to rhyme, as together we tended that beautiful garden. But now, as I look out these windows, I see that the ground all around is just . . . dust.

(And, no, Book, I wasn't too worried about being spotted as I looked out those windows. As a climber of trees, it has been my experience that almost nobody ever looks up.)

Then (I don't know why exactly, perhaps to consecrate my endeavor), I draw forth my Music Box. And without even switching the switch, what should come forth but the old song. And to be sure, it steadies me some. And as I sing it, it sounds so very like a prayer, so sweet and sad and spare, and the music and my singing ever so gently stir the air . . .

But then, I think I hear something!
I hush . . . I listen . . .

From far off at first, yes, from the farthest end of the Empress-Queen's Wing, I hear . . . well, it sounds like *a flock of screaming women* – yes, like a horde of females screaming in fury! And this cyclone of screams is coming closer and *closer* and, *ohhh*, it is *blood-curdling* as it comes hurdling up the stairs . . .

And then these deafening, shrieking voices *blast* open that big oak door, slamming it hard against the wall, and they come screaming into the room, rushing and screeching round and round me in a cacophonous *whirlwind!* Why, I thought they'd nigh on split my doggone head open with all that racket!

Now, Book, I must note: Although these squalling voices were certainly jangling my nerves a-plenty, I have encountered quite a few invisible spirits in my travels throughout the Whirld, and, by and large, I have found that although they generally have a grudge against *somebody*, it has never once been against me. I have also found that there is generally good reason for the overly cantankerous behavior of such-like upset spirits. So I don't take it personally that these phantoms are obviously aiming to terrify me with all their noise and their ridiculous theatrics of busting open the door like that. (As if any spirit ever needed a *door* to get into a room.)

What I *am* a-fearing, however, is that the shattering volume and piercing, potent pitch of their screams will endanger my much-beloved hearing, thank you very much. So, finally, in the midst of all their carrying on, I yell:

"ALRIGHT ALREADY!
YOU'RE EXTREMELY LOUD AND FRIGHTENING!
YOU'VE MADE YOUR POINT!"

Well, *that* prompts a mighty fine chorus of gasps, I can tell you. And now they are all whispering and whispering, whooshing by me in a tizzy.

"Who is she? Who is she? Just who does she think she is?"

Well, I am a breath away from introducing myself, Book, but I halt my tongue. It comes to me that: A) considering I have come to try to take back the Kingdom, and B) considering the circumstances of my leave-taking of the Kingdom, this may very well be the first time I encounter upset spirits who *do* have a grudge against me personally. So I takes it slow, and I say to them gently, from my very heart:

"O Invisible Lady Spirits, I'm ever so sorry if I've disturbed the peace hereabouts. But, you see, this most wonderful room was so dearly cherished by my Mother . . . "

Well, at the very mention of the word "Mother," them formerly furious spirits begin to appear in the air, one after the other, more and more *there*. And they all have wide, black eyes and long, shredded hair!

And I go on, "You see, my Mother gave birth to me, and then she died, and I grew up without knowing her. So I took my refuge in this room, where I felt that she were always hovering about, to soothe me and cheer me, as I missed her so very much . . . "

And now there is much sniffling all around me, and all them spirits' wide, black eyes are sparkling with tears.

"She died of a broken heart, on account of my Father turning his back on her. He despised my Mother – and me too, because I were a girl."

And they explode into such anguished *howling*, such a frenzied agony of rage, why, it is as if I'd thrown a red hot spear into their collective belly! Once again they are rushing and *whooshing* all around me and, oh, yes, their outraged screaming is harrowing in the extreme. But I can feel, Book, that this fury is not aimed at me at all, but at my Father – and, most likely, at *their* father.

Yes . . . it is beginning to dawn on me just who these tormented spirits might very well be.

After a few moments, they calm and slow and settle some, and by twos and threes and ones, their voices now soft and whispering, they braid their sad facts together in a mournful fugue:

> *"We were born, we were born,*
> *but we never got to be, not to be, never to be,*
> *we were smothered, smothered,*
> *we were never, ever mothered,*
> *we went unnamed, unknown, we were buried all alone*
> *in the ruins, in the ruins of the Empress-Queen's Wing . . . "*

So, it's true! These tormented creatures are the spirits of those poor murdered infants. Yes, there are thirteen of them, to be exact – *thirteen!*

> *"They call us the Furies, yes, we are the Furies!*
> *Our screams of fury scare everyone away . . .*
> *Far, far away . . . "*

And one of them floats by, sniffling:

> *"But we so dearly want our mother to come visit us some day."*

I ask softly, "Does she live?"

And they moan, and they groan:

> *"Ohhh, her body lives, but her spirit, ohhh, her spirit is dead.*
> *She's a slave to that beast! She will never be released!*
> *Our poor mother, poor Raynna Ravinnia . . . "*

"What a beautiful name," says I. "My Mother's name was Lilliana."

> *"Ooooh, pretty . . . That's very pretty too!"*

And then they all suddenly stop stock still in the air, and one of them fixes me with a piercing stare:

> *"Wait, then – just who are you?"*

"Why, I'm Lillian. How d'you do!"

They all gasp:

> *"But Lillian is dead!"*

Funny, eh, Book?

"I beg to differ, ladies. Consider the evidence!"

And, oh, then there comes another terrible tale they tell by ones and threes and twos:

> *"Oooooh, there's a story about you,*
> *but the People must not tell it, must not know it, must not think it,*
> *but still we hear it, yes, we do,*
> *when they dare to come and whisper here, which most mostly never do,*
> *we hear them sadly say,*
> *their dear little Lillian was thrown out, thrown away, just like us,*
> *dead and buried, dead and buried,*
> *just like they will be, if they even speak your name!"*

"No, that can't be so . . . "

But they weren't through.

> "Oh, yes, the subject of you is taboo!
> No, don't say Lillian whatever you do,
> or you'll be dead and buried too!"

Then a single Fury zips right up into my face and says:

> "And you were singing! You must not sing!"

Three more of them sweep in.

> "It's against the law!"

Then all the rest rush forward in a flurry of furious worry.

> "You must not sing or dance or read or write!
> Or pray to a candle in the dark of the night!
> And laughing is forbidden too . . .
> You must never laugh, whatever you do!"

Oh, the unthinkable evil of it all . . . The horrors going on inside this Kingdom wall!

"Now then, listen here, my fine Furies . . . "

And at this tiny endearment, they smile. And though it touches me deeply to see a flash of happiness cross their tormented faces, I have a most significant truth to declare – a truth that needs a speaking out, loud and clear into the air:

"I am the firstborn child of the Emperor-King and the rightful heir to this Kingdom, and I have returned to put things right."

At that, the Furies all turn to confer with each other, stunned, their big black eyes blinking.

"But how does she dare?
How does she dare to declare such a thing?"

And then, suddenly, they gasp and turn to me in alarm.

"Our mother's hateful husband
claims the Kingdom, claims the throne,
officially, forever, for his very, very own!"

"What! Where? When?"

"Now! Now! His coronation is today!
They're all there, in the town square . . .
The crown will soon be his! Yes, the deed will soon be done!"

And I say, "Thank you kindly, ladies. Now I really have to run!"

And do I ever run! I go a-tearing out that door, flying down into
the deep, dank darkness of those steep, spiraling stairs, aiming
to take the well-remembered labyrinth of doors through here
and doors through there. But, oh, so many of the doors and the
heres-and-theres are there no more, as so much of the wing lies
in rotting, blackened ruin.

"Ah, that's right," thinks I, "from the fire . . . "

And there I am, racing through the remains of the Empress-
Queen's Wing, with them thirteen Furies panicking, swirling,
rushing after me, yowling, howling, warning me not to go! But
I do not slow my pace for even a moment, and I fast leave the ruins
and the Furies far behind.

And, *ohhh*, as I am tearing through those colorless, cadaverous
streets, what meets my eyes further fuels me for a fight. Why,
there's been such a ghastly, ghostly *greying* of everything in sight.
There's not a single trace of green or purple or red or yellow or
blue or even white! Why, I feel downright *criminal* because my

clothes are so colorful and bright! Still, there's absolutely no one anywhere in sight.

Then, I near the square . . .
I sneak a peek around the corner.
I see the silent crowd packed in tight.
I also see the beginnings of the goings-on beginning to go on.

So I slink back into the shadows, and I twirl my Cape – turning the entirety of my Traveling Costume into the dingiest, dullest grey, so that I'll blend in with everything, in every which depressing way. Then I pull down the brim of my now dull grey hat to shadow my face, and I slips into the square, into the back of the crowd.

The first thing I notice is the awful, stone cold quiet. Why, when I were a child, gatherings here used to be so boisterous and happy, but the People are now so silent and sad. The change in their demeanor so distresses and appalls me, but I force myself to calm and to concentrate.

I steal a glance around the square. I see armored guards stationed everywhere. And, oh, there it be:

That still majestic stage!

As I stand there and behold it, how vividly I am remembering that last, fateful spectacle I saw take place upon it.

Thinks I to myself, "Oh, how the shameful past has planted the seeds of the shameless present . . . "

Ahhh, there they are! Just look at them up there: the Chancellors. Yes, the very same greedy, grasping group of parasitic politicians as ever they were, whispering here, smirking there, patting each other's backs. The scavenging hacks. How very fat they've grown. How they smile so smugly, as if everything is going so smoothly and so well, at so long last, aren't we just so *wonderful.*

"So, it's all coming off without a hitch, is it?" thinks I. "So pleased with ourselves, are we? *Well*, we shall see, boys, we shall see..."

Just then, a stray memory flies back to me. Why, I know *exactly* where I need to be! So I scan the back of the square to see if the merchant wagons still line themselves up there and – *aha*, there it be! – what used to be a favorite perch of mine: the roof of Quincy's Apples & Oranges Wagon.

"*That's* the ticket," thinks I.

And I edges my way through the back of the crowd – *oooh*, slip-slidey like quicksilver am I – and I keeps my eyes averted so as not to catch the eye of anyone I know. Which is all too disheart-eningly easy, Book, as everyone is looking at the ground.

And as I approach the Apples & Oranges Wagon, I see, with great relief, that good ol' Quincy is, as ever, nowhere to be found. No, there is only an old mule who pulls the wagon, standing ever so still and patient, and who so reminds me of Millie, who used to pull this same wagon long ago. I pat the mule on the neck as I pass, and sadly note that even *she* seems thoroughly exhausted and defeated.

Then, moving ever so slowly so as not attract notice, I climb up onto the wagon roof. And when I arrive there, I crouch down low behind the Apples & Oranges sign, and I peeks up over the top of it in order to case the place. And from that vantage point, I observe that the guards seem to be rather lackadaisical – apathetic even. Yes, that one is eating, those two are snoozing, those three are playing cards.

Then my eyes are drawn to a pocket of frenzied activity near the stage, and I notice, from this new height, a fenced-in area that didn't used to be there – a sort of a pen, in fact – in which I see what must surely be: *Hoppers*. My, what a strange, unsettling sight they are, all smashed together in a pack like that, madly scritch-scratching with their quills, each one jumping up now and again to see above the crowd. Why, they put me in mind of a bevy of bugs! And who do you think I should rightaway recognize in that unsavory bunch? Why, that smirking, snickering, horrible Hopper who so disconcerted me the day of my Horse Thief trial, all that long while ago. And, Book, the moment I lay eyes on him, I see the whole ugly picture.

"Of course . . . " thinks I. "You were the one who told the Weaver that I was still alive! And *that's* why he sent those three men after me . . . "

And, look, there he be: the Head Lord High Chancellor, the pompous windbag, waddling to the front of the stage. He surveys the crowd with that big, fake, fatherly smile of his, then proceeds to start the show:

"Greetings, friends! Welcome! I'd like to thank you all so very much for coming to show your support today!"

What unmitigated tripe! It is so obvious that it were compulsory to attend this sham ceremony. Why, there isn't a single smile to be found amongst this cowed crowd.

"What a beautiful day it is for such a grand, historic event, eh?"

He applauds and, as if on cue, the People instantly applaud with him. It is chilling to witness – it's as if he's got them trained.

Meanwhile, all those other phonies onstage stand gazing up at that awful grey Cloud, admiring it as if it is a clear blue sky.

"At last, the moment has arrived! I am so excited, so honored, so – well, so *moved* to have this privilege. I truly am. May I present to you a man of utmost integrity, this most devoted leader who has cared for all of us so tenderly, given of himself so generously, protected us so paternally – well, I could go on for *far* too long. So, with no further ado, I give you: our Savior, our Friend Forever, our Most Esteemed and Heroic Highness, our Dearly Beloved Emperor-Regent Master Weaver!"

And with far more enthusiasm, he applauds again, and again the crowd follows suit. And then the perfidious idiot tacks on an afterthought:

"Oh, yes! And, lest we forget, our adorable little Duchess Raynna Ravinnia!"

Then the Head Chancellor cues a drum roll, which is followed by an off-key, sour little fanfare. He indicates that still louder applause is required. Still louder applause is delivered.

The curtain at the back of the stage parts:
And there stands the murdering fiend himself.
Cloaked in the royal ermine.

My gut clenches into a fist.

"The Weaver . . . " thinks I. "*Ahhh, yes,* however could I have forgotten *you.*"

With such a self-satisfied smile, the Weaver strolls forward, then stops center stage, all the better to soak in his completely coerced ovation. Then, in quite a leisurely fashion, he strolls to the foot of the stage – oh, yes, very much as if he owns the place. He looks out at all the People, then he spreads his arms wide, as if to send us all a great big odious *hug*. Then he raises that grasping claw of a hand and hushes the crowd.

"Thank you for that warm reception, my dear People! How nice to see all your smiling faces on this *very* special day, which marks a brand new beginning for us all, eh?"

Ughhh, that *voice* of his . . . How it made my skin crawl then. And how it still does.

The Head Chancellor applauds.
The People follow suit.
The Weaver continues:

"Now, you all know my story. I came to this Kingdom long ago, having had the premonition of a great future here. How lucky I have been to be embraced by all of you, and to have been able to be of service to our poor, dear, soon-to-be-former ruler."

My Father . . . I wonder what they've done with him . . .

"Oh, yes, I am so deeply grateful to have been befriended by all these noble, intelligent, *honorable* gentlemen that stand beside me now. I'd like to take this opportunity to tell you, my wise friends, how touched I am by your loyalty and your devotion. How I cherish your love."

And the Chancellors blush and smile and elbow each other.

And, *ohhh*, it is sheer agony to keep silent! But I calm, and I concentrate, and I watch, and I wait . . . Oh, yes, I were quite long enough in the Theatrical Profession to know that *Timing Is Everything.*

The Weaver then motions for the little raven-haired Duchess to step forward. And, oh, it is all too tragically clear from her hollow, anguished eyes that – just as her ghostly daughters said – Raynna Ravinnia's spirit is well and truly dead. As if in a trance, the little Duchess moves to join that repulsive old husband of hers, and I note with horror that she is once again heavy with child.

"As you can see, my good People, my little Empress-Queen-to-be is bound and determined to give me my heir!"

The Head Chancellor cues the People to applaud. And the Weaver turns upstage and casually seats himself on the throne. And all the Chancellors dress around him, as if they are posing for some pathetic portrait. Then one of them steps forward, beaming as he carries the coronation pillow, upon which sits the Crown.

And then, with a sudden solemnity, the Head Chancellor steps forward, brandishing a royal scroll. He breaks the seal, unfurls the parchment, and commences to announce:

"Hear ye, hear ye! The Abdication Proclamation!"

Abdication? *What?*
But I mustn't be distracted . . .
I feel the moment fast approaching.

"I, the Emperor-King George the Twenty-Second, being no longer of sound mind and body, have come at last to the unfortunate understanding that I am no longer fit to rule our Kingdom. Thus, I pass on, with such confidence, such gratitude, such pure, unbridled pride, the Ruling Crown of the Emperor-King and All Powers Thereof to – "

"THE ONE AND ONLY RIGHTFUL HEIR!
AND THAT HAPPENS TO BE ME!
GREETINGS, SCOUNDRELS, LONG TIME NO SEE!"

And as every face in the place turns to stare at just who would so foolhardily dare to speak such daring words, I twirls my Cape so theatrically, with such a *sweep* – and I turn my dull grey self back into the criminally colorful Lillian of Everywhere, with her feet planted firm, with her hands on her hips, with the clarion ring of her declaration still echoing through the air!

Well, the whole place is now a still life painting, o' course. Why, nobody can even begin to believe what they're seeing!

So, sure, I takes full advantage of their stupendous stupefaction, and I declare:

"THAT'S RIGHT, BOYS,
THAT'S MY THRONE AND THAT'S MY CROWN!
NEVER THOUGHT YOU'D SEE ME AGAIN, EH, WEAVER?
YOU MURDEROUS, LARCENOUS LIAR!"

Oh, the looks on their faces – why, sure, it's as if they've seen a ghost! And they shout:

"Stop her, damn you!" "Seize her!" "Take her away!"

And a whispering, like a wild, fresh wind, goes rushing through the crowd:

"It's her!" "Aye, it's she!" "It's true!" "But how can it be?"

"HELLO, MY FRIENDS! IT'S LILLIAN . . . IT'S ME!"

And I seek out and recognize old familiar faces. That looks like Walter! Could that be Carlotta? They're all staring up at me so helplessly and, well, I know not what else to do, do I? So I just start firing my monumental rage at all those vile scoundrels on that stage!

And as I do, I see them armored guards come clattering down from the walls – with a good deal of difficulty, it appears, as they have been caught entirely, well, off-guard.

But, alas, sluggish and slow though they be, a few of them are closing in on me, and – *ohhh, no* – one of them guards reaches out and grabs the mule's harness, and I hear such a honking, angry *bray*, and the wagon jolts and, why, that magnificent mule just *bolts!* That's right, she tears off at breakneck speed, and the sea of People parts for her as we go tearing around the square! And I grabs onto that Apples & Oranges sign, and I finds myself a wide, sturdy stance upon this racing wagon, and, why, I become a *fire-breathing dragon* – that's right, I ROAR!

And then, *ahhh,* there comes a sight I shall delight in evermore . . .

See, all these armored guards are gathering, gathering by the score, huffing and puffing and panting as they come lumbering after us. Then one big lummox catches up to us, and with a triumphant *"HAH!"* he grabs hold of that wagon's back door, and the sheer dumb weight of him *yanks* that old door right off its hinges, and – *ohhh, yes!* – all them apples and oranges go rolling out into the square! Why, there are apples and oranges, oranges and apples rolling everywhere!

And then, *well* . . . first *one* guard slips and slides and crashes, then *another* guard slips and slides and crashes, then *another* guard slips and slides and trips and smashes smack on top of the ones before – and then comes more and more and *more!* Oh, it is the most heavenly feast of trippings and slippings and tumblings and stumblings and crashings and smashings – why, it were marvelous beyond measure, that's what it was!

Now, Book, I ask you, what else could I do at such a moment but *laugh?* I tell you, it is a guffaw the likes of which I've never heard come out of me before. And I notice that some of the People cannot help but to start laughing with me, and I am so heartened!

But then, in the space of an instant, their faces freeze with fear, their hands fly up to cover their mouths, and their heads bow still lower than before. And I am so *sickened* to see that the People are, indeed, too terrified to laugh.

Well, the mule stops running, and I stop laughing, and I look around at all the People, and I say:

> *"MY FRIENDS, LISTEN TO ME . . .*
> *AS YOUR RIGHTFUL EMPEROR-KING,*
> *I TELL YOU IT IS NO CRIME*
> *TO LAUGH OR SING OR REASON OR RHYME!*
> *FOR LOVE OF THIS KINGDOM, I HEREBY DECREE,*
> *NOW AND FOREVER, YOU ARE FREE!"*

Then I feel the wagon tipping sideways, and the guards grab hold of me.

And as they proceed to haul me away, the Weaver shouts:

"Stop! I want this *traitor* to see who rules the roost now!"

And he takes the Crown off the pillow and jams it onto his head like a spiteful brat.

"See? *I'm* the Emperor-King now! And that, traitor, is *that!*"

And with that,
and with no small amount of rough handling,
here I now be,
in this cold, dark jail cell,
writing the end of my life history.

I should say right off that it has been announced that I am to be hanged tomorrow in the town square, right after breakfast. But all is well with me, Book. I had no army. I did what I could do. 'Twas my duty to do my best. I only hope I've planted a seed that'll grow to do the rest.

Now, I must tell you that Bill – a beloved old friend who was the Kingdom Gatekeeper when I were a child – is now the Jailer here. Bill brought me this candle and something to eat. I feel so bad, because each time he comes to the cell to see if I need anything, he is weeping. He is so very happy to see me alive, and so very sad to see me die.

"Both things are coming so close upon each other, Lil . . . It is altogether too much to bear."

I tell him it's alright. And it is.
I have met up with Destiny, at last.
I can feel it. And I am at peace tonight.

And, Book, who should be in the cell next to me?
Why, none other than my Father!

I can see him through the bars. As before, he does not see me –
though this time not by royal decree, but because, just as Jimmy
said, my Father is quite mad. I have been gazing over at him now
and again as I write. It seems he lives in happy dreams, which
is something of a comfort.

Yes . . . I am now recalling those few times we looked into each
other's eyes that long ago day when I were banished. I noticed,
even then, such a surprising sweetness deep down inside him.
And somehow that sweetness permeates his presence even here,
in this dreariest of all possible places. And, well, it brings me an
even deeper measure of peace tonight.

And, oh, so very noteworthy, Book, is the astonishing *wonder* of
his hair! Yes, his hair and beard have most miraculously, most
magnificently, and most *helpfully* grown all the way down to the
ground – for it seems that he *still* hasn't put on a stitch of clothing!
But his floor-length tresses are such a shining silvery-white that,
even in this very dim light, why, he glows like the moon.

I am so very moved to see that Bill has cared for my Father so
devotedly all this time, in these most spare of circumstances.
Yessir, I could always count on Bill. And tonight that is a profoundly soothing thing to know.

Now, Book, in the morning I will leave you with Bill. I have asked
him to keep you safe.

I have also asked him to wait until I am gone and then to please
go out to where Hank waits and tell him what has happened to
me. I do so hate that Hank should have to hear such sad news,
and I do so hate giving Bill such a sad task, but I feel sure that
they will be a comfort to each other.

Yes, my childhood friendship with Bill came back so easily that I naturally ended up telling him the story of how Hank and I met, and how he were a captured Wonderhorse and such. Yes, just the way I used to tell Bill all my little adventures back when I were a small child.

Book . . . my Father has come to the bars and is staring at me!

I must go!

My Coronation

No, in this moment, my Father is not wandering in any dreamy reverie. He is *seeing* me, yes, in the here and now.

I stand slowly. I move to him slowly. It feels to be a holy moment, that it does. And as I come closer, I smile as I note that I am just as tall compared to him now as he were tall compared to me then.

He is staring and staring at me. He blinks.

"Lilliana?" says he, at last. "Have I died?"

I am a-feared to say that I am not my Mother, and still more a-feared to call him Father, so I say:

"You live, Your Majesty. And glad I am of it, indeed."

At this, he smiles a little. Then he looks at his hands, and then at me.

"But am I here again?" he asks. "Am I back?"

Aye, he *is* mad, Book.

"We are both here again," I answer. "We are both back."

And then we smile at each other for no reason I can explain. And he reaches through the bars and tenderly touches my hair, ever so lightly running his fingers down the length of it.

And then his eyes light up.

"*Ohhh*, I know who *you* are . . . of course, I do!" says he, with such a charming laugh.

"Alright then, who am I?" says I, laughing easily along with him.

Ah, yes, this waterfall of silver hair is now my dear conspirator. And he whispers with such delight, his eyes twinkling:

"You are my one and only child. You are my heir. You are Lillian."

Book, I am wonderstruck. He *knows* me. He is crystal clear!

"Why, yes!" say I. "That is exactly who I am!"

And then we have ourselves such a hearty laugh, as if we have both just understood the most wonderful joke. Then, says he, merrily:

"So, where have you been?"

As if I had just left yesterday or this morning. I breathe . . . then I steady myself to say:

"Well . . . Father . . . "

In the whole of my life, this is the very first time I speak that word to the very man himself. Yes, in this dreary place, at the end of the Whirld, we are family, at last.

"I have been a-journeying here and there and everywhere," says I, "and I am finally come Home."

And then I see that he is suddenly remembering something of our dark past. His face slides into such melancholy and his spirit into such remorse.

"They told me you were dead."

I smile at him softly.

"No, Father. It just took me a very long time to find my way back."

And his chin trembles, and his eyes gleam with tears.

"I'm so . . . awfully sorry, sweetheart."

He reaches out to me through the bars. And I take hold of his hands, surprised by how warm and strong they feel.

"Oh, Father, I must tell you, I've had the most marvelous life. Truly I have."

And he raises his thick, silver eyebrows in wonder. And I nod, assuring him of the absolute fact of it.

Then he says, his voice now stronger:

"Kneel, Daughter."

And I do. And he reaches further through the bars and places his hand upon my head. Then I feel his hand shift a bit.

"Hmph. Is this *my* hand on your head, or someone else's?"

"It is your hand, Father."

"Oh, good," says he.

And then comes His Majesty's voice, so clear:

"I, George the Twenty-Second, pass on the Ruling Crown, the Title of Emperor-King, and All Powers Thereof to my rightful heir, Lillian the First. *Arise*, King Lillian."

And I do. And when I do, he smiles at me proudly and says:

"Yes, daughter . . . you will make a wonderful King, indeed."

And at that I dissolve, and the tears flow, as I know what I know.

"Oh, Your Majesty, it has been decreed that I am to die tomorrow."

My Father wipes my tears and pats my cheek and says:

"No, no, now, you mustn't worry . . . that won't do at all! There's a good girl, don't cry, no . . . Why, it's the *loveliest* lake, surrounded by daffodils. I used to swim there when I was just a boy. Why, you could see clear down to the bottom . . . "

And it's apparent that, yes, he's gone away again. So I say:

"Your Majesty? Perhaps you'd like to rest a while."

"Did I leave again?" says he. "Am I still here?"

"You're still here, Father. Why don't you lie down now and have a nice nap."

With that, he turns and walks over to his little cot, lies down, and goes straight to sleep. I have watched him for a long stretch now. So soundly does he slumber . . . Yes, listening to the rise and fall of his breathing brings me such solace tonight.

Oh, he did wake once, that's right . . . He sat up and asked the darkness:

"Am I on tour?"

"Why, yes," says I, "and you're having the most *wonderful* time!"

And back he went to sleep, leaving me smiling.

Oh, Destiny . . . how eloquent of you to have given me the glory of my Father at this, the very last.

Life is so very beautiful. I am ever so glad to have lived it.

My goodness, Book, suddenly I feel so tired.
I'll just close my eyes and rest for a bit.
I still have so much more to say.

How It All Ends

Oh, no, I've slept too long – the guards are already here! Why, there's Joe, a Palace guard I once knew so well. I am yanked to my feet, pulled from my cell. There sits my Father on his cot, staring after me. I call out to him:

"Goodbye, Father!"

They grab my hair, shove a balled-up rag into my mouth, tie a rough cloth around my head to secure it. They tie my wrists *so tightly* behind my back, and then – *oh, no!* – they pull a sack over my head! I can't see – I can't breathe! I am pulled, pushed, dragged along, up a flight of stairs, across a landing, then up more stairs, doors opening and closing, then down a hallway – where *am* I? I hear Joe whisper:

"I'm right behind you."

And then I am pushed out into open air. I am on cobblestone. Yes, I am in the square. I can feel the crowd – so deadly still and silent they are. A guard shoves me forward, and I hear a mocking voice nearby:

"I told you death'd catch up with you one day . . . didn't I, duckie!"

Ughhh, it's that loathsome Hopper! I stumble and nearly fall on my face, but then I'm jerked back up onto my feet, dragged up more steps, then pulled, pushed, turned – and then I am left to stand on my own. I am reeling. I am feeling so cold, so cold, I can't stop shivering . . . There is some movement behind me, a few steps away, and I hear Joe say:

"Here. Give that to me."

And, *ohhh* . . . my old friend is putting the noose around my neck. Well, better him than them. Yes, ever so much better. I am so cold, and when he comes close, he feels like the sun. As he's adjusting the noose and the sack around my head, he whispers in my ear:

"You are loved, Majesty."

I must not cry! *Do not cry, Lillian,* or you will not be able to breathe and you will faint, and you will not make a good death! *I must make a good death.* That's all that's left. Stand tall, Lillian. Tremble if you must, but *stand tall.* The People are watching, children are watching – they will remember.

"At the beginning of this great new day for our Kingdom . . ."

Ah, yes, there's the Weaver, starting the show. Take in some air, breathe deep, breathe slow.

" . . . let me tell you a truth. It's an ugly truth that I have known for a very long time, and the time has come for all of you to know it too. This woman is absolutely no blood relation to the Emperor-King George!"

It matters not – it matters *not at all* what he says. *Stand tall.*

"Oh, yes, the disgusting fact is that her mother was such a shameful tramp, she would lay with any man who would have her. And rather than admit to her treason, she took her own life when she gave birth to a child who was so *obviously* not fathered by the King!"

Oh, Father, I wonder if you'll remember me . . .

"What's the matter, traitor? Nothing to say today? I didn't think so. And why does she say nothing in her own defense? Because there is no defense against the *truth!*"

And what would you know of truth, you depraved wretch! Would that Judge Augustus T. Abernathy were here – he'd make mincemeat of you.

"And, yes, of course, just like her mother, she is treachery itself! Why, it was not until we pulled that dagger from her murderous little claw that her Father fully understood the betrayal of which she was capable!"

What! What ridiculous tale are you weaving now?

"By his mercy, she was not executed, but only banished. And now, like a foul plague, *she has returned*. And *still* she stops at nothing in her mad desire to seize the throne! Well, I say this is treason of the *vilest* sort, and you may be sure I will deal with it as such. I hereby sentence this traitorous witch to be hung by the neck until dead!"

There it is, then. Oh, Donovan . . . I will see you soon, my Beloved.

"So let us all rejoice in this historic moment, as we vanquish and crush this venomous evil – now and forever!"

"Now and forever!"

Ah, that would be the Chancellors, parroting and applauding. But something is odd. The applause sounds so *thin*. Why . . . it sounds like no one else is joining in?

"So," the Head Chancellor prompts the People once again, "let us rejoice in the vanquishing of this evil from our midst!"

Again his cronies applaud, trying to rouse the People:

"Huzzah!" "Hurrah!" "Hip-hip-hooray . . . "

But it seems their farce won't play today. Why, there is such a Silence coming from the crowd, a Silence so defiant and so *loud*.

Can it be? It seems that they are refusing to cheer my death!

Oh, what a gift is that brave, silent "No." I can bear what I must bear now, that I can. Yes, and I must make them see that their protest has emboldened me. *Stand strong, Lillian, stand tall.*

And the Weaver says, "Let's get this over with. Goodbye, traitor."

The time has come, indeed . . .
Goodbye, Life!

And the Chancellor says, *"PROCEED!"*

I hear the heavy lever creak.
Oh, Death, please take me fast!

The floor falls away and I drop! I choke, I *choke* . . .
Blackness, such *pressure – ohhh*, my head will pop!

Spots of light, flashes of color . . .
"Goodbye, Little Girl!" Mad Aunt Harriet?
Galloping hooves, galloping, galloping . . .
"Why, hello, there, Miss Horse Thief!"
"We are impressed by you, Lillian of Everywhere."
Floating, floating up the green hillside . . .
The Peacocks! All those eyes beaming Light!

Ohhh, there you are, my Beloved . . .
Your Eyes so blue, they shine clear through me!
Endless blue skies . . .
How I fly!

But what? I'm falling – I hit the ground!
I'm gasping, coughing, gulping air – there's *air?*

Am I alive? I must still be *alive!*

I'm in someone's arms.

The sack is pulled off my head – why, it's Bill!

"You're alright, we've got you, Lil!"

The ropes around my wrists are cut, and I hear:

"Majesty! We must *hurry!*"

It's Joe! And as he pulls the cloth off my head and Bill takes the rag from my mouth, I look a-way up above me to see, perched all the way up on the very tip-top of the gallows, waving down at me – can it be?

Says I, "Is that . . . ?"

"A friend of yours, come back to do you right!" says Joe.

Why, 'tis none other than Jimmy the Dodger, sitting on top of the gibbet, holding up the severed rope, smiling his fool head off, while the guards are pointlessly trying and failing to grab him. And wouldn't you know, that daredevil of a lad is saluting me with my very own Pocketknife!

"Can ye run, Majesty?" says Joe. "We must get to the south door – *that* way!"

And of course I recall exactly which way that door is, as it is the infamous door they threw me out of. And to think it could now be the door to my liberation – *ha!* Well, sure, I jumps up with much new wind in my sails, and Bill and I tear off after Joe, who is expertly bashing one oncoming guard after another out of our path.

And then, above us, loud and clear, we hear Jimmy calling out from his high perch in a mighty impressive Stage Voice:

"HEY, WEAVER – SCUM OF THE WHIRLD! REMEMBER ME?"

Oh, he is fearless! And it is so exhilarating to listen to him as we make this mad dash for our lives! But then – *oh, no!* – here comes a rushing river of guards. There is naught to do but turn and run in the other direction, while Jimmy holds forth from up above:

"AS A YOUNG LAD, I WAS APPRENTICED TO THIS MISERABLE, ROTTEN CROOK, AND I HELPED HIM ROB THIS KINGDOM!"

Oh, no, from the other direction, here comes *another* rushing river of guards! Oh, we are done for . . .

"I WAS HIS KICKED DOG AND HIS SLAVE – AS ARE ALL O' YOU! AND IN YOUR HEARTS, YA KNOW IT!"

Joe presses the handle of his dagger into my hand, then shields me from the front, brandishing his broadsword, while Bill shields me from the back, brandishing his axe. And we three are now one canny creature, circling, circling, surrounded by a sea of spears and swords and chains. And as this sea of guards closes in, as they raise their weapons high, why, I hear a strange, bellowing *ROAR!* A sound I've never heard before . . .

And right then and there, out of pure thin air, appears a fearsome Wonderhorse, rearing up in a mighty rage – yes, *roaring* in a vivid blaze of fiery color! Good ol' Hank . . . he sure knows how to make an entrance!

Well, o' course, that sea of guards instantly rolls back, so stunned are they by this shocking counterattack.

Shouts Bill, "Met this friend o' yours outside!"

Shouts Joe, "Ride, Majesty, *RIDE!*"

And in a flash, I am upon Hank's back. He tells me to hang on tight, whereupon he rears up and rears up again, sending out brilliant, near-blinding rays of color – and in that one triumphant moment, it feels as if I too am made entirely of dazzling light!

But then – *oh, no!* – I turn to see the guards overpowering Bill and Joe. And as I turn back they are throwing thick, heavy chains around Hank's neck, pulling him *so roughly* to the ground . . .

I am yanked off him, I am grabbed by the hair, I am forced to my knees, and I am dimly aware of the Weaver laughing, but I no longer care, for all is lost . . . Bill and Joe don't have a prayer. And there be Hank in chains again. And it's all because of me. And it's more than I can bear. And a tidal wave of black despair rises up and drags me under, and there is no light *anywhere*. And there on my knees in the square, the one dull thought I'm thinking is:

"Just . . . get it over with."

When, just then, there comes a *sound* . . .
an ominous, *spine-chilling* sound,
resounding through the air above us,
rumbling through the ground.
And it crescendos and it grows, and, finally, it explodes
in an ear-splitting *THUNDERCRACK!*

And then, *oooh*, it is so eerily *silent* . . .
Every soul in the square stands petrified, listening, waiting . . .

And then, from far off at first, I hear a wailing, whistling wind.
Is it some kind of storm?
Wait – that's no storm!
That there is a screaming swarm of Ferocious Female Spirits!

Why, them Thirteen Furies are *ten times* the size I saw them last! They come screaming and soaring through the air, shrieking and swooping down into the square – yes, it seems they are dead set on scaring the living daylights out of all them guards, who are now madly dashing for *their* lives! And as we free Hank from those horrible chains, I tell Bill and Joe:

"Have no fear, fellas, it's fine! Them there ladies are friends of mine! Gimme a boost back up there, will ya?"

And so Bill and Joe lift me right back up through that open square of air through which I formerly fell to my death mere moments ago. And just who do you think should have somersaulted so deftly down off that high gibbet and onto the platform to lend me a helping hand but a certain daredevil of a lad, who flashes that smile at me and says:

"Now, aren't ya glad I stole your knife?"

And I laugh and hug that gallant thief with all my might.

And standing up there in the open air, we turn to behold those Thirteen Furies diving and screeching all over the square. And I am so moved, and I feel so proud that such magnificent, mighty creatures have come to my defense. Oh, the rampaging *glory* of them! Why, here and there and everywhere, there are yelping guards in desperate flight, rushing, pushing, scrambling to get away, *get away* from these swirling, shrieking spectres tearing through the air, with their piercing, fierce, black eyes and their wild, shredded hair!

And the People herd themselves together at the center of the square. But as it soon becomes apparent that *they* are not the targets of these vengeful screaming spirits, they begin to applaud and whistle and cheer the primal wonder of these savage saving graces flying through the air.

I then turn my attention to the goings-on going on across the square . . .

The stage is now littered with abandoned spears and swords, along with two – no, *three* stray Chancellors. Oh, yes, I spy those quivering bellies protruding from behind the curtains.

And over there next to the throne, all alone, stands the Duchess Raynna Ravinnia – still so like a sleepwalker, even amidst all this pandemonium.

And, *ahhh, yes,* there he be: the Weaver. In the throes of a full-on tantrum. Stomping back and forth across the stage, shouting and sputtering in a red-faced rage. Though of course nary a word can be heard above the cataclysm of sound all around him – and no one is listening to him anyway. But he does not seem to be aware of anything but the sound of his own voice, and he just keeps on spewing vitriol, to no effect whatsoever.

And soon after I spot him, why, he spots *me.* Whereupon, sure, he turns the full force of his monomaniacal outrage onto me – terrible, traitorous witch that I be. And as I watch him foam at the mouth, with his eyes bugged out and his face as red as a turnip, I am amazed by how suddenly small he seems.

My gaze is then pulled skyward, and I am instantly transfixed. The Furies have stopped stock still. All thirteen of them are floating high above the square, just hovering there in the air, each pair of sad, sparkling eyes staring stageward at the object of their affection:

Yes, the Furies have spotted their mother.

Oh, how beautiful to hear their screams soften, becoming keens and wails and woeful howls. No longer are they wrathful spirits, no – how they shrink and sweeten and sigh. How touching it is to watch this now tender tribe of sisters swirling down, down to their mother on the stage. And as they draw near her, they coo and coo and cocoon themselves around the delicate little Duchess.

Then . . . can it be? Yes, one by two by three, they dive and disappear into the sleepwalking shell of their much-missed mother. And as they do, *ooooh,* there comes such a *sound* from the now round "O" of Raynna Ravinna's mouth – one unbroken, ear-piercing, blood-curdling *SCREAM.*

Well, the Weaver bursts at the seams.
He whirls around and *wallops* his wife across the mouth!

Her scream stops. The crowd gasps.
And then, *oooh,* it is so eerily *silent . . .*

And the Weaver turns back to the crowd,
and just as he opens his mouth to – oh!
Ohhh?
Ohhhhhh . . .

Well, there's no other way to say it:
Raynna Ravinnia begins to grow.
And *grow . . .*
And *GROW!*
And, oh, how the lightning flashes, oh, how the thunder cracks!
And though she is so fast becoming so fearsomely *colossal,*
everyone knows who's the only one here
with anything and everything to fear.

At last, the Weaver turns to behold
his wife's astonishingly altitudinous state.
And he gapes all the way up the everlasting length of her.
And when their eyes at long last lock, the Weaver freezes in shock!

And the now-gargantuan Duchess reaches down,
and with one gigantic hand she seizes him,
and she lifts him way up high, and she looks him right in the eye.

Then she *rattles* him and *throttles* him 'til he's very nearly dead!
Then she raises him still higher, so high above her head,
and swiftly, savagely *slams* her tormentor down onto that stage!
And with a wild-eyed, ferocious fury,
with a hair-raising *howl* of rage,
she seizes a spear and hurls it downward,
piercing the precise place in the Weaver's chest
where his heart ought to have been,
impaling him
and nailing him
to the stage floor.

And with that, the colossal Duchess ever so quietly shrinks back to her diminutive self – blinking her big black eyes as if she has, in fact, come back to herself after a long absence. Then she meets my eyes across the square and nods ever so slightly, as if to say, *"There. That's done."*

The little Duchess then spots something lying at her feet. She bends to retrieve it. Then she rises, reverently holding the Crown. And I do believe I see a small smile curve her lips.

She walks to the edge of the stage, leans down, and passes the Crown on to the People, who then silently, ceremonially pass it one to the other to the other, all the way across the square . . . until it finally lands in the hands of a man who passes it down to his young son. And then the man leans down to whisper in the boy's ear. And with a great solemnity, the boy walks up the stairs to the platform, over to where I stand. And when he reaches me, I kneel. And the child sets the Crown upon my head.

And at that very moment, it began to rain . . .

Yessir, I tell you, Book, that dreadful Cloud burst into a zillion raindrops right then and there. And it went on ahead and rained for thirty-three whole days and nights! Why, this is the first chance I've gotten to write and tell you how it all happened, I've been so busy and everything's been so wet!

But when the rain stopped, *ohhh,* everything now looks so fresh and clean and dazzling in the sunlight. Yes, the walls and the towers and the streets of the Kingdom are now that same warm, elegant ivory they were when I was a child. And because that awful Cloud has entirely evaporated, why, that sky is its ol' Wild Blue Yonder self once more.

Oh, that reminds me . . . *Schlufenschlagen!* You heard me, Book . . . *Schlufenschlagen.* That's the original name of our fair Kingdom.

Yes, *that's* why I were always so annoyed whenever I heard that stupid, long, pretentious, artless name, "The Biggest and Best – " *Hogwash!* Turns out Zenzi's map was right about the name, after all – how do ya like that? Schlufenschlagen . . . I know, isn't it just the most marvelous name you ever heard?

And, sure, we have been in the midst of one delightful celebration or another ever since the rain stopped. O' course, you won't be surprised to hear that one of the very first things I did was to have that stage floor replaced. After all, we can't be putting on fine theatrical productions with bad blood on the stage, now, can we?

Oh, Book, I am overwhelmed! There's *far* too much to tell you, and I only have these last few pages left, so I guess I'll just gab away and say what comes out until we come to our natural end. You oughta be well used to that by now, eh, Book?

Alright, so let's see . . .

My Father is now living in a lovely, sunlit room in the Palace and seems much happier, indeed. And Bill takes care of him, as we have no need of a Jailer in Schlufenschlagen anymore.

And, oh, *my*, Bill and Jimmy and Joe and I, how we love to tell each other the tale of what happened over and over – how Hank appeared so blindingly out of the blue and how the Furies appeared so fearsomely out of the sky! Why, they were all so magnificently brave, I get teary-eyed every time I remember it. Though Joe and Bill and I have noticed, with no end of fascination, how Jimmy's telling of the tale takes on all make and manner of fictional variations every time he tells it.

Alas, though I told him I'd be most proud if he'd stay and make his Home here, Jimmy told me he had places to be and things to do, and he needed to be off and away. I felt truly sorry to see him go and had a mind to thank him with some marvelous parting gift. So, when Jimmy quite formally presented me with my Peerless Pocketknife, why, I quite formally presented it right on back to him, along with my pledge of eternal friendship and endless gratitude. But do you know, Book, Jimmy insisted with such intensity that everything that is mine must be returned to me – and by that he meant my Pocketknife, as well as the Kingdom.

Well, I were still without a gift to give him until the night before he left, when we two happen to be taking a stroll through the Emperor-King's Wing of the Palace . . .

So, there we are, reminiscing about that momentous moment when our childhoods collided, laughing about how I'd chased him through these very halls. And as we are walking amongst my Father's outrageous proliferation of clothes and jewels and frippery, Jimmy spots a massive gold ring, just silly with diamonds and a dazzler of a ruby, big as a robin's egg. And, *oooh*, there gleams such a gleam in the Dodger's eye. And though he is clearly at war with himself, I can see that he is purely *aching* to pocket the gaudy thing. So, o' course, I flat out give him the ring with my heartfelt thanks. And I must confess, I were also secretly hoping he'd maybe get the idea that with this ring, he'd now have the means to retire from the pilfering profession altogether, should he so choose.

Aw, I miss him as I write, Book . . . but I'll always smile at the thought of him, that I will.

Oh, and I must report: One day, in midst of those torrential rains, Raynna Ravinnia gave birth to a strapping set of twins – a boy and a girl. What a tender mother she is. How she shines with serenity and contentment. And the babies are quite breathtaking, with their raven black hair and their big black eyes! So often, when I gaze into them sparkling black eyes of theirs, I am put in mind of the Furies, sure . . . And every time I kiss those babies, in my heart I send my love to the glorious warrior-spirits of their predecessors.

Wherever they are, I pray they are at peace now, and I hope they can feel my gratitude and my awe at the mighty army they were on behalf of us all.

Awww, dagnabit, I suppose I oughta tell ya about them Chancellors, though who wants to waste paper on 'em at this point. Well, the whole crooked bunch of 'em come to me – the *gall* of 'em all! – and they have the nerve to stand there with their bare faces hanging out, bowing and scraping and blathering all over me:

"Oh, make no mistake, Your Majesty, we hated him too!" "And we all went looking for you long ago, didn't you know?" "Oh, yes, we had a *massive* search party – exhaustive, really!"

Anyhow, I banished 'em. Yup, I sent 'em out into the Whirld with nothing but a few sandwiches between 'em. And, sure, while I was at it, I banished that horrible Hopper too. And I told all them other Hoppers we had no more use for 'em here in Schlufenschlagen.

Oh, and o' course I must record *this*, Book: A few days after the rains began, Hank and I had such a hankering for a victory ride that we decide to head on out of the Kingdom, rain or no rain. And whaddaya know, but the moment we clear the gates we find our dripping wet selves greeted by the clearest blue sky and the prettiest day as ever there was in all Creation! We'd clean forgotten that dreadful Cloud were hovering *only* above the Kingdom!

And when we look upwards at that Cloud behind us, right off we both notice that it is already a good deal smaller than when first we laid eyes on it. And I tell you what, Book, right then and there it suddenly felt to me as if that ol' Cloud were crying with relief, crying its heart out.

Anyhow, sure, Hank and I proceed to have ourselves what might well be the wildest, whompingest, rip-roaringest victory gallop in the whole of our history together. And that sure is saying something, ain't it, Book?

So, here I now be . . . just outside the window of what is officially my very own Tower Room, at the topmost tip at the furthest end of the Empress-Queen's Wing. Yessir, I am a-lying here so cozily, so contentedly, in my Scarlet Velvet Hammock, as in my traveling days of yore, up here at the top of my favorite Red Rose Oak Tree, just a-gazing at the glory of the sun beginning to set and at my all-time favorite view of anything anywhere:

The Great Big Beautiful Whole Wyde Whirld Out There.

Including that sleek blue sliver of the Calico Sea . . . Yes, he is here with me. I can *feel* him. Even now, I have only to close my eyes to see his Eyes, gazing into mine with so much pride.

You know something, Book, it's really quite remarkable how this dear Tree's branches are now in such perfect reach of my window – almost as if we agreed long ago to meet here at this very spot just so's I could tell you the very end of my story! Though, for an ending, this sure feels like the *beginningest* beginning that ever was.

But you know, I'll bet from somewhere down that ribboning Road, I'll look back and read that very line I just wrote, and I'll say, "Lillian, you are so silly. You weren't at the End or the Beginning of anything! Why, you were smack dab in the *Middle!*" And I'll probably be right.

Life makes me laugh, Book, no doubt about it. Oh, how I would so love to write a Great Poem about Beginnings, Middlings, and Endings someday. I wonder if I've gone through enough Life now to write a truly fine Poem, at last? Hmph. We'll see. I'm doubtful. For now, I'll leave it be. Life writes much better Poetry than I ever will, that's certain.

And, *ahhh,* Destiny . . .
Now, what do I have to say to you with just this one last page left? Hmmm . . .

Well, aside from the many times I have thanked you, praised you, and courted your collaboration and good opinion of me, you know all too well that there have also been many times in my travels and travails when I truly didn't think you knew *what* in the Whirld you were doing, other times when I judged you to be completely cold and uncaring, and still other times when I was absolutely convinced that you had a *whopper* of a cruel streak. Yes, I often thought it painfully plain that my admiration for you went woefully unrequited.

But, oh, in this round, eternal moment, in this here beloved tree-top, as I watch that rose-gold sunset, as I bask in the perfect peace of this gloaming light . . . well, I see that I were just a fool, and that you are and have always been so lavishly, outlandishly good to me. May I always see so clearly. May I always do you right.

Mmmm, delicious . . . I just took that moment to stick my nose into this big, fat, red rose that's peeking over my shoulder as I write. I tell you, Book, it's good to be King. I dunno why exactly. I feel it just suits me, like an old pair of slippers.

Yessir, I have felt at Home all over the Whirld.
Friends have been family, strangers have been friends.
And though I shall be always, in my soul, a wondering wanderer,
I am, at long last, come Home.

My dear Book, how I do thank you.

Love evermore and then some,

Lillian

Greetings, dear Reader!

So, at last, we meet again,
at what appears to be the end of The End . . .

But stories (like people) do not always chart themselves
in straight lines, now, do they?
No, the fullest, truest tales are far more partial to *circles*.

After all, the Truth is *round*.

Ergo, herein lies . . .

III: The Beginning

Once Upon a Time...

In a picture perfect Kingdom, Lillian was born
to the picture perfect King and Queen of this pretty place.

But soon after the birth of their daughter,
the delicate little Empress-Queen Lilliana lost all interest in living.
You see, the Emperor-King George felt cut to the core,
because Lilliana, whom he'd formerly adored,
had given birth to a useless *girl*,
obviously on purpose, obviously out of spite.

He called his wife a fool and a traitor
and a villainous threat to the Crown.
Why, every other self-respecting Empress-Queen before her
had had the half a wit in her head to produce a firstborn *boy*.
The King refused point blank to even think of speaking to her again
or to so much as look anywhere in her direction
as long as they both shall live.

Now, the People didn't mind a bit
about having a Girl-King for their Heir.
As a matter of fact, they thought it might be a nice change.
But, as usual, the King didn't care what they thought.
He felt insulted. He felt betrayed. He felt humiliated.

He would be the very first Emperor-King
ever in the history of his entire ancestral line
to pass on the Ruling Crown to a *girl*.

But there it was, you see. That was that.
Whether the Emperor-King George liked it or not,
the Chancellors and all the People knew
that Item 37 of the Royal Manual plainly stated:

The Firstborn Child of the Emperor-King
Inherits the Ruling Crown,
the Title of Emperor-King and All Powers Thereof

Firstborn "child," you see.
A loophole large enough to leap through.

And in her feverish dreams, the failing, ailing Lilliana leapt.
As she lay sleeping in her bed of guilt, she looked up and saw,
standing at the wide-open window, a dream-memory of herself,
still rosy and round and shining with child,
gazing contentedly down upon the Kingdom,
a soft breeze in her hair.

And her dream-self laid hands upon the globe of her belly,
and made a silent wish . . .
Then she turned to look at Lilliana, lying there in bed,
and she smiled at her, and she nodded,
as if to say that everything had gone just *perfectly*.

And this vision soothed the soul of the little Empress-Queen,
and it brought her peace, but it did not save her.
Not even her rapture at the radiant health
of her miraculous newborn daughter was enough
to buoy her up or to stand her strong
against the ceaseless, pounding censure of her husband
and the mindless, smirking malice of the people at the Palace.

And so, the Empress-Queen lay dying of sadness and shame,
accompanied only by the mocking shrieks of laughter
from her husband's dinner party down below.
And when she knew her time was near,
Lilliana held her newborn close and whispered in her ear:

"Remember, my dearest darling-dear,
you are the rightful Emperor-King,
and a Girl-King for this Kingdom might be . . . just the thing . . . "

And Lilliana closed her eyes and quietly slipped away.
And as that tower bell tolled the death of the Empress-Queen,
BONG by *BONG* it began to dawn on the Emperor-King,
mid-toast at his banquet downstairs,
that with the knife of his own unkindness,
he had killed the love of his life.

Now, some stretch before all this,
when Lilliana was an alive-and-thriving young newlywed,
George had gone off on a diplomatic visit
to a faraway jungle kingdom
and gotten himself stung by a vicious Vanity Bee,
thereby suffering a severely debilitating bout of Vanity Fever
in all its manifold madness.

He'd tear his hair and weep at the thought
of wearing anything at all more than once,
so he'd incessantly change clothes throughout the day,
and through most nights too,
and he could never actually leave the Palace
because he was forever going back to change his hat
or to have his coat re-lined.

George weathered the Fever just fine.
He came through it right as rain.
Or so it *seemed*, at the time.

But the Fever had, in fact, shivered his timbers, shall we say.
Loosened his support beams, so to speak.

Well . . .

When that bell began to knell its low, slow echo,
the Emperor-King George, at his banquet below,
right then realized, with shattering surprise,
that the light of his life had gone out.

But he refused for even one moment to grieve,
refused for even one moment to believe
that he might have been even one little bit wrong.

And so, with each clanging, banging *BONG*,
George cracked a little bit more,
until, at last, he snapped like a dried twig.
And the bats all flew from his belfry
and all his demons, reborn, did a jig!
And George jumped up on that tabletop
and tore off his powdered wig,
and he laughed, and he cried:

"A blinding new sunrise is blasting behind my eyes! There are
a trillion brilliant *everythings* I've just now realized . . . Oh, it's
so clear to me, I must hereafter always be a dazzling expression
of divinity – *hee-hee!* Oh, yes, I understand, *I see* . . . So, I
now hereby decree that this Court henceforth shall be dedicated
solely to adorning me with an evermore transplendent, evermore
transcendent new wardrobe! That's it, *by George,* that's it!"

Well, that *was* it, indeed.
The sky, as they say, fell in.

Yes, the Emperor-King's old Vanity Fever
sparked and flared and flamed through his veins,
and once again consumed the lion's share of his royal brain.

Life with George became an intricate, infinite, emotional minefield,
carpeted with eggshells.

   Coursing through it, of course,
      was the requisite river
         of silks and velvets and laces and
            buttons and bows and boots
            and hats and trims and feathers
            and cuffs and curls and
               diamonds and pearls and
                  watches and sketchings and
                     tantrums and etchings and
                     ravings and rantings and
                     rantings and ravings and
                  fittings and fittings and
                  fittings and fittings and
                  fittings and fittings
                  and fittings and fittings
                  and fittings and
                     fittings and fittings
                     and fittings and
                     fittings and
                     fittings and
                     fittings and fittings
                     and fittings and
                     fittings and
                        fittings and
                        fittings and
                        fittings and
                        fittings . . .

                           Exactly.
                           Sheer madness.

Now, far, far, away,
all the way over on the other side of the Palace,
this rushing river of royal ridiculousness branched off
into a nearly harmless, distantly babbling brook,
at the quiet end of which lived . . . Lillian.
Safe in the shell of her own child-universe.
Sprouting into healthy little Girl-Kinghood.
A sparky little person right from the get-go.
Rangy and rosy and full of wild red hair and big ideas.

Her Mother's parting words had planted a seed in Lillian's Soul.
And her Soul, as all Souls do, kept watch.
Tended the seed. Helped it grow.

And, oh, the Girl-King had a way of seeing what was what.
Yes, she saw what those Chancellors were trying to do.
They were trying to keep her stupid.
Turn her into a pawn and a doll, not a ruler at all.
The only tutor they ever sent her was a kindly man named Ed.
Poor Ed had been kicked in the head by a mule at some point
and couldn't even spell "Ed."

Oh, they gave her only the most paltry education,
the most perfect preparation for her future weak and wifely station.
Heir or no heir, the Chancellors were plotting to marry her off,
make a powerful alliance, expand the Kingdom,
bring in revenue, turn a curse into a blessing,
and try, try, *try* to get the Emperor-King to concentrate on
remarrying as soon as possible, and doing it *correctly* this time.
No more half-breeds to muck things up.

So they engaged a fine Lady to teach Lillian:
How to use a fan.
How to cross her ankles.
How to speak with downcast eyes.
How to fake a laugh.

"Excuse me, ma'am, but . . . what is all this supposed to teach me, exactly?" inquired the girl.

"Why, it's to prepare you to do your duty, of course," said the Lady. "Get married, bear sons, live happily ever after! Though that will be quite the trick, I must say. You're going to be *obscenely* tall."

"But I'm the Heir to the throne! I've just *gotta* learn to read and – why, there's a whole Whirld of Big Ideas I've gotta know about!"

Well, this outburst so disturbed the Lady
and so perturbed the Chancellors
that they locked up all the books in the Kingdom.

Lillian saw.
Lillian heard.
Lillian understood.
Though she acted blind and deaf and dim,
and played possum and passive and pretty-as-you-please,
so they'd focus on her Father and leave her be.
Both of which they definitely did.

Meanwhile . . .

Hans, the Seventh Palace Under-Gardener,
for love of future King and Kingdom,
at the risk of his scrawny old sunburned neck,
secretly taught the girl to read and to reason.
He stole books to sneak to her in his gardening sack.
She'd read them, they'd discuss them, then he'd sneak them back.

Now, every now and then,
the girl saw her Father from a distance.
However, he never, *ever* saw her.
He forbade any and all reminders of his wife or her betrayal.
To that effect, when she died, he issued an ironclad edict:

- The Emperor-King -
Most Vigorously, Decisively, and Incontrovertibly
Refuses to Ever Lay Eyes Upon the Heir-Apparent

The child was therefore and thereafter:
Banned from participation in all pomp and ceremony.
Banned from entering the Emperor-King's Wing.
Banned from being anywhere remotely near the Emperor-King.
Whenever she came too dangerously close to crossing his path,
the nearest Lord or Lady or Steward or Servant would
pull her back in a breathless panic and hide her.

Ah, but the girl was miraculously matter-of-fact about it.
She knew her Father to be so imbalanced
as to be downright upside-down.
And she knew that everything and everyone else in the Palace
was therefore likewise upside-down.
And she knew that the only thing in her power to do
was to survive, to thrive, to grow up,
and to someday set things right.

So, knowing what was what, Lillian flourished.
And the powers-that-were thought her to be such a cipher,
and their hands were always so full of her Father,
that her coast was usually clear.
So she'd slip out of her scratchy, poofy Palace costume
and into some comfortable homespun:
white shirt, green leggings, brown boots,
and her beloved purple felt hat,
given to her by the Second Scullery Maid's third cousin.

Thus transformed, she'd look in the mirror and laugh with joy.
Then she'd climb out the window and down the ivy
and disappear into the town to take her solace in the People.

And the People, for their part, took their Girl-King close to heart.
They treated her like one of their own.
Taught her how to get on.
How to jump rope.
How to tell a joke.
How to slide down bannisters.
How to eat an eclair in four bites.

Oh, the People loved their little King-to-be.
They saw their hopeful future in her strength and in her smarts
and in her sparkling auburn eyes.
Yes, she was a scrapper.
They were sure she would save them in the end,
not from her Father's tyranny exactly, no,
but from his criminal self-absorption.

So . . .

There came, of course, a time when the Emperor-King
got so worn down from getting so dressed up,
so wiped out from wearing this and wanting that,
that he crawled into bed one particularly fine afternoon
and refused to get up ever again.

Waving away medicinally intended hats and shoes and scarves,
George whispered weakly to the Head Lord High Chancellor:

"*Ohhh*, there's only one thing that can soothe my soul and save
my life . . . "

And as the whole room craned and strained to hear,
too scared to hope, too tired to fear, he said it:

"The Most Beautiful New Suit of Clothes Anywhere Ever in the
History of the Whole Wyde Whirld! *Ohhh*, I want it for my
Birthday . . . *or I'll have your heads.*"

Well, the Chancellors closed their jaws, collected their wits,
and gave him their most heartfelt vows
that his will would most dutifully, indubitably, be done.

And they bowed, and they scraped,
and they solemnly scooched out of His Majesty's bedchamber.

But the instant they hit the hallway:
Three of them fell to the floor and began to sob.
Two of them started shoving each other.
One of them started whacking himself in the head with his shoe.
All of them were unraveling.

Please.
Somebody.
Come and fix everything.

Then they turned what was left of their minds
completely inside-out, and came up with a solution
that they fervently prayed would bring them salvation.
From somebody.
Somewhere.
Somehow.

And they called all the People together in the town square
and stood side-by-side onstage, looking sanctimoniously on,
while the Head Herald proclaimed:

"Hear ye! Hear ye!
This be the Proclamation of the Search for the Suit!
His Completely Serene Majesty
desires and requires
for the maintenance of his continued robust health,
and for the celebration of his upcoming Birthday,
The Most Beautiful New Suit of Clothes
Anywhere Ever in the History of the Whole Wyde Whirld!"

"Aw, for Pete's sake . . . " said Lillian, up a tree at the time, reading some contraband poetry. "Can't a person get a little peace and quiet around here?"

And she stuck her fingers in her ears.
And she went right back to reading.
And upon hearing this "Search for The Suit Proclamation,"
the People looked at each other and shrugged.
And, as usual, they left the madness of the Palace to the Palace.

Well, the Chancellors sent out all the Kingdom Criers,
who cried and cried, through every last town and village,
all throughout the countryside.
And soon suits, suits, suits came streaming in from far and wide.
But, alas, no suit, no suit at all would suit the Emperor-King,
and his Birthday celebration was all too fast approaching.

Now . . .

One frenzied day, just outside the Palace grounds,
the Chancellors were locked in a feverish huddle,
wringing their hands, tearing their hair, blaming each other.
And as Fate would have it (and doesn't Fate always have it?),
a man who called himself "The Master Weaver"
just happened to be passing by.
Sniffing the sweetest opportunity whiffling through the air,
he stopped to listen . . .

He'd come to the Kingdom that very day
with his apprentice in tow,
an orphan called Jimmy the Dodger.
He'd heard all the ruckus about some king and some suit
and, most saliently, about a king's ransom for said suit.

"Master Weaver, sir," said the boy, "shall I go pick pockets?"

"Quiet! I'm *listening* . . . " said the Weaver.

He smelled the desperation dripping from the Chancellors' brows.
He heard the panic screaming from between their whispers.

Oh, this could be so much more than a touch-and-go sort of sting!
Why, the maestro of lies and deception was willing to bet that
even if he played with one hand tied behind his back,
he could orchestrate this entire off-key Kingdom
and be strumming those Palace purse strings
for a long, *long* time to come.

Make no mistake,
the Weaver knew himself to be destined for greatness.
They would tremble the day they finally understood.
Oh, yes, they would . . .

And the man knew his moment, indeed.
He moved in on that huddle of rich men in their muddle,
pattering past all the raised eyebrows,
all the questions about him and his apprentice
and their shoddy clothing,
effortlessly weaving a tall tale telling how
they had been ruthlessly robbed en route
and left only with these hideously shabby clothes,
a state which *deeply* offended
his all-too-finely tuned aesthetic sensibilities.

After all, he was:
Life-Long Head Potentate of the Whirld Weaver's Guild!
Sixty-Four-Time Winner of the Most Exquisite Royal Garb Contest!
Incessantly Sought-After Creator of Kings' Costumes!

But no matter about any of *that*.
The really essential thing was:
He'd had the most amazing premonition,
the most compelling precognition
about this very Suit, this very Palace, this very Emperor-King!

"What a coincidence!" "My word!" "*Unbelievable . . .*" "You don't *say!*" cried the Chancellors, so completely swept away.

"Oh, but I most definitely *do!* I must tell you, after I had that dream, nothing in this *Whirld* could have stopped me from coming to the aid of this Emperor-King of yours. And let me tell you something *else . . .*"

Well, tears leapt to the Chancellors' eyes.
Talk about prayers being answered!
Talk about getting what you wish for!

So, in a matter of mere moments, the Weaver convinced them
that he and his poor young apprentice had traveled
all that long, terrible, arduous way from hither and yon,
from just so far away and just so far beyond,
just to sew the Suit,
just to save the day,
just to fix things.

And as he spoke, so fast and so sure,
the Chancellors saw that, in all sorts of ways,
this calm, collected savior of a Weaver knew
just *so exactly* what to do.

"So, now, if I may be so bold as to say . . ."

"Oh, please, *do* say!" "Most definitely *say!*" "*Shut up!* Will you let him say?"

"Alright, first I'll need to see his Majesty's wardrobe so I can see what he likes. Then I'll whip up the perfect, prize-winning Suit, and then – oh, I am so sorry, gentlemen! I didn't mean to be so . . . *aggressive.*"

"Oh, please, *do* aggress!" "By all means, *yes!*" "You mustn't digress, Mister Weaver, just tell us what to do!"

"Actually . . . that's *Master* Weaver. And, of course, I'll be more than happy to."

And that's the way the Weaver began to play the Palace
for all it was worth.
And they wined him and they dined him,
and they really didn't mind that he never actually told them
what sort of Suit he would actually whip up.

And then, oh yes, *then* the Weaver oh-so-seamlessly wove his way
into the heart and soul and dressing room of the Star of the Show!

Yes, George and the Weaver, the Weaver and George . . .
the Emperor-King and Master Weaver became ever so very close.
Keen, cozy collaborators, crazy for color and fashion and fit!
Why, the King was so smitten with that wonderful Weaver,
he was up and out of bed in no time
and skipping down the halls again.

All was well, after all.

Well . . .

On the day before the big event,
Jimmy the Dodger was in the town square,
handing out announcements for the King's Birthday celebration,
pilfering small items here and there.
In fact, when Lillian the Girl-King first laid eyes
on Jimmy the Dodger, he was picking Walter the Baker's pocket.
Jimmy was mid-pinch when Lillian stepped up
and tapped him on the shoulder.

"Why, hello," she said.

He froze. She grabbed the pouch.
He started to run. She tripped him.
He fell flat. She sat on him.

Just then, one of the Palace Guards happened to be strolling by.
He stopped, regarded the children,
looked at Jimmy with a particularly narrowed eye,
then said to Lillian:

"Anythin' I can do for you, Your Highne – ?"

"No thanks, Joe! Everything's just fine! Here y'are, Walter . . . "

And she handed the pouch back to the Baker.
Hearing her fib for him, the Boy-Thief held professionally still.

"Why, I didn't even feel it come loose!" said Walter, so dismayed
and so relieved all at once. "Thank you so much, my little Hi – "

"Oh, you are *so* welcome, Walter! What say we help this lad up
here? He seems to have fallen."

So, Walter and Joe helped Jimmy to his feet.
Walter, being Walter, dusted off the boy's shirt a bit.
Joe, being Joe, looked down and said, in a stern, fatherly tone:

"Are you behavin' yourself, laddie?"

"Real nice to see you, Joe! G'bye! S'long!" said Lillian, as she
quickly pulled Jimmy across the street.

"Hey, thanks for not turnin' me in," said the Boy-Thief. "I owe ya!"

"Why were you picking his pocket?" asked the Girl-King. "Do
you need money? Are you hungry?"

"Nope. Just practicin'," said he, as he stooped and picked up the
scattered announcements.

"*Hmmm . . .* " said she, wondering why anyone would practice
stealing. She picked up one of the announcements. "What's this?"

"Some show, I dunno," said Jimmy.

"You're handing them out, and you don't know – "

And as she spoke, she suddenly realized that he couldn't read.

"Oh, I see . . . You haven't had a chance to read them!"

She smiled, and she glanced around.

"Follow me, if you please!"

And Lillian darted into an alley, and Jimmy darted after her.
And she gestured for him to have a seat on a big barrel.

"Now then, for your entertainment, sir!" said she, sweeping her
hat off with a big, theatrical flourish.

"Y'have red hair," said Jimmy. "I fancy red hair."

"Why, thanks! Hold this, wouldja?"

She threw him her hat, and he put it on, and they both laughed.
Then she unfurled the parchment
and read the announcement aloud:

On the 'morrow there will be
a Birthday Celebration in the town square
for the Emperor-King George,
at the climax of which
Our Most Beloved Majesty
will, at last, show his subjects
his brand new Birthday Suit,
which will forevermore be known as:
The Most Beautiful New Suit of Clothes
Anywhere Ever in the History of the Whole Wyde Whirld!

And Lillian murmured to herself, "*Doggone* it, Father . . . "

And the Girl-King felt the Boy-Thief's round eyes upon her.
And she saw that he saw who she was.

"*Why, you're that little Princess . . .*" he whispered.

And with that, Jimmy jumped off that barrel,
ran out into the street, and left Lillian in the dust.

"Aw, shucks," she said, sad to be solo once again.

Then she looked back down at the announcement.
Seeing more print at the bottom,
she further unfurled the parchment.

> Attention: The Fabric of the Emperor's New Clothes
> is finer than any fabric ever known
> It has been officially certified by the Whirld Weaver's Guild
> as an Absolute Miracle of Delicacy.
> Those who cannot see the Splendor of this Fabric
> are to be considered
> Fools, Traitors, and Threats to the Crown,
> and will be dealt with in no uncertain terms as such.

Lillian frowned. And then she shrugged.
Oh, they were always saying and doing things at the Palace
that never made an ounce of sense at all.
They were all always acting as if the sky were about to fall.

And the sky looked so breathtakingly blue that day
that she walked off gazing up at it,
idly wondering what sort of fabric could cause such a stir.
Then she froze in her tracks and said:

"Hey, wait! He's got my hat!"

And she dashed off to nab the Boy-Thief.

She ran into the square, but she didn't see him there.
So she climbed a nearby ladder to the roof of a nearby shop.
She squinted, she scanned . . .
She spotted her hat streaking through the crowd
toward – could it be – the Palace?
She was off that roof and after that hat in a heartbeat.

Meanwhile . . .

The Chancellors and other Palace dignitaries
sat in the Weaver's spacious parlor in the Emperor-King's Wing,
spellbound . . .
adoring their Weaver-Savior,
who was at the apex of an intricate spin,
describing the exquisitely delicate nature
of that *fantastic* Fabric of his!

And in that heady moment, from that totally transplendent tip,
the Weaver felt himself to be in such omnipotent form
that he allowed himself a touch of god-like glee.
He had them all sewed up, you see.
He'd mingled and tangled all their egos together,
and he'd trussed them up real tight,
and now they all scurried for his favor
and competed for his compliments,
all in cutthroat competition to see
just who his newest pet would be.

Then, smirked he, "Oh, I must warn you, there are some pathetic,
provincial, completely *ignorant* people . . . Well, you're not going
to *believe* this . . . "

"What? Tell us!" all the glittering Ladies pleaded, laughing
along with him. Oh, the Weaver was always such a stitch.

"Well, believe it or not, truly vulgar, *stupid* people *don't see any fabric at all!*"

"At *all?*" said the Chancellors.

"Believe it or not," smiled the Weaver.

"Oh, my, that *is* pathetic!" said the High Chancellor.

And the whole room laughed itself into a lather.

"The thing you've got to watch out for with these devious fools is that they're always *traitorous,* always *treasonous!* I've seen it so many times before. They're not just stupid, they're *evil* to the core."

"Oh, isn't that always the way?" "But of course!" "That is a *fact.*"

They all concurred,
feeling all cozy and superior,
so sure of how clever and sophisticated they all were.

And the Weaver smiled, as if he had a special secret.
And they smiled, so happy to be in on it.

And the Weaver said, "So, would you . . . like to see a swatch?"

Well, the whole room burst at the seams with excitement.

"Oh, good! My dear Emperor-Friend left it entirely up to me. Now, let's see . . . who will I show it to? Who truly *wants* to see?"

Meanwhile . . .

Just outside and down the hall a-ways,
the Girl-King had caught up with the Boy-Thief,
who was rounding the corner into the Emperor-King's Wing,
which was where the Weaver was,
which was, of course, strictly off limits to Lillian.

There hung a tapestry overhead that said:

Ghe Emperor-King's Daughter
Shall Not Enter the Emperor King's Wing
Upon Penalty of Death

Upon seeing such a menacing sign for the very first time,
such a debate ensued in the Girl-King's heart:

Her head or her hat.
Her hat or her head.
Oh, she really almost didn't know . . .
She did *so* love that hat.

So she looked around, and since she only saw
empty halls to the left and empty halls to the right,
just for a hat, she risked her neck and peeked around the corner.

And what she saw was the Boy-Thief listening at a door . . .

Behind which, the Weaver was playing with the urge
to further toy with all these pretty sitting ducks of his.
Make them beg and whimper, maybe,
or sit up and bark like dogs.
But he decided not to risk it.

So he produced a sample of that fabled Fabric of his.
Yes, right then and there, he presented them with
an undeniably glamorous swatch of:

Air.

They blinked. They hesitated. And then:

"Oooooh . . . is that it?" *"Ahhhhh* . . . " "Oh, isn't it just *exquisite!"*
"Where now?" "There it is, indeed!" "Isn't it just *incredible!"*

- 344 -

And so they all began absolutely, positively, clearly seeing
something that wasn't even slightly there at all.

Then Jimmy the Dodger burst into the room – too fast, too loud.
All eyes turned away from the Weaver to see who it was.
Awed by all those glittering people staring at him,
the boy took off the purple hat and made a little bow.

The Weaver's eyes threatened murder,
but his voice spoke sweetness and light:

"Ah, Jimmy-Boy, come in! Come over here to me."

"I'm sorry, Master Weaver, sir, but I just *had* to – "

"Interrupt?" smiled the Weaver, ruffling the lad's hair.

And the Ladies also smiled at the Weaver's loving care.

"Did you sew on those last few buttons, boy, and move the trim
just that bit, like I told you?"

"I did, sir, uh . . . That's why I've come, sir – to tell you that the
Emperor's New Clothes are . . . finished!"

Well, the room went wild with the triumph of it all!
And the Weaver laughed with joy!
And as he hugged the boy and chucked his chin,
he smiled and said, through his teeth, amidst the din:

"You just saved your scrawny neck. You know that, don't you?"

"But – but I saw the Princess, Master Weaver, sir . . . "

Instantly, the Weaver said, "My dear friends, do excuse me for
just a moment! Please help yourselves to my delicious new
sherry. Drink up, enjoy yourselves, be my guest!"

And as they feverishly drank, he yanked the boy outside.
But the door banged into something, and there was a little yelp.
And the Weaver peered around the door
and then down to the floor to see,
sprawled on her backside:

Lillian.

She looked up to see the Boy-Thief, collared and docile,
in the grip of a glassy-eyed, bony-faced, crooked-looking man.

The Weaver closed the door.
He took stock of the little girl on the floor.
He walked very slowly all around her, and he smirked.

"Well, *that's* a funny costume for such a *rich* little girl."

"Yes, sir . . . " Lillian said, so very softly, as she stood up, with
her eyes so very far downcast.

The Weaver assessed the child . . .
Oh, such an awkward little lamb.
But she would do. In time. In a pinch.
Such a cinch for a wife of the puppet-queen-type,
when she grew – yes, probably far too tall. No matter.
She'd stay meek and she'd stay small – *inside*, where it counts.
Yes, she'd learn to live to aim to please.
Ahhh, little girls were such a breeze . . .

"Now, just what are you doing in *this* part of the Palace, Princess?"
said he, so silkily, so that he could watch her tremble.

"I'm sorry, sir, it's just that – that's my hat."

And with a bowed red head, she shyly pointed
to the crumpled purple felt in the Boy-Thief's hands.
And the Weaver turned his glassy gaze down upon the Dodger.

"Well, you've been *completely* stupid today, haven't you?"

"Yes, sir . . . " the Boy whispered.

And the Weaver took the hat from the boy,
and with it, slapped him in the face.
The girl gasped.

Then, slowly, the Weaver turned on the girl,
with his hooded eyes and his very softest smile.

"Now, I'm sure you saw that big sign that says, quite plainly,
you're not supposed to be here."

"I'm so sorry, sir . . . it's just – I don't know how to read."

And she felt the Boy-Thief's eyes upon her.

"*Aww* . . . a rich little girl like you can't read?" needled the Weaver.

And at that, the Boy-Thief paid her earlier favor back in kind,
and he looked deliberately away.

"Maybe," said the Weaver, taking her firmly by the chin and
tilting her face to look up at him, "if you're very, very good, if
you *never* question me, if you always *obey*, I'll show you how
to read . . . someday."

"Oh, *sir*," she breathed, her eyes growing wide. "*Thank you*, sir!"

"The girl's an actress," thought Jimmy. "Impressive."

"That's *Master Weaver*, sir. Say it, please." The Weaver smiled.

"Master Weaver, sir." Lillian smiled back.

"Yes, that's right," he said, still so very like a friend. "And they
told me you weren't very bright! "

Lillian shrugged and sighed a little,
and she looked down at the floor,
desperate to get her hat and get away.

"So, Princess," he said, "you want this back?"

Her stomach fell flat to see her hat so helpless in his hands.
And he tossed it lightly up in the air.
Up in the air and down.

"Yes, please, Master Weaver, sir. It – " and she stopped herself.

"What? *Tell me . . .* " he said, soothingly.

She didn't want to, but somehow it came out anyway.

"It was – a gift."

"Oh, a *gift* it was, now, was it? From who? Who gives you gifts?"

She hesitated to say, but, again, somehow she told him anyway.

"One of the kitchen maid's cousins. She . . . knew I liked the color."

And the Weaver looked at the girl.
And then he looked at the hat.
And then, with his fist, he pushed it inside-out, and he said:

"The thing is, it isn't a very *nice* hat, is it?"

And as he talked, he played with it,
bending it this way, twisting it that.

"You risked your neck for this piece of cheap felt?" he asked, as he fondled the felt, watching her eyes watching her hat. "You know what they said about you not being very bright? I'm not so sure they weren't right. Oh, don't look so pathetic! *Here . . .* "

And he held out the hat.
She reached for it, naturally.
Naturally, he snatched it away.
She felt the fool. She flushed.
He liked that . . .
So he held out the hat again.

"It's *yours,* isn't it? Have to take what's yours, don't you?"

She felt ashamed. She felt confused.

"I . . . don't know."

"You don't know? Well, goody-goody for me then, eh?"

And he had himself quite a good laugh at that.
And that was when Lillian reached for her hat
and grabbed a fistful of felt!

But the Weaver didn't let go, no . . .
Instead, he pulled her close to him, far too close.
And as he hovered above her, he said:

"I'm a *very* close friend of your father's, Princess. And soon . . . "

And he took hold of a hank of her hair and yanked it just a bit.
Then he leaned down and put his lips right up against her ear.

" . . . *I'll be an even closer friend of yours.*"

And she felt his words whip through her,
as if they were wind and she just . . . air.

"And you're going to do everything I say, aren't you? Answer me."

"Uh-huh."

Then he slapped her hat back into her hand.

-349-

"I'm *so* glad we met, Princess! Now, you run along before somebody who's not as understanding as me catches you here."

And as the Weaver watched her run away, he said:

"You know something, boy . . . little girls are the cherry on top of the sundae. You'll learn that – one day."

And the Dodger, hanging his head,
followed his Master back inside.

Well, Lillian ran alright,
to the highest point at the furthest end
of the Empress-Queen's Wing,
to her Mother's private Tower Room, to her secret sanctuary.
Oh, the whole wing had been sealed off when Lilliana died,
but Lillian had long ago found her way in though a side window.

And now she flew around the corner,
took this left and then that right,
and then the door through here,
and then the door through there,
and then up, up, up into the deep, dank darkness
of those steep, spiraling stairs . . .

And she felt for the cold, iron doorknob,
and fairly fell onto the warm, wooden floor
of that most profoundly peaceful Tower Room,
made bright by sunlight streaming through the vaulted windows,
dust dancing in the beams.

Lillian crawled into the armchair, curled up into a ball,
and with her hat in her hands, she cried.
And she cried and cried and cried.
And then, she sat up and said, quite resolutely:

"Now then, that'll be enough of that."

And she dried her tears with her soft purple hat,
and petted it, and told it gently:

"You're alright now," said she. "You're with me."

Suddenly, she remembered the Weaver's words in her ear
and tried to shudder them away,
but the memory was stubborn and determined to stay.
So she reached for the thing that always soothed her,
and from a gilded drawer in a curvy-legged table,
Lillian lovingly lifted out her most cherished treasure:

Her Music Box, with its tiny jewels sparkling and flashing,
and its exquisite, intricate silver filigree.

She'd originally discovered it a long while ago,
lying on its side under the table in the dust.
At first, she didn't know that it was a Music Box,
and thought it simply the most beautiful thing she'd ever seen.
It was when she tilted up its lovely lid
that she saw the engraved words inside:

Sigh Unto Me
That I Might Sing for Thee

And so the girl sighed into it . . .

And, oh, that delightful, waltzing melody rose up
and danced through the air around the room,
and it thrilled her through and through.
But what thrilled her still more was how the song
seemed to dance through *her* too!
See, somehow she knew all the words of this song
straight through from beginning to end,
and from the first time she sang it, she felt it to be
the longed-for return of a long-lost friend.

So, here and now, after that horrible scene with that terrible man,
Lillian once again sighed into the Music Box,
and then she sank back into the armchair, this time just to listen.
And as she stared out the tall tower window into that Wild Blue,
a cloud floated by . . . a skylark flew through . . .
She wondered where he was flying to.
She wondered if the song was wondering too.
And with the song and the sky and the wondering,
she fell into that soothing someplace just south of sleep . . .

> . . . that felt . . .
>> . . . so deliciously . . .
>>> . . . deep . . .

And as she dozed and listened, as the melody floated along,
Lillian suddenly felt the gentlest breeze,
carrying with it the scent of . . . *mmmm*, lilacs . . .
And she heard a distant, lilting voice singing along with the song.
And then there came such a tender breath of air,
as if someone ever so loving had ever so lightly kissed her hair.

And then her mind's eye opened, and she looked up to behold:

Her Sweet Mother
shining there,
white light streaming through fields of red hair!

Now, if Lillian had been wide awake,
she'd've said, "Who are you?"
for she'd never even seen a portrait of her Mother, it was true.
But wide asleep, Lillian knew.
And, of course, her Soul knew too.
So it sat right up to admire the view.
And neither Soul said a word, at first.
Why, sure, they felt no need to.
They just smiled and shined, the way Souls do.

And then her Mother said:

> *"Change is coming, my darling-dear.*
> *Whatever happens, fear no fear.*
> *Your present is past. Your future is here."*

And then the girl's mind's eye closed shut.
And all became the darkness from which all dreams are born.

Then Lillian's eyes snapped open, and she woke with a start,
so surprised to see that the Sun was starting to set!

She looked around . . .
She could've sworn someone had been standing – just there?
She rubbed her face.
She stretched her arms.
She mewed herself awake.

Then she turned to behold her sanctuary in the setting Sun,
everything so lovingly bathed in that rose-gold light.
The very picture of perfect peace, it was.

Ah, that gloaming-light . . . how it always seemed to promise
that things would always come out right,
that all bad things would mend with the quiet of the night.

As was her custom at sunset, Lillian sat on the window seat.
And, ah, yes, there it was, in all its thrilling, inspiring splendor,
her very favorite view of anything anywhere:

The Great Big Beautiful Whole Wyde Whirld Out There.

How often she had dreamed herself out and about in the Whirld.
Oh, then she would be free! How fine a feeling that would be!
Not a princess, not a daughter, not a nothing . . .
Just Miss Nobody from Nowhere,
cut loose on the whirl of the Whirld!

Yes, be careful what you wish for. So they say.
But what do they know, anyway?

Well . . .

The very next day was the day of the Big Birthday Bash.
The town square was bursting with color and laughter,
and people selling wares, watching performers, enjoying life.

Lillian sat on the roof of Quincy's Apples & Oranges Wagon,
her favorite spot for such festivities,
watching as the jugglers juggled,
the dancers danced, and the singers sang.
And the weather was sublime.
And it was time.

The Birthday Suit Processional was all set to begin!

The drums rolled . . .
The fanfares fanned . . .
The Girl-King's gut clenched like a fist,
and her heart turned heavy as lead.
And though her head didn't understand why,
her body ached with sudden dread.

The Weaver stood on a balcony high above,
looking down on the crowd in the square.
Jimmy the Dodger was standing beside him up there.

Down on the stage, the Head Herald entered,
and the Conductor looked up to the Weaver for his cue.

Oh, how the Weaver adored telling people what to do.
He'd always known he was meant for commanding things,
for controlling the masses, for bossing around kings.
And it had all come off without a single hitch.
And he'd done it all without sewing a stitch!

Said the Weaver to the Dodger, "Glory be to me, boy. Just you wait and see . . . "

The Weaver merely lifted a finger,
and the processional music began,
and from the Palace doors emerged:

A

long,

slow

train

of

Palace

Processional

People,

all looking

particularly pale

and

peculiarly perturbed.

And then, a dramatic musical crescendo!
And *then*, a dramatic parting of the curtains
at the back of the stage, dramatically revealing:

The Birthday Boy Himself.
The Emperor-King George.
Naked as a needle.

Who then made his now legendary way
forward and onward and into the lap of his People.
Who had, of course, frozen into a still life painting.
Which had, of course, escaped George's notice entirely.

Oh, George took center stage with the greatest gusto.
George was in his Glory.
George was in his Prime.
George was Radiant Like The Sun.

Lillian was stunned into still life, along with everyone else.

The Weaver cued the Chancellors to applaud.
And the People tried to follow suit in a scattered sort of way,
as they shuffled and coughed and looked down and away,
and fretted about treason and the real reason for all this madness.
And the Head Herald mumbled and stumbled blindly on,
through a detailed description of
this Most Beautiful New Suit of Clothes
that the Emperor-King wasn't even remotely wearing.

But, oh, how George posed,
and, oh, how George peacocked,
showing off the cut off the vest,
the drape of the coat,
the heel of the shoe,
the lay of the lapel.

And as Lillian watched this shameful show,
she suddenly saw that she and her Father
and all the People of the Kingdom
were nothing but the butt of a big, fat, rotten joke.
Why, someone was making fools of them all!
This supposedly Historical Suit wasn't even a snippet,
wasn't even a scrap, wasn't even a shred!
Why, this foppish fabrication of a Suit
wasn't so much as one single solitary thread!

Well, the Girl-King just saw red.
Yes, she just plain old lost her head.
Such outrage blazed up inside her,
blasting through her earlier dread,
and she stood up on the roof of that fruit wagon,
and she stomped her foot, and she said:

"THE EMPEROR HAS NO CLOTHES!"

Oh, such a silence petrified the crowd.
No one moved a muscle. No one drew a breath.

"What's that?" said George, smiling, thinking that he must've
missed some compliment, some pretty posy from his People.

Still completely beside herself, Lillian shouted:

"THE EMPEROR HAS NO CLOTHES!"

"Oh, good heavens," thought George, "some silly peasant doesn't
see the genius of my prize-winning suit! That clever Weaver said
this might happen, and that I must absolutely ignore it if it did."

But, ever his own master, particularly on his Birthday,
the Emperor-King demanded:

"WHO SAID THAT?"

The People cringed.
The sun went in.
Some sort of bird cried out.

And when Lillian heard that bird, it suddenly seemed
that she had just dreamed that someone had just screamed
at the Emperor in front of everyone.
And then she realized that the heckler had been her.
Her hand flew up to cover her mouth!
She had entirely forgotten about the ironclad edict:
The Emperor-King must never, ever lay eyes upon the Heir-Apparent.

And *then* she realized that losing her head
and proclaiming the truth
might have just actually cost her and actually lost her
her actual, factual head.

"I SAID," said George, *"WHO SAID THAT!"*

Lillian let out a small, sad sigh.
Then she lifted her head and raised her hand up high.
And as the Emperor-King scanned the square,
his eyes soon fell upon her.
And for the very first time ever,
Father and Daughter beheld one another.

And George was the sole soul there that day,
who hadn't the smallest clue as to
who was really beholding who.

All around the square, the People stood stock still.
Too terrified to blink.

Up on the balcony, above it all, stood the Weaver, thunderstruck.

"Play it out . . ." he said, softly. "Let it ride . . ."

Beside him, the Dodger thought, "I hope she buries ya, y'bastard."

The Emperor-King stared across the square
at the skinny, red-headed girl,
and then he burst out laughing.

"WHY, YOU'RE NOTHING BUT A GIRL! COME HERE, GIRL!"

Lillian just blinked.
She just couldn't think what to do.
But George was used to people jumping
the instant he told them to.

*"YOU DARE TO DAWDLE, GIRL? YOUR KING HAS JUST
SUMMONED YOU TO THE STAGE!"*

So Lillian scrambled down off the roof of the wagon.
And as she passed the sweet old mule that pulled it,
she whispered:

"Wish me luck, Millie . . ."

And, standing up there at his Master's side,
the Dodger said a prayer in his heart for the Girl-King
as he watched her make her way through the People.
Who, not so by the by, weren't feeling at all comfortable about
giving their girl up to this mad, naked fellow.

But he was who he was,
and she was who she was,
and they were who they were,
and they didn't know what else to do.
So they just let her through.

Meanwhile, George smiled at the Weaver and winked and waved.
And the Weaver winked and waved back.
And he watched.
And he waited.

Lillian arrived at the foot of the stairs leading up to the stage.
She took a breath, then raised her eyes to the Emperor-King,
who stood glowering good-naturedly down at her.
She took off her hat, and she started up the stairs.

And when she reached the top,
the King bowed to the girl with great elegance,
as if she were a visiting Queen.
And the girl curtsied deeply, with great elegance in return.

And as the People watched this courtly courtesy,
they thought (nakedness notwithstanding)
this odd reunion was, somehow, a beautiful sight to see.

And the King found himself chuckling at the charm
of this funny little unexpected girl,
and he smiled benevolently down upon her.
Then, playing it full out to his People,
the Emperor-King George said:

"Oh, I feel so very good today – so blessed, so expressed, so fin-essed, yes, so very fortunate to be dressed in such an undeniably incredible creation as this! Why, I feel strong, I feel free, I feel so divinely *me!* In fact, I've never before felt quite so – wide open! So, yes, of course, I wholeheartedly permit the dissenting opinion of even this funny little ragamuffin . . . "

And he smiled broadly at his People.
And they tried to smile back.
And, as oblivious as ever to anyone else's discomfort,
George turned ever so buoyantly to Lillian.

"So, tell me, my young critic . . . why is it you so boisterously disapprove of my beautiful New Suit of Clothes, enough to shout it out in front of everybody – and on my *birthday*, no less? No, wait! I know, I know why! Don't tell me, I'll tell you . . . Here it is: I think you're jealous!"

And he laughed at that one quite a bit.
And Lillian, to be friendly, laughed along with him.
And so it was that Father and Daughter shared
their very first laugh together.

And as they laughed, their eyes met.
And they smiled at each other . . .
And Lillian was so surprised to see
such a sweetness deep inside her Father's eyes.

And as she wondered at his wondrous warmth,
her newfound friend spoke in a voice so clear and so all-knowing:

"What's your name, girl?"

Lillian froze, terrified.
She had no idea whether to be or not to be herself.
All she could do was stare down at the hat in her hands.

Up on the balcony, the Weaver grabbed the Dodger by the ear.

"Expose her! *Now!*" he ordered.

"Well, girl?" George said. "Don't you know your own name?"

"Damn you, boy – *expose her!*" snarled the Weaver to the Dodger.

Meanwhile, suddenly noticing the tag in the lining,
Lillian pulled a name out of her hat: *Hats by –*

"Henrietta! Your Majesty . . . "

"*Henrietta* – well done! I was worried there for a moment. Why,
I thought you'd quite forgotten your own name!"

And he laughed heartily at his joke, it was *that* clever.
And, once again, Lillian laughed along with him.
And as they looked at each other and laughed together,
George took a liking to this funny little girl,
and he gave her an extraordinary bit of free rein.

"Alright, now . . . What exactly is it about my outfit you object to?
Is it the color? Do you feel it's out of season? Come now, you
have my permission to pan me in public – just this once, mind! –
and I *promise* you, you won't be charged with treason."

Lillian brightened.

"That's it, Henrietta, be fearless – say what you want to say!
Come now, have at it, seize the day!"

So, Lillian took a deep breath and stood up tall, in a regal way.

"Well, it's like this, Your Majesty . . . I don't much admire your
new clothes because, well, there aren't any. Why, as far I can
see, Sire, you're naked as a baby!"

And that's when it happened.
It was bound to, of course.
Considering.
Oh, yes, Lillian got the giggles.
She buried her face in her hands,
seized by uncontrollable laughter.

Now, the giggles, as we know all too well, are contagious.
Most especially in nerve-wracking situations.
And these giggles were no different, for if there ever was one,
this was a nerve-wracking situation.
So, when Lillian started to giggle, all the children started to giggle.
And though the grown-ups tried desperately to stop them,
alas, they too were stricken.
Soon, Laughter reigned supreme throughout the square.

And Lillian finally dared to look up to see
that it was only her Father who didn't at all understand
what could possibly be so funny.
He seemed so very confused,
as if he were just beginning to sense that,
for some very shameful reason,
he wasn't at all in the loop.

And Lillian thought he suddenly looked so old and so very lost.
And the People's laughter faded into sad silence,
as they noticed their Emperor-King starting to search his forearm,
trying to determine if there really was a jacket-sleeve there . . .
or if, in fact, that really was forearm hair.

The Weaver held the point of his dagger to the Dodger's ribs.

"Do or die, boy, *do or die* . . . "

Up on the stage, George began to feel terribly self-conscious,
sensing that he really might, in fact, be totally naked in public.

And Lillian, feeling a protective pull, handed him her hat.
And the poor man took it so gratefully,
and he covered himself with shame.

The Weaver pressed the dagger into the Dodger's ribs.
The Dodger felt the point pierce his skin, and he panicked,
and he screamed out to save his life:

"DON'T LOOK, YOUR MAJESTY – IT'S YOUR DAUGHTER!"

Once again, the crowd turned into a still life painting.
The Weaver stalked back into the Palace.
The Dodger buried his head in his hands
and sank to his knees in shame.

The Emperor-King glared at his disowned Daughter,
who stood there so stunned to see
just how fast her Father had flashed from friend to foe.

"I *looked* at her, *ohhh*, I *looked* at her! *WHY DIDN'T ONE OF YOU
STOP ME?* What's the matter with all of you – *ARE YOU MAD?"*

Tears came into his eyes, and he pointed at the girl accusingly.

"You . . . you killed my wife. You ruined my life. *You betrayed me*
the moment you were born . . . *TRAITOR!* That's what you are,
you're a *TRAITOR!"*

Lillian started to cry.
The People grew agitated.
The Head Chancellor suddenly swooped in.

"So, let us all give our beloved Emperor-King a big Birthday
cheer! What a day, eh? What a day!"

And he prompted the People to applaud and hurrah.
And they did the best they could, considering.

And as he escorted the weeping Emperor-King off stage,
the Head Chancellor hissed down into the orchestra pit:

"Play something happy, you idiot!"

The other Chancellors grabbed the girl and dragged her off stage,
leaving the People standing there, looking at each other,
wondering what they were supposed to do about any of this.

Moments later . . .

Back inside the Palace,
the Chancellors were pacing and yammering,
trying not to trip over poor old George,
who was wrapped in a blanket,
sitting on the cold stone floor,
up against the cold stone wall,
shivering and softly moaning.

Lillian was in a corner, sitting up tall in a gilded high-back chair,
pretending not to be scared, pretending not to care that,
even if they didn't cut her head off,
they would surely lock her up forever and a day.
Oh, she would never again drink in fresh air,
never ever get to see the Whole Wyde Whirld Out There,
or feel the sun on her face or the wind in her hair.

Then she noticed that her Father's blanket had slipped,
leaving his back and shoulders bare against the cold stone wall.
And the sight of him pulled at her heartstrings.

"Why, he's just a sad, broken old man . . . " she thought.

Checking to be sure the Chancellors' eyes were riveted elsewhere,
she surreptitiously slipped off the gilded high-back chair
and sidled softly over to George,
who was gazing off in a vacuous stare.

And, as if she were nothing but a gentle stirring in the air,
he let his Daughter put the blanket right.
And, as she regarded her Father's very tousled hair,
she sighed and softly said:

"Oh, George . . ."

And then, why, the funniest thing . . .
George turned to look deeply into Lillian's eyes,
as if she were his best friend there, and he said:

"I am so sorry, sweetheart. This is a such a very sad affair, isn't
it . . ."

And a small smile shadowed the end of it.
And Lillian looked into her Father's eyes for a bit,
and she saw something familiar mirrored back,
something so similar, in fact . . .
Why, this was the first time ever that Lillian became aware
of what it truly felt like to be an Heir.
And for the very first time in her very young life,
the Girl-King felt more formidably *there*.

The Weaver blasted through the door.
The sheer shock of him shushed the Chancellors,
who shrank back into the corners of the room,
while George shrank back into the corners of his mind.
Only Lillian held her ground.

"Get away from him!" snarled the Weaver. "Stop torturing him!
Haven't you done enough?"

Suddenly confused, ashamed, guilty, all at once,
Lillian retreated to the high-back chair.

"Now, now, hold on there, Weaver . . ." said the Head Chancellor,
so upset but so unsure.

After all, he'd imparted so very many secrets to this man,
who'd become so very close, so very quickly.
And, after all, they'd made so very many plans.

"You made us all look like *fools!* His Majesty was completely – "

And with that, the Weaver went wild-eyed.
Played the betrayed savant-artiste.
Looked them all dead in the eye,
as if he'd been stabbed in the back.

"You didn't see it, did you? Oh, I do not *believe* this!"

"But there was no . . . " "But he was . . . " "But he wasn't . . . "
"I mean, you – he . . . "

The Weaver turned on them ferociously.

"You *lied* to me! You *betrayed* me! You said you saw, but you
didn't see – you didn't see a thing! Oh, what did I expect?
This Kingdom is so *pathetic*, so *provincial* . . . You know what? I
should just wash my hands of this whole lousy place!"

They all protested, in a panic:

"Wait! No, Master Weaver – we *saw!*" "We *so* saw!" "Of course
we did!" "It wasn't that we didn't *see*, you see!" "Oh, we saw . . .
everything!"

And as the Chancellors further sold their souls,
and as the Weaver further turned their heads,
Lillian turned to George,
who had now retreated to some faraway place in his mind.

And she wished herself right there next to him, right now.
Maybe sitting on the banks of some cool, clear stream,
laughing, with their feet dangling in the water . . .

No such luck.

"We're so very sorry, Master Weaver, for the misunderstanding.
The Emperor's New Clothes were incredible! Sheer genius!"

And the Weaver heaved a martyred sigh.

"Alright . . . Apology accepted."

Oh, the Chancellors were so relieved to be back in his good graces!

And then the Weaver posed a question:

"Well, I think it's obvious what has to happen now, don't you?"

The Chancellors gaped at him, waiting for a clue.
They were so toasted and so scrambled,
they didn't know what to do.

"Oh, it's so simple. Come on, *guess* . . . " smiled the Weaver.

He didn't want to say it. The clowns should take their cue.

"It's a fateful little matter concerning You-Know-Who."

"You mean . . . " ventured the Head Chancellor, pointing behind
his palm at George.

"No, you *dimwit*, not him! *Her!*"

He glared down at Lillian with a scalding eye and an acid tone.

"This spoiled brat here, who thinks she's so *bright*."

And Lillian turned from her Father to face the Weaver,
burning with brand new insight:

It was plain to see this fight was going to be hers alone to fight.

And she looked him straight in the eye and said,
so certain she was right:

"Well, I'm bright enough to know that you're a crook! Why,
you're nothing but a big fat pack of lies!"

Those glassy eyes flew open,
every muscle in his bony face died.
And the Chancellors were on her in an instant,
snarling and snapping in a toothy pack:

"Shut up, you stupid brat!" "How *dare* you – you little traitor!"
"She's a traitor!" "Why, you *traitor!*"

And the Weaver's face raced back to life,
and he cut to the chase in a voice like a knife:

"Listen . . . You all know as well as I do that what this crooked
little rat did out there was an act of High Treason! And I happen
to know that she's planning to *murder her Father* and *take the
throne* – oh, yes, I have friends who've been keeping an eye on
her, and they have plenty of evidence to back that up. And, sure
enough, yesterday I caught her lurking around the Emperor-
King's Wing with a *dagger* in her hand!"

The Chancellors gasped at the felonious act.
Lillian gasped at the treachery.
The Weaver delivered the verdict.

"She's a traitor. That's a fact. His Majesty said so. Traitors must
die. Period."

Then the Head Chancellor chimed in:

"Why, you're absolutely right."

And Lillian knew that she was through.
The very worst was coming true.

And as she wondered whether they'd hang her,
or *what* they'd actually do,
from completely out of the royal blue,
cried out the other You-Know-Who,
in a voice surprisingly clear and true:

"I COMMAND YOU TO RELEASE THAT CHILD! LET HER GO!"

Well . . .

Everyone – even the Weaver – froze. They stood stock still.
And Lillian felt the most magnificent thrill!

"YOU HEARD ME – LET HER GO! Just . . . let her go . . . "

Instantly, the Weaver tried to trivialize the King's good will:

"Ha! What can he possibly authorize? The man's a lunatic!"

The Head Chancellor answered in a bureaucratic hush:

"Weaver, even so . . . he still is King around here, you know."

"Oh. Yes, of course. So, what would you advise, my friend? I
yield to your expertise."

And, right then and there, the Head Chancellor
cleared his throat, smoothed his hair, inflated his ego,
and turned to officially and formally banish
the Kingdom's Rightful Heir:

"You have proven yourself a Traitor
and disloyal to the Crown,
having defied the Royal Edict issued by His Serene Highness,
the Emperor-King George the Twenty-Second,
and you are hereby Banished from this Kingdom
Forever and a Day.
And should you ever dare to return,
we'll kill you and the horse you ride in on!"

And as the other Chancellors were leading her to the door,
Lillian regarded her shipwrecked Father,
still sitting on the cold stone floor.

"Thank you, Your Majesty," said she. "Goodbye . . . "

Her Father didn't hear her. But somebody else did.

"Oh, *goodbye.*"

The Weaver leaned his face in, far too close to hers.

"If I ever lay eyes on that ugly little mug of yours again, I promise
you, you will be on your knees begging me to let you *die!*"

And do you know what Lillian did right then?
Lillian spit in his eye.

As the Chancellors dragged her down the hall in one direction,
the Weaver stalked off cursing in the other direction.
Oh, he was on a now urgent mission!
The People had to see the great man who'd restored order.
It had to be incontrovertibly clear just who'd saved the day,
that the Weaver's in the business of making everything okay.

So he spoke to the People like a true friend,
weaving a tale that told them everything they wanted to hear.

" . . . and it was so very moving to see our dearly beloved Emperor-
King and his precious little daughter sharing Birthday cake and
planning how they're going to make up for all that lost time!"

The People had no idea who this smiling stranger was,
but they were most heartened by this very happy news.
Might they be seeing the strange new dawn of a brand new day?

Then somebody asked a very good question:

"Excuse me, sir, but who are you?"

Why, the Weaver was more than happy to explain and explain
and explain and explain and explain half the day away,
so vaguely and so monotonously
and so without content and so without sense
that the People just wanted to go home and put their feet up.

They were now just too completely exhausted
to remember exactly what it was
they'd been concerned or confused about
in the first place, anyhow.
And everything seemed to be just fine now.
After all.
In the end.
Pretty much . . .
Didn't it?

Meanwhile . . .

The Chancellors were busy shoving Lillian out of the Kingdom.
They slammed that big wooden Door behind her.
And dead-bolted it, to boot.

And the girl stood face to face with the Door.
Now, she had always loved that Door before,
so comforting to lean on when the Sun baked the wood warm.
But it looked so mean and rotten now,
shut against her like that.

And so, most decisively, she turned her back on her Past.
And there she stood, facing her Future.

Suddenly, she felt in her belt for her –

"My hat! *Oh, no . . .* "

Tears rushed to her eyes.

"Now, now," she instructed herself, "this is no time for that. I must go round front and see Bill and tell him what happened before I go."

So she ran around to the ornate front gate of the Kingdom.
And there stood big old Bill, the Gatekeeper.
Asleep on his feet, as usual.
With his visor shut, as usual.

She blew on his big old hand a little, so as not to scare him awake.

"HALT! WHO GOES THERE?" Bill shouted, scared awake.

"Shhh, Bill, *shhh . . .* It's only me, it's only Lil," said she. "See?"

And Bill lifted his visor and looked way, way down at Lillian.
And his big ol' face burst into a big ol' beautiful smile.

"Why, hello, Lil! Lovely to see ya! How are ya?"

Yes, obviously Bill was completely uninformed.
Always on the outside of things.
Always had to wait 'til supper to hear it from the wife and kids.

"Aw, Bill, I sure will miss your smile."

"Miss? Why, no need for that, my dear Lil, I'll smile at you all day long, I will."

"Well, see, Bill, it's like this . . . There's been this awful big commotion about the King . . . "

And Lil told Bill the terrible tale.
And somewhere in the middle, poor Bill got so upset,
he took off his helmet and slid down the wall to the ground.

" . . . and so, you see, Bill, they've given me the boot."

At this, Bill burst into tears.

"Aw, please don't be sad, Bill," said Lillian, as she patted his big old shaggy head. "Now you know I've always had a mind to see the Whirld, right? Right?"

Bill nodded just the tiniest bit,
but his broken heart just couldn't quit.

"Please, Lil, *please* come live with me and the wife and kids! We'll take real good care of you. We'll hide you 'til you're grown!"

And Lillian leaned her head against Bill's,
and she kissed him on his big old tearful cheek, and she said:

"Aw, Bill . . . You're the very finest pal a girl has ever known. But, no, Bill, that's too dangerous. I can make it on my own."

At that, Bill bowed his head and cried his heart out.

"Bill, listen! Am I still your King-To-Be, Bill, am I, huh, am I?"

At this, Bill wiped his face and sat up straight.

"Indeed you are, Lil, you know that."

"Alright then, Bill . . . listen, 'cause this is real important, 'cause somethin' awful bad's afoot, y'see. You tell the People what's become of me. Tell 'em I got the boot for saying what was so. Tell 'em I'll go away, I'll grow up, and I'll come back someday, and I'll put everything right. Tell 'em I'll miss 'em all, o' course . . . "

And tears rushed in, for her heart began to break,
but she fought them down for the Kingdom's sake.

"But most of all, even if you forget everything else, tell 'em to watch out for this Weaver fella. Tell 'em he's the rottenest rotten egg we ever saw. Y'hear me, Bill?"

"I do, Lil," Bill blubbered, "I do."

"Alright then, stand up now. There you go . . . Now, wipe your face and look real sharp, and don't you fret for me. It'll all turn out alright someday, just you wait and see. Well . . . I guess I best be going now."

And with that, the weeping giant handed her his lunch pouch.

"There's two egg sandwiches left, I think, and an apple."

And the little Girl-King kissed the knuckle of that giving hand.

"G'bye, Bill," said she.

"G'bye, Lil," said he.

And Lillian headed off,
and left Bill the Gatekeeper sobbing inside his helmet.

Well, having done what needed doing, she truly *meant* to leave,
but just as she was aiming to walk out into the Whirld,
she stopped short.

"Oh, *no* . . . I can't – well, I *won't*, that's all. I just *won't* leave without it, nossir!"

And she ran around to the foot of her old friend,
the mighty Red Rose Oak Tree.
She climbed up the Tree and over the wall,
and then slipped back in through a side window
into the hall of the Empress-Queen's Wing.

Then she flew around the corner,
took this right and then that left,
and then the door through here,
and then the door through there,
and she ran up, up, up into the deep, dank darkness
of those steep spiraling stairs . . .

She felt for the cold iron doorknob and dashed into the room,
making a bee-line for the windowsill,
where her Music Box was sitting so prettily still,
waiting for her.

"I couldn't have left without you, now, could I?"

Treasure in hand, she turned to her beloved Tower Room
to memorize the welcoming wood and light and warmth:
the writing desk, the fireplace, the armchair, the wide, soft bed.

Then she raced back down the stairs,
back through the doors, taking the lefts and the rights,
and then . . . she heard voices!
She stopped.
So did her heart.

She knew she ought to slip out that hall window right now,
but something ever so much more insistent inside her
insisted that she simply *had* to hear
just what those voices were saying.

So Lillian crept up the hallway of the Empress-Queen's Wing,
behind this plant, behind that sculpture, behind those drapes,
to hear what all too soon became all too clear.

Said the voice of a guard – a guard she didn't know:

"Yeah, the Weaver's movin' in here, takin' over the whole place."

"Is that right?" said a familiar voice.

"That's *Joe!*" thought Lillian.

Said the first voice, "We're gonna cart away all the paintings,
the books, the works. The Weaver wants to start fresh. Y'know,
do things his way."

The Girl-King grew so furious so fast,
she thought that she might faint.
But perhaps that day she'd learned a little something
about restraint.
So she waited 'til she heard the guard's heavy boots
clomping off into the distance.
Then she peered out from behind the drapes
and, seeing she was safe, whispered:

"Hiya, Joe!"

Poor Joe was so startled he almost cried out,
and his eyes went round as plates.

"Your Highness! What're you doing here?"

"I heard what that man just said. I can't let that crook move into
my Mother's Wing – and I sure won't let him *ruin* everything!"

"The Weaver's men are everywhere," said Joe, as he scooped
Lillian up and ran with her down the hall.

"No, Joe, don't you see – "

He reached the side window and hoisted her up.

"Someone's coming! Climb back down there. I'll take care of
them. Hurry now, *go!*"

So Lillian slipped out the window
and jumped down to the ground.
And, crouching there, she heard a strange, *crackling* sound
from somewhere just around the corner.

What was that smell . . . Was that smoke?

She slipped behind this bush, that wheelbarrow, this bench . . .
And then she saw, a short stretch away:

Another new guard she didn't know,
looking bored and put upon, holding a torch.
He had just started a bonfire of – *oh, no!*
Paintings and books and carvings and beautiful, doomed things
from the Empress-Queen's Wing!

The guard stared into the fire for a bit,
as if it were merely burning garbage.
Then, satisfied, he set down the torch and walked away.

And, in that moment, it seemed to the Girl-King
that her body had made up its own mind.
And she ran over and snatched up the flaming torch
that fool had left behind, saying:

"I will not let him live here – NO!"

And with uncanny aim,
she threw that torch through the hall window.
And it might've been Fate (who's to know),
but suddenly a furious, tumultuous wind swept up,
and all at once the Empress-Queen's Wing erupted
in a raging inferno!

Well . . .

A commotion began and Lillian ran.
And soon she was over the wall,
safely back in the arms of the Red Rose Oak Tree.
She clung to a mighty branch, gasping and trembling,
feeling herself to be one beating, pounding heart.

And, after a while, the Tree soothed her
with its silence and its certainty.

And Lillian lifted her eyes to see . . . *ahhh,* yes . . . the welcoming
splendor of her favorite view of anything anywhere:

The Great Big Beautiful Whole Wyde Whirld Out There.

No windows or walls in the way now, no . . .
Oh, right there before her, so majestic,
she saw that bountiful, beckoning Beyond!
All those hills and dales and mountains and trees,
and that elegant, ribboning Road
she'd so often imagined traveling upon.

So Lillian climbed eagerly down,
from limb to limb to limb to the ground.

And she looked up and saw a skylark in flight.
And she wondered where he was going.
And then she realized there was no more need to wonder.
Because now she could go too.
So she made up her mind to follow him.

But, just as Lillian started down the hillside,
she heard a rustling behind her in the Tree.
She turned around and saw, in the bottom branches –
No, it couldn't be!

But there it plainly sat:

Her dear old purple hat,
hanging calmly off the branch's fingertip,
as if it had been waiting there for her all afternoon.

And she hooted and hollered and ran and
leapt up and grabbed it and kissed it and hugged it and asked it:

"Now, who threw you over the wall?"

And as she put the hat back on her head, she said:

"*Awww*, I'm just so glad to have you back, that's all!"

Then she looked way up at that mighty Red Rose Oak Tree,
and she called out:

"Thanks for everything, Tree! I'll be back some day, you wait
and see . . . I'll remember you, if you'll remember me! Well . . .
so long!"

And then, Lillian, the little vagabond Girl-King,
strode off into that crystal clear mid-afternoon.

Off to where the sun gets shone,
and the wind gets blown,
and the thunder gets thrown.

Off to find out where that lark had flown.

Off into the arms of Destiny . . .

ACKNOWLEDGEMENTS

Vast, Eternal Thanks to

Hans Christian Andersen

for the wondrously wise story
"The Emperor's New Clothes,"
the timeless glory of which planted a seed in my soul so long ago
that has, at long, long last, bloomed into
"The Return of King Lillian."

---◆---

Endless thanks to all the great and powerful storytellers
of faerie tale, myth, folklore, literature, and film,
who have uplifted my spirit and so very ingeniously shown me
that we are all, indeed,
the sum total of the tales we tell ourselves.

---◆---

Exuberant, everlasting thanks to Kristin Overn,
who, with the greatest respect, kindness, humor, receptivity,
intuition, imagination, devotion, discernment, and fun,
has made it possible, through this remarkably joyous collaboration,
to manifest a tale that I had always intuited was far too daunting
for me to birth all on my non-linear ownsome.
She has been Producer, Editor, Dramaturge, Midwife,
Fellow Adventurer and Golden Friend.
She heard the heartbeat of this tale that had been growing inside me
for decades, and tuned perfectly to the sound of its style,
and for this reason, I call her the Story Whisperer.
I am forever grateful to her for being so gracious, diligent, and
crucially instrumental in finally bringing King Lillian into the world.

- 381 -

Made in the USA
Middletown, DE
02 November 2020